Saving the Earth and forming a kinder, gentler society reminds us of the value of human connections. Ron brings a message that transcends time and place.

—A. K. Frailey

Dedication

To all my loyal readers who have enjoyed reading these chapters and commenting on them as I serialized my draft copy before final editing and proofing for the book. Also, to all of those brave people who are willing, when faced with disaster, to pull themselves up by their bootstraps and go to work.

Finally, to Lark Pogue who carefully reviewed and edited these chapters to make them better than my original writing ever could.

LA 2032
Starting Over

by

Dr. Ronald W. Hull

Equus Publishing LLC

www.equuspublishing.com

The characters and events in this book are fictitious. Any similarity to real persons, living or dead, is purely coincidental and not intended by the author.

Table of Contents

The winds of change tear at my edifice door,
strange new changes never heard before.
Keeping house in order a much greater chore.
Starting to wish change would come no more.
—R.W.H

Prologue

No one saw it coming and no one believed what it was doing when it did. But I, Drake Hutchins, bearing witness to what happened, am writing this so everyone will know what my partner, Derek Jones, and I did to try to create some sort of a new beginning from the wreckage of the old world.

But first, let me begin with how it all started… Who we were before. Our fathers were unlikely roommates in their freshman year at California State-Long Beach when they were assigned to the dorm to share a room and began their college studies in STEM, science, technology, engineering and math. My dad, Cal, for Calvin, Hutchins grew up in the Central Valley and wanted to go to school near the coast so he could surf.

Cal's father, my grandfather Ralph, was a small farmer who grew various crops according to the season to market. He had a few small stands of fruit and nut trees. All suffering from various crop diseases and the occasional drought. It was hard to keep ahead of large landowners trying to buy him out.

Derek was from Watts but received scholarships and a Pell grant for his studies as he worked hard with his father, Josh, for Joshua, Jones, an apartment manager for a slumlord. Both of our fathers were no strangers to hard work and making do when they met that day in their room. They introduced themselves, and almost immediately, developed mutual admiration as they started going to classes and competing with each other for grades in classes they shared. To save money, both were soon rooming together off-campus with other students and each had jobs to help pay the rent and for their schooling.

Upon graduation, my dad was hired by an Internet startup and found himself deeply involved in creating a commercial website for what the company was attempting to do, hoping to become, one of the leading brands in the brave new world of Internet business, evolving at lightning speed. Dad had nearly burned out in 2001, desperately coding 24/7 when the Internet imploded, the company failed and Cal Hutchins, along with many others in the cyber industry, was jobless with few savings.

Likewise, Josh had fared better, joining one of the infrastructure companies creating the Internet on a heady ride with stock options that involved getting out into the community and installing the company's equipment, getting the Internet into every home in the greater L.A. area.

Joshua Jones was proud to be able to even provide Internet services to Watts where he grew up. But also, a bit worried the drug dealers would soon find the Internet helpful in doing their business. Josh also hoped that Internet use would help young people with their schooling. He had been bussed away from the very beginning because he tested high on IQ tests.

When nothing else came up in a market crowded with unemployed Internet engineers, Cal turned to a maintenance job for a large apartment complex to make do. Learning as he went about his various tasks, he hatched a plan to start his own maintenance and construction company. He rented an abandoned warehouse space and mounted a shingle, Hutchins Construction and Maintenance. Created his own website for the business and soon found himself bidding jobs big and small, growing to the point where he had to hire workers. Finding many from south of the border eager to work for low pay in the city maintained labor locations. Many of these men had good skills already learned. Soon, he also needed management help supervising crews.

In 2003, Josh's company reorganized and he was out. He thought about a lawsuit for a while, but after talking to a couple of attorneys, thought otherwise. He had been in touch with Cal all along and when Cal heard, he made an offer to Josh. "I need to expand, and I need someone to help me manage all this work. If you throw in your savings and your severance, I can make you an equal partner and we can expand our operation here."

Josh thought for a minute, and replied, "That sounds like an offer I can't refuse. When can we draw up the paperwork?" Cal was all smiles hearing that and they chuckled together over the reference.

"Anytime you like. Let's meet for dinner at 8 pm at Sand Pier in Venice. And then, tomorrow morning at 9 am, we can meet with my lawyer to make sure that the paperwork is correct and legal."

They soon were doing contract maintenance work for some buildings and remodeling others. The company was growing. Dad married Julie Hughes, who he dated in high school when he found her by accident working in L.A. at a company he had a contract with. They began dating again. Soon, he hired her to work for the company and the rest was history. I was born in 2014, four years after my older sister, Erica, who looked after me like I was her child.

Josh married a schoolteacher, Sharonda Wilkes, while he was at the Internet company, but they held off having children with their busy lives. It wasn't until Sharonda quit teaching that they started to have children: Derek in 2014 and Angel in 2016. Once the kids were in daycare, she began working with Josh and Cal's company, too.

But I'm getting ahead of myself. When the mortgage debacle happened in 2008, many properties came on the foreclosure auction market at reasonable prices. Cal and Josh jumped in and started buying houses and flipping them. It wasn't long before the Construction and Housing Network, CHTV, spotted them and asked them to create a TV series.

With the producers' help they came up with the title, Cool Flips. With as much as 30% profit on each flip and projects taking as little as three months to complete, the two entrepreneurs were making big money and getting national attention because of their TV show. Bringing their wives into the show made it even more popular. When Derek and I came along, that popularity grew with our antics on the show.

Two of the houses they flipped were on Pacific View Drive in Malibu. The street followed a curving cliff three miles from the Pacific, overlooking it in the west with fabulous sunsets far below. The properties were built in the 1920s for movie moguls with high wall enclosures of two acres that had fallen into disrepair with age. There was one property between the two and all three of them were about the same size.

First, Cal, and then, Josh, bought the properties to renovate. And then, they completed the year-long task of restoring them to their former glory while working on other projects at the same time. Both homes retained the original California Spanish design with the latest conveniences: large vegetable gardens, infinity pools with diving boards, adjoining hot pools, barbecue patios and fire pits for outdoor living in the large, very private, backyards.

As a result, both of us were born into luxury and the California lifestyle only because of the hard work and perseverance of our parents. From day care through high school, we were inseparable, often called the D Bros by classmates. At an early age, shown off with our sisters on the

TV show and helping out with our fathers' work by the time we were 10.

One time when I was working on layouts for one of the buildings we were renovating on my smart pad, Dad took me aside and told me, "Enough of that, we have a punch list to do tomorrow and I want you to go along with me and start learning how to write with a pencil on paper. You'll never know when it may actually come in handy."

Oh, how those words come back to me as I write this with pencil on paper! As though he were visionary and looking over my shoulder right now. The next day, Dad showed up with a clipboard, paper and a pencil. He gave it to me and had me write, awkwardly, what he keyed on his notepad inspection form, as we systematically inspected the building looking for things that needed to be corrected or replaced before releasing the project for sale. He showed me both architectural lettering and cursive writing that he used in high school and college. Methods of writing that weren't being taught in our school.

I was so awkward trying to write with a pencil that Dad insisted for a month that I go over to Aunt Sharonda's, as I affectionately called Derek's mother, in the evening after dinner. She then spent an hour with both of us helping us learn both cursive and architectural writing and lettering. We both took to drawing easier with a pencil because we had been doing it all along with our fingers on our touch screens. I was even quite good with a stylus for more precise work. It was refreshing to leave our busy Internet and social lives to learn older ways of doing things.

But the D Brothers were not just all work and study with no play. We surfed, spent time in the Sierras, both in summer at our cabin and winter skiing. Dad took us to Grandpa Ralph's to hunt quail in the Central Valley in season. We did rock climbing, skateboarding, parasailing, parasurfing and other wild activities.

When we were sixteen, we both acquired electric sport cars that, fortunately, had enough built-in AI safety features to keep us from wrecking them when we got a little too reckless, sometimes racing each other through the hills. And we traveled, first to Hawaii, and then at least once a year, off to some other country for a week or two–an education in itself. Girlfriends came and went. We were carefree, loving life.

But not always… Getting ahead of myself, again. In April 2020, when we were only six years old, our private school was closed and we were forced to stay home while Dad and Uncle Josh shut down their construction company for a few months.

But we were often together at home until it was okay to go back out in public. Dad insisted that we all get vaccinated, but Derek and I couldn't get ours until late in 2021. We all got some form of Covid-19 in 2022, but by that time Dad's business was taking off again.

Our illnesses were brief with few symptoms and nothing lingering. Our families were lucky. Some of our classmates lost loved ones. At my age, I heard that there was a lot of political discord that I didn't fully understand at the time. Some of the kids we knew went through divorce. We knew nothing of that, either.

Congress passed a huge infrastructure bill to get the economy changing from fossil fuels to more efficient ways of providing energy for all of the luxuries that we enjoyed and people missed during the pandemic. That huge expenditure kicked off what would be called later as the "Roaring 20s of the 21st century."

A period of unprecedented growth of the United States economy, often disrupted by a rapidly changing climate. Bringing both drought and floods to California and destructive storms throughout much of the country. The seashores were rapidly eroding and the ocean began to eat away at shorelines everywhere in North America and the rest of the world.

The urgency to change became a new war on the environment. Young people like us in high school knew that we would have to change the whole way we were living. Even though Derek and I were already living it because we were so wealthy and so many others weren't.

Uncle Josh often reminded us about his upbringing in Watts and the terrible riots back there in 1969 before he was born but still bore the scars. "Protest like that with all that burning and looting doesn't solve our problems, it makes them worse. We had a lot of rebuilding and repair to do."

We had solar arrays on our rooftops that made enough electricity giving us a surplus that was sent back to the electric company. Dad showed me the check that he got each month. We had a 10 foot-high concrete block wall around the property from the front to the back that was covered with stucco and overgrown with colorful bougainvillea blooming nearly year-round. Mom kept our large garden full of fresh fruit and vegetables nearly year- round, too.

Behind the house was our very large pool where we had many parties with neighbors, friends, clients and classmates. Beyond that our property dropped off like a cliff that was crumbling a bit so there was no need for a wall. The original wall hung out over space about 5 feet because of the back of the property gradually eroding away with every earthquake and rainy season.

We often hang glided and repelled from there, sometimes causing our neighbors below distress when we landed in their backyards and apologized for the intrusion. Hang gliding took us all the way to the beach. Where ou sisters or friends would drive down and pick us up to take us home for another flight if we wanted to.

Fortunately, most of the property was solidly steel-piered in bedrock and only that edge was dangerous. Dad built a fence and rail there so that anyone visiting would not get too close to that precipice and accidentally fall off. We also had a fence around the pool to prevent small children from drowning there.

Dad also put in a large ceramic cistern to provide water for the garden. During the rainy season with its gully washers, the cistern would fill up and provide water throughout the nine months of nearly no rain, just a little mist off the ocean from time to time with the fog.

But it was much cooler there than L.A. with always having a sea breeze in summer. While in winter, huge windows to the south sunroom provided heat for the rest of the house even when it was quite cold by an ingenious duct system bringing the heat from the top of that huge room to the rest of the house.

Derek had lined up studies at Cal Poly San Luis Obispo, and I was going to USC as we approached our high school graduation. It was a time of joy graduating from our private high school together and a sober thought of being separated while going to college.

But fate would enter in and everything changed.

ာຄ)(ຊ⌒

1

The Pandemic of 2032

The rumor was that it came out of the South from teeming Mexico City or the Amazon Rain Forest as animals crowded together escaping fires on what little forest was still left. When I saw it on the news they called it Amazonia-9 and described it as "lethal."

Like its predecessor, Amazonia-9 was airborne, but had an incubation period in the body that didn't show any serious symptoms for five days or more. Therefore, since the start of the Roaring 20s of the 21st century had left nearly everyone wealthy or better off, people were on the move more than ever.

Inexpensive travel became available to more and more with transportation that left no mark on the atmosphere while the atmosphere continued to grow hotter from inertia and wouldn't cool off for another 50 years or more. Climate disasters continued to grow both in quantity and intensity. People young and old were fulfilling their dreams and bucket lists with ready cash as though they were all fiddling like Nero while Rome burned.

Our family was no exception. By that time, our construction and reality show businesses had us traveling worldwide during every break in the seasonal show with the hired help keeping the construction going while our fathers and mothers were gone.

Derek and I were busy going to huge parties heralding our high school graduation. Escape drugs were everywhere at those parties, but we were smart enough to avoid them. People tired of online interaction in their work craved human physical interaction and good companionship. Whenever our contemporaries wanted, they had free time to mingle. Online work gave them more free time to do it. But the loneliness and grind of online work just wasn't human enough for most.

Almost every business that had people on site working had a nursery and early childhood education center for the preschool children of the staff and administration. Most of the elderly had caregivers coming into their own homes on a daily basis giving them all the care they needed, regardless of their ability to pay, thanks to legislation providing that service, both under Medicare and Medicaid. Grandpa Hutchins at 82 and still working his farm was the only elderly person left in our family. We visited him often in the Central Valley. He claimed he didn't need any help.

But secretly took in a young lady to do his cooking and cleaning for him. When the news warned of the pandemic, there was a brief run on stores where people stocked up on what they thought they would need, closed their doors to strangers and wore masks like everyone had worn with some controversy back in 2020. If they had to go out into public at all, and most did, they wore their masks.

Unfortunately, 90% of those masks still let the even smaller A-9 virus spore to enter through the tiny gaps in the fabric. Even the touted N95 masks were inadequate. Nothing short of a HAZMAT suit would stop the rapid spreading of the virus. Few had them and wore them.

Derek and I were too busy to catch much of the news, but from what was reported that I saw, the hospitals were immediately overwhelmed as loved ones brought their dying to the emergency rooms where within five days much of the hospital staff were infected and dying. I heard one report that described the death rate from the infection as "Exceeding 90%." Panic was setting in fast for those who had been rushing around getting ready only to find they may have been infected while doing that necessary task. Some even went out again; sure, they would run out of supplies very soon if something like what was predicted would happen. We were getting ready to go to our graduation that morning when Derek called me and told me that he was feeling bad. "I woke up this morning with a splitting headache. I took some Advil but it won't go away. I'm starting to feel a bit feverish, too. As much as I want to go to graduation, I don't think I should. Don't want to infect you and any others if I have it."

I hated to tell him, but I did. "I'm starting to feel the same way. It must've been that party we went to the other night when they told everybody not to gather in large gatherings. I have to tell Mom and Dad and isolate myself in my room. You do the same. See you on the other side, pal."

Derek shuddered. "I hope you don't mean what Dad preaches, do you?" "Hell no. I mean when we are feeling better again. I'll text you first and then we can VuMe until we can leave our rooms and the house or vice versa. Savvy, Kemosabe?

"Savvy. See you on the flipside." Derek closed his flip phone and headed for bed. Fever chills were moving up his back. Sharonda was ready with hot soup and prayers. For her, prayers helped speed healing. They always worked with a little bean soup.

After I put down my flip phone, I looked around for something to wrap around my face. A hand towel in the bathroom seemed to do the trick and I walked to the kitchen where I saw Mom making bacon and fried eggs for Dad and me.

From the entrance, 10 feet away, I called out. "Mom, I'm starting to feel sick. I've taken some Advil for my headache and Tylenol for my fever, but I need to isolate myself from the rest of you. You can put my breakfast by the door and knock but don't come near. I've already got a big jug of water and some more Tylenol. I even found some of that Covid medicine you kept and will take it before going back into my room. Like you always told me, I'm going to take care of myself and get some fluids, rest and sleep. It will be over soon, I hope."

With a sadness in her voice Julie couldn't hide, knowing that Cal had awakened with the same headache, she called out to the side rather than directly at him, "That sounds like a good idea, Dre. I'll put your eggs by the door as soon as you are inside with a big pitcher of orange juice that you will need along with the water to keep hydrated. I'll be there for you if you need me."

As she hurried to finish the eggs, get some to Erica, and take the rest to Cal in their bedroom Julie started crying, hoping for the best, but fearing the worst.

I went to the bathroom and took some of the Covid medicine. When I got to my door, Mom had already placed a small platter with my toast and eggs, along with the pitcher of orange juice. I got everything inside and ate the eggs that were already quite tasteless. Took two capsules of both the Advil and Tylenol and drank most of the orange juice. It no longer tasted refreshing. It just seemed to burn my already raw throat from the growing fever.

I crawled into bed and covered myself with a sheet and blanket. My window was open a crack letting the fresh sea breeze in. I was totally covered, but sweating from fever and trying to keep warm. It wasn't long before I found that my nose was so congested I couldn't breathe through it anymore and I had to breathe like I did while swimming, through my mouth. My stomach started churning and I wondered if I would throw up the eggs I had just eaten.

I don't remember when I dozed off but it was welcome. My dreams came very vivid and they were torturous as my body and immune system struggled to fight the beast of this virus. Finally, after what seemed like three days of my occasionally seeing light and darkness through my eyelids, the fever finally broke, my throat and sinuses were opening back up and I started to feel much better but weak. I still had a very dry throat and muscles that felt like I had been through an Ironman Triathlon. My flip phone told me that it had been seven days since I went to bed, not three.

I reached for some water and drank nearly all of it that I had by the bedside. I dragged myself out of bed and headed for the kitchen. But nothing was cooking there and the house was silent. I went to my parent's room that I had never been in except when I was very small. I knocked and got no answer, so I carefully opened the door and saw my parents sleeping. I approached them cautiously, but to my horror, they both were very cold and stiff to the touch.

I started crying uncontrollably. I remembered clearly the last time I cried years before, when I left childhood to stand up and be a man. But the emotion that swept over me couldn't be denied. I feared for the worst as I approached my sister's bedroom. Another place I never ventured into since I was about twelve. Once again, I knocked, with no answer. And once again, aghast, I saw Erica dressed in just panties with no bra lying on the floor face down, as if she was trying to get out of bed and fell there. Her tanned legs already had a blue cast.

My anguish only increased. Wondering if I would find anybody alive. But I went to the shower and took a hot one for some time while thoughts ran through my head that I never thought I would ever have. I had felt grown- up before, but now I had to take charge of my life, fully, without any help from my parents or my sister. I was so dehydrated that I was surprised that I still had so many tears flowing. I drank heavily from the cold-water faucet. But I didn't feel any better.

Trying to think of what to do next, the first thing that popped into my head was Derek. We had been together at that party, and probably had brought the contagion home with him like I did. I gave him a call on my cell phone rather than texting. Wanting to hear his voice, first.

I found my phone working like nothing had happened. But it rang and rang. I hung up, rang again. Derek still didn't answer. He always answered within two or three rings, even if he was on the phone with somebody else. The thought that I was truly alone was too much to bear. I had to find out what happened at his house. Ringing his phone that much should have caught somebody's attention if they were alive. I had to go find out.

2

Strange New World

I left the house in a hurry, still weak but getting stronger with each step, really worried about what I would find. As I realized my weakness going down the steps from the front entrance, I slowed down to let my legs keep up with my mind racing at light speed trying to figure out what I needed to do after going to Derek's house. Too many things popped into my mind to mention. I had to focus on one thing at a time.

Suddenly, a shadow came over me in the bright sunlight and I was startled by it. I looked up and saw a vulture, not ten feet above my head! I often had seen vultures drifting in the thermals where the sea breeze ran up against the coastal mountains, especially while hang gliding. Sometimes we soared on the same thermal. As if they enjoyed being with us as they searched for food with their keen sense of smell and eyesight. The ones I saw in the city fed on roadkill from the many cats and dogs and the occasional bird that unfortunately, committed suicide by chasing its own reflection in the shiny façades of many buildings and even our large windows overlooking the ocean.

This was different. As though this vulture was circling me in anticipation of me dying very soon. From what I saw in the house, that thought wasn't too far-fetched. But as I looked out further, I saw many vultures circling all over the city. This was not normal. They probably came in from the Mojave Desert and coastal ranges because new food was everywhere here. Nature's undertaker. I soon appreciated what they were doing.

I hit the button that opened our beautiful steel gate that showed passersby the quality of our construction company as well as our own gated enclosure or compound, if you like. There was a button on the outside that linked to the house intercom so that occasional visitors who came unannounced could be viewed and talk to whoever answered and be let in or not. Even on our phones.

You couldn't be too careful in 2032 Malibu. There were just too many marauders out there looking to take an easy buck. Cameras everywhere didn't seem to stem the tide of the poor becoming desperate or opportunistic.

Most had guns.

When the gate was only partway open, I rushed through it and hit the button to close it, as I passed and started uphill towards the Jones's place. The street was silent as far as I could see and nothing was out of place. Actually, quite normal for this time of the morning. But it was really quiet except for the melodies of songbirds as they flitted from tree to tree in the neighborhood and the sharp piercing calls of seagulls far below three miles away at the coast.

What was really strange as I struggled up the sidewalk, really noticing the weakness in my normally, strong body, near fainting from the sun's heat and the exertion to push my legs forward, was that there was no background traffic sound that was usually quite evident if one listened. Nothing was apparently moving in the greater city except wildlife. Occasional dogs barking and, of course, an enhanced ability to hear songbirds and seagulls.

When I passed the Rosenbergs' gate, I looked in and saw nothing unusual. Jake was 83 and Martha was 81. They had both worked in the film industry and had inherited this place from Martha's father way back at the turn-of-the-century. They had hired a young immigrant woman doing things for them that they were having trouble doing alone, like getting their groceries.

I made a mental note to check on them later, hopefully to find them alive. Thinking of them made me think of Grandpa Ralph in the Central Valley. Was he still alive? So many things had to be left until later for now.

I reached Derek's home and, ignoring the intercom, immediately coded in the correct code to open the gate. And then, hurried to the house without closing the gate. Something I learned to do religiously after that. I knocked on the front door. Nobody came to the door. I feared for the worst and tried the handle. It was locked.

So, I headed around the house to the back and found a sliding glass door leading out to the pool was unlocked and I slipped inside. As I had done a thousand times before, I climbed the steps from that level to the one above leading to Derek's room, worried that I would find the worst.

I opened the door with trepidation, slowly, and peeked in. Derek was lying in his bed on his side with his back to me. I moved to the bed and touched his shoulder lightly. He was warm and let out a slight groan. And then, he mumbled, "Is that you, Mom?" "No, it's me, Drake. Are you okay?"

"Are you in a dream? I was dreaming you were here. Where have you been? I've been really sick and only this morning was having dreams of you coming to save me."

"Are you delirious? I didn't come to save you. I came to see if you were alive. Called and you didn't answer."

"I had ringing in my ears but I couldn't wake up enough from dreaming to answer. I was too heavy." Derek turned over and looked at me through squinting eyes. He wasn't fully awake yet.

"Slow now, don't try to get up too fast. You'll get dizzy and fall over. It's been seven days since we got this thing and we are both dehydrated and in need of refueling.

"First things, first. We have to check on your family and see if anyone else is alive or needs help. But I'm going to get you some water right away, because you'll need that to check on your folks and your sister. I didn't hear anything coming in the house, but they may be up walking around."

Derek swung his feet off the bed and took off his sweat soaked pajamas while I got him some water and he drank from it slowly like I told him to do so that he wouldn't choke or throw it up. And then, I walked him into the shower where he, like I had done earlier, enjoyed the hot water pelting his skin and washing the grime and sweat off so that he could feel like a human again.

I had Derek drink some more water, and then, walked him to his parents' bedroom and let him go in alone. Like me before, I heard him sobbing loudly and knew that they had both, like my parents, succumbed to the killer that stalked us all and killed quickly and silently without remorse.

I pleaded with Derek to come with me and check on Angel. He was reluctant to pull away from his parents, but I assured him that there was nothing he could do to bring them back. We just had to see if Angel was alive. I helped him to her room and, once again, she was lying there in bed cold, just staring up into space like she was looking for something or someone to come and take her away, but didn't.

I cried right along with Derek as we worked our way to the kitchen and found eggs and bacon in the refrigerator. We found some dry cereal and oatmeal and decided to make oatmeal because I knew our stomachs were not ready to eat a lot after being sick for so long. But the rumbling in my stomach told me I needed food.

We also made a big pot of coffee to both hydrate and wake us up for what we had to do. From the freezer, got out some frozen orange juice and made a big container of that to drink, too.

While eating, we discussed what to do first. Since our families hadn't been worried about death, we didn't remember any discussion about where anyone would want to be buried. On my phone, I did a search and got a listing of all of the funeral homes in the greater L.A. area. I made a list of the phone numbers of all of those that were within reasonable distance: about forty within twenty miles.

I had my cell phone with me and Derek retrieved his. I started from the bottom of the list of mortuaries and Derek started from the top. All we got after letting the phone ring for some time was a polite, "We are not in the office right now, please leave a message at the tone." Worse, when we got no answer at all or, "This phone is no longer in service."

Finally, nearing the end of the list from both ends and nearly lunchtime, Derek got an answer from a harried sounding, "This is Hiram Berkowitz of Heavenly Rest Funeral Home in Alhambra. Can I help you?"

Derek put on the speakerphone and said, "Our parents are dead. Can you give them a proper burial?"

"You can get in line. I've got over 100 requests like yours. We have to use HAZMAT suits to do our work and we can't come and get the bodies. I had to bury my wife and brother-in-law already, myself, so we are short staffed." We could hear him breaking down on the phone.

I stepped in and said, "That's okay, we'll bury them ourselves. You take care and take care of your own."

"Thanks, I will," and he hung up.

I saw the disappointment on Derek's face. While Derek wasn't, his parents were devout Baptists and funerals were a very big deal for black families and churches. "Should we call your Church in Watts?"

"I don't know. But maybe they know of a funeral home or a way to bury them there. I'll call."

Derek rummaged for a minute in his mother's things on the kitchen counter and found something from the church with the number on it. He made a call, but got only the "Please leave a message" message, so he did.

We both knew that we wouldn't be getting any call back; miracles weren't happening. We would have to make our own.

"Let's get busy and bury your folks next to your mother's garden. I know that it was planted because I saw new sprouts coming up the day before I got sick. Are you up to it?"

"I don't know, but I can't think of anything else to do right now. I feel pretty weak but getting out there in the sun and drinking more fluids might get these muscles to work better. I hope the digging won't be too tough."

"I wish we could get to the warehouse and bring back a backhoe or trencher, but I don't think that would be a good idea right now and like you said, physical work might make us feel better and get our minds off what's happened to us."

"Dammit! I forgot I need to call Grandpa Ralph! I hope he's escaped it so far." I gave him a call with the speakerphone on.

The phone rang about 10 times. Ralph Hutchins, a bit out of breath, finally answered.

"Drake, boy! Is that you? I've been calling almost every day and couldn't get your dad. What's going on? What little I get of the news is that almost everyone is dead? Is that right?"

"Yes, Gramps, everyone here except Derek and me. And we just came out of it this morning after seven days of delirious fever and an inability to breathe. We can't even get anyone to bury them. That's what we are about to do."

"At least you're alive. That's something. I'm about dead or getting there. That little woman that I hired, Alicia, what's her name, that's been so sweet and cute that I thought of marrying her, hasn't come around for four days now. Don't think she's going to come again, either.

"If I see anyone come to the gate, I yell to them from the front porch. Come to think of it, nobody has for a few days now. I'll be needing some groceries soon. Alicia always brought them for me. But I can rely on the freezer and the garden for what I need right now. Thank goodness your dad put in that windmill and the solar panels so that I have power when the power goes out. So far it hasn't."

"Gramps, we got a lot of work ahead of us today. But I'll check back with you every day and see how you're doing. We may even try to get out there in a bit when we get everything squared around here. That may take some time."

"Yeah, some time. When times get tough, the tough get going. Getting a little choked up so I'll sign off." We could hear him choking and sobbing in the background. He was a tough old coot, but what we told him happened really got to him.

We just stared at one another for a moment. Hoping against hope that that old man, our beloved, Gramps, could make it on his own at his age. We just didn't know. We were starting to struggle, too.

We went downstairs to the workshop at the back of the garage and found two shovels. Started digging a single hole nine feet by six feet alongside the garden that was in dire need of weeding and watering. So, we did that first.

The digging went quite well because the volcanic light loam caused by millions of years of erosion of the Pacific Range had resulted in it building up on the bedrock near to the coast like this. That's why the back of the properties here were eroding away with rainstorms and earthquakes.

Still, the sun was really low in the west when we finished the hole to six feet deep. The vultures that hovered over us all day had gone off to rest for the night, thankfully. We decided not to dress the bodies or do anything to protect them. We got a wheelbarrow from the workshop to make it easier to carry the bodies and placed them carefully, Joshua first, and then, Sharonda, and Angel, next to her.

We filled in the graves quickly knowing that we would make grave markers later. We had been snacking and drinking to hydrate all day, but we were really hungry. Grabbed some food from the refrigerator and we headed down to my place to bury my folks and my sister before nightfall. Finishing that, we were not only hungry, we were dead tired.

After grilling some steaks and taking showers, we were in bed by 8 pm It was 8 am when I opened my eyes the next morning. I felt much better than the day before, but I was very stiff from all the exertion grave digging. And knowing that we had to do it again and so much more scared the hell out of me.

3

Reality Sets In

I stumbled into the kitchen and found Derek already up. He was gathering things to cook for breakfast. I joined him. We both were starved and prepared about twice what I normally would eat because I thought I'd eat it. We made extra bacon because it was already getting some green spots of mold. The milk had a tinge of tang that it was going sour, too. We didn't have to worry about the refrigerator and freezer failing because it was all running off our solar panels. Mom wouldn't be running to the grocery store to replenish our supplies. As we cooked our food and started eating it we began to make plans.

"You know," I said. "We're going to have to go to a supermarket and get food if we can. These perishables won't last and we won't be able to make weekly runs to the store anymore. I'm so glad that our moms got their gardens in and growing. We'll have fresh food in excess this summer. From the window I can see that we have to cut lettuce and some other crops are already producing."

"I've been thinking the same thing, Dre. There's so much we've got to do. We need to prioritize, and maybe, split up. I'll take the bacon out of the wrappers and wrap it in daily amounts, and then, put them in the freezer. What we can't freeze, like my mom's leftovers, we'll have to bring here and eat right away. Something tells me, it's going to be hard to get food."

"You've got that right, Der. But there's other priorities first. We've got to text all of our friends and relatives. And then, start calling them, one by one. See who we can reach. I have a feeling services like our phones won't work after a while and we'll have to contact people right away if we're going to reach them. That's huge."

"Some of them may be in trouble. Did you hear that popping last night?"

"Yeah, just before I went to sleep. But I had only wild dreams about everything not working that I can't really remember right now after that."

"I think it was gunfire. Sirens off to the distance, too."

"Yeah, you know better than I. Lot of poor folks in the L.A. area. Living day-to-day. Must be rough for them right now. I expect they are breaking into buildings to get what they want and need."

"But we will have to break into places to get what we need, too. Won't we?"

"We will. But remember, we are the Brothers D. We are builders, not takers or destroyers."

"I get it, Dre. We'll take only what we need to build."

"Right. Who's going to do what, Der?"

"I ate too much already. I can't finish this." Derek waved his fork over his remaining platter of fried eggs. "I'm wasted from yesterday. Why don't you go check on the neighbors and get the perishables from our house. I'll stay here and start the emails and calls. Maybe get some veggies for lunch."

"That's a deal. I'm afraid I'm going to have to leave what I've got here, too. Maybe heat some of it up for lunch. Fresh veggies sound good. I'll get going after I shower and brush my teeth."

Ten minutes later, still stiff, but stretching my legs with each step, I started up the street after seeing a coyote cross the street far below, more vultures in the air and smoke rising in pillars from several distant places. Smelled it in the air. Fires burning uncontrolled, I thought.

I stopped at the Rosenbergs' gate when I heard the whir of an electric lawnmower. I peeked through a small crack in the heavy wooden gate and saw Jake out mowing the small patch of grass that he kept in the front of the house for a putting green. Most everyone had gone desert landscapes to save water.

I yelled, "Hey Jake! Are you okay?"

Jake turned around and started walking towards the gate.

I yelled again. "This is Drake Hutchins from next door. Don't come any closer! Let's talk at a distance."

"That's good to hear, boy. How're your folks doing?" he yelled back.

"They're all dead. Just Derek and I recovered from our two families."

"That's really, too bad." I could see his face drop even at that distance and his voice was no longer loud. "Really, too bad. Did you bury them?"

"Yesterday, here. That's all we could do." That deep sorrowful feeling crept over me once again and my eyes began to tear. I wiped them from my cheeks with my hand.

"That's awful. No rabbi to speak over them. But it's that way all over. In the first days there was lots of news. We watched it online continuously. So many rushing to the hospitals. Long lines of cars and people trying to get in. Ambulances couldn't make it. So many dying right there in the street. People with HAZMAT suits running around, unable to do anything. We saw looting like we never saw before in all the riots. Everybody just taking stuff. It was terrible…"

I regained my composure. "But are you all right. Do you need anything?"

"Aleta, that young woman we hired to help us hasn't come for five days now. She always brought us groceries, cleaned and helped with the garden and meals. Sure could use her now."

"I was sick for seven days, so I don't want to come close to you now. But Derek and I will do what we can to help you out. I've got to go and check on the other neighbors. But will be back later."

"Okay, thanks for your offer of help. You guys were always good to us. Good kids."

I hurried on to Derek's house, gathered up all the perishables out of the refrigerator, put them in a garbage bag and carried them back to the house to give to Derek.

As I approached the kitchen I called out, "Der, the Rosenbergs are alive! I just talked to Jake. That girl that helps them, Aleta, hasn't come for five days. We will have to look out for them."

"I sent a bulk text to everyone on my contact list. Haven't received anything back. Made a few calls and got no answer and had to answer voicemail on most. This isn't going to be easy." I could see the concern on his face. I couldn't encourage him.

"You've got that right. And I'm afraid it's going to get a lot tougher."
"I'd better get going to the neighbors. I'll see you around noon."

I left the house again, picking up a six-foot ladder that I tied a rope to in case I had to climb over walls.

Beyond Derek's, there was a turnaround and a large estate at the end of the drive. It was the home of a major 20th century mogul that he willed to his daughter, Barbara Wilkes-Hodges. She was about 70 and quite a socialite, living off the family trust. Our families didn't socialize with her, so her place was unknown territory for me.

When I got there, I rang the doorbell that had a view screen intercom and waited. I pressed the intercom button and called out a hello. Rang again… And waited… Nothing, the screen remained blank. I climbed over the fence with the help of the ladder. At the bottom of the ladder, I was startled when a large afghan came running up to me. I was glad he wasn't a pit bull guard dog because he licked me in the face. On his collar he had a nametag reading, "Regis". Regis followed me to the house.

I climbed the stairway to the front entrance of the palace-like building to the decorative glass double door and found it ajar. Once again, I called out and no one answered. I climbed a magnificent, curved staircase to the second floor and found the master bedroom. She was lying in bed like she was sleeping, but she wasn't. Her eyes were open, so I closed them and glanced briefly at her well-preserved body and a thin negligee at her age. *What a waste.*

Her Regis was with me and I couldn't keep him from sniffing her face and then whining. Instinctively knowing that she was dead. I quickly searched the rest of the beautifully decorated rooms and found nothing. Regis and I then went downstairs and searched some more but found no one, even at the basement level where there was a near ballroom size entertainment room and a private gym that could rival a commercial one, complete with an Olympic size pool viewed through huge windows outdoors. Just lots of exotic birds in cages, some flying free.

At the end of the pool, I found guest quarters. Inside, I found her caretaker and his housekeeper / maid wife. Both of them also dead. When I came back out of the guesthouse, I saw Regis drinking from the pool. In a nearby utility room, I found some dry dog food and poured some out for him. The way he gulped it down indicated to me that he hadn't eaten in several days. And then, threw up a little bit after, looking up at me and panting vigorously.

My head was spinning. If this is what I find in the first house, what am I going to find in the others? I really wasn't sure I wanted to know. It just looked like a lot of work ahead that I wasn't sure that Derek and I could handle. What else am I going to find? I wasn't sure.

I hoisted the heavy bag of dog food over my shoulder and Regis followed. When I got to the gate, thankfully, there was a button there that I could push to open it. I grabbed my ladder and took it outside and propped it up against the outside wall. Left the gate open a bit. Regis and

I headed back to my house so that I could introduce him to Derek.

We burst into the kitchen and surprised Derek making calls. "Hey, Der, Look what I found!"

Regis didn't hesitate and ran right up to Derek and gave him a greeting kiss.

"Unfortunately, his mistress, her housekeeper and groundskeeper are dead. You should see that place! It's a real palace! And Regis, that's his name, isn't the only thing there. I believe I saw a large birdcage with some macaws or parrots. Will have to go back and decide what to do with them. I'm beginning to think that it's going to take a lot of work just to deal with our neighborhood."

"Yeah, I know what you mean. These calls are killing me. I only got about five texts back so far and they are desperate. I made about 15 calls since you're gone and only talked to two people. One was a cousin that you don't know in Watts and the other was Daphne from school. She was crying so much during the conversation that I didn't get all that she said. We will have to help her if we can. But she's about ten miles from here in the Hollywood Hills. I don't know what the streets and roads are like to get there."

"Maybe we should tend to the living first and take care of the dead later."

"I'm thinking that, too. Let's go there this afternoon and see if we can help her. In the meantime, before lunch why don't you check a couple more houses while I make some more calls? I'm beginning to think this is going to be very hard, what to do first… Or even next."

"You've got that right, Der. I'll leave Regis here and check out a couple of houses like you said. Not sure what we'll find on the way to Daphne."

I went back to where the ladder was and went to the gate of the house directly across from Derek's. I peered through the gate and saw nothing moving. And when I tried the intercom, got no response. I didn't know the people in the house because they were a young couple that recently moved in with two small children after the house had been gutted and renovated by a home flipper. But it was not our family business. We were now doing much larger projects. At least we were… Nothing happening now, or ever again, from what I could gather.

I used my ladder again to climb over the wall and watched more carefully for possible dogs as I climbed down onto the property inside. Once again, I knocked on the front door while peering through the window and seeing nothing but a large open space with sparse furniture and what looked like a kitchen off to the right. The door was open. I called out again and heard nothing.

There were toys and clothes strewn around the living/family room and in the kitchen was a mess. I sensed that someone was alive in the house but wasn't answering me. I approached the master bedroom with much trepidation. I found what I expected. The young couple in bed and dead. And then, I went around to the four other bedrooms one at a time, frightened by what I thought I might find. The first two bedrooms were empty. In the third bedroom, also empty, I found it decorated for a boy but there was no boy in the room.

Arriving at the last bedroom in that hallway next to the bathroom, I found it decorated for a girl. That room was in shambles like the kitchen. I heard whimpering coming from the walk-in closet that led to the bathroom.

I opened the door a bit further and found a young girl in pajamas, her hair all matted and unkempt. She was hiding in the corner, afraid to even look at me. I could see she was both hungry and hurting. I panicked for a moment, not sure of what to do. *She still could be contagious…*

I called out gently, "Little girl, what's your name? I'm here to help." She turned shyly and glanced at me. "Melissa." She started crying.

"Mommy… Daddy… Tommy!" She cried out through her tears.

"I know. I know. I want you to come with me. You need to leave here with me, Melissa. I had to think fast. *What should I do with her? … I know, the Rosenbergs!"*

"How old are you, Melissa?"

"I'm seven and my brother Tommy is three." She stopped crying. "Where's your brother? I didn't see him in his room."

She put her left index finger to her mouth and pointed past me. "There." I held out my hand and she took it. I followed as she left her room and down the hall into her parents' bedroom where I had just been. She pointed to the bed and said again, "There."

I went around the end of the king size bed and found the toddler on the floor on the other side. He was dead, too. I couldn't tell whether it was from the virus or from lack of water and food. My eyes glazed over and I tried not to show Melissa, but I was in the presence of an orphan. Instinctively, I knew there would be a lot more. I took Melissa's hand again and back into her room where I gathered up from the closet as much clothes as I could carry in a large clothes bag that I found and asked her if there were any toys that she would like to bring with her.

Melissa pointed to this thing and that thing, and then another, and then another until there was so much I couldn't take it all in one trip. I took her hand and we left the house. I knew I had to come back for more of her things, but not now. She had to know her heritage. It was in that house and I had to find it for her. But not now.

As we crossed the street to the Rosenbergs', I asked Melissa, "Do you like dogs?"

"Daddy and Mommy told me they were going to get us a dog when we got settled in. I like doggies. We had one back in Ohio."

"We have a real nice one that you will like. But for now, I'm going to have you meet your new grandpa and grandma until I can find out if your real ones are still alive in Ohio. Okay?"

"Okay, where's that doggy?"

"You'll see him soon. And maybe, some colorful birds."

We arrived at the Rosenbergs' gate. I pressed on the old-fashioned intercom and heard Martha on the other end.

"Who's there?"

"It's Drake. Drake Hutchins from next door. I talked to Hiram earlier about how you were doing."

"What do you want?"

"I have a huge favor to ask of you. Can you take care of a seven-year-old neighbor girl who has lost her family to the pandemic? I don't think she's contagious. Derek and I are trying to locate our friends and family and we can't really take care of her right now. We will try to find any relatives she may have that are still alive. But that will take some time. Melissa's in need of being cleaned up and eating right. I got some of her things so she will have something to wear and to play with."

Martha softened quite a bit on the intercom. "Okay, we will come out and see this little girl you're talking about. I think I've got a room she could take. But you have to promise me that you'll find someone she can go to because we are old and unable to take care of young children anymore. Never had any."

The gate began to open and we met Hiram and Martha about halfway to the house. Martha knelt down and hugged the girl when she saw her pitiful condition. Smeared with dirt, strawberry jam and peanut butter.

"Don't you worry, Melissa? Grandma Martha will take care of you. I want you to come in the house and we'll get you settled in, give you a bath and some milk and cookies if you like later. Okay?"

Melissa's eyes lit up at the sound of cookies. "Okay, I like cookies."

It was with great relief that I crossed the street again to the next house, knowing that I had done the right thing by giving the Rosenbergs a chance to help us out while we helped them out.

The next house was well known to us. Rodney Owens and his family owned it. He had a large used car lot and was often seen on television doing the local advertising. Once again, I went up to his view screen intercom and pushed the button. The screen lit up and it was Rodney, with a stern look on his face.

"What do you want, Drake? I heard you rummaging around next door and saw you on my surveillance cameras. What are you doing, scavenging? What are you gonna do with that little girl? I saw you take her across the street?"

"No, I'm just going around the neighborhood trying to find out if anyone's alive. Next door, I just found a seven-year-old girl whose parents had died and I took her to the Rosenbergs across the street where they took her in until I find if any relatives of hers are still alive."

"Well, that was really nice of you, but I'm not having any of it. Where have you been? The world is coming apart. We are prepared here, but we can't take in anybody else. My wife and son are dead already. But me and my daughter are going to hold out as long as we can. Just go away and don't come back. I'll shoot any trespassers, even you!"

"Okey-dokey, we'll do that. I lost my parents and Derek Jones did, too, as well as our sisters. But if you're ever inclined, get in touch with us again because we want to help bring some order, at least in the neighborhood."

"No more talky talk. Just go away!" The intercom went dead.

I just shook my head and crossed the street again to lunch with Derek and a story he wouldn't believe.

❧∙⊰⊱∙❧

4

Daphne's Rescue

I was really torn about what to do while we ate lunch. But I was regaining my strength and trying to focus on the neighborhood while thoughts of Daphne kept nagging me to go get her. Daphne was one of those privileged kids who grew up in wealth and inherited beauty from her celebrity parents. Her father was Walter Hughes, one of the top grossing actors in Hollywood and her mother was the supermodel, Vanessa Wiles. She was an only child and grew up with nannies and private tutors. Both Derek and I had crushes on her in our private high school, but neither of us ever dated her because of her social standing and ours.

I shared my thoughts with Derek as we ate.

"Der, it's going to take a while to check on the remaining houses on our street. Frankly, it's taking time and after what I've found this morning, it isn't going to be easy. I've already saved a dog and a little girl. Don't know if anyone nearby is dying of thirst that we should save or not."

"Daphne sounded desperate."

"But it would take all afternoon to get there and back. We have to know if anyone is still alive or maybe in trouble here. That's my problem."

"We could call them. I've got a couple of numbers from the Eversons and Waltons. I'm sure your dad and mom's phones have some more numbers if we can open them."

"Sorry, I never had their access codes. Just respected their privacy like they respected mine after they confiscated my phone that time and we had a good talk."

"Yeah, I remember that. When I heard what happened to you, I cleaned up my act, too. It would've been much worse for me if my dad found out. So, in a way, you kind of saved me, bro." They both chuckled.

"I have an idea." Derek offered. "We could print some flyers and either make airplanes of them and toss them over the walls, or we could tie rocks to them and throw them over the walls."

I thought for a moment… "That's a great idea. Mailboxes won't work. How about, 'Derek Jones and Drake Hutchins, If you need help, call us, and then, give them our mobile numbers.' They can call us while we are on the mission to help Daphne."

"Great idea."

Derek went to my computer, typed in the message, colored and enlarged it for a standard piece of paper and printed 20 copies.

We rolled each paper up and tied it with some ribbon we found in my mom's work area. Then, with some string, tied some rocks to each roll so they would be heavy enough to throw over the fence. Paper airplanes would be nice, but the updrafts that we parasailed on here would make them land in the front yards very iffy.

While Derek gathered up what we would need or might need for the trip, I went to the part of the walk-in closet in my parent's bedroom where Dad kept his guns. I picked out two pistols with holsters and loaded them, leaving the chamber empty for safety. Also, a shotgun and rifle that I loaded the same way. Strapped one holster around my waist for the 9 mm and dropped it in. I took the rest of the guns and additional ammunition to the garage and put them in the cab of Dad's utility truck that had a range of 600 miles. The double cab truck also had a generator that ran off gasoline to run all the electrical power tools and welder on the truck as well as recharge the batteries if there wasn't a plug-in around and the batteries got low.

We put Regis in the backyard with some water and food. Double checked if there was anything we'd need, and left the house, driving slowly down the street, throwing our flyers over the fences of about 20 homes until we ran out. Soon after, as I drove east by northeast through familiar streets to the 2 and on to the Hollywood Hills, we passed few cars in the streets that were mostly empty. Eerily quiet compared to its usually bustling traffic.

And then, once in a while, there was a car parked strangely out of place and we could see someone slumped over the wheel that we knew was dead. Probably really sick people who are trying to drive to the hospital or to a loved one and didn't make it. As we passed expensive shop areas we saw occasional windows smashed and in the distance along the way we saw a moving car or two. Other people out like us.

The spiraling vultures in some places told us where something dead was out in the open–where the dead were. We weren't drawn to them to find out what they were eating. We just knew. I shuddered at the thought and drove on. Here and there, we saw dogs and cats running loose. But no one walking them like before.

From various vantage points we could see the fires that left the smoky haze in the air. But thankfully, there weren't any fires along the path we were taking as we left Hollywood and I drove up into the hills where Daphne lived.

Not wanting to get her hopes up, we waited to call her until we got close.

Daphne's home was in a neighborhood of large walled compounds of the stars. Walter and Vanessa's compound was as expected. Neither of us had ever been there. From the gate, there was a long drive curving out of sight up into the trees. There was so much vegetation that no buildings could be seen. We called Daphne…

The phone rang about five times and she answered. "Dre! Where are you guys?" She sounded anxious.

I answered, "We are at the gate, let us in."

"Oh gosh, yes! Right away. I can't believe you're here!"

The gate opened and we drove up the drive past the luxurious greenery until it opened up into a large circle drive with a fountain in the center that we took to the right and up underneath the awning where there were already a couple of expensive cars.

I saw her come running from the house down the stairs as I was getting out of the cab and she reached Derek first, jumping into his arms barefoot and in a body revealing nightie that seemed inappropriate for midday. Something more like that seven-year-old, Melissa had on when I rescued her earlier. After kissing Derek profusely on his cheeks and then a bit prolonged on his lips, as I rounded the cab, she turned and ran to me with mascara stained cheeks, giving me the same treatment while gushing…

"Oh, Dre! I'm so glad you came. My folks and my brother are dead. I couldn't stand it in the house with them staring like that. I didn't know what to do. I'm running out of everything and no one is here to help me get it. I don't know if I can stay in this place. I've been in the guesthouse until I knew you were coming."

"Do you want us to help you bury your folks?" The thought of doing it again was dreadful to me but I didn't want her to know it.

"Oh my God, No. I just want to leave this place and all that's in it. The memories would haunt me too much. Can I go with you guys wherever you're going?"

Derek put in his two cents. "We're staying at home for now trying to figure out what to do to make our neighborhood a place we can stay in. We've already rescued a dog and a seven-year-old girl. Our next-door neighbors, the Rosenbergs, are still alive."

"Oh, geez, you guys are lifesavers. You have it so together. That's why I've always liked you so much."

I wanted to believe her a little bit but wasn't sure if I should.

I suggested, "Do you have any family or friends that you need to get in touch with before we leave. They will want to know where you are."

She had a puzzled look on her face while she thought for a moment. And then, she started to whimper a bit, as she said, "No, nobody but that, Wondah, who called me two days ago. She was in our group at school but I never really liked her, she was a nosy bitch." She scowled.

"Well, if you think of anyone, let us know. I'm sure you called everybody already, didn't you?"

"Oh, oh, I forgot!" Daphne reached for her phone. "There is my uncle Louie Hughes, my dad's older brother who lives up in Laurel Canyon. He's kind of a recluse artist who does work for the studios. I haven't seen him since I was a little girl. I have his number here on my phone that Dad gave me before he died.

"Go ahead and give him a call, it won't hurt." We waited while she sniffled and rang him.

The phone rang about five times when a gruff old voice came on the phone. "Who's calling and what do you want, Daphne?"

"It's me, your niece. Do you remember me? The last time I remember seeing you was when Dad took me to your place when I was about six, do you remember?"

The voice on the other end softened a bit. "So, it is you, child. I thought someone had taken your phone because I never got a call from you before. With finding everybody dead around here I thought that might have happened to you, Walter, and Vanessa. So glad to hear your voice after all these years, so grown-up." She started crying.

"No, Uncle Louie, Dad and Mom and my brother, Scott are all dead. I can't even bear to be in the house with them. Two of my friends from high school are here to help me out."

"Poor child, you need to come here and stay with me. You shouldn't be running off with guys from high school. I can take care of you. And we can live a long time here without the help of outsiders. See if you can get them to bring you here. If not, get in one of your cars and drive to my place."

"Okay, Uncle Louie, I'll come. You may need me as much as I need you. I promise I will learn to cook and help you around your place if you teach me."

"I will, child. I will." He abruptly hung up.

Derek had a disappointed look on his face. "You can still go with us if you want. Okay?"

Through her tears, "But he's my uncle?"

I interjected, "Der, she's right. But remember, Daphne. If this doesn't work out, just call us again and we'll take you in. And, it sure looks like we are going to be taking in others that will be needing our help too. But, from what it looks like we will have to do, everybody's going to have to pull their own weight."

Derek sighed. "Well, let's load the truck with everything that you will need to take and we'll drive you up to your uncle's place."

Daphne led us to her bedroom that was unruffled because she had been staying in the guesthouse. We went into her closet and she began gathering up loads of clothes and accessories to take until I told her…

"Daphne, we are in a different world now. Only take what you will need that will be durable and washable. Don't take too much right now because you can probably come back and get more as you get situated rather than a lot of stuff you'll never wear or use again."

From her closet, we went into her bathroom and took all the essentials but none of the extravagant amount of jewelry, cosmetics and other beauty stuff that Daphne had in abundance. While Derek was helping her with that, I did a quick survey of the house including her parents' palatial bedroom and closets looking for anything that we might need, but didn't find anything that I thought she might need. We gave her time to take a shower, snack on some food we brought and dress appropriately in shorts, one of her many pairs of walking shoes and a light blouse. Obviously without a bra. She didn't seem to care about taking all of that fancy underwear with her.

It took about an hour and there was way too much stuff, but we were all too tired to argue. We put it on the truck and drove up to Laurel Canyon where we found the small, almost hidden, drive leading uphill with a strong metal gate with a big "**No Trespassing**" sign on it and an old-fashioned voice intercom.

Daphne pushed the buzzer and called out, "Uncle Louie, we're here!" A crackling response came back. "Okay, I see you. I'll be right down."

We could hear the sound of a gasoline powered four wheeler start up and come roaring down the road to the gate. Louie was a thin but strong looking man with a full head of white hair and long beard wearing a black T- shirt showing the arms of a sculptor. The first thing he did was jump off the four-wheeler and run up to Daphne.

"My, my, how you have grown!" He hugged her and she struggled a bit before hugging back. "I can't believe you're here. After that falling out I had with your father, I thought I'd never see you again. But you were only six and neither of us wanted to let you know. Welcome to my humble home!"

Louie unlocked the padlock on the heavy chain securing the steel gate to the concrete anchored heavy steel pole and swung it to one side. He had Daphne hop on to the four wheeler with him and we followed with the truck up the long drive rubbing and breaking tree limbs on each side until we reached a more level spot where a couple of vehicles still left room for us to park under the trees. Before us was a midcentury redwood beam structure reminiscent of Frank Lloyd Wright. The perfect artist sanctuary.

Louie announced upon our arrival, "I'd invite you in for tea but it's a bit of a mess, so if you don't mind, you can just unload Daphne's stuff right here on this table…" He chased some leaves and branches off the top of the table with his hand… "And we'll take it all into the house."

I wondered what he meant by not allowing us in the house, but I didn't ask.

Derek and I quickly unloaded all of Daphne's stuff on the table and after saying our goodbyes to her and waving at Uncle Louie, we beat a retreat back to our house.

As we got underway, once again, scraping the sides of our truck until we got to the Laurel Canyon Drive, I saw in the rearview mirror that Louie was already there closing and locking the gate.

Derek said, "I wonder what that was about? Why didn't he let us in and why he hadn't seen Daphne in twelve years?

"I thought the same things. It must've been something really bad for her father to disown him for so long?"

"Oh well, I guess we'll never know, now that she went with him instead of coming with us."

"I don't know about you, Der. But I had mixed feelings about her coming with us."

"Yeah, I know. I would've been fighting you for her affections."

"But remember, she was pampered all her life up until now. How could anyone turn her into a hard-working housewife?"

"That's a very good question. I was wondering how we might share her, somehow. You know, like all of the babies that were black or colored were mine, and the blue-eyed white ones, yours…" He laughed out loud and I joined him. What a pleasant thought.

We spent the rest of our time on the trip back with Derek making some more calls and trying to think of what we needed to do next.

We certainly needed to clear the street all the way down to the end where it entered the boulevard and maybe put up a barricade there so that we wouldn't get unwelcome visitors.

Somehow, I just suspected that they would be coming. At least, I believed we had time before they would come. Perhaps, after their easyraiding for supplies, food and water would run out in midsummer and they would need to range further into more secluded neighborhoods to get what they needed.

We also engaged in a little good-natured banter until I saw dogs and cats roaming along the way and knew that we would find dogs and cats, and even, other pets like Regis. I tried to think of ways that we could help them without them becoming a real burden of maintenance and birth control.

And then, we passed it, the local Fairway grocery store where our mothers always shopped. It appeared abandoned, so I did a U-turn and we drove into the parking lot, mostly empty except for three cars. Two of them were empty and one contained a dead body behind the steering wheel.

As expected, the double doors were not working, so we took a crowbar and pried open the door to the disabled access entry for wheelchairs. Once inside, there was air conditioning running and the lights were on, but otherwise the place was eerily quiet.

We each grabbed two grocery carts and started going through the store. The produce section contained a lot of very wilted greenery that we didn't need much of because of our gardens. But we picked up some fruit that we didn't have growing in the neighborhood and then headed towards the meat department where we got both fresh and frozen meats. I recalled that our freezer in the garage was only half-full from our last deer hunt in the Central Valley with Gramps. So, we loaded up with frozen fish, steaks, hams and other meat that would quickly spoil if the electricity went out.

There was a distinct odor of rotting flesh that didn't come from the meat counters. We didn't see any bodies but there may have been some in the back rooms where there may have been a lot more food. It was unpleasant, but we had to do what we were doing while we could.

Like those contests where people were allowed to take something like fifteen minutes to grab all of the groceries they could, we had trouble deciding how much of what we would gather. I really felt guilty taking the food because as a young child when I followed my mother, she scolded me if I tried to pick up any little candy or other treat without paying for it. It was even worse for Derek, because he always hated watching young black looters during the protests and riots in various parts of the country.

As we left with all four grocery carts filled with bags of groceries, I made a note to come back soon before others started destroying the store while taking their share. And I knew that the power would soon fail, and all of the perishables would start to rot.

We arrived home to more new challenges that we hadn't foreseen.

5

Bodies and Pets

I was already late afternoon and we had much to do. We busied ourselves with unloading the groceries, and then filling the freezer in the garage and our two refrigerators. The rest, we put in the trailer behind our electric four wheeler and drove up to the Rosenbergs; first, to see what they might need, and then, take the rest to Derek's house for storage there.

When I rang the bell at the Rosenberg gate, Melissa, with her health already restored, but still skinny as a pretzel stick, came running out to greet us.

I called out, "We've got groceries for you! Do you want to tell Mrs. Rosenberg to come out and see what we have?"

Melissa reached the gate, near breathless. "Drake…" She paused to catch her breath. "Grandpa Jake is sick! He got to feeling bad this afternoon and went to bed!"

"Can you have Martha come out? Maybe we can help?" I didn't have a clue on how to help.

Melissa ran back into the house and came back with Martha. Martha had a very serious look on her face as she also reached the gate a bit breathless.

"How is he?" I asked, waiting for her to catch her breath.

"He… He… isn't good. He never gets sick. Hasn't even gone to the doctor for the last few years. Even though he has been complaining more lately about aches and pains as he goes about his daily chores. He started complaining a lot this afternoon and went to bed. He's having trouble breathing."

"That's too bad. Sounds like it might be Amazonia. We've got groceries. Pick out anything you want and we'll take it in the house for you."

Martha Rosenberg opened the gate and I drove the four-wheeler up close to the house. She went through the bags of groceries that we had and picked out what she wanted. We had gathered some different kinds of kids' cereals, but Martha objected. "Just some good old-fashioned cereals like Quaker Oatmeal, Cream of Wheat and Malt-o-Meal."

I could see Melissa squirming a bit and asked her what she would like. She thought for a moment, and then, rattled off, "Fruit Loops, Capt'n Crunch," and a few others I hadn't heard of.

"We only picked up store brand oatmeal and some boxes of the kind of cereal that Melissa wants. I don't think that store even stocks Cream of Wheat or Malt-o-Meal anymore. But I do recall having those hearty hot breakfast foods when we went hunting in the fall at grandpa's. Remember, Der?"

"Yes. I also remember them when Grandma Jones made them for me when we stayed down in Watts when I was a kid. Grits, ever heard of that?"

We unloaded the groceries that Martha pointed out and carried them into the kitchen to put away for her. I asked, "Martha, just make a list of what Melissa wants and you need for the next time we make a run to the grocery store. I hope what we brought here today will help you for a few days."

"It sure will. I don't know how to thank you kids for doing this. I was scared we were going to run out of food until Jake got sick. That reminds me. I've got to check on him. Do you want to come along?"

We followed her into the master bedroom where Jake was struggling with his breathing and wheezing. He smiled but said nothing when he saw us hovering over him and me holding his right hand with my left hand and patting the back of it with my right hand. His eyes were very red and swollen. There were beads of sweat on his brow. All of it giving me the idea that he was very sick and feverish.

Martha confirmed it. "His temperature is 103°."

We waved Jake goodbye and left the room with Melissa following. I asked her, "Would you mind if we left Regis with you and Grandma Martha? He was terribly lonely when we got back this afternoon."

"I'll ask Grandma Martha. I like doggies and he is beautiful!" I turned the four-wheeler around and we drove off to Derek's house and quickly unloaded what we had left into their refrigerators, freezer and shelves. Before we left I remembered…

"Remember that I told you that I saw some exotic birds in a big cage at Barbara Wilkes-Hodges estate next door?"

"Yeah, I remember when you told me about the place and what you found there. I'd like to see it and the birds."

"I think we should let them out or they will die in that place without any care."

We drove the four-wheeler over there and the ladder was still where I left it the day before up against the wall. We both climbed over the wall and entered the palace. Immediately, I detected a faint smell of decaying body. While that odor was revolting, it wasn't yet strong enough to be unbearable.

"We have to do something about Barbara."

"I'm too beat right now to do any grave digging."

"Der, you're right. We can't be digging graves for everyone dead on this street. But we can't let bodies rot in their houses or we won't be able to use any of them for some time. We could find some plastic garbage bags to put them in, couldn't we?"

"I read somewhere that the Zoroastrians always placed their dead on sacred high places for the vultures to eat like the Dakota Indians, I think. We've got plenty of those buzzards around here… Seagulls, too."

We climbed the sweeping stairs to Barbara's bedroom and I found that parts of her well-preserved aged body were turning blue at the surface where blood coagulated under the skin. She was no longer beautiful; looked every bit a cadaver out of a horror movie. Thankfully, not becoming a zombie like so many wild stories with no basis in reality, whatsoever. *This was reality*. How do we dispose of many decomposing bodies?

"Der, I think you're right. Let's let the vultures do it for us.

Silently and reverently, we wrapped Barbara in one of her very smooth, satin sheets and tied it tight at her head. Then, we both grabbed the sheet at her feet and pulled her off the bed carefully to not hit her head hard on the plush carpet. And then, pulled her unceremoniously down the curving stairway with her head bobbing and bumping as it dropped off each marble step. No use pampering the dead.

We pulled her through the large dining room and out on the open veranda overlooking the grounds and pool. Finally, we dragged her down the stairs to the pool level and to the far end of the pool where we left her. We pulled the sheet off her leaving her naked body open on the edge of the pool for the vultures and seagulls above to see, smell and swoop down to feed. Already, they were forming the well-known spiral pattern above our heads. Waiting with their bird brains for us to end our feeding so they could feed without our interruption.

On a hunch, I motioned for Derek to follow me as we walked down through the beautiful gardens that were no longer tended and starting to show weeds to the end of the property where there was a gate in the wall. I manually opened the gate and saw that a trail there led down the ravine and into the natural wildlife preserve in the distance. It was a beautiful sight watching the sun settling in the west lighting up the hills to the east across the valley below.

"I've been thinking we could put all of the pets we find here. We can provide them with food and water and let them fend for themselves. They could leave through this gate on their own and go wild."

Derek answered, "I don't have a better idea. And I'm also thinking we had better get to all the other houses on the street tomorrow or we may find bodies where we could've saved someone."

That thought had bothered me since I found Melissa.

"I think before we go we need to call every house on this street that we can get a phone number for. Save time finding anyone alive.

"One more thing, Derek. Let's get the caretaker and his wife out here, too."

As quickly as we could, we wrapped each one in sheets and dragged them out into the open for the vultures and gulls, too. I worried about coyotes, but we couldn't do everything all at once.

We returned to the house, opened the huge indoor cage door and walked to the small hanging cages for two macaws, a beautiful parrot, a trio of peafowl and several other exotic birds I couldn't identify. We took the birds, except the peafowl, in their cages outside and hung them from hooks under the veranda that were probably used for hanging plants or even the birds' cages before. The peacock and his two paramours followed us out of the big cage and onto the veranda like they had done it many times before.

We opened the cage doors to let the birds out. Some of them were already flying around the house and we left the sliding glass doors and French doors in the back of the house open to the outside so that the birds could leave, and unfortunately, the wild world could come in. Coyotes, feral cats and foxes would feast on a supply of tame, naïve birds.

We would have to come back later and remove very valuable things like paintings, sculptures, books, jewelry and other things that we might put in museums in the future. For now, with plenty of bird food spread around outside, water in pans as it started to get dark was all we could do as we left the place to the birds and animals for the night and near future. People were more important. Seagulls and vultures were already feasting on the former owner and caretakers.

After we made something to eat from all the groceries we brought, we showered and went to bed, exhausted again. Finishing one very hard day, expecting many more to come.

I woke up. The clock said 10 am. I shook off foggy sleep from my head and stretched my aching muscles. I smelled bacon again and found Derek, once again, cooking breakfast for us.

"I thought you were never going to wake up, Dre!" He laughed. "It must be all this exercise and clean air." I chuckled.

"So much for an early start today. We'd better check on Jake next door before we start tackling those bodies you found across the street. And, we had better start calling those phone numbers and names of our neighbors from the Internet."

I was already eating as fast as I could so that we would get out on the street quicker. Derek had already finished much of his breakfast. He would be waiting on me.

Fifteen minutes later, we were at the Rosenberg's gate with our four-wheeler trailer loaded with tools we thought we might need for the day's work. I knew it wouldn't be easy.

Melissa ran out to the gate again crying to greet us.

"Grandpa Jake died last night." She didn't stop crying when she opened the gate for us and we drove on in, jumped out and hugged her, before running inside.

As we came into the bedroom and saw Martha holding her husband's head in her lap with a determined look on her face, softly crying, she told us, "Jacob had a good life. He had a number of problems in recent years that the doctors couldn't cure. It was his time. He didn't believe in Jehovah anymore, anyway. So, I guess it won't matter if he isn't buried with the blessing of the rabbi."

I told her. "We can bury him here, like we did our parents. But it will have to wait. We need to find out if there are any more living people on our street like Melissa, first."

Martha waved her hands as if motioning us to go. "Thank you. I don't know what I would do without you boys. Go ahead and look for others alive. I will prepare Jacob for burial here.

We left, taking the four-wheeler and the ladder from the wall at the estate. We called the numbers we had gathered from an address search for the next house on the right and the house on the left at the same time from our cell phones as we moved down the street. We got no answer from both. The Astors lived in the compound next to ours. We didn't know them. They didn't answer my call, so I put the ladder to the fence and climbed to the top, calling out to them.

No one came, so we both climbed down the ladder and went to the house and knocked. No one was there. But in the bedrooms it looked like someone had been packing with doors open. We heard a cat meowing and saw a cat outside. We found some milk in the refrigerator and put a bowl outside for the cat to drink. We left the cat outside and crossed the street where the Waltons lived.

Once again, we called from the top of the wall and no one came. But when we got in the house we were greeted by their German Shepherd, Mike, but no one else. He led us to the master bedroom where we found both Rosalie and Walter dead in their bed. Our friend, their son, Hunter, who was sixteen, was also dead in his bedroom where we had visited him many times before.

We both were shook up over what we saw. Mike had loyally led us around and showed sorrow and hunger in his face, whining. Silently, we got him a large pan of water and some meat from the refrigerator that we took outside for him to drink and eat.

Then, we silently wrapped the bodies in sheets and pulled them out the sliding doors in their bedrooms to outside where we left the three of them for the vultures while Mike gulped down the meat. He followed us outside where we opened the gate and took him with us to the next two houses. Our grisly task was only beginning. We split up to speed things up. I used a stepladder we had that wasn't as good as the ladder, but it worked.

I started with the house directly below the Waltons, hoping for the best. The occupants had moved in only a month or so before, so I had no idea who they were. But the street number gave the phone number for the surname of Bloom.

I called the number but got no answer. I called over the fence and still got no answer. So, I climbed over from the Walton side and found the front door locked. Then, I walked around the house and when I came to a sliding door for a bedroom, I could see a small girl sitting on the bed with a disturbing man appearing to be dead on the floor between the bed and the sliding door that was open about six inches.

I waved to the girl and she waved back. I called out, "I'm here to help, what's your name?"

She shyly returned my call, "Flower. Can you help me? Mama's very sick!"

As I entered, I could see that she sat next to a sheet covered woman. "Is that your mother?"

"Yes, her name is Melody. She's very sick and I don't know what to do!" She started crying.

I came close and looked into the woman's half opened eyes, obviously feverish. "How long have you been sick, Melody?"

She opened her red eyes a bit more, coughed and wheezed, "I don't know, but it's been days. This is the first day that I've been talking to Flower. She's really scared that I might die like Spike."

"Is that your husband on the other side of the bed?"

"Yeah, the bastard. Lying womanizer. Should have never married him at 17. Glad he's gone." She coughed again and fell silent.

Flower said, "She peed."

I knew it, because I could smell it. I lifted the sheet and found that she was wearing only a beige colored panty that was soaked with urine along with the sheet and mattress beneath. I couldn't say I hadn't been in a date's thong before, but this was entirely new.

"Flower, she needs to be cleaned. I will help you do it." I didn't want to, but knew I had to.

"She's tried. Just take off my panties and wash me. Don't be shy young man, I'm not." Melody fell silent again after choking those few words out.

I reached under the soaked from sweat sheet at her beautiful womanly figure. Grabbing the band at the top began to pull it, and then had to grab the other side at the bottom, to gradually pull her panties down her legs and off her feet. I told Flower to wait while I went to the bathroom where

I found a bucket and put them in it followed by some warm water that I added some hand soap to. I found another pan and filled it with warm water. Got a couple of washcloths and threw a bath towel over my shoulder.

When I got there, I gave Flower one of the washcloths, and I showed her how to put some soap on it and work up a lather. We both began washing. Flower went to her feet and worked her way up, so I was tasked with starting on her lovely stomach and moving down into the completely shaved region where I applied the soap carefully and I heard Melody moan in her misery when I touched a sensitive part.

I told Flower to come with me into the bathroom and we rinsed out the washcloths, poured out the soapy water from the bowl and filled it with fresh, warm water. And another bowl to ring out the soapy water we would remove. I found myself at Melody's hips again rinsing the soapy water from her nether parts and finding that she responded favorably through her fever. Flower rinsed the soap off her legs.

I asked Melody, "Do you want me to put something on you?" "Heavens, no, boy. I feel much better already. I will have to thank you later when I recover." I wondered what that meant? But, had something more to tell her.

"I want to move you to the dry side of the bed. Is that okay?"

"Yes, but please get rid of Spike's body first. I don't want to see him anymore."

"Right away. Mrs.… ah…"

"Bloom, Melody… You can call me Mel."

I went to a dresser in the room and found a clean sheet. I pulled the sheet and blanket off Melody and with Flower's help, put the clean sheet on her naked body, followed by the blanket that was already warm to get her covered again.

Then, I took the sheet that had been on Melody and placed it over her husband, Spike. Rolled his heavy body with the sheet and had Flower help me drag it through the sliding glass door onto the grass where it slid easier, to the far end of the lot near the back wall where I hoped Melody would not see the vultures and seagulls feeding. During the whole time, Flower was crying softly about the only father, as he appeared to be, she had, now dead.

That accomplished, I had Flower help me drag and roll her mother to the dry side of the bed where she went to sleep.

I whispered to Flower, "Make some soup for your mama if you can. If not, make sure she gets plenty of water. I have to go with my friend down the street until it is dark to see if we can find any more people like your mother and you are still alive. We will be back as soon as we can."

Flower hugged me and whimpered, "I will, but be back soon. There's nothing to eat and I'm hungry."

I reached in my pocket and found an apple and granola bar that I was going to eat later and gave them to her.

She smiled again and hugged me again. I slipped out, not wanting to waste any more time.

Derek had already covered two houses across the street, so we were parallel again, going house to house. As we moved down the street we found three more vacant houses. And three more houses with dead bodies.

We found Robert Emerson, his wife, Eleanor and their two children, Michael, 12, and Elizabeth, 10, all alive and working hard to secure themselves in their house like we were doing.

The Emersons apologized for not answering the phone when Derek called earlier, because they suspected that our parents were dead. Unfortunately, like so many, they had recovered and found out that people they knew call my like the Hutchins, didn't. They had also raided the same grocery store for food. We told them that we would keep in touch as we began to make all these houses sustainable for the near future, hoping they would work with us.

Robert assured us. "While I feel really sad about your folks, I'm really impressed with what you two have done already in spite of your grief. We are with you all the way wherever that takes us."

We thanked him for that assurance and moved on, it was getting dark.

Along the way, we freed seven cats. Four of them in one house with dead bodies. We took with us six dogs. Two poodles, a pit bull, a German shorthair, a beagle and a Pomeranian that threatened to bite us until we fed him some water and food.

They all followed us readily up the street by the end of the afternoon to the compound at the end of the street where we took all of the dog food that we had gathered through the gate to the back of the house where we filled up pans of it for them to eat under the veranda in case it rained.

It was a ramshackle pack of strangers I knew would get along and maybe fight off predators and become wild themselves. Those dogs were already chasing the vultures off the dead bodies and the exotic birds to their cages, the trees and the wall. Since Mike was special, we took him home with us. He seemed to regret leaving the other dogs behind but was soon wagging his tail at Martha Rosenberg.

When we stopped off at the Rosenbergs on the way home with the sun going down, we found Martha struggling with half of a grave dug for her husband by her garden out back. We were dog-tired, but we took two shovels and finished the job for her. We all dragged Jake's body down to the grave and lowered it in with a sheet and covered him with it. Martha said some words over him, dropped some mementos and we quickly shoveled the dirt back in.

As I recall, Derek and I felt a deep sadness and concern for those dogs that we knew would not live well on their own. Some would surely die. We vowed to try to find a way to take care of them.

In spite of being so tired, I didn't sleep well and had bad dreams throughout the night even knowing that I had done my best. I hadn't gone back to see how Melody was doing. Hopeful that she was getting better and that Flower would have a mother as I tossed and turned until morning would find out.

6

Rescuing Melody and Wondah

That night, the sirens had almost disappeared. Many of the fires that started had burned out, but some had grown, uncontrolled, and were still burning. The sound of gunfire, both single shots and automatic, continued to grow. It reached a crescendo before midnight, and then slacked off toward morning. But I knew little of it except when I got up to urinate and check outside if anything was out of order.

I woke in the morning with much on my mind. I actually beat Derek up. So, it was me who started cooking and thinking while I waited for him to wake up. Smoke rose up under the burner for the frying pan. I opened a window to let the kitchen air out a bit. Where we live, the dry conditions and sea breeze means there are really no bugs to speak of; hardly anyone has screens on their windows.

Suddenly, the room was full of flies. We didn't have a flyswatter so I rolled up a magazine and went around swatting them. Finally, had to close the window because so many were coming in to the smell of bacon frying. I knew why there were so many. All those bodies we had dragged out in the neighborhood had now had enough time to attract hatches from earlier rotting bodies looking for new egg laying sites. As I looked out the window I could see them in swarms and I could also see seagulls and other birds attacking them with zest. I thought of those dogs experiencing them for the first time in their lives, swatting away with their tails and covering their eyes with their paws.

And then, Derek appeared…

"Sorry I'm late, got a call from Daphne. She told me that her uncle has been after her to pose in lingerie for his painting and sculpture… She said he's being creepy like she's beginning to remember from before… And, she had another problem…

"She told me that her nosy, precocious, geeky friend, Wondah Mohammed, keeps calling. Telling her that she's all alone, out of water and food and has had to hide in the crawlspace under her family house to escape armed marauders. She said they're going house to house and killing people for what little they have. Took all the food she had in her refrigerator and pantry."

"Where does she live?"

"Daphne said over in Inglewood on the east side of Edward Vincent, Jr., Park. Daphne gave me her phone number and address. Said, 'You need to rescue her.'"

"That's near our company yard and warehouse in South Los Angeles. We need to swing by there anyway to get some things for the barricade or we'll have half of Los Angeles coming here after what we have. Why don't you give her a call and tell her that we will try to come by as soon as late this morning after we do a few things here, first."

"Will do. What's with all the flies Dre? I heard you swatting them in here and I can hear them buzzing outside… See them in swarms."

"The result of leaving bodies out for the vultures. At least I saw the local birds having a field day eating them. I'm not sure how long we'll have them around… I hope not long."

"Me, either."

While we made and ate breakfast together, we discussed what we would do for the day. Wondah presented a whole new interrupting challenge among many we had facing us. We left the house as early as we could after tending to the garden. Fighting off flies as we did. Martha and her charges were okay but forced to stay in the house. Some of the dogs were eating flies as though they were good protein and otherwise okay along with some of the exotic birds who were also big fly eaters.

I called Robert Emerson to see how he and his family were doing.

"Bob, just checking in to see how you are doing." I left the speakerphone on so Derek could join us.

"Not well. I can foresee, even with that grocery store, that our food won't last. Finally, don't think it's safe to stay here, even with your efforts. I applaud you for staying, but we are packing. My hybrid truck should be able to make it to Albuquerque where my brother says they have a mountain retreat that we can go to. So, we are leaving this morning so we will have a lot of daylight getting out of the city and on our way into what we hope won't be in dangerous country getting to Albuquerque."

"I think that's a good plan, Bob. My grandfather is in the Central Valley at his farm. If things get too bad here, we can go stay with him. But for now, I'm going to try to make this, our home, livable and sustainable. Is it okay to use your place for growing food and gathering water?"

"Go ahead. I know you guys are resourceful. Anything you do here will be an improvement if we come back in the future. I just don't have the energy that you guys seem to have."

"Have a great journey with no trouble, okay?"

"I'm sure we will… Bye."

"Bye."

I had the keycode to the Bloom compound, so we didn't have to climb over the wall. We just opened the gate and drove the four wheeler in. We knocked on the door though, rather than just walking on in. We heard Melody call out…

"Come on in guys! What took you so long… We're already packed."

As we entered the bedroom, she was dressed in white denim shorts, a light yellow top short at the bottom that bared her taut, tan midriff. It was almost transparent and clearly showed, not only that she wasn't wearing a bra but she was wearing a shoulder holster with a pistol under her right arm. On the bed were packed suitcases.

"We've been up since before dawn. I left the sliding glass door open like I usually do, and suddenly we were being attacked by flies! Took us a half-hour of swatting to get rid of them. I guess it must be Spike's revenge. Look, the vultures are on him. Have been all morning. I want us to get out of here." She pointed to where they had dragged Spike. It was the first time that Derek saw what was left of him. A man he didn't know. He winced at the thought of what he was seeing.

I changed the subject. "Why are you carrying?"

"Because I can, sweetie. Have you heard all the shooting out there like I have? Spike was a detective for the L.A. Police Department. The only reason we were able to buy this place was kickbacks he got for special favors for special people. Part of the reason he was rotten to the core. This is his service FN 509 that he forced me to learn how to fire. Now, I'm glad he did. There're also his police issued rifle and shotgun in the closet. I suggest that you take them if you want to protect us."

"You're right. We were just planning to beef up our defenses today by covering those open gates we have so that intruders can't see into what we have. We'll take the guns and get you out of here."

Flower took the opportunity to run over and hug me. Then, we began picking up their things and taking them to the trailer behind the four wheeler. Derek and Flower walked while Melody rode with me.

I turned into the Rosenberg place and Martha and Melissa came out to greet us. Derek and Flower soon caught up. Flower ran down ahead to hug her friend Melissa, so glad to see her alive. Although in different grades, they were in the same school together. Melody got a sour look on her face. "Are you expecting me to stay with that old broad?" She said it loud enough so that Martha could hear.

"Yes, I thought it was best because we have to leave and go to our father's business where we will pick up supplies to barricade our gates and the entrance to the street. It will take most of the day and we thought you would like it better here with some of Martha's great cooking."

"We're both starved, but I thought I was going to stay with you!" She gave me one of those looks like a spoiled child but I knew it wasn't. It was more like jealousy.

"Okay, you can stay with us, but what about Flower?"

"She can stay here. Did you see how those two hugged? She'll be happier here. Look at that gorgeous dog…" Pointing at Regis, the two girls were petting. Mike was dutifully sitting by the four wheeler licking Melody's bare toes. "I like this German Shepherd and I think he likes me. Or my perfumed nail polish. Vanilla?" She laughed that raunchy laugh of hers.

"That's Mike, I think he'll make a good guard dog. Might need some training though… he's too friendly." I chuckled.

We unloaded Flower's stuff and took it into the house and dropped it off in the same room where Melissa was staying. In the background, I could hear them already discussing what they were going to be doing while swatting flies.

Martha brought some breakfast for Melody and Flower and some hot coffee all around. We relaxed while they ate and, while watching them devour it, she declared, "Not bad for an old broad." We all laughed.

Once Melody had finished three cups of coffee, we were able to return to my house.

Before we left, I told her, "Mel, you can use my sister's room. You could take Mike with you for company, but we have to get on our way to

South L.A.to the warehouse and shop and then make a rescue in Inglewood."

Melody got that look on her face again. "Why can't I go with you?"

I thought for a minute… "Okay, we could use another hand loading material. Are you up to that?"

"I sure am. And, I believe I'm ready for any action." She patted her pistol with her right hand like it was a pet. "Don't you think you guys need to be armed going out there… All those shots we've been hearing?"

"That's a good idea. I'll get Dad's 9 mm Glock and Der; will you take the Beretta?"

"You know how I feel about firearms and shooting people. But this time, I believe you're right, Dre. It's only sane for us to be armed for self-defense. I'll take a shotgun with birdshot, too. That wouldn't kill anyone, but it'll sure hurt."

"Another good idea. Let's pick them up on our way out. We're burning daylight. Der, you take your dad's truck, and I'll take mine. You lead and I'll follow."

Melody interjected, "And I'll ride with you Dre. It's okay to call you that, isn't it." She chuckled.

"I guess so, I've been calling you, Mel." I smiled, looked over and saw a bit of envy in Derek's expression.

As we drove down familiar streets to the yard where the warehouse and shop were we encountered several burned out areas and some areas still burning. We didn't hear any shooting, but we saw evidence of shops broken into and debris on the street that was evidence of looting. Shot up cars and bullet holes in walls and storefronts.

The smell of death was everywhere and sometimes overwhelming so we rolled up the windows, thankful for the air conditioning. When we picked up any speed, flies were splattering on the windshield. Requiring frequent washing with our wipers to get them off.

We even saw coyotes roaming openly and dogs eating bodies. They were somebody's pets but had already turned wild in their hunger and probably were forming packs for protection in their wild state. It made me wonder about the zoos and people that had exotic pets. Did they let them out before they died? I didn't know but wanted to. Would we see lions and tigers in the streets?

We arrived at the yard and found that the padlock on the gate had not been breached. From the gate it didn't look like anything had changed inside. We sat down for a moment in the second floor office and made a lunch from the food and drink that was there, thankful that the refrigerator was still working. While eating, we put together a list of what we would gather and then began doing it. The first items were power tools that we would need. Most of them were already charged and ready for use.

And then, we started loading materials. Plywood, two by fours, cement, rebar, construction barriers and other supplies on both trucks until they were fully loaded. We left with the hope that the heavy construction equipment would not be destroyed or damaged. Hopefully, we would be able to come back and get it to do work later.

It was about 4 o'clock when we finished all that loading. I was so glad that Mel was willing to pull her weight with the rest of us. She was sweating so much her breasts were clearly defined like in a wet T-shirt contest. We both noticed and she didn't seem to care. We were all exhausted; so glad to get into the trucks and get moving with a/c on again.

Wondah's address was on West Boulevard and her house was on the park. All of the houses along that stretch had been remodeled or even rebuilt. The garages had been turned into living space either for rent or for increasing the square footage for second mortgages or equity loans. As a result, both sides of the street were lined with parked vehicles. Along the way, we had to push aside three cars and one pickup truck that blocked our way with bodies inside. Wild vermin and the smell of rotting death were everywhere. We couldn't escape it even with the a/c on.

When we arrived, we found that Wondah's house was much larger than the others and had been obviously rebuilt on two lots and updated by the looks of it. We rang the doorbell that didn't work. It was a camera doorbell and the camera probably didn't work either. Then, I noticed that the door had been broken at the deadbolt so when I pushed on it, it opened easily.

We called out, "Wondah! Wondah!" A few times and got no answer. Finally, I called out, "We are Derek and Drake from your school! Daphne told us that you needed help. We are here to rescue you."

From back in the recesses of the building we heard, "Okay, okay… I'm coming out… I'm really glad to see you guys, just afraid from what I've experienced. Some of our classmates aren't so nice."

I wondered what that meant. But I didn't want to waste time, so we greeted her with hugs and told her that we were there to take her with us where we had food and water and she would be protected.

As we gathered her things in her room, Wondah told us why she was alone. "Mom called from the school district office and told me that she volunteered to help out caring for kids in the high school next door. They were too sick to go home and were in the infirmary in the gym where a temporary care unit had been set up by other school officials and the school nurse.

"Dad came home from Cal State U., Long Beach, sick. I cared for him, but he died in three days telling me that he was sorry. I told him it wasn't his fault. I buried him in the backyard." She broke down crying while Mel hugged her, knowing somewhat what she was going through.

After we had gathered all of her personal things, Wondah lead us to her office that was partly broken up and gathered a bunch of computer gear that she wanted to take with her. She explained…

"I have an online computer business where I consult with and help companies with their automation needs. It's been quite lucrative and the website is still up. But I need a safe place to continue working. You guys seem to have given me a chance to rebuild what I started."

She looked directly at me as she said it. Those huge, technically enhanced eyes tearing up in gratitude when she did. It was obvious she could be a huge asset for us. A genius with AI skills in our midst. The first thing I had in mind was an autonomous camera security system.

As we carried Wondah's things and gear to the trucks, Mel had something to say…

"Dre, I'm going to ride with Der on the way back. Wondah can ride with you."

I couldn't challenge that one. Didn't want to. I was already getting too turned on catching glimpses of her boobs and nipples so clearly defined.

It gave me time to get Wondah's story as we drove back. She told me that her mother met her father in college at Long Beach State when both of them were seniors. But when she went into teaching after college and they had her out of wedlock, they separated. Her mom, Becca Mayes, converted to Black Muslim, changing her name to Mohammed. She gave Wondah her surname, Mohammed.

Wondah's Dad, Oliver Anderson, went on to UCLA for a master's degree, and then, to Berkeley for his PhD in physics. Upon graduation, his alma mater hired him to teach physics. That's when her mother and father reconnected, but never married, and bought this house.

Wondah also told me a bit about how frightened she was when twice, gangs broke into her house and ran through it very quickly while she hid under the house in a crawlspace hearing their loud voices and their footsteps overhead with rats, snakes and spiders crawling all around.

Fortunately, they took only valuables. Unfortunately, they took most of the food she had. She ended up eating noodles and cake mix. The power had gone out so she couldn't begin to repair her electronic equipment and check on her online business. Her cell phone had run out of battery just before we arrived. She was really desperate.

Wondah said that her mother had her tested when she was about five and her IQ was in the genius category. As a child, she was skinny, short and had thick glasses, so she was continually picked on until she got Lasix surgery for her eyes with high tech implants, started doing bodybuilding, and transferred to private schools where they appreciated her abilities with language, music, math and science.

Wondah wasn't immediately attractive, but as I listened to her and saw what a mind she had, I began to get interested in her for what she knew about things that I didn't. She was much more interesting than Melody. And I knew she would be a real asset to our growing family.

But, while we were talking we almost missed it! Actually, had to turn around, and go back to a Wireless Alley store with the storefront window broken. I quickly called Derek and told him what we were doing.

Soon, we were in the store that still had a lot of equipment that hadn't been looted. Wondah had me filling a shopping cart full of cameras, computers, modems and monitors for our security set up. In the back, we found a huge storeroom filled with boxes of equipment that hadn't been touched. I made a note of it to make sure to come back later to get more. Before returning home, we stopped at the grocery store again. Inside, it stunk, the power was off, and it was filled with flies. What produce hadn't been taken, was rotting. I let Melody and Wondah gather any home and kitchen supplies, while Derek and I grabbed food that was in cans packaged or, otherwise, not perishable.

We arrived home after dark and were all too tired to do anything but drop Wondah and her stuff with Martha where Martha fed us all with a hot meal and fresh produce from her garden and fruit trees. We were starting to depend on her to feed us. While there, Wondah fell in love with the girls and dogs. Also, found that Jake's den would make a great office, with permission from Martha.

Returning to my place the three of us rushed to the shower in the master bath. I let Derek go to the one in the second bathroom when he offered, while I politely let Melody shower first. When I handed her a towel, she made sure that I saw her all over tan before moving off into my sister's former room to bed.

After dark, the flies disappeared, so I was able to open my sliding glass door that led to the pool we had neglected using these past many days.

I awoke when I heard splashing. When I looked outside, I could clearly see that Melody was swimming in the pool. And she wasn't wearing any-thing. I slipped out of my briefs I was sleeping in, snuck out across the deck to the pool, and slipped in. She knew I was coming.

⚜⚜⚜

7

Marauders: Great and Small

Swimming pools in the area, including the one where the animals were being housed, lost their chlorination and become stagnant. Creating an ideal environment for hatching mosquitoes.

Melody was on the other side of the pool standing in water up to her shoulders with her back to the wall watching me when I dove in and swam over to her underwater. By the pool LCD underwater light that automatically came on at night, I could easily see her bare legs, midriff, breasts and her shaved vagina approaching and surfaced right in front of her, hoping to surprise her.

Instead, she grinned mischievously, put her arms around my shoulders and gushed, "What took you so long? Kiss me…"

I closed in, feeling her nipples on my chest and my hard on growing up between her legs as I put my arms around her back and pulled her to me making sure that my kiss would be memorable.

It must have been, because at first, after her lips matched mine perfectly, she went limp against me and then, reached down and started rubbing the end of my penis against her clitoris with a heavenly look on her face in the full lamplight. I responded by slipping my right hand from behind her back, still holding her close with my left arm and kissing her lips, neck and under her ears, began cupping her breasts and massaging them while playing with my fingers on her nipples. They were rigid, not from the bathtub warm pool, but her arousal.

Suddenly, we both stopped when we got sharp bites on our foreheads, necks and shoulders–mosquitoes! We were being swarmed by them. We both ducked under water to escape.

I heard Melody yell bubbly underwater, "Let's get out of here!"

Without surfacing, we both pushed off the wall behind us with our feet and swam underwater to the other end of the pool. We emerged from the pool in a single leap and raced each other to my open bedroom sliding door, with me slamming it shut behind us. We were laughing hysterically over what happened, but glad we were inside. There was no time to scratch our mosquito bites or towel dry, we had other things in mind. We just jumped in bed together, grabbed each other and rolled with me on the bottom and her on top.

Melody taught me things I never thought I would ever do. She was clearly n charge and I let her. I came inside her twice, while she had multiple orgasms. After about an hour, we both tired, settled down and she wanted to talk while we held each other without any sheets on we were so warm from exertion.

"I want to tell you Dre, that was amazing. But I don't want you falling in love with me. I've seen Der look at me, too, and I don't want to leave him out. Do you understand?"

"I think I do, but we never shared girlfriends."

"You'll have to with me. And here's the long story why…" I shut my mouth and listened.

"I was pregnant at seventeen with Flower about two months in May of my senior year in high school, just before graduation. When my parents found out, we had a big fight and they told me to leave the house. They had warned me not to go out with that jock troublemaker, so I did to spite them. It was the last straw for them. They had enough and threw me out. I got a garage apartment but was desperate with only a waitress job to pay the rent.

"My boyfriend at the time, Flower's father, told me that he was going to college to play football and he didn't want any baby or me dragging him down. He wanted me to have an abortion and came over one night in early June to take me to an abortion clinic. When I refused, he beat me like I'd seen him beat other guys and left me bleeding to go outside and smoke. I knew he would come back to rape me.

"I called 911. The patrolman that showed up, scared him off, but got the license plate of his car. And then, he knocked on my door. When I opened it up, there was this handsome young man coming to my rescue with a name tag that read "Cpl. Spiro Bloom, LAPD." He took down my complaint, all the while sizing me up as though I were something he liked.

"I don't know what came over me, but I invited him into the bedroom and we had sex. Flower's father was arrested and served two months for assaulting me. I never heard from him again. But Spike Bloom came around often after his shift to have sex with me. When I laid down the law, he agreed to marry me.

"But marrying Spike didn't solve my problems. Spike turned out to be infertile and a womanizer. Often came home drunk and beat me, even in front of Flower. I had a couple of affairs that he nipped in the bud by getting his buddies to intimidate anyone who even looked my way. I was trapped until this pandemic came along and solved my problem for me. That's why I like you, Der, and any other healthy man I find. I want to have babies–lots of them. Repopulate the world!"

All I could say was, "Wow, what a noble gesture!"

She smiled broadly in the dim light. "Not noble, perhaps selfish, but it's time I looked out for myself and maybe did something good in the process."

"And Der?"

"As soon as there is an opportunity, I will sneak into his bed before morning."

"Be my guest. I'd love to keep holding you like this. But I think I understand what you mean and I'll try not to be jealous."

Melody kissed me deeply to seal the deal. We were interrupted from the kiss by gunfire at the lower end of the street and we heard something crash into our makeshift barricade. I jumped out of bed and looked for my Levi's in the dark. As I was pulling them on, I yelled out…

"Der, we have company! Meet me in the gun closet." The shotgun and police rifle were still in Derek's truck so all we had was the pistols and what hunting guns we had in the closet.

Derek met me in the closet and I picked up Dad's old reliable Winchester .30-30 rifle that had shot many a black tailed buck. Derek picked out Dad's Browning Auto-5 and some slugs as well as birdshot.

I cautioned Derek. "I'm going to climb up on the roof. Don't leave the house, they can shoot you from the gate. I heard an automatic rifle or machine gun. While you and Melody are behind the drapes pulled just enough to see if anyone comes to the gate to shoot, give Martha a call and tell her to lock all of the doors and hide everyone in the small garden tool shed out back, including Regis and Mike."

I slipped out my sliding glass door and Melody locked it behind me. It was relatively easy to climb up on the awning and then up on the roof, even with Dad's rifle with a scope that should allow me to see better in the dark.

The shooting was moving up the street slowly as I climbed on the roof. They appeared to be just doing random destruction until they got across from Rodney Owens' place. Then, all hell broke loose!

Both sides were firing at one another with automatic weapons. It sounded like war and louder than anything I had ever heard in the movies or seen on the news. As I reached the crest of our tile roof and peeked over, I could see that it was a double-cab pickup truck with a guy firing what could've been a 45 caliber machine gun mounted in the back like all those Middle Eastern war movies. He was pumping deadly fire across the road with his back to me.

There was no time to hesitate. I braced the rifle on the crest of the roof, aimed for high on his back and squeezed the trigger. I had killed my first man as he slid down off the gun to the floor of the pickup bed. Immediately, another guy climbed over the side and got up on the machine gun to fire in the same direction.

I, just as quickly, dispatched him. I fired five more shots into the roof of the double-cab where I thought guys' heads might be. Holding the last shot for anyone that might try to retaliate my way while getting ready to duck down out of sight and reload.

I didn't have to. The pickup took off up to the cul-de-sac at the end of the street, spun around, squealing tires, and then, raced back down the street and away, firing no more shots as it did. I pumped off my last shot at the roof behind the driver but missed and they got away.

Adrenaline was still pumping into my blood stream and my heart was beating nearly out of my chest. I soon felt great relief and calmed down having killed at least two of them and driven them off. But without Rodney firing from the other side, things might've been much different. I knew right then, we had to spend much of our time on barricades, arms and surveillance, to prevent any more firefights in the neighborhood.

When I got down off the roof, I realized there were no mosquitoes. And thankful that there hadn't been that late at night with a cool breeze off the Pacific feeling refreshing and cooling me down. I met Derek and Melody in my bedroom and we all hugged each other and cried.

But we couldn't stop there. We had to see how Rodney and Stephanie were. Derek called Martha and told her that it was over and that she could go back to her house with the kids and dogs. We all left my house with headlights and our pistols loaded with one in the chamber, just in case.

There were two bodies in the street. One was an attractive black woman as tattooed as the other one. I don't think I killed either of them. We couldn't tell in the dark but would be able to determine what killed them in the morning. Obviously members of some gang. I remembered them yelling obscenities in English. So, they weren't Spanish from Central America even though their tattoos appeared to be from there with those symbols I had seen before on the Internet. Strange?

We approached Rodney's Place with caution. We tried the doorbell at the gate but it was destroyed. Parts of the wall were battered so heavily concrete blocks were knocked out of place or broken leaving holes in the wall. I went to one and yelled out…

"It's Derek and Drake from across the street! Are you all right, Rodney? Are you all right!"

At first, I got no answer. But I didn't stick my head in the hole for fear of being shot at. Finally, I heard Stephanie call out, "I'm shot, but my dad is dead! Please help me… Please…!"

The gate wouldn't open because the touchpad had been destroyed. There was a guy hanging dead on it. Another was dead in the yard. All of the dead had AR-15 rifles with high-capacity magazines and more on their bodies. Shell casings were everywhere. I climbed over the wall and rushed to the house that had been battered heavily by that gun on the pickup and rounds from the assault rifles.

Rodney was dead below the living room window with multiple wounds and a big hole in his back, lying in a big pool of his own blood. Stephanie was behind the kitchen island with the granite top purposely taken off and tilted in front of it–broken. She was shot through by her right shoulder and her left calf where it was broken and bleeding. We got some towels from the bathroom and some bandages from the war room and patched her up to stop the bleeding. I spotted some morphine in the war room and Melody gave her that, too.

I carried her over my shoulder in a fireman's carry because of her broken leg all the way to where Martha had the gate open letting us in with her. She then guided me to her bedroom and had me lay Stephanie down gently on Jake's bed.

Martha said, "I was a nurse in Baghdad during the Iraqiwar. That's where I met Jake. He was a wounded colonel that I cared for. Cared so dearly for him, he married me." She sighed.

And then, she examined the wounds and while we applied pressure to them, got a suture kit from her bathroom and began stitching Stephanie up. Once the wounds were closed and no longer bleeding, she expertly set Stephanie's leg and with some lath that we found in the garage, made a splint that kept the leg stable enough to heal, and maybe, walk on later.

When she was finished, Martha declared, "I've got some crutches, somewhere. You'll be up and around in no time." And patted Stephanie's hand as she did. "I'll get you some soup to replace that blood you lost."

Still keyed up from the morphine and the wounds, Stephanie engaged us in conversation until Martha came back with the soup.

"Dad got excited when he heard the shooting. He told me to wait in the kitchen until they got in the house and put that countertop in front of the Island for me to hide behind."

"Did you stay there?"

"No. From the kitchen, open to the front room, I saw Dad put on his bulletproof vest and grab his AR-15 with a 40 cartridge magazine and run out the front door leaving it open. I ran to the door as he reached our front gate and opened up on something I couldn't see. I heard other guys shouting in English evil words and shooting at him. I saw sparks coming off the steel gate where bullets hit.

"A machine gun was blasting at our wall and I saw a guy climb over and onto our front yard, so I shot him and he dropped. Dad came running back, bleeding on his legs and arms and yelled at me to, 'Get back behind your barricade in the kitchen!'

"I saw him go to the window and shoot a guy that was trying to climb the gate. And then, I saw a big hole open on his back and blood flew out as the spent bullet slammed into the countertop in front of me, breaking it.

"I prepared for the worst, but then, I heard you shooting and the shooting stopped. And then, I felt pain in my leg and realized that I couldn't stand on my left leg and just slid down behind the counter bleeding until you guys saved me."

We all went back to bed, but I don't believe any of us slept. All I could think about was that I may have opened a hornets' nest where gang members from all over L.A. may come after us. That was until I realized that those gangs probably suffered great losses from the pandemic, too.

And that group had gotten together to try to get food, water and other resources as far as where we lived. Just trying to survive. But at what cost? Our lives? We had to do something. As I lay awake, a plan formed in my mind.

Derek was smiling at breakfast because Melody was with him, also smiling. I didn't ask them how it was because I knew. I had other things to discuss as we made breakfast and ate.

"Der, any ideas on what we need to do to keep those gangsters from coming back?"

"We need to put up a surveillance system on the streets approaching ours and then, maybe have a booby-trap using dynamite that we have in the yard, to set off if anyone tries to come onto our street violently again. The surveillance could help us tell the difference."

I agreed with what Derek suggested. And told him so. He called Wondah and she agreed and told him, "I can do all of that with what I gathered yesterday. First, I'll set up a Wi-Fi modem and network for the whole community so that everything can work without any wires. I'll get started right away."

"I've got something more aggressive in mind, Der. But first, we have to remove all of those bodies, including Rodney, so it will look, except for that wall, like no one was ever here. Who knows, they might be so decimated they will never come back. Or just gather more gang members and come back for revenge."

Derek got us back on the immediate subject at hand.

"Let's take the bodies out through the gate past where we are keeping the dogs. There are already too many flies as it is, and the meat might help make the dogs wilder, sooner."

"Well, let's get to it, the sooner we clean up the mess, the sooner we will be able to protect this street from whatever may come our way. Mel, can you help us?"

"Sure. I told you I can carry my weight. You guys can both count on me." She winked wickedly. We both understood too well.

The three of us took the four wheeler, charged up from its last duty, with the trailer, out our gate to the street and began picking up bodies. We photographed their tattoos to see if we could identify who they were and where they were from. We stopped by the Rosenberg place and asked Stephanie what we should do with her father. She thought a minute…

"That's a tough one." She yawned having been awakened from a deep sleep. "I've experienced the smell and the flies. Didn't count on that. He wasn't my friend in recent years. I resented all of this that he and Mom created, with their thought that the world would come to an end.

"But, not this way. Not what happened last night or even the pandemic. He was wrong. He should be buried so he won't stink or cremated. But you guys are such angels, I'll let you do whatever you are doing to the others. It will have to be right. I'm in no position right now to tell you." She shut her eyes and drifted off into sleep again.

We left the house and proceeded to the Wilkes-Hodges estate where there was a driveway going around the back of the house all the way to the large ground care and storage building on the back wall. The grass was already growing knee-high without any attention from ground-skeepers.

We drove out through the open gate some distance down the trail until it got too steep and stopped. Several of the dogs followed us anticipating food. We unloaded the bodies there, hoping that the flies from our neighborhood would find better places to lay their eggs with these bodies.

We also hoped that the dogs would find them as a way to get something to eat other than the dog food we were providing that, eventually, would run out. We wanted them to go wild. Like the birds and the cats. As we drove off I looked back and saw them licking the blood. It wouldn't be long before they would be tearing away at raw flesh and liking it like the dried blood. Vultures were already circling above.

In case the gang that was massacred decided to come back, we quickly placed plywood over the front and back of our three ornamental gates using only the cameras on our doorbell intercom as a way of seeing who was at the gate. By placing plywood both on the front and the back of the wrought iron gates with bolts from the front plywood to the back plywood holding them in place and making the gates much stronger and nearly impossible to see through in the process, we felt more secure if anyone else came looking for plunder.

At the lower beginning of the street, we put up the construction barricades and a big sign that read, **"Under Construction: Access Prohibited**." Mounted a steel gate with a padlock that would certainly slow down any intruders. But as I thought about it more that morning, I had a solution in mind that would be more offensive than defensive.

8

Dealing with Murderous Gangs

About 11 o'clock we retreated to Martha's kitchen for lunch. I decided to reveal my plan I had for dealing with the gangs I knew would be coming again.

"Der, you come from Watts by way of your dad and grandfather. Did they ever tell you how bad it was when the Brown Lions and other gangs came to the neighborhood?"

"Dad never told me anything, but I heard a little bit from grandpa. The crack cocaine problem in the 1980s was when it really got bad and the Blods and Grips formed and fought over all that money. No one was safe.

"It's worse today with all of those immigrant gangs that formed for protection and then, while gaining power with numbers, have begun warring and terrorizing. The way I see it, they have no skills to fend for themselves when the power goes out, there is no running water, and food is no longer easy to find in stores or rotten. I see them surviving by doing what those guys did last night. We have to help the good and eliminate the bad, I'm afraid to say. Law enforcement won't do it for us anymore.

"Der, did you get a line on those guys last night?"

"I gave it to Wondah before we went to get the bodies."

Wondah was glad to help out… "From the pictures that Derek gave me, I easily found out from the tattoos. It's a gang from Belize that calls itself the Blips, affiliated with the Grips in Belize City and here. They're one of the most vicious in all of L.A. They are located off Washington just north of the 10, not far from here."

Derek interjected… "I remember a job we were working on in that neighborhood two years ago. Had to drive by that place every day on our way to and from the job. Really bad neighborhood." He shook his head.

I said, "I think we have a way to teach them a lesson. Dad's decommissioned Abrams tank he got in an auction after the Iraqi war from Fort Ord is in the yard."

"Isn't that a bit extreme?" Derek was doubtful.

"We don't know what we're up against. I think for now we'll have to hold them off. But in time, when they can't find water, food or gasoline, they will begin to die again and get even more desperate. I hate to say it, but we must meet force with force.

"Dad bought the tank for military parades since he was a Marine veteran of that war. He had it made fully capable by a company that did that sort of thing. We went out on a Nevada firing range one time two years ago when I was sixteen. I got to drive the tank and Dad fired off a few rounds from the big gun. It was deafening. We still have that ammunition as well as some rockets and ammunition for the two machine guns.

"What I'm proposing is that we go get the tank that has rubber treads on it, go to where they are, and make sure that they don't come back here, ever again. As unfortunate as it may seem, we will be at war between good and evil. What do you all think?"

Derek spoke first. "I know that Dad would disapprove, hoping there was a better way. But I know you're right. I'm in. You will have to tell me how to operate the firepower while you are driving." He still sounded scared of the whole prospect and looked it.

"Normally, operating that tank requires intensive training, but I'll show you how to do it and I know you can because these kinds of things are easy for you to do and you do them better than me. It's just like driving the heavy equipment you do well already "I reassured him.

"Can I come along?" Melody excitedly asked.

"Yes, you can drive us there and then follow us on the way back. If something goes wrong, we will have to count on you to get us back here. Okay?"

"Okay."

Wondah spoke up again. "Can I come along too? I'd love to learn how to fire one of those guns. I'm pretty good at those online war games. The thought of handling all that firepower? Wow!"

She had ambushed me. "I was thinking I'd have you stay here and begin installing that wi-fi network of cameras and monitors, as well as remote booby-traps we can set with dynamite we can bring from the yard. But, now that you have suggested it, the tank needs three people to run it well anyway. I will put you on the machine guns."

"Cool! I won't disappoint you." She smiled a broad smile.

With a plan set in place and lunch finished, we gathered up water and other essentials after I said, "Let's roll…" Leaving me wondering, Why did I use that overused expression from the movies? Thinking about it more, I realized the phrase was appropriate.

I let Melody drive Dad's truck so she could get used to it in case she had to drive it hard in an emergency I hoped wouldn't happen. This time, Wondah joined Derek in the backseat where they chatted about what kind of a defense system she would engineer. I sensed that they were flirting with each other when they talked, and I was glad for that.

Melody turned out to be a great driver, dodging growing trash in the streets along with abandoned vehicles that ran out of gas or their batteries died, left where they stalled. There was more water in the streets from broken pipes the summer heat and ground heaving had caused with no one to repair them. They would provide water for the unfortunate and gangs for a while until the water system, itself dried up and no more water could be found in the pipes all over town.

Losing city water was a big concern of mine that I didn't tell everyone about but had a plan ready to address in my mind. By August, L.A. was a desert. It wouldn't be until November before the annual rain would fall again. Going was easier on the 10 and we arrived at the yard just past noon.

We took the tarp off the tank and removed the plug keeping birds and squirrels out of the big gun barrel. We found some batteries that were well charged and replaced the four that were in the tank, still remarkably well charged when we hooked them back up to solar powered battery chargers.

While Derek and the girls brought some ammunition to both the tank and the truck, I cranked up the engine and the diesel started with a lot of black smoke at first, but then settled down to a steady knocking sound from the high compression cylinders. It was much louder than an 18-wheeler with little or no noise suppression from its exhaust pipes. Part of the tank's intimidation factor.

I rolled the tank out from the overhead shed it was parked under and did a spin to see how the controls operated. A cloud of dust rose and everything was good. We really were ready to roll. I took a while to show Derek how to load the big gun and fire it upon my command. And then, I showed Wondah how to operate the machine guns and fire the rockets we installed on the rocket launchers in the front of the tank. That took about an hour. And then, we were really ready to roll.

Melody not only helped us carry ammunition, but she also listened closely when I instructed the others on what to do inside the tank. When we were ready to go I told her…

"Mel, I want you to follow us closely and stay on the phone with us continuously so that I can give you instructions, if needed. Never get yourself boxed in where you can't turn around. Some of these streets are so full of cars that you can't turn around. Make sure that you have a place to turn around always in sight. In case you have to quickly turn around and pick us up running to you."

"I hope that doesn't happen. I wouldn't want them to get a hold of your tank." Melody replied.

"If that happens, I will try to drop a grenade in it as we leave. But, keep the truck away because there might be a terrific explosion after." We all laughed to cut the tension.

Very soon, we were on the 10 with the tank running its top speed smoothly and as silently as a rubber tread can make a tank run. As I took the Washington exit after about 5 miles, the butterflies in my stomach started to crawl up my throat and I steeled myself to carry out this mission as best I could. I tried not to let the others know my trepidation. I had to be stronger than them.

Those thoughts receded from the front of my mind by constant bantering back and forth with Mel in the truck behind. It wasn't long before we came down the street that Derek knew well. The houses along the right side of the street with their graffiti and appearance let me know that it was the real thing.

When we came up to what Derek remembered was the headquarters, an old three-story theater building, the truck from the night before, showing many bullet holes was parked in front. No one was stirring on the street and was grateful for that.

"Guys," I said. "Let's focus all we've got on the building. Wondah, fire your rocket right after I have Der fire the big gun. I'll then drive up the street, turn around at the next intersection and come roaring back down this way with you firing the machine guns as we go.

"Mel, turn around at that last intersection and wait on a side street for us to come running or the tank to come by and follow.

"The big gun is aimed at the truck. Commence firing!"

I saw the truck ripped in half as the shell slammed through it into the theater behind with a force that shook the building as though it would fall down. But the rocket did the trick and the building blew up in a way that we would've been hurt or killed had we not been in the tank. Scared me!

I drove up the street to the next intersection, spun the tank around and with Wondah on one gun, and Derek on the other, we strafed the entire gang side of the street as relief flowed off my shoulders and we roared past Melody waiting for us at the next intersection. Seven miles and a half hour later, we opened the gate to the end of the street and I drove the tank up to the cul-de- sac on the end. I then backed up close to the gate leading to the Wilkes-Hodges estate with the big gun pointed down the street as an additional deterrent to future marauders.

I didn't tell anyone as they cheered in victory, that I feared we may have killed innocent women and children. But without any law anymore, we had to kill or be killed. Sad to say. I sincerely hoped that all of the bad element that was still alive would die from lack of knowledge about how to stay alive in the new world we were in. Die off peacefully, too weak to try to take anything from us again.

But I knew from what I read about history, people in the past have survived horrendous hardship and even the bad could do that. I just hope not, so we could save the good. We were already running out of some staples. We had to continue to improvise, grow and build. Not waste any time with war anymore.

We spent what was left of the day helping Wondah install wi-fi cameras along the wall and on the walls facing the street below ours. Each camera had a solar panel hidden behind the wall to charge it and she had already started to set up a series of monitors in her office at the Rosenberg house where piercing alarms would occur when no one was watching the monitors indicating someone was moving or coming on the street down there.

From the truck, we unloaded ammunition for the tank, dynamite and electronic caps that could be set off remotely from the monitors when necessary by wi-fi. The bombs we made were encased in camouflaged, waterproof enclosures so they wouldn't be spotted easily by anyone looking at them and kept dry. We placed four of them down by the end of the street. We hoped we would never have to set them off because of the destruction they would cause.

After an early evening meal, something we hadn't had in days, we all retired to my place and took a swim in the buff. Derek swam up to me on one side of the pool where the girls couldn't hear.

"Dre, I'm going to leave the house tonight to sleep in my house. Wondah wants to go with me. I find her exciting, do you?"

He had a way of asking me questions like that and I wasn't sure what to say. "Now that you mention it and I've seen her over there without her glasses, jeans and male buttoned-down shirt, she is, to say the least, sexier than I thought."

"That's what I was thinking–brainy, too!" And he punched me in the shoulder, hard. I smiled.

Melody found my bed before I did and after making frantic love like the violence we had experienced that day, we both settled for sleep with some nightmares along the way.

Derek was surprised at the knowledge this little geek had about sex. She taught him a thing or two and he sure liked it. His affection growing by both her touch and his touch of her taut little body that was barely out of puberty. But even after three or four sessions where they both were satisfied, they too drifted off to sleep.

When his phone read 4:15 am. Derek was jolted awake from a deep sleep. Wondah reached for it first, but, when she saw "Daphne" was calling, handed it to Derek with a puzzled look on her face. Thinking, Does she know we're sleeping together?

Derek sleepily looked at the phone and answered, "Hello Daphne, what..."

She interrupted him, whispering… "They're here! I'm in the woods behind the house. Uncle Louie is shooting at them and they are shooting back, lots of them." Derek could hear the guns in the background firing." He immediately put me on a three way call.

I was in a deep sleep; my mind was running through options of what was to come. The reason our phones continued to work was a result of USpan, completed in 2026, bringing in G6 software and eliminating the need for land-based relay stations and hotspots from competing companies, literally wiping them out unless they agreed to merge and share the immense profit. The solar powered satellites were in self-correcting geosynchronous orbit and would last a long time. AI ran the whole operation without the need for human intervention. But that, too, would fail in time. Everything that we relied on daily would fail.

So far, electricity had not failed in our neighborhood, but I feared that failure would come before we could make sure that all of the buildings on the street had adequate solar power to even heat the houses during the brief cold winter. Natural gas was still okay, too. But that, too, would fail in time and could become a real hazard, causing fires and explosions.

Water, of course, was our most pressing concern. Even our cisterns were inadequate for the rest of the long summer and city water would soon disappear with all of the water breaks we had been seeing in our travels. Those breaks would provide temporary water for those that didn't have any but would present real problems for those drinking from them if the water wasn't boiled.

There was a ringing in my mind and before I realized what it was, Melody was shaking me. She handed me the phone… Derek was calling at 4:16 am! When I started to answer, I heard Daphne's voice and stopped; switched the phone to speaker so Melody could hear.

She was whispering. "We were sleeping when we heard one of Uncle Louie's alarms go off and it jarred us out of bed. And then, I heard an explosion down by the road. They had set off one of his booby-traps. As I pulled on my jeans, Uncle Louie yelled, 'Daphne! Go out the back door and down into the woods as far as you can go. I will be shooting at them. Hide and wait until morning before you come back or if I call you back. Hurry! Get out of here!'

"I heard a lot of shooting and yelling as I ran. I'm a long way from the house now. The shooting continued for a long time, but it isn't as loud now, maybe stopping. But I don't hear Uncle Louie calling me back. Der, what should I do?"

"Stay right where you are and wait until dawn like your uncle told you. Go to sleep if you can. Based on what you told me, I don't think your uncle will survive all the shooting. After they take what they want, they'll leave. Wait until dawn, or if he calls you. You don't want them seeing you. So, sneak back very carefully. Then call me back. Okay?"

"Okay. I'll try to sleep. And call you back when it's light out. Thanks, love, Bye."

"Bye." Derek hung up.

We heard Wondah in the background. "Geez! And I was calling her for help! We need to go get her."

Derek sighed. "Yes… It looks like we'll have to go get her, again." He thought, Here comes trouble. But didn't tell her.

Melody had a puzzled look on her face checking my expression. I sighed, hung up and told her.

"Our high school prima donna. We went to save her earlier, but her uncle intervened. Let's try to get some sleep until morning. It looks like we're going to have to rescue her again putting off some things we need to do around here, pronto."

Melody put her arms around me again to comfort my thoughts. But they kept me awake anyway while she slept until the sun reflected off the light poles above the pool as the sky turned from black to blue and I knew it was dawn.

popos

9

Rescuing Daphne Again

The last thing I wanted to do was rescue Daphne again with all that needed to be done running around in my head. But, at breakfast, I was outvoted. Even Wondah wanted to go get her and bring her back to be with us. So, I relented.

"Okay then, somebody has to stay back and continue work on our defenses. We still aren't fully protected from attack. And, there's a lot of other things to do."

Derek volunteered. "I'll see Daphne when she gets here. You guys can go and get her. I can work on the drones and more booby-traps. We have to make sure those booby-traps are out of the curiosity of children. That will be tough. Kids get into everything."

Wondah piped up. "In that case, I'll stay, too. Der will need a lot of help from me if he is going to do what he says. I'd like to see if we can make that old tank fire remotely." She clapped her hands joyfully, so we joined in. What a great idea!

"I was thinking more of infrastructure. I know, the boring stuff." Everyone laughed. "It will take some doing to get this old neighborhood self- sustaining before the end of summer." I could see sober looks on their faces. Dad had a long list of subcontractors. I was thinking that maybe we should call as many as we can find to join us here with their families so we can have a real construction firm again. Rebuilding, not only here but all over. Based on the number of people out there still alive and struggling, I see this neighborhood, while sound for us, inadequate for all of them. I even have an idea for how to contact them. But that will have to wait till later when we get this place self-sustaining."

"I see what you mean. Wondah and I will make some calls today when taking breaks from the work outside. Okay with you, Wondah?"

"Dre, you certainly are ambitious and visionary to say the least. Of course, I'll help out, look up their websites, locate them if they are alive."

"Der, call Daphne and tell her we will be there are about nine, 9:30

am. Tell her we'll be armed in case there is still trouble there. We'll take the AR- 15s along with our pistols and a shotgun."

Melody piped in, "I can't wait." Adventure ran in that woman's veins.

Very soon, we were on our way. We were pulling the trailer, "In case Daphne wants to bring her Ferrari," I quipped. Mel laughed. It wasn't that far-fetched.

I was glad to leave the mosquitoes and flies behind, but the windshield soon became filled with suicides. I had to use the washers and wipers to smear them off. Thankfully, as the sun got higher, there were fewer of them swarming in the air.

There were more water leaks where sometimes the high stance of our truck really helped, fires that kept burning, probably because they were fed by natural gas, and generally more trash and abandoned vehicles from people still trying to find resources or treasure that probably wasn't worth the price of water. Or, what drinking water would eventually cost. Occasionally, neighborhoods stunk of natural gas leaking or dead bodies rotting. There just weren't enough predators to get rid of all the rotting flesh.

There was more rubbish along Laurel Canyon Drive, indicating to me that gangs were expecting to find wealthy people and had made several raids into the canyon. Gates were smashed and bullet holes pocked every one of the entrances, large or small. But all was quiet and eerily silent. We saw no bad guys on the road, thank goodness!

Halfway up into the canyon where Daphne was, there wasn't as much destruction. I saw that as a good sign until we came upon Louie's hidden entrance. A pickup truck with a swivel machine gun on its truck bed was all crumpled up across from the entrance as though blown there by a tremendous explosion. There were three dead inside and body parts on the road.

The steel gate had been rammed and broken off where it pivoted. Two male gang members and a heavily tattooed woman lay dead there, all with AR-15 type rifles still in their hands. I decided not to drive in, but to walk in carefully with our guns ready first so we wouldn't be surprised by anything or anybody. I cautioned Mel…

"Don't close the truck doors when we get out. Be careful not to step on anything that makes noise like a piece of metal or a twig. You walk up on the right side of the drive and I'll walk on the left, not in the middle. Don't say anything. If you see something suspicious get my attention by waving your hand and pointing. I will go very slow. Keep pace exactly with me. Make sure your gun is fully loaded and that you have the safety off when we are on the road going up."

"Yes, sir, Sarge!" She laughed. And then, got a serious look on her face. "That's exactly what I would do but thank you for making sure."

We left the truck as quietly as we could and proceeded up the drive trying not to disturb the overhanging brush that was often in our way and our line of vision. There were two more bodies, both men, on that drive, mangled by obvious booby-traps. There were countless shell casings that we had to be careful not to step on or kick as we climbed the steep road. When we reached the top, everything seemed to be quiet. Ahead, there was a rock wall that was part of the circular drive. One spot on the wall showed evidence of heavy bombardment.

When we got there, we could see that all of the vehicles had been shot up except for a couple of the classics that he had that were now gone. Uncle Louie lay dead behind that rock wall with his head nearly blown completely off. Around him were three automatic rifles and a few unused magazines on top of a great pile of expended shell casings. It looked like he lost by being outnumbered, not his superior position and firepower.

With everything appearing to be safe, I yelled out, "Daphne! Daphne are you there! It's Dre, coming to get you!"

Daphne came out with a rifle in hand. Threw down the rifle and came running to me, jumping up on me wrapping her legs around my waist and showering me with kisses. Saying, "Oh, Dre! Why didn't I go with you the first time! It's been a nightmare! I'm so glad you came. I want to get out of here…" She looked over at Melody who was standing there with a surprised look on her face. "Who's that?"

"That's Mel, my neighbor who lost her husband to Amazonia. She's with us now. Derek and Wondah stayed back to beef up our defenses from attacks like this."

"Hi Mel, you're cute! But this guy, he's the man! Wondah is with you? I just wanted to have her stop calling me with her sob story."

"Well, we rescued her and she's become a great asset. Will you?" I could see Melody smirking a bit out of the corner of my eye.

"Of course. I'm great at organizing activities. And I promise I will work hard, because from my experience here, food and water will be hard to find. Louie was well stocked, but I could see that his stores would run out in about six months and we would have to go hunting."

"Are you ready to go? Do you want us to do something with your uncle? Bury him?"

"I'll have to get a few things. As for Louie, there," she pointed at him with disdain, "That letch can rot in hell! It slowly dawned on me that I had forgotten the trauma he caused to me. That bastard stuck his finger in me repeatedly when I was nine. That's when I lost my hymen!"

Daphne started crying. Melody came forward to hug her, understanding better than I.

"I was so ashamed for not having a hymen that I told all the girls at school that I had lost my virginity at 13 with a guy that I met when we were on vacation in Switzerland. I fooled them, but I'm still a virgin!" Her tears flowed freely admitting it, she hugged Melody tighter and I began to understand why Daphne was so standoffish and conceited in school.

We entered the house that, from the front, exhibited lots of bullet holes and broken windows. Inside was no better. A wild party had taken place with bullet holes in the walls, ceilings and artwork. Some of the artwork was slashed with knives, paint was spilled everywhere, making the floor sticky in places. Liquor bottles were empty and broken all around. All of the food and liquor that Louie had put away for the long run was taken. The place was cleaned out. Even his inventory of guns, explosives and ammunition.

When she returned earlier that morning with great trepidation, Daphne had found her closet invaded with most of her clothes taken along with her computer. She worried about all of those pictures and videos she hoped against hope they wouldn't put on the Internet. Glad that she was way off out in the woods out back where they couldn't find her when she saw some of her ripped clothes with blood on them. These were real savages. From their graffiti, she told me…

"Dre, I think they were Blods. I know that graffiti, those symbols. We were warned about them in school to avoid association with them. Most of what I had here is ruined. Let's pick up a few pieces and go back to Mom and Dad's place where I can get some more. I will need clothes that fit and protect me if I'm going to work."

We hurried up and gathered up all she wanted. We didn't have to drive the truck up the drive. As we left the house, I noted that several vehicles that were heavy had made deep impressions in the soft soil of the unpaved circle drive. Probably why the classic cars were gone–trophy cars. But gasoline cars and gasoline wouldn't last much longer without parts and newly refined gasoline.

We left the bodies as a deterrent but gathered up all of the guns and ammunition and drove back to Daphne's home. Typically, she jumped in the front seat between Mel and me, to Mel's disdain. Then, she put her hand on my leg to brace herself and seemed to feel obligated to tell us the rest of her story along the way there.

"I'm sorry, Dre, but I'm bad at making decisions. For some reason, I thought staying with my Uncle Louie would be a way to reconnect with him from my happy remembrance of staying with him as a child. At first, he was really nice. Giving me that back room over the deck where he had a bird and squirrel feeder. It was always pleasant in the morning to wake up there with birds singing and the dappled light coming in through the windows. He helped me fix up the room and fed me, mostly canned rations that he had a huge store of.

"He had a large water tower and an outdoor shower on the deck, 'To save water,' he said. And then, the first time I used it and found that the water was pleasantly warm, but without pressure, I lathered myself up and saw him in the bushes peeking at me. I yelled at him and he left down the hill for something.

"I heard some shots with a shotgun, and when I got dressed he came back with two quail for breakfast. That fresh meat was great and I skipped the cereal with water because there was no milk except powdered milk he normally ate. After that, I got on my computer in my room trying to contact folks and he went off into his studio working.

"But then, the next morning over breakfast, he asked me if I'd like to pose for some photographs that he could turn into paintings, 'If I liked.' I foolishly agreed. He had me go to my room and put on an outfit and then come out into the studio where he would take several pictures and poses. Sometimes, he would come up and move some fabric here or there, do something with my hair and brush up against me accidentally in a way that I knew was intentional.

"By the end of the morning, he was having me pose in my nighties, bikinis and even bra and panties. All the while, he took pictures and kept saying things like, 'That's great. Beautiful. You make a great model,

Daphne. Smile, look as beautiful as you are.'

"In that single morning, he already had me nearly undressed and I was actually liking it, getting all that attention. At lunch, Louie told me he thought I had a great body and he wondered if I wouldn't mind posing in the nude for him so he could paint me. I had seen some paintings of nudes and some he made of me as a child in cute outfits and I liked them. I hadn't been painted by anyone since. He explained that it might be boring to sit so long, so he would have me change poses and I could use my cell phone to occupy me while I waited.

"I don't know why I fell for that line, but I agreed. I went in my room, undressed and put on a bathrobe. Uncle Louie got me a stool for me to sit on it. My feet didn't touch the floor and if I had to sit there a long time, I was worried I would get dizzy and fall off. Louie thought for a minute, and then had me go over to a red mohair antique couch. He had me lounge on it like a Victorian lady. I took off my robe and handed it to him and he positioned me for the first pose. All the while eyeing my blond pussy hair that I hadn't shaved.

"Louie shook his head, 'I guess that will do for this 18th-century style painting, today. But I think I'll have to shave you clean for something more contemporary tomorrow.' He said it so matter-of-factly, it got my mind stirring on what it was that made him so obsessed with seeing me naked and wanting me to be shaved clean.

"That old couch was quite comfortable while I sent out text notes to people who didn't answer back until I dozed off… Only finding him in my face adjusting my body in a way that was obviously more for his pleasure than the painting. By late afternoon, he had finished a painting that certainly did look like it came right out of Victorian America. Louis was talented. He added my nude to his collection of nude paintings of women that he had painted.

"When I put on the robe he said, 'Why don't you go without it. I usually go naked around here when it gets as warm as it's getting. Keep my clothes handy in case I have to go out or somebody is at the gate.' Again, so nonchalantly that it unnerved me.

"I kept the robe on and got dressed back in my room. He told me that he was going to his bedroom to take a nap. I suspected in his bedroom he had monitors with cameras around the place so he could peek at me whenever he wanted.

"I looked for a camera in my room and found one neatly disguised behind a two-way mirror. One that I had used to look at while I was changing outfits earlier in the day. I began to wonder if he would be putting videos of me on the Internet on websites that might still be operating that sort of smutty thing.

"I was incensed. Put on some clothes in the closet while checking for a camera and went outside for a walk where the air was clean of smog and there weren't any flies or mosquitoes. Just the kind of tick that carries Lyme disease. But under those oak trees there were no grassy areas that they like. From blades of grass, those ticks grabbed onto anything with blood in it that passed by. Some say they jump… Maybe so. I checked later and didn't have any on me.

"At dusk, I heard him calling me and he had brought out some venison steak and prepared quite a feast for us. In addition to the wine, he suggested after dinner drinks. I told him that I saw the cameras, and he apologized. 'But they were originally for security for the place when they came available. Once in a while a starlet would come here to have a portrait made, and I would admit to spying on them, like I spied on you… I'm sorry.'

"I told him that I wasn't going to pose for him anymore and that I was going to leave as soon as I could find someone who would take me… You! But that damned Wondah kept calling and you rescued her, first. Oh well." She sighed, shrugged her shoulders and patted my leg too close for comfort. "It's okay now."

We were pulling into the long drive leading to her parents' house. When we got to the gate, I was surprised when it opened to her cell phone code. At least some things were still intact and working well. I was glad there didn't seem to be any signs of marauders.

The place smelled of death so badly that we had to tie kerchiefs over our noses just to run around her bedroom and closets gathering up more clothes for her. I told her to take only work clothes like shorts and jeans, blouses, jackets, but most of her clothes were not utilitarian so we had to dig around in everything to find what we needed. We all were glad to get out of there with a couple of suitcases and a few dresses on hangers. There was no Ferrari to pick up. That was a joke among us at home. I didn't tell Daphne. I remember she had sold it before graduating, wanting to buy a new car to take with her to college.

Occasionally, we stopped and picked up useful things that were in the street, like garbage cans that could hold water. Basically, a scavenger hunt. It slowed our progress and filled the trailer.

When we were about three miles from home, we came upon some people hiding behind an electric station wagon. They looked really scared when we drove up, so I yelled out, "Hello! We mean you no harm!" While I was pointing frantically to Melody to get her pistol out. And then, I pulled mine out of the holster and had it ready on my lap as I ran the window down a little more so that they could see my face better.

The big man called back, "Hello! You won't find me any harm! It's just me and two of my kids. We're desperately trying to get to the beach. We are out of water and hope we would find food there. I'm running out of options." His head dropped and he started crying.

I went back to the truck to get my thermos of water. The boy and girl came out from behind the car and ran to me as I handed them the thermos and they both drank heartily before giving it to their dad. They were clearly desperate. Soon, Melody and Daphne joined me as I reassured them.

"You ran into the right people. We are here to help. I'm Drake, this woman is Melody and the other one is Daphne. We just rescued her from a bad situation." The guy nodded hopeful recognition to both of them.

Regaining his composure, the man responded, "I'm August Palmer, but my friends call me Augie. This is my son, Rocky. He's fifteen, and my daughter, Clowie, she's thirteen. We were all sick with Amazonia. My wife, Sharlotte, and my little girl, Jeny, didn't make it." He burst out crying again.

"I know." I patted him on the shoulder with my left hand. "I lost my parents and my sister. We all lost someone. That was a vicious virus. But we're trying to get back on our feet and making progress."

"I was an analyst for a tech firm you may have heard of, USpan. I made good money and we lived a comfortable life in Pomona. I didn't see this coming. We weren't prepared. Ran out of food two days ago and only got water from broken water lines and got sick from that. And then, thinking that maybe we could catch fish or dig up clams on the beach, we couldn't find any charging stations that worked near here and ran out of power."

"You're really lucky that we came along. We have water and food with us and were headed back to our home. You're welcome to join us if you're willing to pitch in and work hard so that we all have enough water, food and everything else we might need by working together. We, with my partner, Derek Jones, who also lost his parents, are both sons of contractors and are building a community of people like you who need help. What do you say?" Augie stopped crying and a relieved look came over his face while his kids, their thirst quenched and munching on almonds that Melody had given them, fairly beamed with anticipation.

"The beach was a desperate choice. And look where it got us. I'm willing to take your offer. Any strings attached young man?"

"Only that you are a team player and you and your kids give us more than you take. My trailer is equipped to carry vehicles for my family construction business. Let me take your station wagon with us and we will get it charged up. If you don't like living with us, after we feed you and show you where you might live, you are free to leave. Derek and I are not going to make anyone stay with us that doesn't want to."

The negotiation over, we busied ourselves with getting the electric station wagon on the trailer and were soon on our way. We answered questions from them as I drove home.

When we arrived at the main gate and opened it, Augie was impressed. I told him. "Our houses are filling up but we have a couple of great teachers for your kids. Right now, it's more tutoring than classes. I'm thinking that you could occupy the house directly below mine. I would expect you to put in a garden and help me give you power and water on your own. But for now, you could eat with us, because there is no food in that house. What there was we have taken."

Amazingly, Daphne had kept quiet the whole time with these new people horning in on her parade. But she was squirming alongside me when we arrived at Martha Rosenberg's house to introduce everyone to her and see if she had any food ready for us to eat. I parked the truck in front of her place and automatically opened her gate from my phone with her code.

Martha, Wondah and the kids all came out to greet us and Derek was with them, too. When Daphne saw Der, she broke from the rest of us and ran down, jumped up with her legs around his waist and kissed him like she had me. Gushing…

"Oh, Der. Thank you. Thank you for saving me! I don't know what I would've done without you and Drake!"

She clung to him as we walked into the house.

I asked Martha, "Do you have enough food for this gang?"

"Of course, I do. I expected you to be hungry when you got back, so I made a stew using some of that frozen venison and young carrots and onions from the garden. I'm running low on potatoes and the ones in the garden are nowhere near harvesting. Also running low on meat, the frozen stuff is disappearing fast. Soon will have to rely on those survival foods that Stephanie brought. I'm already using the powdered milk if you hadn't noticed. Even with that, it won't last very long if we keep bringing people in with us."

"Thanks for the assessment, Martha. I think it's time we'll have to see about getting some fresh meat or fish. I think we should all think about what we can do to replenish our food sources. It's not going to be easy."

Everyone sat down around two tables. One for the adults and another for the kids while Martha and Stephanie served us. My mind was full of what to do next. So, while I was eating, I stopped and tapped on my glass to stop everyone from chatting to announce what I thought.

"I think, since my house is full, that Daphne, you should stay here and room with Stephanie while I get the Palmers situated in the house directly below mine."

Daphne suddenly piped up, cutting in to what I was saying. "I don't want to stay here. I want to stay with Derek in his house!"

I could see Wondah squirm in her chair and get a mean look on her face.

Derek saved me when he spoke up. "Ah…Ah… I'm afraid that wouldn't work. I've been staying with Drake because my house, after my parents died, is unlivable until we get it cleaned up and haven't had enough time to do that."

Daphne replied, "Well, I'll help you clean it up. But I don't want to stay here with a bunch of kids around. I've been to the house on the top of the drive a couple of times at parties when Barbara Wilkes-Hodges invited my parents over. That's the kind of place I want to live. Is anyone there? Is Barbara still there?"

I stepped in again. "Unfortunately, Barbara is dead. And we've left the property to all of the neighborhood dogs and released all of her exotic birds outside."

"That's fine, whatever, Dre. Just take me over there and I will make do with the way the house is. I remember those birds. They were fabulous. I hope they all haven't flown off and some are still around."

"Some of them are still around because we have bird food that we put out. You can help us by doing that and feeding and watering any dogs that are still there. I guess it's okay for you to stay there, but since the place is so large, maybe you can accommodate some other people with you, later."

"That's a deal, Dre. And Der, as soon as I get the place cleaned and fixed up, I want you to come over and see it. And then maybe, maybe we will clean your place?"

Derek joined us after dinner and we put the Palmer car on Derek's garage charger and walked Daphne with her suitcases and dresses over to the estate. Once inside, she ran immediately upstairs and into Barbara's bedroom where she jumped on the satin sheets as though she had arrived at a posh hotel and was testing out the bed.

She exclaimed! "I love it… I love it!" And then, she looked around the room and said. "You guys can go now. It looks like I've got a lot to do around here before dark. I sure hope the plumbing works, I need a bath. But, I know you guys are too busy to join me… Maybe later?"

After that, we got the Palmers into their house needing quite a bit of work for them to stay and they started working on it right away. I told them they could come over to my house for breakfast. Afterwards, Derek and I returned to the Rosenberg house and continued working with Wondah until it got dark and we were all tired and gritty.

Ready for another swim In the pool and a good night's sleep. Once again, Derek excused himself and he and Wondah went over to his place for the night. I could see she was happy going, but I wondered how the situation with Daphne would play out. Just another thing to worry about. Maybe I needed to intervene. But how?

And then, Mel swam over and wrapped herself around me, giving me a deep, wet kiss with her exploring tongue that gave me tingles of what would be coming next.

Instead, she whispered in my ear, "Don't you think that Wondah is hot! She tells me that she is bi and really interested in me! If you don't mind, I'm going to join Der and her tonight. You won't be too lonely without me, will you?" Giving my ear a nuzzle with her lips that only increased the tingling.

It was hard to resist going with her, but I knew I needed the rest. I put on my best Clark Gable response. "Of course, I won't be, dear. Go and have your fun." Actually, I was relieved.

I left the pool, took a brief shower to remove the chlorine smell and hit my bed and sleep for the first time in the past several days.

∾❦❧∾

10

Seeking Food and Others

I slept well at first, but my dreams were jumbled with my plans and they finally forced me awake. As I got up to pee, I looked outside and thought I saw something. When I carefully slid open the sliding glass door, a bevy of quail feeding in the garden took off. I thought, rather than try to go back to sleep, there was something I could do before everyone got up–hunt.

Quail season wasn't until the fall after the chicks had hatched and grown up. But the rules of hunting had changed. I got dressed in some heavy denim jeans and found my hunting boots. I also found my hunting vest with slots for shells and put that over my flannel shirt to fend off the early morning chill. I picked up my father's Browning 12gauge and filled my vest with birdshot shells. I also added a few slugs, in case I encountered something bigger, like a black tailed buck that would provide us with venison for a month. While I was doing that, I reminded myself to take Augie and others fishing for a larger take of seafood protein, too.

I had left the sliding glass door open and went back there to see if the quail had come back. I didn't see them, so I left through that door, quietly closed it and skirted around the house to the street and to the estate. I knew that behind it were thousands of acres of chaparral where I could find multiple targets in a hunt at dawn. It was still dark, but I could sense dawn coming.

As I passed the house, some of the dogs came out to greet me. But some were notably missing. They didn't make a sound except happy panting as they accepted my head rubs and licked my hands in appreciation. I was glad for that friendly welcome because I didn't want them barking and waking up Daphne. The dogs followed me as I walked past the pool and looked everywhere to see if I could see any game in the huge unkempt garden area that I hoped Daphne would help us restore.

Leaving the gate, I walked down the trail in the total darkness to see what had happened to the bodies. As I neared them, the dogs following began to whimper and return to the estate, leaving me alone as I came close. With my phone light, it was obvious that something larger than vultures had been eating them. Perhaps the missing dogs. But more likely, a mountain lion, coyotes, or even the very rare, California bear, re-introduced in recent years to areas like the reserve below.

I turned off the light and walked carefully away from the bodies with bare bones protruding from what was left of putrid rotting flesh. I tried not to step on any twigs as I gingerly made my way through the chaparral hoping to hear quail peeping or even rustling as they fed in the dark before dawn. I also scanned the camera on the landscape ahead in infrared mode where I would pick their warm bodies up, probably before I would hear them. I left it in record mode, too. A record if I shot any.

Gradually, the sun, while still behind the mountains to the east, began to light up the sky and the whole area below. While I still kept the phone scanning for warm bodies, I gradually could see better and possibly, spot one. It wasn't long before I saw something moving and the camera confirmed that it was a covey of about 20 birds. They were about 50 yards off but still within range.

I couldn't risk flushing them because it would be difficult to shoot any more than one or two on-the-fly. That was the way I did it to be fair to the birds all my hunting in the past. But like hunting out of season we were in a time of dire need for protein and I wanted to get as many birds as possible.

With my phone in my left hand and my shotgun held to my shoulder with only my right hand, I fired into the center of the covey, dropped my phone and fired off two more shots as the birds flushed and scattered. It looked like I hit some when I saw them falling. When I got there, I found I had shot five on the ground and two in the air. A couple of them were still trying to run, wounded, and I quickly grabbed them, wrung their necks and put them in the game bag.

Seven birds might seem like a lot, but it wasn't even enough for one meal for us. As I continued walking further, something moving to my right caught my eye and I saw the ears of a jack rabbit hopping above the brush. I waited until it got within range and then shot it in the head so I wouldn't harm the meat.

I knew that rabbits had parasites but thought that perhaps Martha would make a rabbit stew by thoroughly cooking that big guy. He might feed the whole crew for one meal. It was worth a try. I picked him up and put him in the game bag, too. It was getting heavy and getting very light out. I decided to head back home with what I had.

By that time, vultures were descending on the bodies. One flew right over me. I thought, What the heck. And shot him in the head directly over me. The bird fell like a rock and barely missed me. I didn't know if the vulture had been eating rotten flesh yet this morning or had fleas on its feathers, so I put on my hunting gloves. Holding the dead bird with my foot on its head and pulling on its legs with my left hand, with my hunting knife cut the bird's neck off at the body and left it there.

I had to hold the vulture up high and away from me while it bled out. I put a bit of strain on my right arm, but after a couple of minutes it was over, and only dripped after that. A couple of the dogs came back and licked the puddle of blood. Then, they followed me as I reentered the estate with my kill. I saw Daphne standing on the balcony from Barbara's room wearing nothing but a nearly transparent robe that left nothing to the imagination and was slightly open.

She yelled down, "What do you have there? I heard the shots, was a bit scared. Then… I saw you come through the gate…"

"Breakfast!" I yelled back. "But isn't that a filthy vulture?"

"Sure is, but I'm going to find out if we can eat it."

"Eat it? No way… Why don't you come up here and I'll give you breakfast." Even at her distance, I believe I saw her winking at me.

"I'll have to take a rain check. I'll have to see if this bird is edible and clean the rabbit and quail I have for breakfast for everyone. You're welcome to come."

"There's still food in Barbara's refrigerator and freezer for me. But be sure to come and see me when you can. I'll be cleaning all the dust from this place that has settled in after she left. You won't believe it when you see it."

I would have answered her, but I was already out of sight passing by the side of the mansion in a hurry to get back to Martha's place and get all of my kill cleaned for the hungry crowd that would be gathering for the day's work.

As I expected, Martha, hearing the shots, was waiting for me when I arrived. A couple of the kids were awake and with her.

"Oh, Jehovah!" She shrieked. "Is that a vulture? What are you going to do with that filthy thing! "

"I'm going to see if it's edible. We need all the fresh protein we can get. I've got a jack rabbit and some quail that we can have for breakfast if you help me clean them. Can you get me that turkey frying pot that I saw in your kitchen and fill it with boiling water out back?"

She nodded and went back in the house while I went past the garage and around the house to the patio where there was a table that was suitable for cleaning what I shot. I put the vulture down on the pave stones while Regis and Mike, spooked at first by the vulture's appearance, sneaked in and sniffed, and then, licked some of the blood that was still trickling out of the hole where the neck had been.

I laid all of the quail out on the table and began skinning the rabbit. While his skin was soft and easy to remove, I never liked the smell of rabbit being cleaned and hoped that this big old male would taste better than he smelled while cleaning.

Martha and the kids came and went, first with the turkey frying pot and pails of boiling water. And, then, some rubber gloves used for cleaning and garden work, a plastic bag for entrails and a couple of very sharp knives. Once Martha had everything with us, she joined me and started skinning the quail. She encouraged the kids to watch us work and learn how to butcher wild game for cooking.

By that time, I had taken off my hunting gloves and put on some rubber gloves. Grabbed the vulture by the legs and dropped it into the boiling water just long enough to make plucking the bird easier and kill any bacteria that may have been on the feathers and skin. I couldn't think of the use for those feathers, so I just put them out to dry in the sun and would put them in another plastic bag later when they dried in case they would become useful later.

After its feathers were off, the vulture was a pretty skinny bird but weighed about 6 pounds. Maybe 4 pounds of edible meat–if it was edible? I quickly cut it up and cleaned each piece by dipping it into the boiling water with tongs that Martha had provided. Making sure there was no bacteria that survived. I put the pieces in a large pot and told Martha to boil them.

But first, I had to taste the bird to make sure that it tasted good enough to even boil. I cut off a piece of breast held steady with the tongs, went over to the gas range on the patio there and turned on a burner. Quickly cooked a piece of vulture to a golden brown and bit off a bit, while the kids watched with glee and Martha winced as though I were eating poison. Maybe I was but I had to find out.

I was surprised that it tasted so good. "Tastes like chicken, only better, richer!"

The kids laughed out loud and Martha was relieved. All of a sudden, the kids were yelling…

"Can I have some! Can I…!"

I decided to roast a drumstick for them. It was a little smaller than a turkey drumstick but much larger than a chicken's. It took a little longer to get golden brown and I made sure it was thoroughly cooked before I let the kids taste any. I cut off pieces with my knife and let it cool so they wouldn't burn themselves in their eagerness to try it. Even Martha reneged her earlier worry and smiled after she tasted some.

"Mm… It does taste good. I think I'll boil that whole bunch to get the broth and have the meat fall off the bone for a rice and vulture hot dish that I will add some mushroom soup to. That probably will feed the whole crew, for now. Are you planning to bring more people into my kitchen? Her smile turned to a glare.

"I've been thinking about that. I want to save as many good people as I can from dying of thirst or starvation. But I can't strap you with the whole burden of the kids' schooling and cooking. I think I'll have to ask the family I just brought and others to start cooking for themselves and others as we try to figure out how to help as many people as possible survive beyond all the death that the pandemic brought and may still be bringing."

"So far, Wondah has been a big help with schooling. And Stephanie is a whiz in the kitchen. I'll have to tell her about this vulture. It seems bigger than the others. What is it?"

"I saw them when we went to Mexico. It's a black vulture. They're bigger than the turkey vultures around here but smaller than the California Condor. They're not supposed to be here, but they may have migrated here in search of more territory as their numbers grew in recent years with all the death south of the border."

I thought for a moment, and then added, "I don't think we should kill any more vultures for now. They are doing us a great service in getting rid of all these dead bodies. If their numbers increase because of all the food, a year from now or more, we may hunt them just to get enough meat for the table when other sources of food run out."

Martha sighed. "I see what you mean. I remember when we lived in Manhattan. Some of the poor ate those flying rats, pigeons." She turned up her nose.

"I've eaten them. At grandpa's farm. They were nesting in his barn and eating the grain he had for the animals. I shot some for him one day. He showed me how to clean them and wrap the breasts with bacon, so they wouldn't taste so strong. We have to get all the protein sources we can. I'm going to try seagulls next. We need to think creatively about protein if we are going to survive."

Everyone moved everything into the kitchen. Martha decided to make a rabbit stew from the jackrabbit. Others were coming in for breakfast, while they did, she told me, "I'm out of fresh everything. Using powdered milk, egg powder, egg waffles, and some other substitutes for now. But it would be great to have a cow and some chickens so that we could have milk and eggs again."

I told her, "I'll see what I can do. Maybe get some goats."

I joined the others gathering around the table, ready to see what I had laid out for them to do that day. As usual, everyone was chatting while eating. I clicked my spoon on my coffee cup to get their attention.

"As you can see, I went hunting this morning and shot some quail, a jack rabbit and a black vulture that turned out to be quite tasty. So, we have some fresh poultry to eat for now, but we need a lot more. I suggest that Augie and I and some others go down to the beach and see what we can catch or gather today. Fresh fish would be a welcome change in our diet. Any other suggestions?"

"That sounds great." Derek said. "But I think we need to split up. Wondah and I have been making those calls and we got hold of some of the subcontractors. I've given them our address. Two families are desperate and willing to come here and work with us but can't. Wondah and I want to go get the son of the plumber, Harry Hastings, we used to see on television. His name is Harry, Jr. He and his mother are the only ones left of their family. The mother, Frances, knows where all the plumbing supplies are in town and also knows the plumbing trade well, like her son. After running around looking for food and water, they ran out of gasoline.

"And one of our sheet rock contractors, Hector Lopez, his son and daughter, both teenagers, said they were raided by marauders and lost all the supplies they had gathered. Don't even have a vehicle. There are others, but we can wait to go get them or have them come to us. Someone needs to greet them."

Mel spoke up. "Der, I'll do that. Steph and I can watch the monitors and welcome anyone that comes."

"I want Stephanie to ride shotgun with us in the back. We'll be going into some bad neighborhoods." Der looked concerned.

I interrupted, "Der is right. After their morning classes, Melissa and Flower can help you watch the monitors, Mel. I think it would be good for you to work with your daughter on this important task. We had better get going if we are going to do all we need to do today. Any more questions, concerns?"

Martha had one. "I will need those two kids for an hour this morning to water and pull weeds if I'm going to keep ahead of the needs of our three large gardens."

"That's fine, you're in charge of them. I know you will give any newcomers a welcome, too. We'll probably be back by noon. Thanks everyone, as soon as we finish eating, let's go to work."

We took my truck and it wasn't long before we reached the famous Santa Monica pier. On a normal early summer day, it would be crowded with locals and tourists and the beaches on either side would be filled with the same as well as surfers on good days.

The pier was deserted. Except for the incessant cries of the gulls and the gentle lapping of collapsed waves on the beach, it was silent–no calliope music or crowd noise. But there was life as we grabbed our gear and bait and reached the end of the peer. A lone man out there, fishing.

I called out as we got closer… "Hello! It's good to see you! How's fishing going!"

He turned his attention from the water, dropped his pole, and started running to us. He ran up to me, grabbed my hand and shook it vigorously, declaring…

"Man! You guys are a sight for sore eyes! Thought that I wouldn't find any people here, but here you are! What's your name? I'm Ray Dugas. I'm from Iowa. Was a student at UC-Long Beach when this whole thing happened."

"I'm Drake Hutchins." I introduced him to the Palmer family. "We're from up in the hills just two miles from here. We need food, so we we're going to fish."

"Fishing's shitty… Ah… actually quite good without any other people around. But, you see that sign up there? I'm getting a lot of 1s and 0s and have to throw most of them back–too much mercury and PCBs. Deadly to eat."

We walked over to where he had a bucket for his catch. He had one jacksmelt, a California corbina and a surfperch. Providing, maybe, three meals for him.

"Yeah," Ray said. "Not much for fishing since sunrise. But I threw away some barred sand bass and rockfish because, since I've been here, all I've been eating is fish. Seagulls are really hard to snare. Only got a couple so far… They taste like fish, anyway." He turned up his nose.

"Anything else? Shellfish?"

"Yeah. There are mussels and clams on the piers, and crabs. But I'm not much for swimming underwater."

We baited all of our lines from a bag of bird and rabbit entrails and threw them in the water. Rocky and Clowie already had their snorkeling equipment and spears and jumped into the water. Augie and I stood next to Ray at the rail, watching our lines and Ray was more than eager to talk to us. So, we listened.

"When the pandemic hit, all hell broke loose at school. Nearly every-one left for home. After a couple of days, everyone was sick who stayed and the food sources on campus dried up. There was no going home for me. The gasoline clunker that got me here was on its last legs and I was afraid I wouldn't make it. Talking to my folks back on the farm, they told me things were just as bad there, and not to come until they told me. Haven't talked to them since. Afraid to.

"And then, I got sick and was lucky to have my girlfriend care for me until she got sick just as I was recovering. I drove her to her mother's place about 10 miles from campus, and her mother took her in. But later when I called, no one answered there. I got a bit anxious and drove over again. Going in the door, the smell hit me. They were all dead." Ray started crying…

I tried to console him. "I lost my parents and my sister. I know how you feel. But why did you come here?"

Ray wiped his eyes with the back of his hand and continued. "When I first came I was a fisherman back home, so on those holidays when everybody went home, I came here to fish. It's really different from freshwater fishing, but I caught on and enjoyed the people I met out here. Some even let me stay with them. But as you can see, nobody seems to be here now.

"One of the guys I stayed with was a longtime surfer and had a little beach bungalow right up there." Ray pointed to the place. "So, I went there first. There was no one home and there was some food and drink in the refrigerator, so that's where I've been staying. I've run through all that food and I'm about to go on a fish diet if I don't do something. I've been stealing water wherever I could find it, but that's running out, too. You guys seem prosperous. Do you have any greens? vegetables?"

"Yes, we've got three large gardens going. But all we've got with us is camp food and water, some fruit." I reached in my bag and handed him a mango. I could see from his face that Ray was glad to get it. We had some grain and nut bars, too. Gave him one to munch on while we fished.

We continued our conversation while catching fish. Unfortunately, we had to throw most of them back, giving me an idea that perhaps we could raise saltwater fish in our unused pools. But I didn't say anything to anyone about it.

It was about 11 o'clock and we had about 50 pounds of fish low in Mercury and PCBs when we heard Rocky yelling and running up to us. When he arrived, out of breath, he pointed up the beach and gasped…

"Can you see it? There, up the beach! That's a dolphin, a stranded dolphin, and it's alive!"

☞₧₨∾

11

Forbidden Food and Urgent Matters

We all took off running back down the long pier and then along the beach to where the dolphin lay struggling in the sand about 10 feet from the water. Rocky got there first, but I was right behind him, along with Ray. Augie was last, because he stopped running halfway and had to walk, holding his side as he did.

The dolphin was clearly in bad shape. The sand, disturbed, showed where it had struggled to no avail. But it wasn't struggling anymore, just looking at me with that pleading eye to do something. Already showing a distinct skin redness as a sign of severe sunburn. I can only imagine its agony and inability to call out to its pod out of the water.

I looked at the size of it, apparently a male, closely and said, "It would be tough, even with all of us trying, to get this huge guy back in the water. And if we did, he'd either die anyway or try to come back on the beach again. But it doesn't look like he has the strength even to do that. In the water he might drown."

Ray agreed. "What do you suggest we do?"

"I favor putting the poor thing out of its misery. Augie, what do you think?"

"I think we need food, fresh meat. This is no time to be sympathetic when our lives are at stake."

"I agree, Augie. Does anyone object?" I looked around at everyone and they all shook their heads, No, or said so.

I pulled out my revolver and showed it to the poor animal and then aimed at what I thought was his brain below the blowhole. The dolphin exhaled one last time and his blowhole stayed open. His eye no longer had any expression, just stared like a dead human.

Ray ran up to the beach bungalow he was staying in and brought back some coolers to put the meat in. Augie and I got out our knives and began experimental cutting to see if we could butcher the animal right. There was a thin layer of fat under the skin, so we skinned it like we would skin a deer to see if the skin or that fat would be useful, like whale oil.

The meat was surprisingly dark and deeply muscled. I estimated that we cut off about 300 pounds from the skeleton and entrails we left for the scavengers that were already circling. Carrying the meat back to the truck was quite a task, so we went back to the pier, gathered up the fish, shellfish and our gear, and then, drove the truck as close as we could to the carcass to put the meat on it. After lousy fishing, that dolphin saved our day. That is, if anyone would eat it?

As we loaded up, I asked Ray, "Are you coming with us? We could use another hand. You say you're a farmer and we've got crops to put in, cultivate and harvest. Are you with us?"

"You know I like it here. But I can't live on fish alone. I'll come along and help you out if you let me come down here often and fish for everyone. Maybe leave, if I don't like it."

"That's a deal then. You'll like the young ladies. It's not lonely like here. We are all working together to make it to next year and the year after that–starting over."

In no time, we were back in our growing compound and savoring some rabbit stew with homemade bread and all around the table again getting ready for the afternoon ahead. Once again, I checked on what everyone was doing by clicking on my glass with my table knife.

I was interrupted by my phone ringing. I looked at who was calling, put it down on the table and turned the speaker on, so that everyone could hear, and answered…

"Bob Emerson, it's good to hear from you! I hope you made it to your brother's place. I was wondering about you?"

"We made it, but it was rough at times. Since we left on the freeways we really didn't run into any trouble until we got out in the country where everybody has guns. We were shot at, both from the side of the road and by other cars that we came upon along the way. Everyone was so desperate they were shooting for no damn reason. And then, after we left California into Arizona we had to pay to get through a roadblock near Las Vegas. They didn't want money; they took our water and road food."

"Man, that sounds bad. Did you have to go without water after that?"
"We were so tired by that time we drove down to Lake Mead and camped. Boiled water from the reservoir so we didn't have to go the whole way

without water, just without food we planned on."

"How was Albuquerque, like LA?"

"We got there near dusk and I didn't see any lights, so apparently they had completely lost power. Have you?"

"So far, we still have water and power, but we're not sure how long that will last. Our water pressure is low because of so many leaks. I expect the power to go out anytime soon and not come back on. Our plans are to get every house on the street, including yours, fully solar and wind powered in the next couple weeks. But getting our own water system is probably more urgent. With our three gardens, our cisterns will not provide water for all of us before the end of summer."

"Like in LA, we stayed on the freeway in Albuquerque until we got to the state highway we took to my brother's homestead. He was really glad that we got there. Roger and his wife have built that place in the mountains over the past 10 years. We will have to scramble to provide for all of us, but he has a deep well that is windmill powered so we don't have to worry about water. It's large for a homestead house and is fully solar powered. Neighbors are very cooperative and mostly Native Americans. But they've all been hit hard by the virus and lost many. Cooperation helps because everyone here is helping everyone else out."

"Bob, we are finding people that want to join us in an effort to collectively survive, too. But we had a violent gang come up the street and battle it out with Rodney Bloom until he died and they wounded his daughter, Stephanie, who is recovering from a broken leg. So far we are fine, but there's a lot to do if we are going to make it even to next year."

"Just wanted to reassure you guys. I'm so glad that we have this G6 network from satellites, otherwise, before, this was one area where there were no signals and I wouldn't have been able to call you."

"I hope you don't mind if we put someone in your place. Like I said, we'll put in solar power and connect your water up to our own system of water storage and distribution. We've been calling our subs and some are coming to stay here with us."

"You know, Drake, I've always admired the way you and Derek have handled yourselves and I can see you really have taken charge where I thought we wouldn't stand a chance. I'm so glad that I have a brother who has worked very hard over 10 years to be self-sufficient and now has to take us in as well. I'm going to have to sign off. But best wishes and good luck to all of you."

Derek, sitting next to me, answered, "Bob, don't worry about us. We are so glad that you made it okay in spite of what you ran into. We are faced with some vicious gangs but we will use deadly force if we have to. All of us wish you all well, too. Keep in touch. Goodbye."

Bob followed and hung up. I was greatly relieved. Made me think of Gramps all by himself in the Valley… *I need to call him…* I thought, distracted.

I followed that call with checking on what everyone was doing. I told them, "Based on what we caught this morning, fishing at the pier doesn't seem like a very good option for getting seafood. But Ray, who I've already introduced you to, has volunteered to go down there and fish for us so that we may have fresh fish quite often. But this afternoon, I'm going to drive down to the fish market in San Pedro with Ray to see if we can get a lot more fish that are low in mercury and PCBs, like salmon. It's a long shot but we need to explore all the options we have."

I told Ray and Augie to wait for me and caught Derek before he left the room with all the others.

"Der, I've been ignoring Gramps, being involved in so many other things. Will you stay with me while I call him?" We sat back down, while Martha, Melody and Stephanie were clearing the table and doing the dishes. I put the phone on the table again, hit the familiar link, and called.

Grandpa Hutchins rough voice answered. "Hello, Drake. Glad you called."

"I've been forgetting to. Is everything okay there? Derek is here, checking in, too."

Derek got in the picture and chimed in, "Hi, Gramps."

There was a look on Ralph Hutchins's face that belied his cheerfulness. "A neighbor boy, Carlos Ramirez, has been coming over here almost daily and helping me out with things. But it's getting a bit dicey because he told me that the townspeople are shooting it out among each other and he thought it would be only a matter of time before they would be coming out to the farms and raiding for food and water. The nearest town isn't that far… twelve miles. I'm really getting concerned and have my rifle and shotgun loaded on the front porch in case anyone tries to get nasty with me." He coughed to clear his throat.

"We've had a run in here in the neighborhood, too. Fortunately, thanks to the firepower of a neighbor, we were able to kill most of them and drive them off. But there are a lot more gangs here and we are preparing booby-traps and even have Dad's tank here that we used to wipe out the gang that attacked us with a machine gun on the top of their pickup bed. They also carried banned automatic assault rifles we got from the ones we killed. Terrible killing weapons that we can use if we have to, like the tank."

"They've probably got them here, that's what I'm worried about," Gramps said.

"Remember that movie we saw at your place that time, No Country for Old Men? That's where you're at now. You're making me really worried about you. We need food and you have lots of it. So, I've changed my plan for tomorrow and we'll leave first thing in the morning and should get there by noon. Is that all right with you?"

"That makes this old guy happy and relieved. Can't wait till you get here." He looked relieved on the screen.

"We'll be there, I promise. Stay as long as we need to. See you tomorrow. Bye." Grandpa Hutchins said his "Bye" and hung up.

Derek said. "I was wondering when you would be going out there. Are you planning to take anyone else along?"

"I don't know yet. But I know you're going with me. We'll see who's free tomorrow who might go with us. There's a lot of work for us to do there for him. And to get the food he'll give us. It will take hands."

Both Ray and Augie spoke up at nearly the same time… "I'll go with you," they both announced.

Derek answered for himself. "No, maybe some other time, but I'm not sure we are secure here with both of us gone for a couple of days like you might be. I'll stay this time. I'm sure with Augie and Ray along, you'll get the job done, and maybe bring Grandpa Hutchins back with you."

"I doubt that, Derek, Grandpa is married to that land." The others all laughed a nervous laugh. "And Mel, will you come along, too? That would make four of us armed who could harvest and load our trailer much quicker."

"I can't wait. I've heard so much about your Grandpa. To meet him would be an honor. My grandparents died while I was still a small child."

That's what I liked about Melody. She was very adventurous, like me.

"Well, he's one adorable, tough old dude to continue to take on that little forty acre spread alone after Grandma died some eight years ago, when I was about ten."

That afternoon, everybody took off doing various tasks. I got Augie and his kids situated in one of the empty houses. They all agreed that Ray should stay with them for now while he decided whether he would go back to his beach house or not. First, they had a big cleanup job to do. Two of the major tasks ahead were to get the swimming pool back in operation and to dig a garden to plant vegetables.

But first, I had them go with me to a place I thought we might get a lot more fish, the fish market down at the Port. We drove off and left everyone else under Derek's watch and advice. I didn't ask Mel to come along because I knew she would want to come along. I gave them both AR-15s with extra magazines from the ones we had confiscated. It was about thirty miles via the 405 and 110. I didn't know what we would encounter on the way and we had to be prepared.

From the freeway elevation we could see more flooded streets and dense smoke swirling up in some parts of the way, but like the 10 these freeways were relatively free to run with only a few wrecks and abandoned vehicles to avoid. We saw a couple of cars on the other lanes driving north past us. We watched them carefully as they passed, but they didn't fire on us so we didn't fire on them. I was sad that it had come to this. But we didn't know who to trust in this world that was evolving.

When we arrived at Terminal Island we passed a huge cruise ship with beautiful lettering on the side of the ship near the bow, Rambler of the Seas. It looked so pristine and ready to take thousands of passengers on one of those wonderful cruises that the whole family had gone on to the Fiji Islands and Australia. But that was then, and now was now. Still, that ship was so intriguing it stayed on my mind.

Just as was the Fish Market, where Josh and Dad often came to get seafood for parties or celebrations at the shop after a successful build. Lots of memories. As we approached, the market seemed to be vacated. Thinking for a minute about what happened at the grocery store, I'm sure that many came and took all the fish and seafood they could.

But, everything was way too neat and clean for nobody to be around. There weren't even any bodies. I called out as loud as I could, "This is Drake Hutchins! I've come to buy fish! Is anyone here?"

A shrill voice came from the restroom area at the far end of the market. "Okay, okay, I come. I remember your father and uncle coming many times. So glad to see you. We have many troubles. Trying to stay alive."

It was Van Nguyen, a guy I was very familiar with when he catered to some of our parties and celebrations. I ran to greet him, hugged him and lifted his skinny light body in the air spinning him around. Unfortunately, his breath smelled of fish.

Van declared, "Of all people! You and your family have come to save us?"

"Only Derek. The rest of our family died in the pandemic. How about you?"

"I was at sea with my son. When we arrived, most of the fish were gone and the rest were rotten, a horrible mess to clean up. All of the people here at the market were shot, left for dead. The few that survived are hiding in their houses and apartments. All left of my family is my son, Quoc, and my sister, Sean." He started to cry. Once again, my eyes started to tear as well. So, I changed subject.

"This is Augie and Ray. They are fishermen and were going to help me get fish. But I guess there aren't any."

Van lit up. "There is fish. We had boatload of abalone, crab and Chinook salmon. I catch up coast in kelp forest off Santa Barbara. I have stored in lockers where there is still electricity like in rich hotel over there," He pointed to the luxury Wade Towers, nearby.

"I can't stand living in my house after my wife and family died there. I staying in penthouse, for now. I watching over this market until my son and I go out to sea again to catch fish for you and others like you. Friendly and will give us greens and vegetables, rice, mushrooms and onions so we can continue our diet instead of just fish, fish and more fish." He spat what appeared to be the remains of some fish in his mouth.

And then, he looked up to me and said, "How much you want?"

After promising him that we would bring back as much of those foodstuffs that we could bring and would help him start a rooftop garden on one of the warehouses nearby, we left with about 300 pounds of salmon, crab and abalone on ice. Before we left, I told him.

"I have to go see my grandfather in the Valley tomorrow. But as soon as I get back, I will bring what you need and some people who will help you get started with a garden on the roof along with what you will need to pull it off. Kelp is a great fertilizer, and I know you can get a lot of that."

The seafood was on ice so we had to get home quickly. We said our goodbyes and left.

During the afternoon, Viktor Sarnoff, his wife, Viktoria, and his son Peter, sixteen, arrived hungry and thirsty with all their possessions on his welding truck. Viktor was an excellent iron rigger and his son was his apprentice, doing a lot of work for Dad's contracts.

Vik declared upon arriving, "When you called, we were at wits end. We live in an area where Blods have taken control. Since the pandemic, there was a lot of shooting and we feared for our lives and hardly slept at night. The only reason we were able to get out of there today was I know a couple of the gang members who I helped out when they were kids. They let us pass and get out of the neighborhood when they saw who we were. It was the scariest thing I've ever done. Talk about Russian gangs!"

Derek replied, "I can imagine. Do you see that tank at the end of the street? We went into Blip territory a couple of days ago and settled a score with it. I'm sure glad you're here. We can sure use you as we try to rebuild this place and make it self-sustaining additions. There's a lot of work to do and no pay for doing it. We've got food for now but will have to get a lot more."

Within an hour, a pickup with bullet holes arrived, driven by Monsour Habeeb, the mechanic for Dad's construction company. He told a terrible tale.

"My wife Andie and two children died during the pandemic. I couldn't stand to be with them so I packed up all the food and water that I could take and drove to my shop next door to your dad's yard. But I ran out of everything a couple of days ago. Why I was really glad to hear from Derek when he texted me. I packed up everything I had, including all my tools and my junkyard dog, Freddie, this morning.

"But then, along the way before I got to the 10, I ran into a couple of guys with AR-15s in the street who said they wanted my truck and everything on it, Freddie jumped out of the truck window and attacked them. He had one of them down when the other one opened up with his automatic on my poor dog, giving me the opportunity to run him over. But he still managed to fire a few shots at me as I drove away. I hope he died later! Nadhl!" (Arabic for bastard).

All the subcontractors knew one another from various contracts in the city, so Monsour threw in with Gary Hastings and his mother, Peter Sarnoff, his wife and son. They chose the house next to the Emerson house, with immediate plans to make it solar powered with plumbing to provide for the house, a garden and the swimming pool that needed cleaning, first.

Derek had other plans for them and they agreed to work with him to get those accomplished, remembering the power of good management and design. By the time we arrived back from the fish market everyone was in the pool after a hot sweaty day of working and we joined them as soon as we got the seafood put away in various freezers. After everybody cooled down and washed off, wasting water at our outdoor shower, we started a welcome fish fry with the fish that we caught earlier and a few Chinook salmon fillets that amply fed the whole crew. The only thing missing was potatoes. We were out of potatoes but still had plenty of fresh greens–reminding me to get greens and basics together for repayment to Van when I got back from Grandpa's.

I noticed that Derek, while savoring the salmon, wasn't eating very much. So, I asked him.

"Der, you must be hungry after all you did today, why aren't you eating?"

"I got an invite to dinner at sunset about a half hour from now from Daphne. She says she wants to treat me to dinner and 'after.' I've always had a crush on her and she sure is pulling me in. Just can't resist." He smiled slyly.

"Just stay in shape so we can get work done. What about your two other lovers?"

"They know. When I told them they said it was okay because they wanted to have a night alone together. It's a crazy world we're in now and I'm beginning to like it." He winked.

"A lot of responsibility, too, don't you think?"

"Yeah, I'll definitely keep that in mind. The two of us forever, right?"
"Yeah, Der. The two of us are going to turn this place around."

In a way, I was glad that no one was going to be in my bed with me that night. I was sunburned and exhausted and just needed to get a good night's sleep for the long trip in the morning with whatever we would run into along the way. But I didn't let it bother me and slept deeply until…

I was awakened suddenly by a loud explosion down at the end of the street and knew immediately what it was. One of our booby-traps had gone off and my phone was ringing. I reached for my pants.

$\wp\mathcal{EOCB}\wp$

12

Daphne, the Devil and Rescuing Ralph

Derek followed Daphne's invitation to a tee and arrived at the estate just as the sun was dunking its burning red head in the cold Pacific off to the west. There was still a warm glow at the top edge of the three-story building, but the rest was bathed in shadow with no lights on he could see.

Coming through the door, there was a line of scented candles providing a pathway on each step leading upstairs inviting him to follow. Of course, the candles led to the master bedroom suite on the second floor where he found Daphne lounging on the satin sheets in her diaphanous gown that was the former owner's but accented her body beautifully leaving everything to delight Der's eyes. He was glad he had showered off all the dirt and sweat from working all day and dressed for the occasion in a clean pair of jeans and shirt.

Daphne spoke first. "Welcome, Der. I'm so glad you're here. You don't know how much I've looked forward to this moment. I hope you like what I've prepared?" She waved her right hand toward the candlelit table with two settings of food and drink that resembled what you would see in a fine restaurant. The candlelight atmosphere, incense burning and soft music in the background was just right.

"Daphne, you didn't have to go to all this trouble. But this certainly is divine. I haven't seen anything like this for a long time." Derek shook his head in disbelief.

"I'm glad you like it. Champagne?"

Daphne led him over to the table where she had a bottle of champagne on ice and poured a glass for them. And then, said, "A toast to the two of us?" A delightful look in her eyes.

Derek couldn't help but comply and tapped her glass lightly as she swung her arm around his elbow to elbow and they both brought their glasses to their lips and sipped. Eye to eye and body so close to body that he could feel her heat.

There was shrimp cocktail as an appetizer with the main course of filet mignon grilled perfectly with a rice pilaf and some asparagus. Finally, some chocolate mousse for dessert. As Derek savored the third glass of champagne while finishing his mousse, he knew a way more delicate dessert was coming by the look in Daphne's eyes as he questioned her.

"Where did you get all of this? We are down to eating vulture." He laughed.

"I know, I saw Dre kill one this morning from my balcony. I invited him up for breakfast, but he was too eager to eat that dirty bird than to play house with me. He missed all the fun. Do you want to have fun?"

"What kind of question is that? Of course, I'd love to. And I think you might want to, too?"

"I can't wait, but I want you to be gentle with me."

"What do you mean, gentle?"

"I'm a virgin."

"But what about all that…" Derek was shocked. "Talk in our high school?"

"Yeah, about you and every jock in the place. I dated them all, but I never let them get to second base. One, who will remain nameless, tried to rape me, but I kicked him in the balls and had to drive us home because he hurt so much that he couldn't even drive the car to get us home."

"But what about your uncle?"

"My uncle used his finger to break my hymen. I used it to tell all the girls I'd lost my virginity when I was thirteen. The lie gave me bragging rights. They never knew I never let any prick get inside me until now. I've always liked you, Der. So, you will be my first. But not my last, I'm going to give Dre a chance to savor a near virginess, too. The world we have now will need babies. Before, I didn't want babies until I was at least thirty. But now, I see a need for babies, don't you?"

"I do." Derek felt very awkward at this point and showed it.

But Daphne saved him. "By the way, it was all in Barbara's extensive kitchen. I learned how to cook for parties with my mom. Will you take me to bed and call me Daph? All this food and drink has made me a bit sleepy." She winked.

Daphne rose from the table, walked around it and took Derek by the hand to the bed where she turned and melted into his arms. Derek had never felt anything so beautiful and soft as kissing this love goddess's lips while they moved onto the bed and started exploring each other with kisses and caresses.

But about 2 am, Wondah was on the phone with a warning. "Der! One of our sensors on the street down below triggered. The monitors show three pickups coming our way very soon. You have to get to the tank. I don't have it fully remote yet!"

I was sound asleep. But Wondah's call woke me up, too. And then, I heard the explosion, jumped out of bed, quickly got dressed and grabbed one of the AR-15s as I threw off the cobwebs of sleep while adrenaline pumped me up for battle. I quickly climbed to the roof. My rifle had a laser on it that was better than the scope on the Winchester and those armor penetrating bullets that were so lethal. I watched and waited for something to come up the street.

Wondah and Mel had two drones in the air with both surveillance and lethal capability. They could see the truck that tried to ram the gate had been blown across the street and there were bodies in the street. But the second pickup truck was moving to where the booby trap had blown a hole in the barricade and was slowly pushing through with a number of armed occupants and a machine gun mounted in its bed. The drones fired on that truck, but Mel's was shot down.

As the truck started up the street it was hit squarely by a shell from the tank and Derek. The survivors from that hit and blast all ran to the last truck and drove off. I climbed down off the roof and headed for where the truck had a huge hole in the middle where the engine had been and was burning with bodies and body parts everywhere. Augie and Ray were ahead of me but I caught up and passed them.

Still, I was cautious. When I saw someone moving in the truck across the street, I didn't hesitate to put him out of his misery. But as I surveyed the scene, I counted ten dead and three of them were women. Including the one who had a mortal wound before I shot her. It didn't make me feel any better. I was beginning to know what PTSD was all about, and I didn't like it.

I told everyone as a crowd was gathering. "I've taken a look here and there's no one left alive, but there's nothing we can do tonight. We all have to get some sleep and get up the first thing in the morning to cart off these bodies before we have predators all over the place."

Derek arrived. "Dre, don't worry, you and the other guys have got to take off for Grandpa Ralph's in the morning. I'll take charge of taking care of these bodies and make sure I get good pictures so Wondah can find out who they are and whether we will have to confront them like we did the Blips. They'll probably want revenge. We'll fix these defenses right away."

"Thanks Der. I'm headed back to try to get some sleep and I suggest all of you do the same. If anything else comes along tonight, our surveillance cameras will pick it up and warn us like it did with this. Thanks a million everyone, and Wondah. You are the best!"

Everyone clapped and cheered their appreciation for her skills.

I was back in bed, but thoughts of what was going on and anticipation kept me awake.

Derek returned for a second round in the loving arms of his high school idol. Finding her more than what he had ever dreamed. Only because Daphne finally let herself be herself and not have to put on any false airs of who she really was. Just a young woman of childbearing age in a new world where she would have to work hard to survive and adapt.

The clock on my phone moved slowly, but finally, it was dawn and I was up preparing for our journey to rescue Grandpa Ralph if he needed rescue and get food. The four of us gathered what we would need for the trip and grabbed a breakfast of cereal with water with no milk, fruit or sugar to put on it. We still had plenty of energy bars we would take along for the journey as well as large jugs of water, not knowing if water would be a problem or not. Water was always on my mind and I regretted not getting to work on an adequate cistern system for the neighborhood that day.

Before we left, Derek took pictures, gathered up all the bodies and body parts, and once again, transported them to the place out back of the estate where wild animals and carrion eaters would have their way and other smaller animals would also benefit. The flies were terrible, but Derek and his team worked as quickly as they could and the flies settled on the new blood right away.

Returning to the gate, Derek, Viktor and Gary got busy restoring it. With the tank, they pushed the destroyed vehicles completely to the other side of the road where they would be a great deterrent to anyone attempting to enter the compound again. A road sign signaling DANGER! With a skull and cross bones emblem warned of the fate of marauders.

Knowing that everything was in good hands, the four of us began the 200 mile journey to Grandpa Ralph's ranch, all forty acres of it.

My 2031 utility truck, no longer thinking of it as Dad's, had a 450 mile range with its fuel-cell storage system, with higher capacity and efficiency than batteries. In addition to rapid charging ability at self-serve charging stations. The finish on the roof and hood was nano fiber, Charge-Skin, an attractive wrap pattern that, when properly connected to the wiring harness, provided continual charging to the battery or other electrical storage system as long as the sun was shining on those surfaces. The only requirement was to keep the surface clean at all times. The skin was tough, too, with a useful life of twenty years. Much longer than most paints in the California sun.

I didn't need GPS to guide me on this trip, or even a map. From Cal 2, we quickly picked up the 405 that took us to the 5 and rapidly out of Los Angeles. Looking back there was a haze in the air from all the fires still burning. We were fortunate to have the sea breeze from the coast to keep our neighborhood clear of that unhealthy, smoky haze.

I figured it would take four hours conservatively averaging 50 mph, but we were averaging 70 with very few obstacles to push or winch our way out of. There wasn't much through these mountains that would hamper us except for a few abandoned cars. No people by the side of the road, just California state and national forest.

Just beyond the Grapevine, no longer the scary ride before 5 was built, Dad told me, we branched off the 5 to the right and took Cal 99 all the way to Grandpa's ranch, about twenty-five miles short of Fresno.

Although we were prepared for battle and saw some traffic on the other side, across the median, nothing hampered us on 99 except smoke across the road from grass fires. We arrived just before 11 am. Grandpa's mangled gate at the entrance made my blood race to my temples and sweat pour down my back in our air-conditioned truck as I hit the accelerator tearing up the long dirt driveway to the house.

What was worse, were all the bullet holes around the doors and windows of the house. The porch couch and Grandpa's favorite chair destroyed. But there was no blood on that front porch. The door was open and the living room was full of holes inside, the place was torn apart. My blood was boiling at this point and scared to death that Grandpa Ralph may have been taken or killed.

Not finding him there, we left the house and headed to the barn. I called out, "Grandpa, we're here! Are you all right? We're here. We can help."

Gramps appeared in the doorway of a small shed that had held pigs in earlier days. He yelled back. "Drake! What took you so long? Maybe this wouldn't have happened if you had come yesterday. But you're a sight for sore eyes. Glad you're here now."

He began walking toward us carrying his shotgun. Likewise, we were all carrying our AR-15s but those guns were dropped and hugs were in order. Tears flowed. My anxiety eased off a bit.

"What happened here, Gramps? Your house is a mess."

"It's those Brown brothers. They've terrorized everybody in Eunice. Probably ran out of food and water and that's why they came last night. When I heard them crashing the gate, I grabbed my guns and hightailed it for this shack, knowing it would be the last place they would look into. Where I'd make my stand if I had to. But they left after they ransacked the house and even took some mementos along with all the food and some water in all the containers they could find. Even left the water running." Old man's tears started flowing down his face. I joined him.

"Why didn't you make a stand? Save your place from this?"

"They've got automatic weapons and are vicious. I heard they came from Belize or one of those other Central American countries. Not at all like farm workers who live here. I feel badly for those poor folks if they are still alive. Took over the whole damn town."

"I know them, Gramps. We took Dad's tank and wiped a whole gang not ten miles from where we live."

"It's about twelve miles to Eunice. That's why they came here last night. Probably just going down the road and picking on every farm." His tears had stopped, but he sighed in resignation.

"If they raided all night, they are sleeping today, probably still drunk. We need to hit them now."

"No, Drake! They're too dangerous."

"Couldn't be more dangerous than the L.A. gangs that we are faced with. We brought Dad's bazooka and some rockets for their trucks and houses. That will soften them up before we go after them with four AR-15s. You can come along if you like. Just where in Eunice do they live?"

"Okay, I'll go along. But I'll stay in your truck and drive away with you if you come back wounded or dead." Gramps's eyes narrowed. He was dead serious.

"Before we go, do you need any water or food?"

"Got plenty of water and there are some of my garden crops that I snacked on this morning. We can go. That way I can show you where they live."

It took only about fifteen minutes to drive to Eunice and to the small house where the Brown family lived. The town was quiet, but there was evidence of shootouts on some of the buildings. I assumed that most of the occupants had either fled or were killed. Dogs ran loose in the streets and there was that unmistakable smell of dead bodies with some bones in the street picked clean by vultures bleaching in the sun.

There was an old car and two pickups at the house. One of the pickups already had a number of bullet holes in it and appeared to be no longer drivable. I figured that the newer one had been stolen to replace the one that got shot at last night during the raids.

I told everyone to get out, including Grandpa, and get behind the truck so they wouldn't get shot by surprise. I loaded the bazooka and aimed it at the front door of the house. Standing by the front of the truck and ready to duck back behind the truck to avoid shrapnel and bullets when the shooting started.

The rocket blew a hole through the front door and exploded inside. The house started to burn but no one came running out or shooting. I reloaded the bazooka and propped it behind the truck. And then, led the others toward the house, ready to fire at anything that moved.

The fire lit up the inside when we carefully entered. There were bodies in there, none of them were moving. I saw a middle-aged woman, two young men and a young woman with bullet wounds patched up with bandages and one baby. But all of them had been hit by shrapnel from the blast and were dead. Soon, the fire got too intense and we had to retreat.

Inside the shot up truck Gramps saw lots of blood on the seats and found all of his mementos mostly intact in the bed. Apparently, when the marauders returned, they were so wounded they didn't bother to take anything into the house. The truck was full of what they had taken from Ralph and others in that spree the night before.

Gramps hadn't stayed behind the truck like I told him. He was waiting right outside for us with his shotgun when we came out. Told us what he found in the shot up truck.

He pointed to the newer truck I didn't blow up, either. "That maroon one belongs to Cyrus Meyer, 2 miles down the road from me. He bought it just last year… Proud of it. Worked hard to get it. Sure hope he's alive when we bring it back to him."

The ignition was broken to unlock the steering wheel, and the truck had been jumped to steal it. I got it started the same way.

"Mel, will you drive this truck behind us as we return it to its owner. Stay a bit back from us and if we run into any trouble, remember to be turned around and ready to take us back to Grandpa's place."

"Gladly, Dre. I know the routine." She winked. She got in the driver's seat when I slid out and put her AR-15 down on the seat next to her.

As we left Eunice, a few very haggard looking people and kids came out of the houses and waved at us like we were liberators. Gramps knew some of them, waved and called out to them by name. Told them to come if they needed water or food and he had work for them to earn it.

When we got back on the road to his place, Ralph muttered…

"All good hard-working people. They suffered a lot from that gang. Good riddance. I'll help them all I can."

In the rearview mirror, I saw Augie give Gramps a brotherly punch on the shoulder. Everyone was smiling. We passed Gramps's place to the Meyer's place. It was a large farm with lots of outbuildings and orchards in the background. There was no gate or long drive but the house looked okay from what we could see. I parked on the road and let Gramps out to approach them so they wouldn't think of us as raiders. Grateful for the construction sign on the side of our front doors.

When I saw two young men come bounding out of the house followed by a middle-aged woman, I knew we were okay and signaled Melody to follow me in. The young men were shaking Gramps's hand enthusiastically and the woman hugged him. By that time, we were getting out of the truck and the two young men came over to shake all of our hands as well.

Gramps got a curious look on his face after the woman hugged him and said, "Gladys, where's Cyrus?"

Her face dropped and she replied, "He's dead." Shaking her head. "Amazonia-9 got him. And all of us were sick. Thankfully, Cy, Jr. and

Rich came out of it like me along with two of their sisters in the house."

"So sorry to hear that, Gladys. Cy never hesitated to help me. Like my boys just helped me out by finishing off that Brown gang in town. But from what I saw in town, your boys and you had already given them hell, making our job much easier. They won't be bothering us again. Thank goodness!" He sighed and held her hand in his.

"Yes, Ralph. When I saw that girl from my bedroom window sneak down from the road and steal Dad's truck. I saw the other truck waiting on the road and began to worry it was more than just the girl taking the truck, I woke the boys and told them to grab a rifle, go out the back kitchen door and sneak around the sides of our house to ambush them if they came down the drive.

"It only took a moment. When my boys, using the house for cover, saw guns sticking out of the windows of the truck coming down the drive, they opened up on it and its occupants. Suddenly, the truck backed up to the road, turned, and sped off while my boys kept shooting. Those in the truck got off a few wild shots, but were so surprised they missed, and left, taking Dad's truck with them. And now it's come back, thanks to you." She smiled and nodded us her appreciation.

I butted in. "Not entirely, the ignition's broken. But we wiped the whole family out with one rocket from Dad's old bazooka as part of his military collection from his time in service.

The girl that stole the truck is dead from the blast. And the way the other three guys were shot up, I think some of them may have died before we got there. They were a vicious branch of the Belizean gangs that have infiltrated many cities in the States. Conditioned to know nothing but killing and terrorizing. The sooner they are wiped out, the better. It's war now. and, unfortunately, women and children will be killed, too." I buried my thoughts about that.

Cy said, "Thanks Drake for finishing them off in town for us. We were going to follow up ourselves. We expect there will be more. Everyone here in the country has guns and when people get desperate they do terrible things… Even to friends.

"We have a lot of crops that we have no market for right now and not enough hands to harvest them. We are willing to trade with our neighbors and supply Eunice with food and water now that there are only good people there. Do you need anything?"

"That's what we're here for. To harvest some of Gramps's early crops and take them back to the secure compound we are building in L.A. from the street we live on overlooking the Pacific at Santa Monica. Drake and I will rebuild there just like our fathers and mothers would have with the construction business.

"But they're gone like your father in the pandemic. We have to rebuild and move on. Right now, our primary need is water and food. We are here for the food part. We need a water system for our neighborhood that we will build soon. If Gramps doesn't have what we need to take back with us, we may come to you and trade for it. Don't know what that is yet."

Cy replied, "Don't worry about trading right now, whatever you want, we will give it to you, free. Wiping out that gang has saved us all. We could use some of their weapons."

"They're yours. We have plenty, including my dad's military collection arsenal. Augie, would you please go back to the truck and get those guns, knives and hand grenades we pulled out of that house and car before it all burned?"

Augie got the stuff from the truck and brought it to Cy and Rich. There was a lot of shaking hands and happiness. I told them to use remote cameras on the road to give them advance warning. Use drones and booby-traps to catch the bad guys unawares. They agreed and listened to my suggestions.

Gladys fed us with a great big farmers' lunch spread and a lot of left-overs before we left for Ralph's place around three o'clock.

We were too full and sleepy to work but got out in the hot sun to the garden, weeded it, and began harvesting ripe vegetables and greens for both Gramps and us to take home. We slept well that night after cleaning up the mess and slept on his floor, couches and beds wherever we could find a place to rest our weary bones. By sunlight, we were up and at it again.

❧ ❦ ❧

13

Home with Milk and Honey

I was getting used to waking up still feeling in my bones the rigors of the day before. Still, all the heavy work and anxiety had me in the greatest shape I'd ever been in, even as an active guy all of my life and an athlete in high school. I was building muscles I thought I would never have.

The others were feeling the same way when we all rose to the smell of Gramps making a huge breakfast of bacon, scrambled eggs, flapjacks and fresh squeezed orange juice from his orange trees he took out of the freezer for us. And, there were fresh strawberries we picked the day before. What a feast compared to what we had been eating at home, changing each day with declining food resources.

We finished up harvesting from the garden. Picked some fruit from the trees that were ripe and gunny bags of nuts, prunes, dried apricots and other dried fruit Gramps had stored from the year before to sell in town or at the markets. He had only one cow left, "For my milk," and one steer, "For my meat."

I suggested, "Can you raise a couple of steers and get a cow for us when we come again in about a month?"

"It might be difficult. I ain't gettin' any younger. But I'm beginning to see what you need and will see what I can do. I talked to the boy that's been helping me this morning. Now that the Brown gang is gone, I can get some other guys to come out and work here, too. With old man Meyer gone, his boys have too much to handle. I can probably pick up a steer or two and a cow from them. Since they are in a charitable mood." He laughed.

"That's the spirit, Gramps! But the way we are growing we will need a whole lot more than what your little farm can produce. Let's go over to the Meyer farm this morning and see what we can wrangle from them."

After Gramps showed the others what to do, and what they could load onto the trailer, he joined me and we drove over to the Meyer place. When we drove in, Cyrus and Rich came out of the barn and Gladys came onto the front porch.

"Howdy, guys!" Gramps called out to the boys. "We've come to do a little horse-trading. Only we don't have any horses!" He laughed. We all couldn't help ourselves and joined him in the laugh.

I took over. "Seriously, we are here to take up your offer from yesterday. We've got a growing community we want to get self-sustaining in the near future. We may be able to bring seafood and fish to exchange for beef in the future, but right now, we'd like you to give Ralph a couple of steers he can raise for us to butcher in the fall and maybe a cow or a goat so we can have milk for our kids. Gramps has an old horse trailer we can use.

Cy spoke for Rich and his mom. "I'm open to that. If you bring us seafood we can get it to market here in the Valley and to any restaurants that may reopen. For now, it's a really good deal for us, too. We just happen to have three kids we were going to have to get rid of, two nannies and a billy. With the way things are, we are getting way too much milk we can't market right now. We will be distributing it free in Eunice for now, for their labor at harvest time. We have a young Holstein that is producing milk we can let you have based on our relationship developing more."

"That was easier than I thought. What do you say, Gramps, do you think we have a deal?"

"We sure do. Grandson, you sure are one hell of a negotiator." He laughed again. It was good to see him in such good humor.

The Meyer boys loaded two steers and the cow onto their trailer and two nannies about to milk on their pickup. And then, they brought out a frisky little billy who jumped right in the truck with us.

They followed us with their trailer full to Gramps's place and helped us load them onto his trailer hooked up behind our trailer. Making sure the trailer brakes worked. Our truck was fully charged sitting in the sun for two days and would use quite a bit more power going home but make it okay if we were careful with that long, long trailer behind to watch. I set up a couple cameras to make watching them easier.

But when we got back to his place, it was obvious it was rough on Gramps to see us go. At the last minute, he blurted, "I've got about six months' worth of beef in the freezer and I will only eat about a month of it before those steers are ready to butcher when you come back. You can have it and you can have some chickens. I don't need all those eggs, except for Eunice. They have chickens in town, I've seen 'em. The beef won't thaw will it?"

"Not in the coolers we brought. Any milk, preserves, eggs or anything else you can spare we would like to take, too."

With our trailer loaded with produce, nuts, fruit and grain and the horse trailer hooked up to it, we pulled out, fully loaded with food and waved goodbye to Grandpa Ralph until our promised return a month later to get more and perhaps, bring more fish and seafood for him and the Meyer family to use in trade.

In spite of my concern over the length of our two trailers, the trip back went well and we were at the gate by 3 pm with a huge crowd waiting for us to help us unload all of the food and animals. One of the homes on the street had a very large backyard that wasn't developed very much. There was no pool but there was a covered patio and abandoned garden. Derek and I, along with Ray Dugas and a couple of other guys quickly set up some fencing to keep the goats and the cow in the backyard. Fortunately, it was overgrown from neglect. Providing green grass for the cow and brush for the goats. There was a hot tub that would serve as a place to water them.

The billy tagged along with us and tried jumping up on anything he could to get a higher vantage point. He would end up in the enclosure later when he was mature enough to mate with the girls. For now, he made a great pet for the kids. Regis and Mike enjoyed his antics and played with him too.

When we got back to the Rosenberg house, most of the food had already been unloaded and placed in various refrigerators and freezers. Martha started a great big outdoor barbecue meal for the block with the help of Stephanie and, surprisingly, Daphne.

When I congratulated her on helping us out, she whispered in my ear, "After we have eaten our fill here, I'd like you to join me this evening for a real treat that the others won't get after dinner."

Grinning ear to ear. I turned and whispered in her ear, "It's a date. I think I'm looking forward to it." She looked a bit askance for my doubt. I guess she didn't know that Derek always confided everything with me like a real brother.

It was a busy time for everyone setting up for the meal outdoors on the patio. Some wine was found to help lubricate the gathering and we all celebrated the food we had brought from the Central Valley with the hope that we would be able to grow more food and make more runs to get enough food for everyone, including other people we might invite to our growing neighborhood.

It was late afternoon after all of the good eating and toasts all around. I decided to call a meeting because we were getting too numerous to meet just at breakfast anymore. I suggested we get together once a week like this as a whole community and share ideas for what we could do going forward. I took the opportunity to share with them what was on my mind.

"As you all know, our water pressure is dangerously low. And we have been filling all of the cisterns we have so our gardens can make it through the summer. And, we can continue to grow more food in the fall before the rains come. So, I am planning to leave first thing in the morning with Viktor Sarnoff and Gary Hastings to a tank manufacturer in Anaheim to see if we can get a tank for our water tower I've already designed. It will give us water pressure. But we will have to reconfigure our whole water supply system a bit to make it happen.

"In addition, power is out all across the city, and we will lose it, too. I'm surprised that we still have it in this neighborhood, apparently from geo-thermal sources north of here that require very little human management, run by AI. I want Derek and Wondah to spearhead providing complete, 100% solar/wind power to every household on the street who doesn't already have it." A cheer rose from those around the tables and chairs. I didn't expect it, but humbly acknowledged by nodding and mouthing, Thank you.

"I want all of you to work on your gardens when you can and help out with all of these projects whenever you can. I believe our phones and Internet will continue for some time because it's all on satellites now, all solar powered and AI operated. They will fail in time without some sort of maintenance from humans, but then, we will go to Wi-Fi networks to main-tain communication.

"One last thing. Ray Dugas has volunteered to milk the goats and the cow so the kids will have fresh milk every day and we can make butter and cheese with anything left over. For now, I'm asking all the adults not to drink milk until we have enough for everyone with more cows and more goats. I hope at least one of you volunteers to learn to milk when Ray goes fishing and help feed the animals making sure that they are watered, sheltered and protected from predators like eagles, coyotes, and even, mountain lions."

I could feel from the murmuring the statement bothered some. "There are mountain lions, and maybe, wolves and bears in the reserves north of us. We shouldn't worry too much about them coming here. They will have a lot of wild game to hunt and will shy away from us because they are conditioned to know we are dangerous. But if any do come after our animals, we probably will have to kill them to keep them from making more raids.

"I've bored you enough. You are all invited to my pool to cool off and clean up after a hot sweaty day of working to make our little community a happier place to be." Everyone cheered again and dispersed, doing what they were going to do in the evening.

This time, everyone came with a swimsuit except for some of the kids who didn't have any shame about going bare naked in the shallow end of the pool. Having fun with their newfound friends. Most of the adults, like me, were rather subdued and just relaxed, soaking up the cooling water after a long hot day.

Nearing sunset, Daph motioned for me to follow and left the pool. I followed, catching up to her when she reached the gate to the estate. This time, there were no candles to guide us. Just the slanting light of the setting sun angling through the windows on the west side of the house that lit up various portions of the place brilliantly in a warm yellow glow.

Reaching the bedroom with both of us still in our swimsuits, she turned and pulled me into her curvaceous soft body tightly. She brushed my lips gently with hers back-and-forth a couple of times, and then opened her mouth to give me a kiss that thrilled me all the way to my toes. I couldn't help finding my swimsuit too confining as she started exploring with her tongue and hands.

Then, she stopped right in the middle of kissing, backed off, looked down at my growing bulge and said slyly, "I would fix that if I were you. In the meantime, I'm going to put on something more comfortable."

She obviously was teasing me as I struggled to remove my, still wet, swimsuit resisting by pulling it down over my erection that didn't stop growing. I could see her in the closet with the light on in front of a full-length mirror, take off her swimsuit and start trying on various lingerie that had been Barbara's, but now, fit Daphne perfectly. I ended up sitting on the bed closest to the closet watching her try on those outfits and then, turn around, showing me various poses. And then, taking them off and trying on something else. I must say I was holding back an explosion just watching.

Eventually, she found what she wanted to wear, a vintage 1960s baby doll outfit that was completely transparent showing all of her pinkness as she glided out of the closet, pecked me on the lips and glided off to the substantial liquor cabinet where she poured us some after dinner cordials of Harold's Albany Creme.

I hadn't tasted sherry before but found the texture and taste amazingly smooth and sweet. Found tasting it on Daphne's lips even better. It wasn't long before she led me into bed and she told me to be gentle like she had told Derek. I had every intention of being gentle as I drifted off into her until our excitement and fulfillment had us both sleeping until…

Daphne's phone rang. It was Wondah. "I saw you with Dre. Is he there? Can I talk to him?"

Daphne put her phone on speaker. I yawned and said, "I'm here."

"My sensors down the street just took off. Our cameras show five vehicles coming. What looks like a dump truck with a snowplow on the front, three pickups, all mounted with machine guns, and a car. Derek and I are launching our drones shortly and we need you to get to the tank. I have everybody on the line and they're all getting armed."

I grabbed my pants and asked, "Can I borrow your phone, Daph?"

Sure, honey. I think I've got another one around here. I found a couple of pistols and I'll be ready to shoot if they come here. Don't worry about me."

"We all may have to worry." I was worried to death! I gave her a quick peck on the cheek and ran downstairs barefoot to the tank as fast as I could. Once inside the tank, Wondah had provided a couple of view screens I could connect to the drones through our Wi-Fi. It was much easier to see what the convoy was doing. By the time I got there and turned on the displays, the convoy was already at the gate and had stopped. I could see lights flashing all over the two wrecks we left as a warning. The two drones stayed high and over 200 yards back so they would be hard to hit while they gave good views of what was happening on the street.

What the gang didn't know was there were three Claymore mines at the base of the barricade set to be triggered from either of the drones or Wondah's console. Derek held off firing them for the moment. Instead, he gave a booming warning from the hidden loudspeaker in the barricade in his best Darth Vader voice…

"This is a warning. If you touch our gate you will have the fate of those two trucks you see across the road!"

There was some shouting, and the convoy drove off down into Santa Monica and the beach. Later, we heard a lot of gunfire down there. It put us on edge but we were all grateful we didn't have to fight that bunch. Internally, I knew we would have to do something about all of the gangs if we were going to live in peace moving forward. I just wasn't sure what we would be able to do. I just hoped the lack of clean water would kill them all before the rain came in the late fall and replenished water supplies.

I rejoined Daphne for another round of lovemaking. Before we knew it the light of dawn came streaming in and I had to get up and leave.

14

Fresh Water and Rescuing Jerry

We had reached the end of the normally productive spring season for vegetable crops and faced a long dry time where the green grass that grew so quickly in the spring had matured and dried to a golden brown. The fruit and nut trees had blossomed and started their annual round of drawing water from deep underground to hang heavy with their bounty to a late summer and early fall harvest.

But much of the greenery that heralded the beauty of the wealthier part of Los Angeles was heavily irrigated from reservoirs as far away as Northern California. Those reservoirs, due to the changing weather, were either overflowing in years when the Sierras got too much rain and snow or near empty when periods of drought struck with resulting wildfires burning the declining bone-dry forests, grass and chaparral.

Already, we were in a period of drought, and I feared we would suffer if we didn't come up with a way to provide us with water through this summer and beyond. On our forays along the interstates, I had seen the usually green vines covering the banks turning yellow and brown from not getting their usual irrigation. I feared many of the fruit and nut trees in the city we possibly could exploit would die by the end of this summer unless they were firmly rooted to survive drought without irrigation.

At least, Grandpa Ralph had a deep well into the aquifer powered by a combination of a windmill and solar panels our family had provided him in 2010. But much of Los Angeles and the surrounding communities had been dependent on annual water from the Sierras. As parts of that system failed, water to those communities would fail. It was happening already wherever we went and landscapes were rapidly drying up.

These thoughts ran through my mind as I rounded up Gary Hastings, Viktor Sarnoff and his son, Peter. We set off, fully armed, for Southern California Steel and Tank. Where Gary assured me we could get everything for a water tower and plumbing pipe to re-pipe our neighborhood.

Vik assured me he could weld any kind of metal and knew of epoxies that could be used to seal joints. I was glad to have them aboard. Expertise was invaluable. I was willing to try to do anything, but some things were beyond my skills.

Once again, there were still fires and smoke in the air. The landscape from the freeway looked bleaker than before in every direction. The stench of death still prominent in places. I was wondering how many were dying out there from lack of food and water. I wanted to do something about it, but didn't have time with our urgent need for water in the neighborhood.

We left the freeway and took a boulevard to our destination when I spotted a small boy in the shade on a street corner, alone. We pulled up and Peter yelled, "Hello, can we help you?"

The boy was frail, lethargic and very skinny. Didn't answer. All he could do was wave weakly at us. We left my truck and approached him. His lips were parched and he could barely speak. Looked to be about nine or ten.

Approaching with my thermos water bottle, I asked him, "What's your name?"

He struggled, and with a raspy throat muttered, "Jerry."

I gave Jerry some water. A moment later, he threw it up. I gave him some more, slowly, and gradually, he started to come out of the trance he had been in sitting under that awning.

I asked him, "Why are you sitting here and not home with your parents?"

"I was waiting for the bus."

"There aren't any buses running."

"My mother told me to take the bus to Auntie Gloria."

"Where?"

"San Diego, I think. We went there a couple of times. I think I can find it."

"Why would your mother tell you to go alone with no luggage?"

"It was the last thing she said before she stopped talking with her eyes open and I didn't know what to do because she wouldn't wake up. So, I came here yesterday, waiting for the bus. Will you take me to San Diego?"

"What about your father, your sisters and brothers?"

"I don't have a father. And Mama told me they were dead and not to look."

By that time, I understood. Jerry was so weak he couldn't walk, so I carried him to the truck and we took a few minutes to keep hydrating him and gave him an energy bar he began eating so fast he ended up choking. We slowed him down and he finished the bar.

I realized we were losing time on our mission. I drove off with Gary keeping Jerry hydrated in the backseat, and on through the streets to our destination.

Suddenly, there was a loud crack! on my driver's side door. I didn't feel anything but looked down and saw blood on my left leg and a bullet sticking out of my jeans, blossoming from faded blue to red. I made an emergency stop to the side of the street.

Ever alert, the guys got out behind the truck and pumped automatic fire in the direction they thought the bullet came from. I yelled, "Stop shooting unless you have a target! Stop wasting bullets!"

No one could tell me where the shot came from. There were no more shots as we huddled behind the truck, looking for a glint of sun off a gun barrel or movement. Nothing, just silence.

Fortunately, the bullet came out easily. I simply pulled it out when we had our first aid kit open. While a bandage stopped the bleeding, I would have to get it properly dressed later. I was really lucky the bullet passed through our company sign, the steel of the door and the inner door as well as the plastic and fabric door covering. It had slowed the bullet so it only punctured my leg muscle. But didn't cause any serious damage that would have really delayed our mission. The wound hurt a bit, but I could use my leg without any more pain.

Continuing to be watchful and worried we might get ambushed, we arrived at the yard and were relieved when we saw the padlock on the main gate hadn't been cut or broken. Dad had taught me how to pick padlocks like that rather than cut them off with bolt cutters. After about two for three minutes of working on the pins, it opened and I left it to lock again when we left.

Jerry was doing much better. Even getting a bit talkative. He told us he was 11 and was even a little bit fat when he got sick at school and came home to his mother. He kept asking us if we were going to San Diego and Gary assured him we probably would, "Later, but for right now we were going to take you home with us. Okay?"

"Okay. Can we stop at McJohnny's on the way there? I want a Mc-Smoothie with chocolate cookie bits." He remained a bit confused and a lot dehydrated. I hoped the best for him, not sure he'd make it.

The food soon made Jerry sleepy and he was fast asleep in the truck while we worked. The yard was huge. Soon, we located a water tank the size we wanted and it included a tower already built, 30 feet tall, stored alongside. The tank plus the tower would reach 50 feet, providing adequate water pressure for us. We could get the tank on our trailer, but the tower was too big. Fortunately, there was a flatbed truck in the yard with adequate space for the tower and two more tanks we would add to our cistern system.

Best of all, there was a brand-new fuel cell milk truck with a gleaming stainless steel tank covered with near transparent ChargeSkin sitting there to be delivered somewhere but going nowhere. I picked the lock on the office. We went inside and found the key fobs to both trucks. We also found copies of keys to all of the locks. Even the front gate padlock. So, I wouldn't have to pick any more locks, thank goodness.

I quickly wrote a note with an inventory of what we took and that we would find a way to pay for it all to the owners. I placed the note in a prominent place on a desk where it would be found if anyone came back. We left the office to begin the hard work ahead.

Fortunately, the flatbed truck had a hoist that made it easy to lift and place the two tanks and the tower on the flatbed. Getting the tower tank on our trailer required using a forklift we didn't have at home. I figured we would just use a lot of manpower and hope no one got pinched, rolled on, or crushed. We would use the truck hoist and the same manpower to lift the tower and tank into place since the planned location would not accommodate anything other than a come-along.

After we loaded everything on the trucks, we had to do a lot of strapping to keep them from sliding or rolling off in transit. We were quite a convoy when we left, happy with what we had found and planning to come back there often for more if we weren't stopped by the owners, or worse, gangs or thieves. But that was unlikely–they would have no need for tanks with their way of doing business–robbing and stealing what they needed.

Vik drove the flatbed truck behind me and Gary drove the milk truck behind Vik. While Peter watched Jerry sleep and his color return… A good sign. It seemed like no time and we were back home just before noon.

Once again, a cheer rose up as we drove past people working in the yards when they saw what we brought with us. I pulled over to the side so Vik could pass me and enter the gate to the estate. Fortunately, it was a wide gate required when the building was built in the 1920s.

Peter woke up Jerry and took him across the street to the Rosenberg house where the kids and dogs welcomed another and Martha knew just what to treat Jerry with that would make him happy and help him quickly regain his health. She began heating up some hearty soup from a can. One of the items she still had an ample supply of.

I arrived before the crowd and helped Vik maneuver to the place where the water tower would go up in the southwest corner of the estate. I had just maneuvered the truck into the right location, when out of the corner of my eye, I saw Daphne running from the house…

"Dre, what are you doing! You're ruining my front yard with that big truck!"

"I'm sorry, Daph. I thought you knew we were going to put the water tower here, the highest point on the street. And, we are going to have to put a water tank on your roof to give you water pressure very soon. Otherwise, you won't have water."

"I think I see." She looked defeated and calmed down a bit. "But it's so ugly! Can't you make it look beautiful?"

"Maybe, someday. Right now, I'm concerned about all of us just surviving!"

"You're always right. Dammit! I guess that's why I like you so much… Even love you a little…" She snickered, gave me a peck on my cheek and skipped back to the house like the schoolgirl she still was–delightful.

With all that manpower watching, Vik and I used the hoist to lift the tower off the truck that hadn't driven on the lawn. Just the hard baked corner of the property and drive made of paver stones that easily took the weight. Once the tower was approximately in place, Vik drove the truck back out into the street and parked it where we would unload the two tanks later for cisterns for two properties that didn't have one.

It was my turn. I drove up the drive just in front of the tower top where the water tank would be rolled off the trailer sideways to the right spot where it would be welded to the tower. Vik and I could have winched it off, but with all that manpower standing around, I decided we could use them.

Derek and Peter arrived with our two tractors and we were in business, I hoped.

Derek had brought two-by-fours that we placed perpendicular along the bed and nailed them down to make a ramp for the tank to roll off gently. With the two tractors and their front buckets raised high to hold the tank from rolling too fast, I tied ropes to the tank and asked the gang assembled to pull the tank off the trailer slowly. While they did that, on either side, the tractors backed up slowly holding the tank from rolling on either side until it landed gently on plywood we had placed to keep it from being scratched by the pave stones.

I sighed in relief when it was done, but the cold sweat on my neck lasted a bit longer. The next step involved the crowd helping to position the tank to the top of the tower where Vik, Gary and Peter began work to bolt and/or weld the tower to the tank and install all the piping and even the solar panels that would be used to power the pump at the bottom bringing water to the tank from below.

I let their expertise go to work while the others went back to their work. I drove my tractor back to the shop in the garage and installed the backhoe.

Returning to the site, I dug four holes for the concrete base. And then, made some cement to put in the holes with rebar for reinforcement. Before the holes were completely filled, with Vik's help, I placed mounting plates with four bolts for the final pour from my tractor bucket. Placed with bolts upright and welded in place so when the tower was dropped into place, each tower leg bottom plate would have four bolts to hold it firmly in place in the strongest wind or earthquake.

In the meantime, the children came in from their morning chores to lunch and found a new kid on the block. Jerry was loving the treats Martha put before him, making sure that they were small portions so that he wouldn't get sick. As the children gathered around, started eating, they were full of questions for Jerry.

"What's your name," Melissa asked, curious.

"Jerry… Jerry Phillips."

"Where you live? Do you go to school?" Flower questioned, squinching her nose a bit.

"Anaheim. I got sick at my middle school there and had to go home."

"Oh, are you going back there?"

"My mother told me not to. She told me to take the bus to my Auntie Gloria's place in San Diego. That's where I'm going after I feel better and can take the long bus trip."

"Why would you leave your mother? I wouldn't do that." Melissa blurted, upset in her angry eyes.

"Because that's what she told me before she stopped talking with her eyes open and staring at me!" He started to cry.

Wondah, who had been listening to the kids discussion, came over, gave Jerry a hug, and asked. "What is your auntie's name other than Gloria, is it Auntie Phillips?"

"I don't know… Something like that, but not…"

"What was your mama's name before she married to your father?"

"I don't know, don't have a father… But she told me she was going to raise me alone because her mother, my grandmother I never saw, Maryweather Roberts, didn't raise her. It was Mama's grandmother, Eloise Roberts that raised her, she said. She showed me a picture with Eloise's name on it. Stern looking old woman. I miss my Mommy…" Jerry started to cry again and Wondah held him tight, knowing his pain. The other kids grew quiet, feeling the same.

Wondah grabbed her smart pad and had the two girls gather around for their first lesson of the day. "This is how you can find your relatives if you know their name and where they lived. Some of you may be able to find relatives you can go to who may have survived? Let's try for Jerry, first… Okay?"

All of the kids gave a unanimous response, "Okay!"

"First, we do a simple search. The more we know about the person we are looking for, the better. In this case, we know Jerry's auntie is named, Gloria Roberts. We also know she lives in or around San Diego. And she's probably around thirty years of age. She is the sister of Jerry's mommy." The children watched while Wondah turned on speech and dictated the information, ending by the command, "Search."

The search turned up three Gloria Roberts close to San Diego. Any one of them could've been Jerry's aunt. Rather than call all three, Wondah asked Jerry, "Did your mother ever call her sister by any other name?"

Jerry thought a moment. "Yeah, I think I heard her on the phone saying something like, 'Annie.'"

There was one Gloria Ann Roberts. There appeared on the screen an immediate address, phone number and email address. Wondah tried the phone number and made the call.

It rang for some time before anyone answered. And then, the screen flickered and a woman looking tired and gaunt came on the screen. Jerry couldn't help himself…

"Auntie Gloria! It's me, Jerry! I'm coming to live with you… Mommy told me…"

"Oh, Jerry! It's so good to see you, too, child. But you can't come now. Things are too bad here. We don't have any food or water. It's terrible. That woman you're with looks healthy… Stay with her."

Wondah answered her. "I am Wondah (she spelled her name). We rescued your nephew dehydrated and hungry on the street, telling us, 'I'm waiting for the bus to take me to my Auntie Gloria in San Diego.'

"We brought him here where we are providing water and food for a whole community. We even have a school and I'm teaching science and mathematics. You don't sound like you're in a very good place. I'm sorry. I wish you could come here and join our community. If you can, you are welcome."

"It's best Jerry stays there with you. There's nothing here right now. We are struggling so much with so many lost. Keep in touch, I caught your number, too, Wondah. Jerry, you stay there with her for now. If we get better and can take you in, we will.

"Your mama asked me after everyone got sick, to take you in. But we just can't right now, just can't… Wondah, thank you so much for saving my nephew. I will always be grateful. I'm afraid I'm going to have to sign off now." She was crying either tears of joy or sadness as the screen went blank.

Jerry held Wondah tightly and looked up at her. Suddenly, she had a son to take care of. It was a whole new experience for a teenager. The lesson continued…

Melissa found cousins in Idaho and was very happy.

Flower looked for her uncle in Whittier, but no one answered the phone listed. Since it was her father's brother, she told Wondah, "I'm glad we didn't find him. Mama was mad at him anyway like she was with Dad. Don't tell her I looked." Her eyes pleaded…

"Don't worry, Flower, honey, your secret's good with me." Everyone laughed, even Jerry. They would keep it, too. He was fast asleep before the lesson was over and carried off to bed.

15

Water Tower Raising and Quelling Cain

While Vik, Gary and Peter were working on securing the tower to the tank, I looked around for someone to go get water with me.

With everyone busy with their various work, I grabbed Mel and we took off for what I knew was the closest water source, a little private lake just up the coast about 10 miles at the end of Sunset Boulevard. As I recall, when we did work near there when I was sixteen, it was very exclusive and you had to have a membership to the neighborhood. I think it was called Santa Los Lake, but it doesn't matter, I knew where it was.

There wasn't even a dent in the milk truck's charge. That ChargeSkin was doing its job beautifully. In 20 minutes, we were driving up Sunset Boulevard with our guns at ready, not sure what we would find. But, like everywhere else, all was quiet when we came upon the lake. I wondered why, so drove down into the parking lot 4and looked at the water. The lake was unusually low and a bit murky. It smelled. A closer look revealed dead birds and a dead turtle at the water's edge. There had been people there. Dried tracks leading down to the water as the level in the lake dropped. And then,

I saw it…

"Look, Mel! There's a body in the lake over there!" And then, I saw another one. And another one…

I took Mel's hand and we walked quickly back to the truck. This time, I noticed all the shell casings glinting off the sun. There had been a massacre– probably over the water. It didn't make any difference; the water wasn't any good and wouldn't be for a long time. There was a reservoir further up on Palisades Drive, but my map search showed it dry. That reservoir probably got its water from deep wells. And it probably provided water for the communities nearby and the lake, mortally polluted.

When we got back on the road, I told her, "We may have to leave the city behind to find water in a flowing river that won't be contaminated. But today, it's only about 30 miles to MacArthur Park and its large lake. We have to get back home, first. The guys should have everything mated the water tank to the tower and we'll need to raise it."

We arrived without water just as everyone was taking a lunch break. Vik told me he had everything ready and had, with Derek's assistance, set up the necessary winches we would need to bring the water tower into place. Mel and I grabbed some veggie sandwiches and joined the others at the site where the crowd was again, forming… Our man, woman and kid power. Some of it reliable, some of it, maybe not.

Derek had driven a steel girder up against his wall. At the very top, Viktor had welded a pulley for a steel cable that would come from a winch mounted below connected to the top of the tower just below the water tank. At the same time, the hoist on the flatbed truck was connected to the same location. The hoist could only lift the tank about twenty feet. And then, the cable from the winch anchored in Derek's lawn to the base of an ancient acacia tree would have to pull the tower and tank to the vertical. Timing was everything…

To keep the tower's four base mounts on target, ropes were tied to either side where the manpower, divided up, was supposed to keep the everything lined up, according to plan. I was very concerned, because it was a dangerous move. I began wishing we had a crane. But in the old days, horse and manpower raised many water towers. Winches were much more dependable and powerful. My big concern was whether or not the people would keep the four base pads on each of the legs aligned on sixteen bolts without breaking or bending any of them.

When everything was in place, I used the loudspeaker function on my phone to tell everyone what to do next as precisely as I could. Vik on one side and I on the other, would swing the tower into place for it to land properly on all sixteen bolts… A tall order–*I crossed my fingers.*

"Derek, start winching… And Gary, you do the same! Teams, keep your lines tight and make sure you keep the tower and tank on target to the vertical position. Don't let it tip over either way or the other!"

I waited apprehensively as the power of both winches raised the tower to my right gradually while I watched the positioning of the leg pads as the tower rose higher and higher and the pads ground deeply into the two by four placed for the base pads to come up and over before dropping into the four bolts… My job, I hoped.

When the tower and tank reached a 45° angle, I ordered, "Gary, let your line go slack. Derek will pull it up the rest of the way!"

As Derek's winch brought the heavy tower gradually more vertical, I watched the alignment carefully as both of the teams kept their lines tight and in line where the pads would come up over the two by fours where Vik and I could drop them in place.

When I saw the pad holes were not exactly in line with the bolts, I had to push on the leg in front of me while Vik pulled on the other side. We both sighed a huge sigh of relief when the pads dropped firmly onto the four bolts and a couple more inches of winching brought the other two legs firmly down on their bolts as well. All that was left was to get the big nuts and bolt the whole thing securely in place where4 any wind or earthquake would not have any affect.

Everyone cheered. My T-shirt was soaked with sweat. I signaled to Mel and went down to my house where the shower no longer had any pressure, so I took off my soaked shirt, washed myself as best I could from my sink and put on a clean T-shirt for the trip to MacArthur Park.

Once again, the trip was uneventful, but the streets near the park were nearly jammed with cars and debris. Once we got to the lake, it was very low and a deep chocolaty brown with a green scum. There was evidence a lot of people had come to the lake and drawn water, probably by the bucket.

If we would pump that water into the pristine tank, I was afraid it would be filled with small fish, tadpoles, algae and bacteria, making it nearly impossible to drink without a great deal of filtering and screening. The screen we had for pumping left a quarter-inch square gap for the water to enter and to keep debris out. But this was too much.

Our next, and last option that day was Silver Lake Reservoir, northwest of MacArthur Park and another 10 miles by freeway. When we got there, the reservoir was very low for it being only June, but the water was blue and looked like we could use it for now. Melody stood guard while I pumped the truck full in short order and we were on our way back to the safety of our street.

We arrived at the estate and pumped the water we had gathered into one of the new tanks placed at the base of the water tower through a filter that Gary created to make the water as pure as we could, knowing we would still have to boil it before drinking. Vik and Gary then began pumping the water from that tank to the top of the water tower tank using the solar powered pump built in. It was a slow process, taking over an hour.

As soon as we could, we left to get another load at Silver Lake Reservoir. We arrived again around 5 pm, dead tired. Mel and I retreated to my swimming pool, thankful that we still had it. All the others had been emptied one way or another. We ate and went to bed early.

Gary and Vik filled the water tower tank with the two truckloads of water from the milk truck and tested the pressure of the pipe going to Derek's house. With a lot of overhead piping to do in the next few days, they also retired, telling everyone…

"Don't worry, as long as we can find water sources to put water into the water tower, we'll make it last until the fall rains. In the meantime, please cover your pools completely to keep them clean so we can use them as additional reservoirs, along with building more cisterns and ways of capturing all the rain runoff we can. We have a lot of work to do.

Mel and I were sound asleep when my phone rang again. 2:33 am.

Wondah's worried face appeared on the all-points bulletin…

"Our sensors picked up the snowplow gang coming up the street slowly this time. Derek and I have our drones up and we are seeing infrared bodies sneaking up to the fences on the street below us and climbing over the walls. Apparently, to make a sneak attack on us. We need all hands and guns on deck, pronto!"

We knew the routine; Mel and I quickly dressed. She went to the front of the house where we had built a perch for her to stand on allowing her to look and shoot over our front wall. I climbed to the roof again, dragging both my rifle and the AR-15. I could see others climbing to their roofs below me. Whenever one of the intruders was seen coming up over a wall, those that had a good firing line, did. Bodies were dropping from those walls. But, everyone's worry was any who got over the walls and were sneaking up on our shooters. There was a lot of firing going on, but I didn't get a good shot.

There was a roar as the dump truck took off up the street. Derek, from the drone, set off the first Claymore just as the truck arrived, perfectly. The blast tore the truck's tires to shreds, hammered through the door and dump truck bed, knocking out the windows and killing the marauders in the cab, while the surviving crew of the truck bed scrambled to escape down the street.

I scrambled down off the roof and caught up with Mel as she was getting our gate open so we could join the fighting down at the end of the street still continuing. She yelled as we ran…

"I got one sneaking up the street. Did you get any?"

"Didn't fire a shot. And from what I'm hearing, we won't have to."

When we arrived at the body of the one Mel shot, she was quite small and dressed in black with a black stocking cap mask pulled over her gaunt fifteen-year-old face. I found it disgusting what desperation was doing to these gangs. What they were sacrificing for water and food. I had to do something about it. But what? I didn't know.

As before, we left the cleanup for morning after we searched thoroughly for any stragglers from the intruders who might've escaped. When we were sure they had all left, we retired to our various beds to sleep fitfully for the rest of the night. While Wondah's amazing motion detectors and cameras kept watch for us.

Mel and I talked for a bit after we got back in bed. I consoled her for what she did and promised I would come up with a way to help others so they didn't have to resort to violence to get what they needed. I had an idea I had been percolating in my mind for some time but hadn't acted on. Just a possibility. Once again, thought of the idea kept me awake long after Mel fell fast asleep. Morning came too soon.

16

A Village Emerges

Once again, we took ghastly pictures of each of the dead. Most of them looking younger than 18 but there was one with gray hair. They were all tattooed and clearly, Blods, the largest gang, and perhaps, the bloodiest, in the L.A. area. Derek drove the tank down again and pushed the shredded dump truck off the street as another warning to anyone attempting to enter our compound with any intent of violence.

Derek had an idea watching us taking the pictures. "I think we should print some of these pictures and tape them to the vehicles. Show them what happens when they raid us."

Wondah, who had been resetting another Claymore mine to replace the one used the night before, turned around and yelled… "No, no, nooo… Derek! The Blods are a very tight organization. They double down when any member of their gang is killed. No matter what it takes, they seek revenge. Best to just leave them not wanting to waste any more lives trying to raid us. We don't want them retaliating. And don't any of you put those pictures on the Internet! It could bring hell down on us."

Derek reneged. "Damn, you're smart, Wondah! And, are always right. That's what I like about you." He smirked and made a stupid looking funny face at her.

Next came the grisly task of taking the bodies all the way back past the estate to where we had left the others. Fast becoming a boneyard from all of the scavengers' action. Some flies were still there and began immediately attacking the blood on the bodies. Daphne watched my truck and trailer pass, wondering if she would keep seeing this continue behind her backyard she was trying to make beautiful again with very little water. Unfortunately, we had no other choice.

With that most necessary task over, I grabbed Ray and we drove on down to the Fish Market to see if there were any more boats bringing fish and seafood to the port. My idea rolling around in my head I didn't even mention to Ray on the way but continued to ponder.

Once again, there were no fish in the market and I had to call out Van Nguyen from hiding. When he finally came out he ran up to me and hugged me exclaiming…

"Drake! So glad you here. It's been terrible! We been raided every night. Had to hide while they looked everywhere for food. I leave a little seafood out in hopes to please them, but it no good… No good at all…" He was crying, but burst out again, "And the worst, that frickin' bunch with a dump truck, smashing everything for nothin'!"

I tried to console him. "I know, I know. They've been coming to us, too. I have good news for you. We destroyed a dump truck last night, unless there is another one. You need to have defenses like we have. Starting tomorrow, I will put my people helping your people block off the entrance to the market the way we have blocked off our street. Do you think you can handle more people in the market and hotel?"

With the good news, Van quickly regained his composure. "We about twenty-five people in hotel now with my son and me. Mostly fishermen and their families like us. We have two other boats sides mine who are out fishing right now. But we not any food or water except fish and seafood, so we have been trapping seagulls, pigeons and even rats, to eat. The rats are surprisingly tasty."

He finally smiled, showing his crooked teeth. "But we have no fresh greens and are running out of vegetables–do you?"

"Only a few from our gardens we brought because we knew you would ask. But I'm forming a plan of all of these warehouses here at the port and your hotel becoming self-sustaining and thriving again."

"Really! Drake, you genius! How you know all this?"

"Derek and I have been educating ourselves for this work since we were very young. We want to survive as much as you do. But we need to all work together to get back to where we were before the pandemic. How about turning the port into a village?"

"Sounds good, but possible?"

"Only if we all work together. For now, everyone will have to work for food and water."

Ray, who had been silently watching and listening chimed in. "From what I've seen Derek and Drake do already, anything's possible. We just have to reengineer everything. I want to help you farm from your warehouse rooftops."

"But we need water? Lots water we don't have?"

I had an answer for that. "The first thing I see is the need for security. Once we fix that, we will get a crane from a construction job downtown and put a water tower on your hotel roof. And we will add as much solar and wind power as we can, to keep you powered during the worst conditions.

Especially your cold storage and frozen food warehouses. It will be a huge undertaking and need a lot of people."

"I didn't tell before, but like you, during day over hundred customer come and ask for fish and seafood. They been giving us food and fruit but very little water. They also hungry and many ask about the hotel. I not tell them we support them. Should I?"

"Only if you absolutely trust them. I would suggest that we have them all complete a simple one page contract stating they will help build the village in exchange for food and housing that they would help produce. That's all. A simple contract. But they would have to be interviewed, first. Questioned. We wouldn't want to have any gang members, usually easily spotted by their tattoos, entering our community."

"But water, where you get water for tower? Only place we able to get water from is ship."

"The ship? One of your fishing boats has water?"

"No, big ship over there. Rambler of Seas. They big customer before. Fill cold storage with fresh seafood we catch. They kind to give us water when we need. You want to talk to captain… ah… First mate?"

"I sure do. What's his name? What's his phone number?

Van answered, "Jens Jensen." And gave me his cell phone number.

I dialed it and left the speaker on. A young blue-eyed blonde man with a strong accent in a crisp white uniform with blue lapels answered. "Hello, this is Jens, if you're calling for a cruise, forget it. Otherwise, what do you want?" He looked and sounded annoyed.

"This is Drake Hutchins, I'm here with Van Nguyen." I swung the phone around so Van was in the picture as well as Ray and Quoc waiting patiently, listening to us talking. "I thought your ship was empty because I haven't seen any movement there a couple of times when we came by to visit our old friend and make arrangements for getting seafood in exchange for us helping this little fishing community out."

"That's noble of you, but I see things rather hopeless. We have been afraid those pirates every night would find a way, with simple grappling hooks, to climb up onto our ship and kill us all for what we have here. We have no real weapons and have to make the ship look like it's uninhabited."

"That's too bad. But I'm here to change it. Starting tomorrow, I'm going to have some of my people come here and block off the entrance to the port and make it monitored electronically the way you monitor the ship. And, I will bring confiscated arms, mostly AR-15s we have confiscated from those gang members we have killed, for your protection. In fact, I can give you a couple of them with ammunition today. How many people do you have?"

"The virus was devastating. We lost our captain and his wife and so many others. When it hit the ship, we were about to set sail for a 21 day journey with 5000 passengers and 1500 crew. The passengers never showed up or left right after they arrived, many of them sick already. Most of my crew from the Los Angeles area left that day and the rest we nursed as almost everyone got sick. Until they died and we buried them right here, at sea, without going to sea." He halted. We could see the anguish on his face…

Jens continued, "We are now only 46 crew members trying desperately to maintain the ship and keep our food from spoiling while shutting off much of the ship to save running our generators too much. It has been a struggle, but I'm coping and that's about all. I have been in touch with corporate in Denmark. But every ship is experiencing the same problem and some have failed already."

"Okay, we are all in the same boat, and I don't mean, your ship. We all have to survive, together. And saving the Rambler for the future would be a great idea. A great morale booster. So… I will double down with my skeleton armed construction crew to make you secure so you can leave the ship and help create what I want to create here, a village for all of us starting over in Los Angeles."

"That's courageous and we'll help any way we can." His demeanor changed greatly from before. A glimmer of hope crossed his tanned fair face.

"Van tells me you have water. Is that true?"

"Yes, we recycle water here on the ship for bathing purposes and desalinate seawater for additional water while at sea. We can't do it here.

Our water intakes would damage local sea life even with their screens."

"Is your recycled water drinkable?

"Yes, but we recommend boiling before drinking."

"That's good news. I was hoping to put in a water system to provide water pressure for the village. If you have someone who can help us create freshwater from seawater, it would be wonderful."

"We have two engineers who survived. Once we are more stable, I'm sure working with your people we may be able to make a plant for providing freshwater from seawater right here at the port. We are unable to do that right now because of so many bodies in the water contaminating it. But those bodies are providing a lot of food for sharks, crabs, mollusks and other seafood predators and scavengers. We have been catching big fish from the other side where no one can see us fishing. It helps us pass the time and provide us with fresh fish."

"Enough talk. Can we meet you and some of your crew? I want to give you two AR-15s, some ammo and some grenades for now. More will be coming tomorrow."

"Okay, give us some time. We have to take the stairs without the elevators running."

I drove Van and us to where he usually met with Jens on the dock. A door opened from the side of the ship a little higher than the dock and a ramp came out of the ship and onto the dock. Jens Jensen in pristine full uniform, followed by four others, came off the ship and he introduced us to the third and fourth mates, the third being a beautiful young blonde woman, Dani Steffensen and the fourth, a fortyish hardy experienced seafarer, Jahn Johannsen. Then, there were two engineers, Klaus Reinhart, the ship's middle-aged chief engineer and Hans Hansen, the ship's water resource engineer. Just a bit older than me with a very light blonde beard.

I was amazed at their credentials. Suddenly, from out of the opening came several carts pushed by crew members who were obviously from different parts of the world by simply seeing their smiling faces.

The carts were loaded with food of all kinds we were in desperate need of on our street. I gladly accepted the gift from the now, humbly accepted captain of the ship and his crew and promised them we would provide them with more arms as well as fresh vegetables and greens as we continued to expand our gardens and help build gardens right here in the port.

I told him, "With your help, Captain Jensen, I hope the port can become a sustainable village."

"Just call me Jens," he said, as he hefted one of the AR-15s in his hands testing how it felt. "We'll do all we can."

We returned home with Ray and I talking about what we needed to start doing right away to make the dream I had been mulling over for some time around in my mind come to fruition. I had a lot to tell the other ones at lunch.

Our little enclave was just the start of what I felt would be great for the city to recover from where it started eons before. On the beach where the Los Angeles River met the Pacific before they had names. The Los Angeles and other rivers nearby were dried up now, but possibly could flow again.

But when we arrived at lunch, we were met with sadness rather than joy. Selma, Hector Lopez's seventeen-year-old daughter of the sheet rock contractor who was living in the house closest to our defenses had come to the Rosenberg house asking for help just after we left.

During the raid, Hector and his son, Juan, sixteen, went outside and were the first to engage the intruders. Selma stayed inside with a pistol when terrific firing began. When it died down and they didn't come back, she wept and hid, not hearing us when we cleared the street, generally not talking too much.

But in the morning, she ventured out and found her father badly wounded but alive and her brother, dead. Less than fifteen minutes after we had left for the port everyone converged on the home, carried Hector back to Martha to remove five bullets from his body and bury Juan by the garden they had started. Buried him in a quickly made wood box so that Hector, when well again, could decide what to do with his son.

I was doubly sad because Hector and his kids were doing a great job in restoring the Rodney Owens house and were getting ready to move back there where there were a lot of amenities that Rodney had built in as a prepper. If only they had, sigh. If only…

I told everyone gathered I had good news, too. I told them I wanted everyone to finish whatever work they were doing today and think about what they would do if we all went down to the port and began securing it in the next couple of days. Gary and Vik protested. Gary, especially…

"Come on, Drake! Why do you have to be so interested in the port? We got a lot of plumbing to do here before we finish getting water to everyone on the street. Why drop everything now to go down there and help them?"

"You can stay here if you like. But I'd like to introduce you to my plans for the village there. We could easily fill up the street with folks in the next month and be cozy. But in order for us to have a steady supply of seafood and fish, we will have to rely on the market in a place very vulnerable right now.

There are also hundreds of people, maybe a thousand or more, dying of thirst every day, starving out there in the city. Good people we can help, like you. Come down there with me tomorrow morning and return in the afternoon. That's all I ask. We will find other plumbers who could do the work there and here. But I wanted you to step up to the planning with me."

Vik replied. "I see what you mean, boss. I tend to like your big plans, even though they mean a hell of a lot of work for me." He laughed. The first warmth that had entered the room so far. There was twittering in the background.

Before everyone finished eating and heading back to their various work, the room was buzzing with chatter. Martha appeared and told everyone she had removed all of the bullets from Hector. He was alive but would need several days rest and recuperation before attempting to be up and around. In the meantime, Selma was going to give him 24 hour daily attention. Everyone cheered.

Drake and I, along with Wondah and Melody who had both become indispensable in planning, sat down together to plan what we would start to do the next morning. It was an immense task, unlike barricading our street, there were many streets to the west of the fish market where marauders could come from. We decided to begin with the intersection of Harbor Boulevard and Miner Street, the most likely direction they would come from off Cal 47. Additionally, we would block off the entrance to the World Cruise Center to help provide some initial security for the Rambler captain and his crew. Even that was a tall order. The port was vast and there were a lot of potential places for finding food, fuel and materials in the countless tanks, warehouses and shipping containers that remained unopened or vandalized.

Daphne, once again, invited me to spend the evening with her, but I declined. Not that I didn't want to go, but the ideas spinning around in my head were nearly overwhelming and I just needed to rest. Melody returned after helping Selma with tending to Hector and his wounds. Both of us slept fitfully. Our separate worries overcoming our desire for the night. We slept off and on, thinking of the coming day.

17

Multiple Revelations and Big Start

I awoke refreshed from sleep, so I reached for Mel. The bed was warm where she had been, but she wasn't there. Then, I heard gagging in the bathroom. I jerked off the covers and ran into the bathroom to see if she was okay.

I found her leaning over the toilet, struggling. "Are you okay?" I asked.

"Better than okay…" She turned and smiled against her nausea, "I'm pregnant!"

"How do you know?"

"Felt the same way with Flower. It'll go away in a little while and then come back when I least expect it. The price we women pay for having babies."

She smiled broader, came to the sink, poured some mouthwash into a glass and gargled the bad taste from her mouth.

"Well, congratulations! We all will be looking forward to its arrival. I hope you won't be slowed down too much by the pregnancy."

"Don't you worry. You men always worry about us doing our work… Women's work? When we get pregnant. If it's like Flower, it will be a piece of cake. That is, with a dramatic ending!" She laughed.

We joined the others for breakfast and there was a lot of chatter going on around the room. It seems that Martha had collected pregnancy tests when we raided a pharmacy for what we needed and left a note telling anyone who might be still running the place where we were and that we would pay. No one ever responded to our notes. But we felt better leaving them.

Anyway, it turned out that not only Mel was pregnant, so was Daph and Wondah! Melody assured the other two girls she had experience and she would help them get through their pregnancies together. Everyone at breakfast cheered.

I was grateful we had milk and cream for butter from the cow and soon from the nanny goats, growing up quickly. And eggs from the chickens. We would have to try to find baby formula if any of them couldn't breast-feed.

With everyone agreeing to head on down to the port and get started on securing the place and providing water, we got underway with every vehicle we had available.

Derek and Wondah drove back to a couple of looted electronics stores to gather as much as they could to put together a security system for the port. I drove downtown with Vik looking for a construction project and we found one off Wilshire. There was a crane there working on the construction of another high-rise building stopped dead by the pandemic.

Vik climbed up into the cab and found it was open. We didn't know where the key was but he knew how to get it started and soon had it running. There was plenty of diesel fuel to drive it down to the port and that's what Vik did. He was blocked until we got to a freeway in a couple of places by abandoned cars, but with his big steel bumper easily pushed them out of the way.

The rest of us drove on down to the tank company to find a suitable tank to put on top of the hotel to provide water pressure there and for the surrounding buildings. When we arrived, we found that our note from the stop before was still there on the desk collecting dust. We added a couple more.

Ray and Peter drove the milk truck down to the port to begin scoping where they might put planter boxes on warehouse rooftops and figure a way to get water there, either by pumping or water catchment. Something that had to be done for every rooftop in the area if they were to get enough water to last through the long dry summers.

We found an electric forklift and Augie and Rocky helped me get a tank on my trailer. Within an hour we were back at the port and catching up with Vik as he positioned and stabilized the crane for lifting.

Van and some of his people were there to help get the tank off the trailer and in position to be lifted to the top of the hotel. First, Vik and I took the stairs, since the elevator wasn't working all the way to the roof.

Fortunately, there was a helicopter landing platform that served as a great place to mount the tank. With the help of Peter and some others, Viktor set about providing a stable mounting place for the tank to go.

When Van asked me, "Where we to get water for tank and for planters

Ray, he putting in? Ship won't give us … will it?" I had been wondering the same question without daring to stop and think about it. The idea of getting water from drying up sources in the relentlessly long and hot summers we had been having, except for going great distances, hauling water looked pretty bleak until an idea suddenly popped into my head.

From my knowledge of the anatomy of tall buildings Josh and my father built with me tagging along, there was always a standpipe to a roof-top tank providing water in an instant to sprinklers throughout the building if there was a fire. And, there were places where a firehose could be connected or a fire truck to the standpipe to draw water to help fight fire in the building from those levels where a fireplug was built in.

In the current situation, with fires all around the city burning without anyone fighting them, only the high-rises and business towers had any kind of self-extinguishing protection. No longer needed if there weren't any occupants in the building and no one to take care of the building, especially if it caught fire. So, I decided we would go plundering again.

While all that thinking went through my head in an instant, I answered Van. "I know where we can get water. But I'm not telling anyone right now. Let me grab Gary from whatever he is doing. We'll be back with a truckload of water for your tank very soon."

I found Gary finishing the piping to the hotel roof tank with no water to pump to it. All I told him was, "Let's go get some water. Take a break."

He had been working hot and hard up until midday and had welcomed my suggestion with a happy, "Yes, boss, can't wait to get in that air conditioned truck and cool off.."

We got in the milk truck and I drove directly to the nearest high-rise building I could see. Some company I didn't know of alongside 147 that probably dealt with the port because of its location.

I drove directly to the parking area of the building underneath and parked by the stairs. There were no cars in the parking area–a good sign. It would take too long to check the entire building for occupants, but they wouldn't probably know anything about the standpipe unless they were maintenance people. And then, they would be using the water.

I led Gary down the stairs to the basement where I found the fire suppression standpipe. Back up on the parking area it appeared in the same location basically unnoticed by building occupants, but clearly with a way for a fire company to hook onto it to help fight a fire.

We connected a hose to the pipe, and within 15 minutes the tank on the milk truck was full. And, I believed we could come back here several more times before going on to one of the many thousand buildings in the greater L.A. area with standpipes for fire.

I cautioned Gary not to tell anyone where we got the water. There was a danger that people unaware of what they were really doing would open the fire plug and water would come flying out and be totally lost, even those just trying to get some for their own use without knowledge of the pressure.

Like I told Van earlier, we were back in no time and pumping water into the newly installed water tower on the roof of the hotel. Van and the others gathered were ecstatic.

He asked me, "Where you get freshwater so fast?"

I told him, "It's a secret. But anytime you need water, we'll get some for you. You do have some secret fishing techniques you use, don't you?"

"Yes, I do. Only my son knows–family tradition."

"Someday soon, I may be free to tell you. But, not now. All I ask is that you and everyone else who uses this water except for bathing, washing, etc.… For drinking, make sure you boil it first. It may be very good for drinking, but don't trust it unless you have it tested by Hans Hansen or someone else who can test water for purity."

We had to make one more run to completely fill the water tank we figured would last them about a week before it needed to be refilled. When he returned, Gary began, with several helpers from the hotel and from the Rambler, to begin installing catchment systems on some of the warehouses with huge roofs to catch and store water during the rainy season.

Frances, Gary's mother with three willing helpers using their company double cab electric service truck with a trailer, ran trips to their shop and to plumbing supply houses throughout the L.A. area gathering supplies for the ambitious plumbing needed to convert the water-starved village into one that would be drinking water plentiful year-round.

A bonus to their trips the first day was their discovery of two starving plumbers and their families who had already started rigging ways of giving water to neighbors who had none. Both of those plumbers agreed to come and work in the village in exchange for food, especially fish and seafood.

One of the plumbers brought his family, his service truck and trailer, with the intention of staying. The other, after he saw what was happening, brought his family, too. The neighborhood families followed and began working with the plumbers on the plumbing.

Wondah printed contracts and as soon as the stragglers came wandering in Van, Melody and I approached them to sign it if they planned to stay in the growing village. Van preferred that new, especially Asians, would stay in the hotel with his family and fishing friends.

The contract was simple. It merely asked everyone who came for food or water and stayed, be willing to work for only food and water until a reasonable means for barter or even Internet credit or coins, US money, gold or silver could be exchanged.

They must build work equity into restoring the village until such time as they could leave safely back into other parts of the greater Los Angeles community again. They must not hoard, be violent or behave in a way that the members of the village would find unacceptable. Anyone found unacceptable would be banished. The document had to be signed by the person/persons seeking to stay. Anyone with prison or gang tattoos would not be allowed to stay but given food and water for a few days.

Captain Jensen of the Rambler agreed to take 1000 families. Especially, if he could train some of them to help him maintain and run the ship. He agreed to set up the lowest dining room on the fourth level as a buffet from early in the morning until around 9 pm for everyone working on the village projects to come and eat. He had vast stores of food available for multiple cruises that needed to be used.

I thanked him profusely for that extremely generous offer. I showed him plans that I had made to incorporate many of the houses nearby into the village as long as we could barricade the streets enough to keep marauders out. With either electronic surveillance or barricades. Anyone coming with security or law enforcement experience would be asked to become part of a 24-hour per day security force watching the monitors set up everywhere.

Wondah and Derek found as many Wi-Fi security cameras as they could. They gave about 30 to Captain Jensen to install along both sides of the Rambler to catch anyone trying to board either from the dock or waterside of the ship.

With all that help, I got some of the people finding derelict vehicles, mostly older with gasoline engines, and had them brought to block the streets leading into the port area I had decided to encompass and close off as the initial village. Eventually, a wall might be necessary. But thinking further ahead. I didn't want the village to go beyond those initial boundaries.

I wanted eventually for the people in the village to return to their homes and businesses in the greater Los Angeles area or new ones. Restarting the whole city. Why was I thinking like that? I didn't know, I just was. Trying to make the best of a bad situation. Right now, making it to the fall rains again was the highest priority—capture water then.

We all returned late that night to a huge dinner and celebration for all we had accomplished. But a lot of work remained undone. I asked everyone to devote two more days to the project. And then, maybe one day a week to take care of any problems the village wasn't able to take care of itself. It was my project, but I needed everyone's help in making it thrive. They all heartily agreed. I was happy.

I even took an invitation from Daphne that night to spend a little after dinner dessert with Melody and her. None of us were disappointed with the result. But we nearly overslept.

For the next two days, everyone from our compound devoted full-time to the village. We made tremendous progress. The fires had largely burned out, the mosquitoes and flies were gone, and the nightly sea breezes had blown away the smoky air and especially, the earlier, ever present, stench of rotting human flesh.

When the water catchment systems were finished, we focused on finding solar panels and windmills that we installed throughout the buildings we were working on to provide power for the pumps, lights and in the case of the hotel, conveniences like hot water, refrigerators and even air conditioning.

We encountered both people and vehicles, mostly armed and walking the streets looking for food and water and finding little or none. We encouraged those with transportation to go to the port and sign the contract. We needed, especially, people who could do hands-on work as well as teachers and caregivers for children and people sick. So many we encountered were at stages of dehydration or starvation that needed to be reversed. It was sad to see so many like that. But we were glad we could help them recover and help us rebuild a village first, and possibly, a great community again like Los Angeles had been before.

I turned most of the work over to Captain Jensen and Van, to use the new recruits, when they were healthy again, continue the work that we had started, and perhaps have many move into the nearby houses and go back to their houses in the city, with help. Safety was a big issue and it wasn't completely resolved, yet.

It was late, nearly 8 pm, as we returned to our compound for a welcome shower and dinner before attending to our own compound needs in the morning.

But as we drove, off to the left, it wasn't going to be a normal sunset because an ominous round cloud was approaching and I thought I knew what it might be. I had seen those clouds on the Internet.

18

Water, Water Much Too Soon

At dinner, I had Wondah pull up the weather satellite system for NOAA, the National Oceanic and Atmospheric Administration, radar still partially working. What we saw on the screen was obvious. Something that had started to occur in El Niño years more and more often as the waters off South and Central America reached record temperatures.

A hurricane had been building and moving up the coast heading directly for Los Angeles and points beyond. The storm even had a name, Caylee. Automatically selected by the NOAA AI system naming storms of the satellite images, projecting both future path and trail. The storm was overpowering the cold waters of the Pacific Current and was due to make landfall in the morning.

As tired as I was, I couldn't sleep, thinking what might happen. I wanted our men and women to be out there finishing our catchment systems like we had at the port.

Work delayed by us while we were working the last three days there rather than here. From what I heard from collaborating, everyone was awake and trying to figure out how to catch more water.

At dawn, when I looked out, outer bands had already buffeted our elevated location just off the coast. Outside, from my sliding glass door, I could see rivers of water rushing down through the garden already.

Getting outside, sheltered from the strong wind on the patio behind the building, I could clearly see the main wall of the storm approaching within an hour. All the time we had left to secure everything loose before the brunt of the storm would hit.

Before long, the wind was howling like a banshee and anything loose like some of our gutters, were rattling in the wind. Our windmills automatically switched to feathering to avoid damage from spinning too fast and our solar panels were in danger of being ripped off their mountings.

I watched our fruit trees being whipped around by the wind, losing branches, fruit and nuts that weren't ready for harvest yet.

Fortunately, the storm was moving quickly and we were in the eye of the storm with bright sunlight and calm over the noon hour. We took the opportunity to make a few quick repairs before the wind began to blow again. The backside of the storm came again and we received as much rain as before noon.

By late afternoon, the storm had moved on but had left its mark with some of our windows broken, tile ripped off the roofs, and, worst of all, some damage to some of the solar panels providing us with electric power.

The storm had completely knocked out commercial power to our community and I didn't expect it to come back on. There was an urgent need to make sure every home had complete solar/wind power. It would be dark soon, but the time we had left during the beautiful sunset was spent assessing the damage and figuring out where to get what we would need to fix it in the coming days.

When I checked, the cistern at my house, it was full and so was the one at Derek's house. Other cisterns on the block were either full or nearly full. That was the good news. The bad news was, a third of the community had no electric power and needed it to run their air conditioning units in the very hot days to come.

I called Van and he informed me they had damage to the fish market stalls and some of the solar panels and catchment systems we had installed. Their newly planted beds were washed out and needed to be replanted. His good news was that all of the cisterns we had installed were full and could be used throughout the summer without further trips to get water.

When he heard, Ray agreed to spend another day there helping them replant the planters. When he inquired, Van told him that newcomers had told him there was a lot of flooding in the streets. Everyone who was without water was very happy to drink the possibly contaminated water after not having any for so long.

We began work immediately, and by nightfall, had made a number of repairs already.

But when I returned for dinner and we took another look at NOAA, it was a bit disturbing because the hurricane had turned into a tropical storm and stalled up against the Sierras. I worried for Gramps. When I called, I couldn't reach him. It kept me awake.

But about 5 am I got a familiar call and it was Gramps.

"Hello Gramps," I said with sleep still on my voice and my eyes half closed.

"Drake! Is that you? This dang phone hasn't been working all night. Thought I'd never reach you. It's getting light here and still raining cats and dogs since yesterday and all night long. The whole damn valley is flooded! Never seen anything like it! It's right up to my porch doorstep and the barn and shed are flooded with at least 3 feet of water. All of our livestock is standing in water and mostly trying to find something to climb on. Only the goats are doing that.

"I'm going to need a lot of help to clean this mess up and replant my garden. I'm afraid my other crops are ruined. How soon can you come? Are you still there…" I could hear his rapid, raspy breathing and anxiety seeing it on his face.

"Yeah, Gramps, I'm here. But we can't come to help you as long as it's raining. And we can't drive through 3 feet of water, even with our trucks. So, call me when the water subsides so we can come in on the roads to help you."

"Does sound like a plan, Sonny. Guess I'll have to hold out here for as long as it takes. Would hate to have that dirty water come up any further and into the house. I'd better busy myself getting everything up off the floor what's left after those bastards tried to take everything I have…."

"But please call in the meantime, if you have to. We'll head out to the Valley filled with supplies as soon as we hear from you again that the coast is clear. In the meantime, we've got a lot of fixing to do here for what this hurricane has done. But we're okay, just behind on our upgrades and repairs."

"Okay, I'll call. Bye for now…" He hung up before I could say good-bye.

"Bye." I sighed, most aware that things could get a lot worse for him if it continued to rain.

Another sleepless night. I had made the repairs on the house and thought I would take Ray down to the port to assess the damage along the way and what Van had to deal with.

I was shocked when we entered commercial corners where all of plastic signs were ripped away or damaged leaving a lot more debris in parking lots and streets than before. I was dodging roof tiles, whole solar panels, miscellaneous wood trim and other debris in the streets, too. Huge oaks tipped over and even palm trees on their side. Some blocking the road until I pushed them out of the way. Things were now a lot worse navigating around town.

Even Cal 1 was filled with windblown pieces that could puncture tires or fly up when run over and hit windows. Driving was a whole new ballgame.

I told Ray… "I'm going to have to mount some kind of plow on the front of this truck if we're going to clear off the streets and roads we travel every day."

"Yeah, look down at that water washing out the street below! We are going to be running into some streets that have been damaged from that runoff from the storm, too."

"Now that you mention it, I'm gonna drive a little further and take a look at the Los Angeles River. What do you think?"

"Drake, I'm in no hurry to get to the work at the port, I'm as curious as you are. Let's go."

I took the 710 and soon we were approaching what had been the familiar concrete ditch seen in so many movies. Sometimes, with only a trickle of a stream running down the center for stunt drivers and the foolhardy like I had been to drive through spraying water high until I hit a sunken oil can and damaged the under carriage of Dad's new electric Genesis.

I explained to Ray. "I was only sixteen and caught hell from Dad when he had to get a tow truck and I had to pay for an expensive repair. If he could see me now." I started to tear up with that remark when what we saw ahead surprised us.

For a half-mile from the L.A.River's concrete banks it was flooded! The scope of the flood was massive. As we drew closer and came up to the river, turning north and following it we could clearly see the raging torrent below.

Only in movies had I seen such a sight. The river was over the banks and spreading outward from the main muddy swirling current carrying trees, automobiles, parts of and whole houses. It was obvious that reservoirs were either overflowing or may have been breached.

"Ray, get some videos from your side. We need to take them back home and show them to everyone. I don't think a dam broke, yet, but if one does the flooding here could be even greater and could reach all the way to the port!"

I looked at Ray and he looked back. He could sense the concern I had in my eyes. He had that same concern in his. We drove on seeing bridges at street level either clogged with floating debris or even ripped out. I wondered about anyone who had been staying near the river to get water. They may have been overwhelmed and drowned in the night after struggling just to get water after so long.

We continued on to 101. Taking it, it was a mile or two before I could exit and return the other way. Fifteen minutes later, we were taking the exit leading to the port. I didn't see any flooding, but a lot more debris in the streets. Some of it up against our barriers blocking streets.

Thankfully, the Rambler looked the same. Much of its exposed equipment and rigging was meant for high winds.

We hailed Van shortly after passing through the manned checkpoint where they were glad to see Ray coming back.

"Van, how are you doing? I bought Ray."

"Thanks, Drake. It rough night, but we got through, okay. There some street flooding from water all way down from Hollywood. But it was roofs we have most wind and rain damage."

I showed him the video of what we took of the L.A. River.

"Van, that is less than 5 miles away at Long Beach. You need to tell your people to be close to climbing if a dam breaks somewhere upstream and the water comes down the river watershed. It would be really devastating for you. So, keep your guard up. Fortunately, the Rambler probably wouldn't be bothered at all."

"Thanks for warning and bring Ray back."

Ray, a bit rankled, replied, "I volunteered. Dre just came along for the ride." We chuckled.

"He's right, I'll be getting back to our compound and will pick up Ray whenever he wants to get back to work with us. Okay?"

"In the meantime, have you got a load of fish and seafood that we can take up to the Valley with us when we go in a few days?"

Van smiled. "Yeah, two boats come in yesterday, loaded. Just before the hurricane, thank Buddha. We've got more than enough for a truckload in cold storage. Do you need refrigerated truck?"

"Yes, and probably a driver who's willing to drive up into redneck country." We all laughed.

Ray and Van walked off with Van explaining what was damaged and what needed be done. I hopped back in the truck and returned to the compound. Thinking a lot more about the Central Valley being flooded and the River drowning people just trying to survive.

I tried to put the thoughts out of my mind and on the work we had to do.

It didn't work.

19

Disastrous Aftermath

We spent the next two days repairing our roofs, gutters, solar panels and other things damaged by the force of the storm. And replanted all the gardens knowing we would have enough water for a complete crop including corn and potatoes before it grew colder and the rain started again in the fall. We would have greens and scallions within a week as the heat returned every day. The other crops would quickly follow.

Hector had recovered enough to join his daughter, Selma, repairing the damage, including the front wall concrete work and stucco to near normal so they could move into the former Rodney Owens place. Juan was missed but they carried on without him.

Stephanie was glad but wanted no memories of the way that place was under her father's ideas, rather content to stay with Martha Rosenberg who had become her surrogate mother. Everyone wondered who had got her pregnant, but she wasn't telling. They suspected Juan.

On the third day, wondering about Gramps, I gave him a call and he didn't answer. I was hoping he was out cleaning up away from the house and that was the reason he didn't answer. Still, I worried. The storm, I knew, would make it difficult to get there. So much wind and rain could be devastating to the roads with debris blocking them, washouts, and landslides.

But Ray called and asked me to come and survey what they had done as well as bring him home.

"Hi, Ray. Glad that you were able to help Van and help the port out. We missed you here, too. But we got the crops replanted without you." Ray laughed.

"I knew you could do it." He snickered.

Van popped into view. "Ray, he did good. You see when you come. You coming?"

"Got nothing better to do. I'll hop in the truck and head over there right away."

As I drove to the port along the now familiar route, I noticed that I didn't see any street flooding anymore. The streets were dried out nicely and I could hear hammers from people working on their houses in the distance. No more gunfire. They were coming out after the storm with new energy from having fresh water.

At the barricade there were people signing in. They had that sad, giving up, gaunt look of starvation. With help from the good graces of Captain Jensen and his crew they would be restored to health in no time and become productive members of the growing community.

Unfortunately, so many didn't know, couldn't or were afraid to come. They told stories of how they had to leave family members behind because they died or were too weak to come with them. Some who got to the infirmary couldn't be saved. They already had too much organ damage from, malnutrition or intense dehydration.

Nobody was keeping count. It was just too sad to think how many had died from the pandemic and its aftermath. I could only try to keep the living healthy enough to live on. A heavy burden on my shoulders.

As usual, Van greeted me and gave a call to Ray who was up on a nearby roof helping to fix a solar power source damaged by the storm.

"How are you doing Van, everything okay?"

"Some good, some bad. We getting storm damage repair pronto. But we so many sign up no work. And we don't have places them to stay. Some have gall to tell they don't eat fish or seafood." He frowned and shook his head.

"Except for ship; they get other food and place to stay. I'm so glad you make me arrangements with Rambler. Otherwise, we not do what we doing with no food than just what we catch and now, grow soon.

"You ready go up Central Valley? Take fish? We ready here."

"Not yet, Van. I'm worried about the roads. But I've lost phone touch with my grandfather and I'm getting worried about it."

"No need worry, you the boss. Everything you do turns out right. Your grandfather's okay. Wish mine was still to see what happening with us. Wouldn't believe it. He was fisherman in the Tonkin Gulf. He fed both Vietcong and USA troops. Taught me everything about fishing but died in reeducation camp!" He spit on the ground in disgust. Tried to hide the tears coming to his eyes.

Ray arrived and told me that he had to load some netting that Van had given him, along with instructions on how to use it at the Santa Monica pier. While they were doing that, I gave Captain Jensen a call. He was busy, but Dani Steffensen answered. I was immediately struck by her beauty and her accent.

"Hello, Drake. I hope you are okay after that hurricane. We are used to hurricanes, cyclones and typhoons. While at sea, we are usually able to steer clear of them. But when in port we can weather them, even this one."

"We had some damage we have almost repaired already, Dani. Are you handling all the stragglers coming in okay?"

"We are carefully screening them. Something we've always done while traveling to different countries. There are a few who we are watching who have some criminal background. We've put them in work crews where we can closely watch them. So far, everyone is so grateful for the food and lodging that they are all cooperating and helping us keep the ship shipshape." She giggled.

"And the infirmary?"

"So sad to see so many in such bad shape. Some have died no matter what we do to save them. The stories they tell are heartbreaking."

"And your food?" I continued. "I'm hoping to leave for the Central Valley soon to get fresh meat, vegetables, fruit and nuts within a couple of days. But I can't guarantee getting much because I've heard that the entire valley is flooded. The only fresh food we are getting is from the fish market. But we have a large store of frozen food we need to eat before it gets over a year old. The good news is, the captain checked on our food warehouse and it was not broken into. So, we have a lot of basic foodstuffs to last a very long time."

"We are training some of the new people to be crew members. Perhaps by the fall, we can take short cruises, say, to Catalina Island or up the Coast to Santa Barbara. We also checked our methane storage tank and we have ample methane for years to come."

I hated to stop the conversation because I was in love with her beauty and compassion already. Not knowing if she had a boyfriend or even a husband. Told her I would talk to her again soon and said our goodbyes.

It didn't take long to load the netting and we were off. I was still curious about the L.A.River, so we got on Cal 1 leading to 710 to see if anything had changed. Very quickly, it was obvious that things had.

The river was much higher, flooding a mile from its concrete ditch boundaries. Such a raging torrent was both mesmerizing and apocalyptic to watch. Up ahead where we had been on the interchange with 101, there was obvious failure with parts of both highways missing!

I dared not drive any further for fear of driving off a hidden missing piece of roadway into the water below. I turned around and drove back in the oncoming lanes without fear of running into anyone. But, with a new respect for what water, so needed for life, could do.

After helping finish up replanting all the gardens in our compound, Ray grabbed a couple of the kids and headed down to the beach to try out his new nets on hopefully, willing fish wanting to get caught for our food.

I went hunting out back in the park. Everything was muddy so slopes were treacherous. Also, a lot of tracks. I found a heavily traveled deer trail and waited. As evening approach, a buck in velvet appeared and we would have fresh venison to eat that night. I was grateful we could hunt so close to what we could raise or grow.

As I returned carrying the buck on my shoulders, I could see the lights on throughout our compound. Glad we had solar power throughout that we didn't have before. We had seen the last of the CP&E power grid. Good riddance.

While everyone scrambled to help me with dressing the deer so we would have fresh grilled venison, Ray had a dismal tale to tell.

"When we arrived at the beach, it smelled. There was a line of oily substance along the beach sand and the beach was littered with driftwood of all sizes, including whole trees. And there were bodies. We could see them floating in the floating debris… Just part of it. Part of the reason the water stunk of chemicals and other nasty things."

The kids were crying and Ray just hung his head.

I tried to be reassuring. "Van said they have a large store of seafood from recent catches. I'm sure what you are seeing is the result of the storm and flooding of the L.A. River and others spilling all that into the ocean. Eventually it will clean itself, but I think you guys should get busy and clean up as much of it is you can as soon as you can, so the fish will come back sooner."

20

Disasters Multiply

I woke the next morning with a lot on my mind. Still couldn't get a hold of Gramps. I had to arrange a convoy to go to the Valley. I asked Derek if he would help.

"Dre, we're brothers. I've known you a long time. You've taken us pretty deep this time. Don't get me wrong, I like what you're doing. I'm really enjoying working with Wondah on communication and defense for both here and the port. But things are growing very fast and I'm not sure if you can keep up. I'm not going to challenge you, but somebody might?"

"Thanks for the heads up, Der. You always were the levelheaded one. I've been thinking about that. You and I are contractors, not politicians. Before long I'm going to pull together the people of the port and ask them to start their own government like every village has."

"That sounds like a solid plan. You're good at that." He smiled. "Hopefully that will free me, and you, from the place so it can grow on its own."

"Mind if I change the subject? What have you and Wondah found out about the Valley?"

"It isn't good. NOAA radar from space is giving us images of more hurricanes building off Central America, in the Atlantic and Gulf of Mexico. It's already a very busy tropical storm season. We are also seeing lots of very strong thunderstorms all across the rest of the United States. Very high temperatures, followed by strong fronts. Lots of tornadoes being pinpointed by satellite technology with no one at the helm.

"Closer to home, satellite Internet images are showing us that several dams have been breached and at least two have failed with catastrophic results downstream. The Los Angeles River is draining water as far away as the Valley that remains flooded, for now."

"Is Caylee still dumping rain on the valley?"

"No, she finally moved into Nevada and beyond."

"Any sign that the flooding has gone down?"

"We were seeing less flooding this morning from last night. Large areas are still underwater and are draining down all the rivers virtually unstopped overflowing all the dams and destroying some."

"Guess I'll have to wait a while before we go."

"Yeah, Wondah and I will keep an eye on those cameras we can still reach by Internet and let you know when we think it's possible to get there as the flooding subsides."

At breakfast, Ray gathered up any free man and woman that he could find who wasn't occupied with food production, to go with him down to the beach to help clean up. He borrowed my four wheeler, a trailer and assorted shovels, pails and pans to help with the task.

On our way to the shop, I filled Mel in on the beach cleanup, the upcoming convoy and additional work that I expected we would have. But I had a premonition I didn't tell Mel about.

Before we got there while taking the 10, the view below had changed from the last time I drove that way. It was obvious that the hurricane and street flooding had been disastrous in some neighborhoods. Debris in the streets was not just wind debris, but also parts of buildings that had been washed away. In some places there were deep gullies torn through streets as the storm sewer system was overwhelmed and the water ran down the streets the quickest way to the Pacific.

And, what I had thought would happen had. For a full half mile before we got to where the shop was, the streets were flooded from the L.A. River! Melody was shocked having seen it for the first time. But I knew the shop was underwater and there was no going there. My only thought was that the office was on the second floor and hopefully, didn't flood. The supplies and equipment in the yard could be replaced from other parts of town. The tools and power equipment probably damaged beyond repair.

Driving very carefully to avoid driving off a hidden piece of I-10 fallen into the flood below or with a support so badly damaged that the freeway would fail from my truck's weight, we drove across the raging river to the other side.

We took a safe exit, and then came back on the eastbound lanes, once again, amazed at the power and destruction of all that water coming from all that way, no longer held back by dams or diversions.

We stopped over the torrent and both of us got out to look from the rail and take videos.

I found myself saying, "Mel, in spite of losing the shop, there's something awesome about watching the water with all that debris in it roiling below us. Carrying everything to the Pacific it can tear loose."

"There sure is." Mel held me close. "It gives me shivers. Truly awesome. Our own Niagara Falls?" She giggled.

We got back in the truck and headed to see how the crew was doing at the Santa Monica beach. Before we got there we could see smoke rising. When we were in view of the beach, there was fire spewing black smoke up and down the entire coast. Even hurricane beached boats were burning.

"What the hell happened?" I yelled.

Mel answered, "I don't know, but we're going to find out."

We pulled up behind four other vehicles parked at the entrance to the pier. We could see them, men, women and children, all frantically, with pails and shovels trying to put down fires with seawater and sand that had caught on a number of the older creosote covered wood pier supports that weren't protected by steel or concrete.

I grabbed two pails and a couple of shovels from our truck and we rushed down to help them put out the fires while all the way up and down the beach, the shoreline was on fire.

We struggled for another half hour while the oil and gasoline in the water burned out and the wooden debris that was on fire was extinguished by seawater from waves.

Afterward, I asked a soaked and soot covered Ray what happened.

"When we got here, we dragged the wood we could into large piles that I thought we might burn later as bonfires. And started shoveling the oil and tar-soaked sand into buckets and pans I didn't have a good idea where to take at first. There was just too much… Way too much!" Ray shook his head and I agreed.

"When I saw that the greasy gasoline and oil slick was constantly being washed up on the shore, someone suggested that we might burn it as a way of getting rid of it. I thought it was a good idea, so I lit a piece of wood and threw it into the oily slick. There was a flash, almost an explosion, and the fire raced up and down the coast beyond our control. Even the section of the dry sandy beach that had been cleaned earlier was burning. The flames were very hot and reaching over ten feet. The chemical smell of the smoke was overpowering. We all ran down to the pier and tried to put the fire out under it so the whole pier wouldn't burn.

"We were fighting for over a half hour before you two came along and helped us. By that time, everything had pretty much burned out except big jams of wood from buildings and boats that will probably burn a long time."

I sighed when he finished explaining. "Well, I guess that's one way of getting rid of that oil, gasoline and chemicals in the water and on the beach. But if more keeps washing in, we may have to do it again. I sure hope that fire doesn't get to the port. It could do a lot of damage there."

"You're right, Drake, I had the same thought. From what I can see, it'll be a while before we can fish again. Should we take fish to the Central Valley when we may need it here?"

"I promised and we need the fresh meat that they can provide us until we can grow animals here. We might be able to gather enough fruit and nuts from backyards here, but they have a lot of crops and animals we could benefit from until we start sustaining ourselves with your expert help."

"A lot to think about. I'm glad you're thinking and planning ahead. I'm not very good at that. Just what I'm gonna do for the next day and that's about it. By the way, I'm just a dumb Midwestern farmer, not the expert you claim to be with big plans for everything."

Our chuckles broke the tension we had been feeling from the fight with the fire.

Melody, as dirty as the rest of us with no chance of washing off in the ocean that may still be toxic, agreed…

"There's so much to do it's almost overwhelming. I don't know how you do it, Dre."

"Been doing it all my life, watching Dad plan huge projects and carry them out. I had a good teacher. And it really helped to have Der there as my idea bouncing board. He steered me in another direction many times, keeping us both out of trouble," I had to laugh at the memories I hadn't shared.

"Well, we can't do any more here today. I suggest we all go home and work on all those projects we are behind on. Let's come back here tomorrow morning and see if we will have to burn the surf again. Save the Santa Monica pier again."

When we got back to the truck, my phone was ringing. I ran to get it and answered. It was Van.

"Where you been? I calling over hour and you no answer. What's up?"

"We have been fighting fire at the Santa Monica pier. I left my phone in the truck."

"The water start coming up about noon. We saw everyone run for the hotel or the ship. Water come in and destroy the market but not get in cold storage, yet. First floor of hotel flooded. But we are safe, for now. No longer able to give you fish."

I should have expected it. "That's okay, at least you're all safe, for now."

"We have dinghy to get to other buildings. Houses we remodeling ruined. We start snaring seagulls, pigeons and rats for meat. We be okay. Just want you know, that's all." He hung up having said his piece.

We returned home hoping for a hot shower together, only to find out that Martha had sent the kids to another house because she had three of our residents in the house with symptoms of Amazonia. Augie Palmer and his son Rocky, and Viktoria Sarnoff, Viktor's wife. Augie was the worst, having a great deal of trouble breathing.

Martha had secured a few bottles of oxygen when we searched pharmacies earlier and had them in her garage along with a couple of oxygen making machines.

I wondered what else could happen. And didn't want to think about it. To divert my attention, we talked about what we might name Melody's baby. We took a hot shower to get all the grime off together. It didn't work. I couldn't sleep even after making passionate love with her.

❧ ဆ၊℧ ❧

21

Disasters' Aftermath

I was up before dawn. Left Mel in bed and tried to call Gramps. Still nothing. The only thing to do was to figure out how to get there and find out what had happened to him. Was he even alive?

I called Van to tell him about our cases of Amazonia and an unfamiliar voice answered. I said, "Who is this? I'm calling Van Nguyen…"

A young face came into view in a darkened room and the voice said, "This is Quoc, his son. He can't come to the phone right now."

"Oh, why not?"

"I sent him to the infirmary on the Rambler last night having trouble breathing. Had to use the dinghy because the pier is still under three feet of water. We had to take others, too. The captain put them all on quarantine. We are on quarantine, too–one week. But we have to work—the flood…"

I could hear him struggling to talk to me and unsure what to do or say.

I tried to help. "Quoc, I'm really sorry to hear that. I lost my father, so I know. Derek and I hope that he recovers, like we did, after seven days in fever. Stay quarantined and call me at this number if you have any questions."

We had quarantined the best we could the night before when the three infected came in. I wanted to find out about them, so I called Martha.

When she came on the line she looked haggard like she hadn't slept. I asked, "How is everyone doing?"

"I asked the girls to quarantine with the kids. No use exposing them. It's hard, but I'm doing it alone. Augie is dead. I will wrap his body this morning and drag him out back of my house so that you can bury him or whatever Clowie wants to do with him. Rocky and Vicky are feverish but sleeping and stable for now. Only time will tell."

We were in a whole new world. Our only communication was our mobile phones. We had to wait it out until we were all clear of infection or even reinfection. Derek and I might get it if this was yet another strain.

We broke quarantine that afternoon when I got together with Derek and we transported August Palmer's body to the house they were staying in with my four wheeler. After talking to Clowie on the phone, she decided that she wanted to wait until Rocky recovered before they would decide what to do.

Covering Augie's body in a double layer of plastic over the sheets that Martha wrapped the body in, we dug a shallow grave near the garden and buried him there. Ready to be dug up if necessary. While there, we weeded the garden and watered it. By the time we were through it was getting very hot outside. We retreated to our air-conditioned houses and back in quarantine.

The next few days were filled with phone calls and occasional trips away from others to get urgent things done, like tending to the gardens and providing anything that Martha needed. Still couldn't get a hold of Gramps.

Mel and I ran out of things to talk about the next day, so I went hunting in the evening, waving at Daph as I passed. Brought home a young buck and five quail so I was busy until midnight tending to all that meat.

Melody was a big help. In the morning, we left parcels on several doorsteps with Wondah quarantining and Derek opening the gates for us remotely.

The next day, Ray had fifteen of us, in separate vehicles, drive down the beach and assess the situation. What we found was astounding!

On the beach close to the pier was a thousand pound sea lion floundering for its life. Covered with thick oily tar and chemical burns, it was on its last legs and struggling greatly like the dolphin had before. Ray pulled his pistol and put the poor animal out of its misery.

First things first. The sea contained much less oily slick, but the beach was oil soaked as before. So, we immediately set it on fire. I knew that the fire didn't go all the way down to the port because, according to Quoc, "We didn't get any fire here, but had lots of oily mess in the water until the flood washed it all away."

This time, the pier wasn't as threatened as before and it took around ten people to keep the wooden supports from catching fire. The rest of us violated quarantine, including Derek and me, helping Ray cut up the beast. The big male provided us with some very fine steaks and valued organs like the liver and to take back home with us.

I called Quoc. "How's your dad?"

"Not good. He's barely breathing. They have him on oxygen and he's not responding."

"That's not good. The reason I'm calling is we just killed a sea lion that was suffering from chemical burns and we had to put it to death. We are getting a lot of meat. I'm suggesting you watch out for animals like that and kill them before they die for meat until we are able to get animals from the Central Valley."

"That's a great idea, Dre. I will keep you posted on Dad. We are all praying. I hope that helps. I'm not Catholic or Buddhist like some. Already, we have enlisted a friend, Val Le, a fellow boatman, who has agreed to lead us through this trying time. I'm afraid I'm not up to it."

"I understand Quoc, can you put Val on?"

"Sure, on a three-way. That way you can get his number and we can all talk together even though we are quarantined."

I heard him ring, and a Vietnamese face with long blonde hair and a ruddy look appeared alongside Quoc.

"Hello Val! Quoc tells me that you are filling in for Van who is on the ship in the infirmary. Is that right?"

"Yeah I am, bro. You may not remember but I was alongside Van when we were meeting with Captain Jensen the other day."

"Yes, you were the one with all the questions."

"I like to know what's going on. Van actually picked me as a replacement in a meeting we had dealing with the rising flood. Fortunately, the flood has subsided now and I expect, by tomorrow, we can walk on the dock to assess the damage and start making repairs."

"Are your boats okay?"

"They sure are. Quoc suggested we tie them to the Rambler and we did before the water rose. It kept them from breaking their moorings and drifting out to sea like so many other boats we saw being carried out. What a shame." I could see in his face and hear in his voice what that meant to a fisherman–his livelihood.

"Yeah, we saw several that were washed up on the beach at Santa Monica. When we accidentally lit fire to the floating oil and gasoline, fire raced up and down the coast and caught most of those boats on fire. Did you see any of the fire your way?"

"No. We saw the fires up the coast a couple of miles away from the hotel. But we didn't have any. Probably because the flood was so strong, it washed all the chemicals, oil and gas out to sea, I guess."

"That's good news. We've had too much bad news. Let me know when I can come on down and help you out with repairs. We have nearly fixed everything here. Just have to deal with the return of the virus in our community worse than yours. Stay safe."

We said our goodbyes and I knew that the port was in good hands even without Van. I hoped to talk to Val again very soon.

My phone rang. It was Daph. "Dre, I just got a call from two producers, friends of Dad, Sean O'Flannery and Renée DuPont. They've been holding out at his estate in the Hollywood Hills. They have solar power and water from a large cistern but have totally run of food and are starving."

"I understand the problem, but we are under quarantine and I'm not sure what these two people can do for us without becoming a burden."

"Sean tells me he killed every, rat, squirrel and rabbit, as well as some pet peafowl he had on the property. Even trapped pigeons and crows. He says that he will hunt every day for us in the state reserve out back. You know yourself that we can get game from there.

"Renée says that she will teach, take care of kids, garden with me… Whatever it takes to prove her worth. She says they are so emaciated they can't come to us. She says that they'll both be dead in a couple of days only drinking water." The look on Daph's face told me all I needed to know.

"Okay, I wasn't looking forward to another day locked up in here, so give me the coordinates, and Mel and I will try to go get them before they die, today."

Daphne gave me their address and Mel and I left immediately.

This trip was different from the ones to rescue Daphne, twice before. While Cal 2 took us into Beverly Hills quickly, when we got on the streets it was a different matter. Not only were there abandoned vehicles, debris from the hurricane and washouts that had to be navigated. My four-wheel- drive got me through most of them, but in a couple of cases, we had to detour around, slowing our progress.

When we got into the hills, it was worse. Not only were there wash-outs, but mudslides blocking our way. After a half hour of navigating around these we came to a massive one about two blocks from our destination. We had to walk. We both filled backpacks with power drinks, power snacks and some smoked fish and jerky.

We rang the doorbell and the gate opened for us when the cameras, one of which was shot out, showed who we were. It was a long uphill walk to the circular drive in front of the huge house. An emaciated woman greeted us at the ornate double door.

I called out, "Renée DuPont?"

She didn't answer but made a brief motion with her hand for us to come. She had a really sad, defeated look on her face when we got close. Her lips were cracked. All she could do was whisper to us.

"Daphne sent you? I'm sorry, but Sean is unable to come to the door. He is too weak."

Inside the huge entryway I could see three kids peeking from a side entrance. "Who are those kids?" I asked.

"Neighbors… survivors. Sean's upstairs. You will have to get him."

We immediately took off our backpacks and opened them to give Renée and three kids some power drinks and snacks. Then, we ran upstairs searching for Sean and found him in a palatial sized master bedroom with a matching circular bed, too emaciated to get up. He waved his hands and pleaded with his eyes. His throat too dry to talk. Only a raspy whistle came out. He was in bad shape.

I wasted no time and hoisted him onto my shoulders in the fireman's carry I learned in scouts. The first time, other than practice, that I actually had to use it. He was light, seemed like about 100 pounds. I carefully descended the long curving staircase as rapidly as I could.

When I reached the entrance again the kids had run out, being in better shape than the adults, to an awning covered surrey electric cart that could carry us all. I breathed a sigh of relief as Mel helped Renée up on a seat and I placed Sean between them so they could support him.

The oldest boy, about ten, took the helm and I sat alongside of him as he drove us through the gate that opened automatically and down to the mudslide where we carefully put the surrey under the shade of a palm tree that had survived the hurricane and well behind a tall wall.

Once again, we hobbled and scrambled up over the 50 foot high mudslide filled with trees and pieces of buildings and walls that couldn't withstand the landslide.

It was rough going carrying Sean, but he was light and I was very careful not to make him fearful of falling. We all made it to the truck in good shape.

I took the three kids up front with me and Melody tended to Renée and Sean in the second seat. Renée was able to munch on a power bar, but Sean couldn't. Melody gently put pieces of smoked fish in his parched lips and held a sports drink with a straw so that he could sip a little at a time. Sitting between the two women, they both held onto him as I navigated the rough spots. Taking it very slow taking much longer going back then coming.

Along the way, the kids, feeling much better and now chewing on jerky followed by power, were really curious about everything they saw.

I asked the ten-year-old what his name was. He was glad to tell me. "I'm Cruz Martinez. I'm twelve. My sister and I lost our mom and dad, the actor Carlos Martinez and mom, Virginia. This is my sister, Selena. She's ten. In the other girl is Carla Gomez. She's our groundskeeper's daughter, but like family. She lost her parents, too."

"I know your father well; I've seen all of his movies. So sorry to hear that you lost your parents. I lost my parents, too. How did you get to the O'Flannery's?"

"I was sick and my sister and Carla weren't. We searched both houses for food and there was a lot, especially frozen. Carla knew how to cook it. It lasted about two weeks before it got rotten. And then, bad guys came. We ran to the treehouse and hid there while they ransacked everything. All of our food was gone. We all cried, but I had a plan."

"Planning's good. I'm planning all the time, trying to keep up with everyone we're helping." I encouraged him.

"When it was daylight, we snuck along the walls looking for homes that the bad guys didn't get into. When we came to this one where we knew Renée was because our parents told us sometimes that they were going to parties there. But we couldn't go because they had no children–adult parties. We rang the doorbell, and Renée let us in.

"They were so kind. Gave us most of their food and Sean showed me how he was hunting and trapping until he got feeling bad a few days ago. We loved that wild meat that Renée cooked for us. But it didn't last. I tried to hunt after Mr. O'Flannery couldn't, but I didn't catch or shoot anything." For the first time, Cruz looked down like he failed. He had been so upbeat earlier.

But like all kids do, he quickly recovered and started asking questions about where we were going and what we were seeing along the road. The girls started answering questions, too, and I tried to answer them as best as I could.

I called ahead to Martha. She looked even more tired than before.

With her permission, I brought her two IV stands out of her garage where we stored medical equipment we got from a pharmacy with ample saline solution to help Renée and Sean recover from dehydration quicker.

Then, we arrived at the estate. Soon, I was carrying Sean upstairs to a bedroom that Daph had prepared. In another 10 minutes both of them were on IVs and talking again from the power drinks helping their dry mouths recover.

We left them in Daphne's care and returned to our self-imposed quarantine with two days left. I had a lot on my mind. Especially, when I called Gramps again and got no answer. Was he even alive? I didn't know. I had to find a way to get there as soon as I could. I set my day to leave the morning after our quarantine and got on the phone to others to see if I could get everything together in time. For us, it would be leaving our quarantine.

22

Central Valley Odyssey

Another day in quarantine. But things had to get done. I gave Daph a call while Mel made breakfast for the two of us. A little smoke cured sea lion belly that smelled and tasted like bacon with fresh eggs from the chickens awaited me.

"Hi Daph, everything okay?" She didn't look okay.

"No, Sean died last night while talking to us. Renée, so far, is doing okay but she's beside herself over losing him. I can't console her. Don't know what to do."

"Maybe you will need to take her to Martha. But hold off a bit because she is a bit overwhelmed herself… Hold on! … I'm going to have to sign off, got a call coming in from the Central Valley…"

It was him, Ralph Hutchins, looking really tired and not his usual jovial, 83-year-old self.

"Gramps! You had me really worried! I called many times and couldn't get a hold of you. Why didn't you call me back?"

"Just got back here. Found my phone right where it always was. On the table in the kitchen."

"Where've you been? Why didn't you call from there?"

"I don't know, Sonny. It's been a rough few days. When the water started comin' in the back door and into the kitchen, I shut off all the electricals. Before that I wore myself out carryin' stuff upstairs and gettin' everything up off the floor I could. But it was rainin' hard and the water was comin' up fast. Couldn't stop it!"

"That sounds like a nightmare. Why did you leave?"

"Wasn't goin' to. I had the animals to tend to… Save them from the flood."

"What changed your mind?"

"I was barefoot with my pants rolled up in about three inches of water. When I heard a knockin' on my back door. It was Rich Meyer in a motorboat. He told me to get a suitcase of clothes and come with him."

"And then what happened?"

"We motored over to the barn and we roped some cattle and the horses, one by one and led them about a mile to higher ground. But by noon I was so tired, cold and soaked with rain he took me to their place to the second floor because of their place bein' also flooded…" Gramps hesitated to catch his breath.

"Did you save all the animals?"

"Don't know. Still findin' some alive, some drowned."

"Gladys gave me a hot meal and I went to bed. Couldn't get up until the next day. The boys continued to take the two boats they had and rescue more animals. Fear that all the crops are gone. We'll have to start over."

I could see he was about to cry. I never saw him that way before, not even when Grandma died.

"Don't worry, Gramps. We've been waiting to find out if you were okay… Worried sick. I was planning to come as soon as I could and we are planning to head out today.

"But don't expect us until tomorrow, because we don't know what obstacles the hurricane and flood have thrown at us. But I promise we will help you replant and clean up so you can get back to the business of farming as soon as possible. Okay?"

"That sure sounds good to me, Sonny. Okay." He looked much relieved, and we both said our goodbyes.

I set noon as our departure time and began making calls. Quoc had located two refrigerated trucks and three of the young fishermen to help load and unload, as well as drive the other refrigerated truck filled with fresh seafood and fish.

Captain Jensen found another truck and filled it with staples not normally raised in the Valley to be traded for meat, fruit and nuts that the ship could use.

Mel and I took my truck with its winches and four-wheel-drive to lead the convoy because we knew we may come to places where the road may have been washed out and would require the power of the winches to get other trucks through. We would be pulling both the horse trailer and a small trailer with my all around electric four-wheeler with the tools we might need.

Monsour Habeeb volunteered to bring his truck, his tools and pull two trailers as well. Derek and Wondah volunteered to stay behind and make sure that both communities were secure in our absence. They had to repair some of the security system at the port from the flood.

Derek told me, "Say hello to Grandpa Ralph for me and ask him when he's going to come back with you to stay with us."

I replied, "You know Gramps, Der, he'll never leave that place." I saw him shaking his head, yes, in agreement on his face through the phone.

"Yeah, I was just hopin'. Tell him I'll be on the next trip."

"Okay. We've gotta get going…"

In addition to drivers from the neighborhood and from the port, we solicited young strong men and women to help out with unloading and loading the trucks, helping with cleanup on the farms and distributing goods to the villagers in Eunice.

We left the port at noon and had little difficulty leaving taking the 110 to the 405 to the 5 and out of Los Angeles. Most of the highway had been cleared of previous blockage so it was easier going and most of it did not have much debris from the hurricane or flooding to worry about.

But when we got to the Grapevine things were different. Up ahead we saw the first mudslide that had crossed all five lanes of the road on an uphill grade making it more difficult to cross. The mud and rocks were about 3 feet deep over the roadway and about thirty feet wide.

Monsour had mounted a snowplow on the front of his truck for just such a situation. However, the mud and rocks were much more difficult to push aside than snow, ice and slush. I had to help push him through the first slide to open a single lane down to the original pavement for the rest of the trucks to follow us through.

But the second slide was even bigger. Fortunately, it ended after crossing all five lanes, so we were able to skirt around it on the shoulder and by using the winches to get all the trucks back on the pavement and not stuck in the mud off the pavement.

Finally, the third slide was smaller than the first with only about one foot of debris spread out for about 50 feet that we were able to push through as well.

By that time, it was four o'clock and I knew we wouldn't make it to Gramps's place that night. We pushed on to Cal 99 after the Bakersfield bypass until we saw signs indicating Road Closed Ahead.

As we took the detour to the right as directed, the businesses at that intersection all looked vacant and probably were. They seemed long abandoned and had hurricane damage. We stopped and had our evening meal. The only thing stirring was a few blackbirds and buzzards.

Fifteen miles north on that rural two-lane highway, we saw a roadblock up ahead with men armed to greet us. Next to them was a big sun faded sign that read, Welcome to Mondale.

I told Mel, "Keep your hands on your AR-15, but don't raise your hands above the windows where they might see the gun.

"And don't fire unless they fire first," I warned her.

I ran down my window keeping my eyes on the armed man directly in front of me with the badge that seemed to be the one I would talk to.

When I saw him put up his hand for us to stop, I called out as friendly as I could, "Hello! What's wrong with the 99?"

"Flooded out. Road's underwater at the aqueduct. You have to go this way through our village and take the high bridge to get back on 99. Raise your hands high and show us that you're not armed. And then get out of the truck so we can talk."

We both raised our hands high, opened our doors carefully and climbed down from the truck while the others behind us wondered what was going on. No way to tell them what was happening.

We approached until the man with the badge held out his hand again keeping us at length. Three other men with rifles pointed at us stood by.

He spoke. "I'm Deputy Sheriff Luis Ramirez. What's your business in the Central Valley? If you are escaping Los Angeles, turn around and go back. There's nothing here for you."

"My grandfather, Ralph Hutchins, lives up near Eunice. He got flooded out and we are coming to help him get his farm back in order and to bring supplies of food to him, neighboring farmers and the villagers of Eunice."

"That's mighty fine, but we've had a steady stream of folks running out of Los Angeles, thirsty, tired and hungry and we are in no position to help them. Most returned. But those that insisted on continuing sometimes tried to steal from us or take advantage of our good nature." He spit on the ground. "Worse, a couple of times we've had gangs come through and try to shoot up our town. We shot back with everything we had. Lost some good folks after we lost so many in the pandemic. What are you carrying?" He pointed with his rifle.

"Like I already said, some foodstuffs that aren't available in the Valley, seafood and fish." I watched his eyes to see if he believed me.

"Okay, the sheriff ain't here. He's resting from a wound. But about 300 pounds of that seafood and fish ought to be enough to let you pass through. But mind you, no stopping and bothering anyone. We will have guns on you the whole way. Do you understand?"

I nodded and said, "We understand, you will need something to take the load. Follow me."

A pickup truck pulled up and I walked back to where the two refrigerated trucks were with the pickup following. The driver of the first refrigerated truck, who looked to be only about 16, obliged when I told him we had to unload 300 pounds and he opened the rear of his truck.

Some of our guys and some of their guys quickly unloaded the required amount onto the pickup and we were cleared to go. We didn't weigh anything and I was in no position to quibble, but I think they got more like 500 pounds. I told everyone to wave friendly as we drove through the village.

It was a small village with the main street only about four blocks long. We waved. at a couple of heads that looked out of windows as our convoy passed. But we also saw the barrels of rifles and shotguns on the rooftops aimed our way. I shuddered to think of having to shoot our way through. So glad we didn't have to.

About five miles ahead was an incline that led to a long bridge over what had been an occasional rainy season riverbed before 99 was built. It was now the path of the aqueduct and nearly the whole span of the bridge was flooded by what I surmised were dams broken further up the valley. The aqueduct was completely underwater, had disappeared from sight in the muddy and debris filled deluge.

I knew we would have to come back the same way. In a few miles, a sign directed us back on 99 and all around we could see the devastation from flooding. In some places there was a thick layer of dried mud on the road to drive through. Fortunately, in some places other vehicles had made a path we could follow and had cleared the road from debris. Farmers that survived were using these roads.

The sky was full of vultures and eagles again. We saw many dead animals. Some of them were bloated. They attracted not only the vultures, but seagulls and crows.

We saw coyotes and foxes feeding on the carcasses and were surprised to see a cougar with two cubs feeding on a dead horse close to the road, unconcerned by our passing.

It was getting dark and we were really tired, so I stopped the convoy and we camped for the night. We were up at dawn and within two hours had reached Grandpa Ralph's place. It didn't look the same with all the debris and mud.

Gramps came off the front porch waving and yelling.

"Hey guys! Don't come down the drive. Stay out on the road. You'll get stuck down here!"

After introducing everyone, we went inside to plan what we would do and drink some fresh coffee. First, I assigned some of the guys and gals to help clean the house and barn. Then, Gramps told us about some farms that could use the foodstuffs, seafood and fish in exchange for beef recently butchered from drowned cattle. After the cleanup, the same people we left would see what they could save or replant in Gramps's garden. Harvest nuts and fruit from the trees.

And then, we brought in flour, rice, beans, sauces, sugar, cereals, spices, canned goods and other basics that we got from the ship warehouse into the house to replenish what Gramps couldn't get from the store anymore.

He was overcome… "Gosh, you guys are great bringing this stuff all the way from L.A. It's a lifesaver for me. I've nearly run out of all of it." He nearly cried, too.

Leaving Gramps to supervise, we moved on down the road to the Meyer farm and were greeted with lunch from Gladys again. We unloaded seafood and fish and more staples in exchange for two steers recently butchered and packaged. We moved on to other farms with Cy, Jr. driving ahead of us so that we wouldn't get shot at and introduce us to the other farmers to make our exchanges.

At the end of the day, we dropped off all the remaining foodstuffs and some of the meat we had acquired that day in Eunice.

Some of the villagers told us they were gathering animal skins and starting a tannery so that they could make leather goods and crafts. They had also started a pottery factory because plastic containers were no longer readily available from the store. One of the families was making furniture from salvaged wood.

When we arrived back at the farm, Gramps had, with the help of some of the others, a huge barbecue for us with our choice of beef, pork or chicken. We spent the next two days continuing the cleanup, and loading our vehicles with fruit, nuts, and anything else that the surrounding farmers had in excess. We promised to bring more seafood in the future to barter or buy with cash if we could get some kind of money system working again that we all could agree to.

Before we left we could see green sprouts pushing up through the sun-baked mud green and lush. Evidence that under the soil water was retained and that the horses, cows and sheep would have ample grazing as well as hay to cut before the fall rains. Seeds spread by the floodwaters provided much food for chickens, ducks and geese as well.

Even more remarkable was the wildflowers that appeared everywhere, filled with buzzing bees and butterflies. Nature's ability to take advantage of opportunities like this flooding was amazing.

Our return was easier. We cruised through Mondale to friendly waves. When we reached the checkpoint, we stopped and unloaded some of what we had gathered to give to the villagers. I even got to shake hands with a heavily bandaged Sheriff Alex Crockett. He told me, "From now on, you guys are welcome here. Come back all you want."

By nightfall, we made the port and everybody there came out to help unload what we had gathered. The three cows and five goats were the most welcome. A corral had already been made for them. And the five chickens and rooster would begin providing eggs and chicken for the sea-farer's diet.

The rest of us arrived home very late and very tired. As Mel and I relaxed in the pool after eating at midnight, I still had things on my mind we needed to do.

What kind of curveballs would be thrown at us next?

☙❧❦❧❧

23

Town Meeting

At breakfast with Der and Wondah, Mel and I caught up with what was happening while we were gone. Derek asked, "How was Grandpa Ralph?"

I laughed. "He looked like a neglected wet dog when we first saw him. But by the time we left, he was back to his old self. Determined to stick it out there until he died. I'm sure glad we have him. Because he is our entry to most of the Central Valley supporting what we are developing here."

"So, Der, what happened while Mel and I were gone?"

"As of yesterday, eleven more people showed up at the port. We are getting people from all sectors, some with skills that will be really useful, doctors, pharmacists teachers and others too many to mention. They all start right in working for food and water and a safe place to sleep at night."

"That's good. We will need everyone if we are going to revive any part of Los Angeles. Any news from beyond?"

"I'll let Wondah tell you that…" Der nodded towards Wondah.

"The military is in operation all over. Unfortunately, putting down uprisings and mobs. Some communities have become semi-military militias and have raided other communities for scarce resources. Farming areas seem to be doing the best.

"So is the government in Washington, kinda… It's pretty much chaos and every surviving politician for his/herself for now. Most of them asking for more help for their communities. It's the same all over the world. The news on the Internet is pretty bleak, dysfunctional."

She paused, and then started again. "Watching the scuttlebutt online, some of our people are complaining that there isn't any more fish or seafood and that the trip and more trips to the Valley are useless when so much needs to be done right here."

I had considered that happening. "What do you think we can do about it."

She looked over her glasses and said, "I think we should have a meeting to clear the air."

Der replied, "Great idea, Wondah. You and I have other things to do besides work on security systems. We need to get others involved to take that over. I, for one, want to go back to doing renovation and construction."

I agreed. "Okay then, I'll give the Captain a call and see if we can set up a meeting for…?"

Wondah volunteered, "Friday night, two days from now. That'll give me time to get prepared with visuals and a screen set up. I'll get the word out right away so that everyone will know as soon as you find out what the Captain says.

I called Captain Jensen and he agreed to let us use the auditorium for the general meeting and offered a few other rooms for group meetings to hammer out details. I thanked him. Without the ship we wouldn't have had that kind of meeting place. The hotel at the port only had a couple of restaurants. Nothing suitable for a large meeting.

I checked with Ray Dugas. He was on his way down to the port to help get the animals we brought from the Valley started there providing fresh eggs and milk.

"Glad you had a good trip, Mel and Dre. We've got the beach cleaned up about as much as we are able for now. Still no fish and I don't trust the seafood around the pier because of chemical contamination."

"That's not good. Any suggestions about fishing?" I asked.

"I suggest that the fleet go north to Santa Barbara and beyond where all of this industrial crap in the Pacific didn't happen. The fishing and seafood should be okay up there till you get to the Bay Area where it might be bad again."

"I'll be looking forward to hearing how those new animals are doing at the port. I think we should go hunting in the reserve to get more fresh meat for the compound."

"Good idea. It will be a while before we can produce our own meat from the livestock we have. In the future we'll have to run regular trips to the Central Valley as we grow."

"I'm not fond of old goat." We both laughed.

Der and I left to take care of some repairs at the port from the flood that occupied our next two days. In the meantime, with Ray's help, some of the young people of the fishing community took charge of milking the cows every morning at the corral with a convenient small warehouse as a shelter for them at night.

Every morning after milking, they were taken to pasture in vacant lots and big backyards where the lawns had gone to hay earlier and new sprouts from the recent rain provided additional succulent food for grazers. Goats were taken to the places where there was brush they enjoyed.

Every late afternoon they were then herded back and milked again. The community relished the fresh milk and used every bit of the milk and cream. In addition to the pigeon colonies and seagull traps that the fishing community had already established, another area was set aside for chickens and ducks. Sawdust and hay were brought in to provide nesting places.

Scraps from seafood and fish were the primary food source because they didn't have much grain or rice for the birds. They free ranged for that.

Friday evening came and everyone congregated in the auditorium of the Rambler. There were far more people than I thought and filled it halfway. Unfortunately, everyone couldn't be there because we had to have some security that was provided by people from the ship. Our community was left guarded by only its booby-traps and cameras. But we hadn't had any challenges there for some time.

Wondah set up her station on the left side of the stage with her smart pad and Wi-Fi system so she could relay information from the audience to the large screen provided by the ship.

I joined Derek, the Captain and a recovering Van, wheeling an oxygen tank on the stage. When everyone had settled in, I began a speech that I had shared with others to make sure that I was doing the right thing since politics was never part of my life. But we had to start somewhere…

"Thank you all for coming. And especially, Captain Jensen for providing this place for us to meet." I nodded to him and he nodded his head and waved to the audience… They cheered!

"I want to get back into the construction business with Dre. There is an unimaginable opportunity to rebuild most of Los Angeles for those of us who have that kind of vision. But it will take all of us with all of our skills and hard work to make it happen. I'm not going to bore you with details..." I was interrupted with applause again.

"But… But we need to organize in a way that communities have always been organized so we can use our best skills to the best purpose. A few of us got together and decided that we would have some committees work tonight to develop a few details. The committees are governance, banking, business, farming, fishing and any other committees that you would like to see. Any suggestions…?"

Several hands went up and I called each one. The first woman said, "Don't forget education." A second man called out, "Security."

A third woman called out, "We need entertainment."

A nurse from the ship announced, "We need a hospital."

A boy I knew from the beach cleanup, Erik Banks, raised his hand. I called on him.

"My dog, Artie, got attacked by wild dogs and killed. What are we going to do about them?"

An animal committee was created.

Wondah displayed each committee on the big screen and added a room where the details would be worked out. When no more committees were suggested, Wondah displayed the rules and I reiterated them.

"First, you should select a committee to join and go to that room. Second, you should, together, select a moderator to speak for the committee. And a secretary to collect all the suggestions made. Once that's done, everyone should brainstorm ideas and not, at this point, argue which ones are better or not. Once you are finished, everyone come back here and we'll have each moderator make a brief report." Everyone started shuffling out of the room…

"One more thing… If we have time, we will take nominations for Mayor, a governing committee, and police chief or sheriff. Otherwise, we'll convene again next Friday and get that started. Any questions?"

Everyone left the room. Within an hour, everyone was back and Wondah had gathered all of the ideas that the secretaries had on their smart pads. Each moderator was then given 10 minutes to explain what they had come up with. It was getting late, past 9 pm and the little ones were getting restless, so I adjourned the meeting with the promise that we would meet again on the following Friday night.

Der, Wondah, Mel and I left the meeting feeling quite good that we had a start on developing a structure that would eventually have a government, sectors of the society working fully with people that wanted to work in those sectors and hopefully, a banking and financial system that would enable everyone to have a fair shake in the business of rebuilding the city.

Getting there wasn't going to be easy. There were already signs of discord in the ranks. Something to be expected, but I wasn't prepared to deal with.

∽ଌଔ∾

24

Down to Business

At what had become our usual breakfast meeting when we all were present, Wondah had something to tell and show us on the big screen.

"Guys, when we got home late last night I took a look at the system and I saw some red flags right away. It only took a minute to get to the video spot where it happened, about 2:33 am. It seems that three people all dressed in black with masks approached from below and when they got within our warning zone our speakers went off and they retreated rapidly, not knowing that there was no one here. That's the first attempted breach in over two weeks. I wonder if they knew we were away at the meeting?"

Der was first to respond. "That's great work. Shows that our system is working. I'd hate to have those thieves set off our booby-traps. I'm tired of cleaning up the gore. From what you showed us it doesn't look like those violent gangs are still around."

Mel interjected, "I don't know why, but I miss the danger of those violent attacks. Wish I could have shot a couple more of those guys who thought they could take from us whatever they wanted."

"Now, now Mel. I like being able to go throughout the city without someone taking pot shots at us. First, the lack of city water, and then, the flood, wiped out a lot of the gang communities. There probably are some out there still scavenging, but I think they are greatly diminished."

"I hope so, Dre. While my electronic toys are deadly, I don't relish the idea of just killing people because they are hungry. Bloodthirsty? … Hell, Yes!" Wondah ended that train of conversation with that vivid pronouncement. We all laughed.

I turned to more serious matters. "I noticed that there wasn't any spiritual committee started last night. I understand that some people have been going to the chapel in the Rambler on Sunday mornings. But I don't know if we have any priests or pastors in the community.

Wondah pulled up the roster of inhabitants we registered. "There are a couple of monks from the Buddhist temple that served the Vietnamese port community before… Also, a nearby Catholic Church. You're right, Dre, no priest or pastor among us. Just the chaplain on the Rambler."

"I'd like to get our construction firm going again, Dre."

"I'm with you, Der. It's time we started salvaging and rebuilding so the port people can start feeling like they have more than just food and water. We could start by restoring that temple and that Catholic Church if they are restorable. I think our subs and our guys and gals that want to rebuild are ready to work with us now that we have the basics starting to get taken care of."

Mel said, "I'll make some calls, when do you want to start checking on those buildings?"

"We've all got chores to do this morning. Let's agree to meet at the Buddhist Temple at 1 pm. Is that okay with everyone?" Everyone agreed, but only Der and a crew would be with me.

We converged at the Half Moon Temple in Inglewood about halfway to the port right off 101. From the port, thanks to contact with Van, came Quoc and two other Vietnamese lads. They brought with them the two monks that had formerly lived there.

First, with guns ready, we drove through the blocks around the temple to see if there was any activity. Occasionally, Peter Sarnoff with his plow, had to push a vehicle or some windblown debris out of the way. All was quiet except for some cats that were seen and a pack of dogs that scurried across the street in one place.

The temple was already in decline before the pandemic. As we surveyed inside, there was much destruction and some graffiti on the ornate decor so carefully done by several generations of Buddhists. It was a real shame.

Quoc had a lot of discussion with the monks in Vietnamese and he relayed to the rest of us what they wanted us to do or not.

We began with a general cleanup making sure that anything that we swept up or picked up was checked by the monks to see if it had any value for them to keep. We cleared out and cleaned the place in a couple of hours.

Peter Sarnoff had already begun rebuilding the wrought iron fence and gate that formed the entry to the temple grounds surrounded by high concrete block walls covered with white painted stucco and bougainvillea vines in full bloom after all the rain.

Anything that was gold or gemstone had been taken but attempts to remove the gold leaf from the giant Buddha statue in the center of the temple had failed. But graffiti and two gunshot chips to the concrete statue had done further damage.

Given some solvents to try, the monks began trying to remove the painted graffiti from the gold. It was tedious work, but they made progress while the rest of us began to piece together broken furniture and artifacts using glue and whatever we could manage to try to make them whole again.

We cleaned out the monk's quarters and made sure their kitchen appliances were back in operation. Outside of the building, there was a lot of graffiti that had to be painted over with the right colors to match the original. It took two days to complete the work. Der created a solar powered surveillance and warning system like we had so the monks could live there. Our Vietnamese helpers promised to bring them candles, incense, charcoal, food and water until we could get sustainable power and water for them as well. That project took another week.

There was a St. Michael's Korean Catholic Church in Torrance not far from the port we selected for the next day's work. When we got there, we found a rather modern structure rather than a traditional Catholic church.

Our crew, including the Vietnamese guys and one girl, decided it would be better to be a few blocks closer to the 405 to the Our Lady of the Angels Catholic Church, probably over 200 years old. Much more to everyone's liking than the Korean one.

Surprisingly, as we entered we found very little destruction or desecration, probably because many of the South American gangs came from Catholic communities and would only enter churches looking for gold, silver and money, not to desecrate.

We noticed the altar chalices and crosses were missing, evidence of looting. Back in the quarters behind the church we found two dead priests and three nuns. All of them dried out skin over bones. And, in the courtyard, three fresh graves. We buried them with the others.

We then planned to come back to create a well-protected entry and gate so that the building could be used for masses whenever Roman Catholics wished to start a church again. Surely, there were some priests in the area that survived. They just had to be found.

While the Rambler had provided medical and pharmaceutical assistance, the infirmary was small, lacked diagnostic equipment and supplies were running out. I thought our next best bet was to try to reopen a nearby medical complex in Harbor City right of Cal 1. I had seen it every time we drove by. That hospital would be a major undertaking but could provide equipment for diagnosis and treatment that the ship didn't have.

The first morning, we approached the main entrance with trepidation and with good reason. The glass windows and doors were not broken and the main doors were open, leading into a large foyer and information desk.

The smell of the place was what struck me first, followed by the dead bodies on the floor and in chairs in the waiting area all at least two months into disintegration. Again, dry skin stretched tightly over bone like Egyptian mummies unwrapped. Strangely, there was no evidence of worms or rodent attack. Probably because of the nature of the place, usually free from such vermin by design and cleanliness.

The pharmacy was on that main floor. It was untouched and that was a real bonus. As were the rooms used for diagnosis with machines ranging x- ray, CT scan, lithotripsy, MRI, PET, lasers, and bedside monitoring equipment as well as labs all abandoned and without any vandalism whatsoever. Operating rooms and the recovery room were a bonus, too. Something the Rambler lacked.

Our first task was removal of the bodies. There were many bodies in the hospital beds upstairs including some of the doctors and nurses still in their white uniforms and masks. We found some wheelchairs and started moving them out but finding the stairs very difficult to navigate with the head of a cadaver bouncing up and down in front of your face as you tried to drop the wheelchair down step-by-step to the next floor. Oh, how I wished we had some electricity in that building! We needed to get the elevators running again.

We found a dumpster truck and some dumpsters. We brought a dumpster to the emergency center where there was a loading dock and were able to fill it with bodies. For the next two days we removed some 63 bodies. We gathered up in envelopes what personal effects they had on them for identification and chronicled it all on a smart pad with photos of ID cards, jewelry, rings and watches in case there were any living relatives still looking for them. Categorizing it all properly would have to wait until later.

The roster from the village contained a 32-year-old pharmacist, Mary Beth Fong. We found her on the roof of a warehouse where she had already planted some medicinal plants that she had learned of from her grandmother and mother. She was the only one left from a family of six.

We searched the roster again and found some medical technicians, but only one doctor and two nurses.

Hymie Espinoza was 26 and interning at St. Jude's when it happened. With doctors and nurses succumbing to the epidemic all around, he barely made it to his family home in Cerritos only to find his family sick and dying.

Like I got sick, he got sick and was out of it for about five days. When he recovered, everyone was dead except for his 16-year-old brother, Felix, and his 12-year-old sister, Margo. They had kept him alive with water and soups. They began scavenging and slowly starving to death until the storm came and Hymie knew that they would be flooded out because their home was close to the Los Angeles River.

Three days later, keeping ahead of the rising water, they saw posted signs and found their way to the port. We found him recovering with his siblings in a balcony room on the Rambler. He was weak, but willing to go with us.

We took Dr. Espinosa, Ms. Fong, two medical personnel from the Rambler, and three medical technicians and toured the buildings with them. They agreed to start with the main building and open the pharmacy immediately. We set about securing the front of the building and all the other entrances that day. We didn't want anyone upsetting what we had found and started.

Our next main task was to provide power and water to the buildings again. It would be a major undertaking.

৯৵৪৫৪৵৶

25

Labor Day Order to Disorder

It was September, only three months since the pandemic had changed the world. To me, it seemed like a lifetime. Forced to forget my grief from losing my parents and grow up beyond thoughts of college, football, fraternities and the good life our parents had given Der and me. Gone now, but largely forgotten in the perpetual tasks ahead. It was time for a breather.

The calendar told us it was Labor Day, so we sent out a message to everyone not to work, but to play, eat and have a good time for a change on the first Monday of the month. Everyone who heard it from our online broadcast or read it later, cheered.

Der, Ray, and I celebrated by getting up at 5 am and heading out hunting beyond the estate. We all took different stands and waited for the sun to appear, when the daylight animals and birds started to move around and forage. The chaparral was lush from the rain from the hurricane and wildlife was much more plentiful than I had seen it back in the desperate days of needing meat in late June when I last hunted there.

It was still half dark and the sea mist coming in off the coast when I heard firing from the others with the different shotgun sounds of slugs and birdshot being fired.

After he fired, I heard the brush rustle to my left from where Ray was and spotted a young buck trotting my way in the mist. Unfortunately for him, my slug to his heart put him down. I waited. Changed to birdshot. Saw a jackrabbit's ears sticking above the chaparral working his way toward me. I aimed for the ears when he came into the open and fired. He went down kicking up dust, a headshot saving his meat from lead.

In an hour, we were all back together to begin gutting what we shot. Then, putting the meat on the trailer behind the 4 wheeler we drove in on, quiet because it was electric.

There was another buck shot by Der to match mine, seven quail, three jackrabbits, one coyote, a wild pig, and a turkey. The last two, newly feral versions of farm animals. The turkey had white feathers, making it an easy target for coyotes and eagles. We also saw feral cats but didn't shoot any. Perhaps we should have. I knew they would have a detrimental effect on wild game. Like the pigs. Also, mice and small birds, food for the resident predators.

Some like the bobcats, cougars and eagles found cats a good source of food as well. The wild was our predatory place, keeping it healthy. Most of the rest of the morning was spent butchering all the meat as others from the compound helped out. All getting ready for the big barbecue to be held in the afternoon at my pool.

We all ate too much, drank too much of the finest booze and got too much sun in and out of the pool all afternoon. For some it was too much and they returned to their homes to sleep off the excess.

The rest of us headed down to the Rambler where the entertainment committee had put together an hour-long show that began at 6 pm featuring a country band, a comedienne, and some dancers. And then, there was a movie that none of us had seen of an apocalypse greater than we were experiencing where we cheered and laughed at what was happening on the screen.

To top the celebration off, from both the top of the Rambler and the hotel, an impromptu fireworks display took place for another hour. Letting those within eyesight and earshot know some parts of Los Angeles were coming back alive and observing a holiday.

The next day, hung over, we were back working on the medical center. Der, Peter and a surviving electrician working on setting up a massive solar array and two large wind turbines to provide power to the whole complex that would take at least a week to complete.

Likewise, Peter, Gary and I were installing a catchment system, pumps and a large cistern at the top of the hospital to provide water to the building and pressure to the entire complex, n addition to the standpipe system that already existed.

During the following days, another twenty-three people came in, some as far away as L.A. suburbs. Of those, three exhibited gang tattoos and came together on Wednesday. They were emaciated and begging.

As instructed, they were turned away, but as they walked back to their pickup with a pedestal machine gun mounted, the leader and oldest, perhaps 23, fell down on the ground and went into convulsions. Medical help from the ship arrived and saved him. The three of them were then taken on the ship and cared for in a locked state room under guard.

Friday came quickly and throughout the week we began to see signs cropping up from people wishing to run for various key offices from the committees.

As we gathered together in the Rambler theater again, it seemed like our numbers had grown. But it was probably just people coming off the list of sick that had arrived in the last month and were now recovered enough from starvation and dehydration to join in the decision-making process.

There were even some signs in the audience backing one candidate or another. Once again, the meeting started with only Wondah in charge of displaying and recording everything, Captain Jensen, Van Nguyen, Der and me on the stage. That would change when the meeting progressed. At least, it was my intention.

When everyone had settled down, I began, "Welcome to election night. To get things underway right away, we have determined the following offices for the organization. Wondah has put them up on the screen. So, I won't repeat them to you. But first, and please raise your hand or stand up and use your phone amplifier if you have a position and want to talk to us, let us know if we should have any more original key positions."

Three hands went up and three new positions were suggested. Wondah added those to the list.

"Are there any more?" I asked. No one responded. "Okay, let's take nominations for the first position, Mayor."

The audience came alive with lots of names, including those of us on the stage. We all politely declined nomination. But there were three serious contenders for mayor. They all had been working with us and now could show their worth from their backgrounds. I gave each of them the stage to describe why they would be a good mayor in 10 minutes. Thankfully, each of them took less time.

To save time, I asked for a simple show of hands for each of the candidates. We would only count if the show of hands was close. But after I asked for hands for each of the candidates, only one was the clear winner. It was Dr. Joan Roberts, thirty-seven, a former political science professor and associate dean of social sciences at Cal State, Long Beach.

She had shown her worth as soon as she arrived by helping with the infirmary and then later, after the flood, leading groups helping with the cleanup at the Santa Monica Pier. She won by an overwhelming show of hands.

I asked Joan to take over the proceedings and she willingly agreed. The rest of us left the stage except Wondah and joined the audience. It felt good to be there and just part of the voting population again, although I had not voted up until that time except for clubs in high school.

Joan explained that there wasn't time to elect all of the positions suggested. So, she suggested that we only elect a managing secretary for her, a treasurer, and a sheriff to get things rolling. But to hold off elections for the other positions for another week so people inclined to run for office could have time to state their plans for those offices. A show of hands showed that everyone agreed with her.

The next position was managing secretary. Wondah had declined but agreed to help whoever took the position to set up and operate the equipment. There were only two candidates and the audience overwhelmingly selected Monica Peters, 28, who had been the executive assistant to the head of GMG Studios. She had only recovered about 15 days before but was willing to serve rather than cleaning fish the boats brought in. She had an MBA and superior managing skills based on her Internet profile.

The next position was treasurer. Seymour Kaufman, 43, a CPA who expressed his desire to reopen his private business and help establish the monetary system was elected without opposition.

The position of sheriff was contested by three people. A former Orange County Deputy, a sergeant with the Long Beach Police Department and a lieutenant from the Los Angeles Police Department who had manned and led the access gate to the port from when he recovered 2 months before. Lieutenant Morgan Singh, 35, received the majority of the votes.

After discussion about renovating a former business located within the perimeter as the interim City Hall, Joan adjourned the meeting.

***

The next morning, both Der and I were on-site at the building to prepare it to accept the offices of the four officers elected and their supporting staff. The building was adequate for now, but we would look for something larger and more appropriate in the future.

On Sunday morning, Mel and I transported four Vietnamese and one Hispanic woman to the Catholic Church and dropped them off to pick them up at noon.

In the meantime, while traveling to the church, two of the Vietnamese women had expressed that they wanted to open a hair and pedicure salon for the community. We knew of one in a small strip close to the Medical Center, so we drove there to see if it needed any work. Like every other business, it had been vandalized, so we were in the process of cleaning up when we heard a single shot nearby.

It came from the Medical Center. We grabbed our guns and ran towards the front door. Coming around the corner with Melody out ahead of me, I saw the lone security guard who was supposed to be inside lying on his side on the steps and two figures rushing inside the place who didn't see us in their haste.

I yelled, "Mel! Mel! Don't run through that door! Wait for me… Wait!"

I caught up with her at the door with her hand on it about to open. I gasped, "Don't go running in there, they'll hear you coming! We have to sneak in very carefully and catch them by surprise."

But stealth was not necessary, they were shooting at the lock and kicking at the door of the pharmacy making a lot of noise, there was no time to waste, we had to move fast.

26

Preparing for Growth

How can I help you?""This is Drake Hutchins. Glad you were able to answer, Morgan. We've got a mess here at the pharmacy in the medical center. Two invaders killed the guard out front and tried to shoot their way into the pharmacy when Melody and I caught them at it and killed them both. Can you get somebody to come here to attend to the bodies? I'll get somebody to fix the front of the pharmacy– all shot up."

"We'll be right there. We already saw the camera view from alarms we got. He was Orange County Deputy, Marlon Joyner. He ran for sheriff against me. I deputized him right after the meeting. I don't know why he was sitting outside on the steps of the medical center. Must've needed a breather from sitting behind the counter in the lobby for a long time. Would've saved his life." I saw him shake his head and signal to his secretary that he was leaving.

Melody asked, "Mary Beth, are you okay?" She was standing aside, eyeing the dead bodies and shaking as though she were cold.

"I think so… I was so scared when the bullets started hitting the door. All I could think of was to get my gun and get low. So, I got it and crawled on my belly to in front of the counter and lay there as the bullets kept breaking through the wooden folding door above me and showering me with splinters. I kept my gun aimed up at the door hoping I would catch them as they pushed through it. But then…" She started crying.

Melody hugged her to help calm her down. Before long, several people were there and, after many pictures of the dead, the two bodies were hauled off to the dumpster where the bodies from the medical center had been placed and covered to keep rats out.

Deputy Joyner would be given a full shipboard funeral and burial at sea. I was glad I didn't have to tend to the details. Sheriff Singh saw to that. He turned the body over to Captain Jensen's mates who are experienced in such matters.

The next day, I had Hector Lopez and his daughter, Selma, pulled from working on the city office at work demolishing and rebuilding a more secure entry to the pharmacy. The yard at the old company still had the aluminum partitions we needed to do the job quickly so that it would be better and stronger than before.

The security in front of the medical center was beefed up by adding firepower to the cameras that could be triggered from the sheriff's office by the same technology used in our lethal drones.

The raiders had the same tattoos as the three recuperating from starvation and dehydration on the Rambler. Research showed that they were members of an Iranian gang, the Shah's Avengers. We asked some of the village members of Iranian descent about them and they universally told us that those were very bad guys, not only bent on destroying anything Moslem, but were preying on their own country people by protection, kickbacks, extortion, death threats and kidnappings.

Sheriff Singh would escort them far from the village in their truck with no weapons and a couple of weeks of food and water. They would be given what little we found in the pockets of the two deceased as what would happen to them if they tried to come back again violently.

Two days later, a few of us attended the funeral of Deputy Marlon Joyner. It was a fine ceremony for a man hardly any of us knew. We saved his meager personal belongings in case some family member showed up in the future. It was all we could do.

It took a couple of weeks to get the city offices completed. What had been a storage area was converted into a jail that would hold about 10 people. But there were plenty of police substations in the area that would be a police station in the future when the village boundaries would encompass one. But that project, like others, would have to be put off into the future.

The education committee got to work on schooling and decided to create a school where classes were already being held in the meeting rooms on the first two floors of the hotel. Where former teachers and teacher aides were already giving impromptu classes to about 100 students of various ages and groupings. It had been recently cleaned up after the flood and was back in use. Preschoolers had a wonderful place in the Rambler to go while their parents worked.

I decided to send our older kids to the hotel school if they wanted to go. But for now, Martha, Wondah and Stephanie were doing a great job tutoring the kids in our compound and we saw no reason for them to join the larger school until they reached high school age.

Another project for the future would be picking a suitable elementary school in the neighborhood to reopen with a high school nearby. But staffing them, even partially, would take a while with a greater population. Fortunately, stragglers were appearing nearly every day now. Tired of just surviving and coming because they heard the village offered an opportunity to rebuild.

A counseling office was set up by the mayor for any of the many who were suffering mental problems as a result of their experiences during and since the pandemic began. When it opened up, the three counselors that had volunteered with various degrees of experience, were overwhelmed with the number of people that signed up for treatment.

Not wishing to leave anyone out, they set up self-help circles of people with similar mental health conditions to hash it out together and even went so far as to have online sessions using a quorum that would have people signing in wherever they worked and following rules of order with a counselor/moderator to communicate their fears and concerns so that others could suggest a way to deal with them.

Reopening a monetary system was very tricky business. We didn't want anyone hoarding wealth or being manipulated by it. So far, bartering was working quite well, as well as many free ways to get necessary things. But sometimes, what was available was unevenly distributed and that caused some concern among those who were left out.

We needed a bank. So, the treasurer and finance committee had a meeting with Captain Jensen. He had already opened the casino to ship employees and others working on the ship for occasional recreation breaks at the gambling machines. The ship had a large bank of dollars already to support gambling that could be used. Everyone agreed to use US dollars and cents to define the value of goods and services. The big concern was being fair to everyone.

The ship also had private safes for up to 2000 passengers. Initially it was thought that villagers could keep their valuables there but that might lead to heavy traffic in and out of the ship and the captain didn't like that. The only other possibility would be to open, perhaps a nearby bank and/or credit union to start with accounts and safe deposit boxes. Of course, that would require much more security personnel. The committee decided to wait before determining what we might do.

When the fishing fleet came in, there was good news. While they had to go further up the coast past Santa Barbara, the flooding up there, largely through agricultural areas, had fertilized the sea and they were making huge catches of albacore, sardines and yellowtail like never before. With the storehouses filling up and the market providing lots of fish for everybody, it was time to make a run to the Central Valley again to exchange the bounty of the sea with the meat, fruit and produce of the nearby region.

I arranged another convoy, twice as big as the last one, to leave the next day by 10 am to try to make it in one day again. At least, that was my plan. At 2 am, Mel received a phone call and I listened in… Martha Rosenberg was on the line…

"Melody, we've got a problem! Can you come over?"

Mel looked at me intently. I motioned the best I could for her to go. "Okay, okay… I'll be right over… Bye."

She hung up and gave me an inquisitive look before she slipped on her jeans and pulled a sweater over her head as she fumbled for her slippers before she reached the door.

<h1 style="text-align:center">27</h1>

Returning to the Central Valley

I heard the door open and looked at the clock, it was 3:35 am. Mel came in quietly, slipped out of her clothes and slipped into bed with me.

I asked, "What was that all about?"

"It was Stephanie, she had a miscarriage."

"What happened?"

"She told us not to tell anyone."

"I won't. But wasn't it you that told me she was pregnant in the first place?"

"Yes, but…"

"C'mon, you know I like to know what's going on here in the compound so I can head off any problems."

"Oh… Okay, but please don't tell anyone, even Der. Okay?"

"Okay."

"When I got there, Martha was comforting her. I held her hand while Stephanie told us what happened. She said she was having sex when all of a sudden, she started feeling cramps and stopped. She went to the bathroom and got really sick. The cramps increased until she was in spasms and she was bleeding. And then, all of a sudden, she saw her baby come out, all bloody, in the toilet!"

"That's terrible! I can see why you didn't want to tell me!"

"She panicked, pulled the baby out of the toilet and wrapped it in a towel and then ran over to Martha's with it and banged on her door."

"Who was the guy?"

"She wouldn't tell us, but she has a reputation for sleeping around and never told us who the father of the baby was. Anyway, she wanted Martha to revive the baby, but Martha told her it was too young and probably dead. To appease Stephanie, who was hysterical by that time, Martha put the fetus on oxygen, but its color didn't return and, although it looked like a baby, it was in no way developed enough to breathe on its own. I arrived by that time and got Stephanie away from the fetus. I held her and comforted her. Told her that we would bury the baby in the morning. Martha gave her a sedative and she fell asleep."

"Will that hold you up in the morning? You're riding shotgun again."

"I hope not. It shouldn't take long to dig a small grave and make a marker. I think Stephanie has begun to understand. We'll see."

"Okay, I'm going to try to get some more sleep. I hope you can, too."

We were both up at 5 am. There was a lot to do before heading out for the Valley again. This time, the convoy would be double in length and we would have four refrigerated trucks carrying fish and seafood. We planned to bring them back full of butchered beef, pork, mutton, goat, geese, turkey and chicken. As well as more live animals, grain, vegetables, fruit and nuts.

It was 10:15 am when we got everything rolling from the port. The path created by our earlier trip and others taking that route made it a lot easier this time and we reached the fork in the road where the 99 was closed and it was still closed.

This time, Sheriff Alex Crockett and the Mondale community at the roadblock greeted us with open arms. They were in need of just about everything that they hadn't gathered from tolls, so this time we gave them a thousand pounds of fish and seafood and promised that we would give them a similar amount of Valley trade goods on our return. Everyone in the village came out waving they were so happy.

Sheriff Crockett said they had heard from people who tried to take 99 covered up to 5 feet deep in some places with mud and debris and couldn't make it through. But they were systematically working on getting the road opened because they didn't want to be bothered with starving people from L.A.anymore. Some had arrived only to die. They ended up giving more to those people than they took in tolls. Most returned to the city when they heard what was up ahead.

It was 8:30 pm and already dark when we pulled into Grandpa Ralph's place, but the lights were on and when he saw Derek, Gramps cried.

"Oh, Derek! I heard about your parents. Come here, boy. Give an old fool a hug! My how you've grown since the last time I saw you! You both have become such men… I'm so proud of you both."

Mel and I joined Der in the hug. Tired as we were, we didn't get to bed until late with all that he had to tell a roomful of us as we drank some local wine relaxing in the living room knowing we had a tough couple of days ahead.

"Gosh, you guys have sure got somethin' goin' on. The Meyer boys have got together with other farmers in the area and when they heard you were comin' have decided to all come together with what they have to trade in Eunice tomorrow so you don't have to go around t'all the farms. Should make transferrin' goods a whole lot easier."

I answered, "That's great news, Gramps. It will save a lotta time. We'll have to save the salmon and sushi tuna we have for Rich and Cy. It's the best we have this trip. Have a little for you, too, Gramps." I chuckled and patted him on the knee next to me on the couch.

"One more thing, boys. We've been hearin' word outta Fresno that they was wantin' to get the trucks rollin' again East to Las Vegas, Phoenix and Albuquerque where they hear survivors need food. Some parts of town are still under gang control and local farmers have been talkin' about goin' there and cleanin' 'em out so that business can start up again after all we been through."

"When are they planning to do this? Derek asked.

"They'd like to do it tomorrow, but with all that perishable food to attend to they can't. Cy told me that they could use all the man and firepower they could get, so if you could bring some from Los Angeles that would be a big help."

Derek offered, "We've got a tank, but it would be a long drive and a lot of diesel to get all the way here with it."

"Don't have to. There's a fella off 99 with a lot of surplus military vehicles. They are plannin' to use 'em. Some of 'em is in workin' order. Could use someone who knows how to drive and fire a tank. Land a Goshin' Derek! You can?"

"Sure can. You should see what it does to one of those little pickups with the machine guns mounted on the bed. Here, I have pictures…" Derek projected pictures of the pickup that tried to get into the compound that he hit with an exploding shell from the tank on the wall.

"I can't imagine, Sonny. Had no idea you were military."

"I'm not, but I'm a fast learner. We also have lethal drones."

"How soon can you come back and join us?"

"That depends." I cautioned. "Let's talk it over with the Meyer brothers tomorrow, but I'm sure we can help. If we're going to use the ordinance that guy has, we might need a couple of days to get it ready to roll."

Finally got to bed sleeping wherever we could in a houseful of sleepers and only one bathroom.

When we arrived at Eunice the next morning, about twenty farmers had come with all manner of food, alive, butchered, fresh, frozen, packaged and in bulk. All the drivers and their loaders/unloaders all participated in the bargaining right off the backs of the trucks and trailers. In some cases, we were given live animals for little in return because farmers told us they couldn't maintain them without farmhands, so many now dead from the pandemic.

By 3 o'clock in the afternoon, the whole convoy was loaded and ready to leave. But I wanted to find out about what that military surplus guy had if we were going to come back in a week and use some of that equipment to fight the gangs in Fresno. Several of us unhooked from our trailers and followed Cy, Jr. to where the guy was–about 20 miles from Eunice.

When we arrived, Cyrus introduced us to Bob Holcomb, the owner of Bob's Surplus. Bob was in his 70s and said, "I'm too old to get in the fight, but I'm afraid of what's happening in Fresno, so whatever you do to get rid of those gangs is all right with me. And you can use my equipment to do it."

Derek and I were impressed with what Bob had. Not only did he have three fully operating tanks and two halftracks, but he also had some smaller, more mobile rocket launchers and the like, as well as some surplus munitions. It looked like all we would have to do would be to take a day or so to train our guys on how to drive and fire the equipment safely. There wasn't time for what it would really take to get them up to speed. But Cy and the other farmers wanted us in the fight and we were willing to help out.

We left early the next morning and by 3 pm were glad to be back at the port loaded with food and animals from the valley. After unloading, Mel, Der and I, along with others from the compound who went along, returned to the compound with more chickens, another cow and three more goats along with grain to feed them.

At supper, we were glad to hear that Stephanie was feeling much better and back helping Martha with both taking care of any medical needs as well as teaching young kids in the morning.

But while we were gone, our new sheriff had his hands full.

28

Hell Hath Fury

Thankfully, Morgan waited until morning to tell me. But then, he couldn't wait anymore and called… "Hello? Drake? This is Sheriff Singh. I've got terrible news."

It was only 5:34 am and I was a bit groggy… "Yes… What news is that?"

"They attacked last night after 2 in the morning…"

"That same Iranian gang from the tattoos on their dead."

"Oh no, what happened?"

"They arrived with a SWAT truck and four pickups. The video shows them stopping about 200 yards from our gate and then opening fire with all their guns. My cousin, Bertrand Singh, only 20, the only one on duty, was about to launch a drone when they ripped him apart with multiple bullets…." Morgan had to pause to catch his breath he was so emotional. "They wiped out all of the cameras, speakers and blew all of the booby-traps that Derek and Wondah had engineered."

"Did they kill anyone else?"

"They rammed the gate and came into the village firing in every direction. All the explosions wakened everyone, including me, and I was firing from the police station, others were firing from the Rambler and from the hotel. So far, we have 3 dead and about 15 wounded. We killed 5 of them and probably wounded some of the others that got away in the SWAT truck with 2 of their pickups that were still running. It's a real mess here."

Morgan shook his head in disgust. "We have to do something about it."

"Derek, Wondah and I will be there as soon as we can."

Mel and I dressed quickly and headed to Martha's for breakfast to tell the others. But Derek and Wondah arrived just as we did and she had what was left of the video showing the vehicles arriving and the first bursts of gunfire until all of the cameras blacked out.

We got to the ship just in time as the security committee convened. Immediately, we offered our assistance as they discussed what to do. The members were upset and angry. Some of them losing friends and relatives. Some of them even wounded. They wanted revenge, and I didn't blame them.

I told them, "This was obviously an attempt to get food from the market. It looks like they had information that helped them."

Sheriff Singh reported. "Yes, this morning, security on the ship found a cell phone in the possession of the three we have in custody. Undoubtedly, they had told their gang members that there was food to be had here, and that's why they raided. When they got to the market, most of the fish and seafood had been put in cold storage for the night and they got very little food just to get out with their lives while we fired upon them.

I offered my suggestion. "I think we should leave them be. They are starving and probably are dehydrated or sick from lack of clean water. Your response last night let them know that the village can defend itself."

Derek spoke up, "Wondah and I will get busy right away and beef up your defenses again. We will be sure to put cameras and sensors further away from the gate this time to give you early warning of anyone coming. We are really sorry for your loss, Sheriff Singh, and the others who have lost friends and relatives."

But the overwhelming vote from the committee was to seek revenge. To seek out and destroy all of the gangs still alive in the L.A. area. I tried to explain to them that there were ten major gangs and perhaps 200 or more others in the area. They were deeply entrenched in their ethnic communities. It would be very hard to wipe them out and history has proven that when a people are oppressed or attempted to be destroyed, they get stronger… Even gangs. I suggested a lesser strategy. Finally, I agreed to work with what the committee wanted to do if they changed their tactics.

"Okay, we have a tank that Derek drives expertly. We are supposed to go back to the Central Valley in a week to deal with gangs in Fresno, but we've got the time in between to scout for gang enclaves, find them and destroy their vehicles and firepower. But that's as far as we want to go."

Sheriff Singh agreed with me. "They tried to wipe out we Sikhs many times, but we prevailed, even making our way here to the United States and serving as law enforcement officers like me and long-haul truck drivers. I know where the L.A. Police Department has its SWAT vehicles. If any of them are still there, we can commandeer them for the village."

During the final vote, the committee agreed not to try to kill any gang members except in defense and not to destroy their homes, just their attack vehicles and armaments. We all agreed to start the next morning.

Sheriff Singh left a deputy in charge and returned to the compound with us to search the Internet and lay plans for what we would do in the coming days. What we were going to do would be a good training ground for what we would do in Fresno. Fortunately, many of the areas where there were gangs were destroyed by the flood. With our plans laid, we followed the tank to the police garage where the SWAT vehicles and equipment were stored.

We broke in a side door and discovered everything was still there. We secured that door again while we loaded up two armored SWAT trucks with robots, drones, armored suits, shields and ammunition. We had all that we would need to penetrate gang strongholds, hopefully without firing a shot but with enough firepower to shoot if we had to.

Early the next morning, Derek and Wondah arrived at the port with the tank where we filled it with diesel and they picked up a veteran from the Ukraine war who had recently arrived in the port and was very familiar with tanks. Nicholas Eubek was thirty-seven and had operated a captured Russian tank in that war. We then set out for our first target with Sheriff Singh, Mel, me and with three other recruits fully suited to go into our first gang neighborhood, closest to the port.

In Victoria Park there were the Manos on one side and Pit Grips on the other. We rolled up to the obvious entrance of the Manos and no one was stirring. Derek pushed through the gate where the vehicles were kept and nothing was moving there except a scrawny dog. Sheriff Singh used our loudspeaker but no one moved. We sent a team in of three and they came back out with a report that all they found were dead and rats eating them. We found considerable guns and ammunition that we took with us. Destroyed what we couldn't take. I thought, it can't be this easy.

The same proved true for the Pit Grips. But Grips were more organized and those that had been in the Park may have moved to join others. At least that's what we thought. We moved on to check in on the Centerview Pros. Nothing there to worry about either.

We moved on to and arrived at George Washington Carver Park. We began to hear bullets pinging off metal and knew we were being fired upon but we didn't know from where. Something that we would experience often in the coming days.

Near where the Carver Park Grips headquartered there were two pickups out front equipped with machine guns in their beds. Derek, with Nick's help, tore both of them in half with two well-placed exploding shells. A drone soon spotted what looked like a ten-year-old girl shooting from a rooftop.

When Morgan called out to her, the shooter turned out to be a 12-year-old, stunted by circumstance, boy. He gave up and told us that the older ones that survived the epidemic went on raids to get things so they could survive.

But almost every time they left, some of them didn't come back. He started crying and Melody had to console him. He had been shooting dogs, cats and rats to eat and finding water in gutters and cisterns that were drying up fast all around him.

The boy who told us he was Carlos Ramos, came with us and Melody gave him some treats to start regaining his strength. We were just about to leave the park when we heard a pickup coming with two guys with their hands up. We took a defensive stance with our guns on them when they pulled up near us and a man and a woman got out of the pickup and the ones in the bed turned out to be a 15-year-old girl and her 13-year-old sister. All of them were desperately in need of assistance. The last of the Compton Barrios gang.

We called ahead and told them to go to the port to get food. But because of their tattoos they wouldn't be accepted there and would have to continue to live here. The woman, Maria, a cousin to the man, Alfred, began to cry and pleaded with us. But what we had experienced had hardened everyone, and we told her that maybe, if they showed cooperation and traded with the port fairly, eventually they would be accepted. We asked Carlos if he wanted to go with them, but he adamantly clung to Melody and declared, "No!"

As we moved into Watts in the afternoon, I could feel the hairs on my neck stand up as the streets closed in on us the deeper into the side streets we got. A hundred years of poverty had walled in the streets and covered them with graffiti over graffiti making the place very dark even in the bright sunlight, trying to fade all of that paint on paint. The Grips were deeply ingrained here and it showed.

As the streets turned into alleys of disabled vehicles with only one lane we heard something coming up ahead and it was one of those pickups coming around a street corner and firing on the tank as if it had a chance. Derek fired one exploding shell into its radiator and the pickup and its occupants were no more. Then, I saw a Molotov cocktail come over the fence and land on the tank as I heard another pickup coming from behind with its machine gun firing into the SWAT truck behind us.

There was no time to think. Melody and the Sheriff were out the other side firing at where the Molotov cocktail had come from but it was a high concrete wall, so they came back and threw grenades over the wall as I grabbed a fire extinguisher and begin putting out the fire before Derek and his crew would be roasted alive inside.

Meanwhile, behind us, that SWAT crew opened up on the pickup behind only to find to their horror that there was only a teen driver and a teenage girl at the gun. Both, dead for nothing. We blasted a door open to that wall. And then, with some flash bangs over the wall ventured inside.

Back in the labyrinth of rooms, we found what was left of the mighty 112th Street Grips. Two followers who had been shot and were bleeding out beyond our help and a grizzled old, tattooed warrior confined to bed from wounds and malnourishment. The room stunk from the infected wound in his side crawling with maggots. He begged us to kill him. Morgan put him out of his misery.

The trappings of his leadership around him in the room, guns, drugs and bling did him no good anymore. What was really disgusting was that bones he had apparently been chewing on and thrown aside were from human arms and legs. In the kitchen behind, more grisly evidence of cannibalism was found. That's how far this group of survivors had come to eat. We couldn't wait to get out of there after making sure no one could use any of the ammunition and guns left there.

We had seen enough for one day, so decided to head back to the port so that Morgan, Derek and Wondah could begin to restore the entry to the port before nightfall. Burial at sea for those who died would be the next morning. Carlos told Melody and me much about what it was like growing up without a father and thinking he would join a gang because that was all that anyone in the neighborhood could do. The snacks he was eating seemed to energize him and he asked us a lot of questions.

After introducing him to the kids at Martha's, we met Ray. He and I decided to go on an evening hunt taking Carlos with us to relax. Carlos proved his skill with guns by taking two quail and one rabbit. Ray got a deer and I shot a wild pig. We had wild meat again for the compound and everybody pitched in with cleaning it when we arrived back for a late barbecue.

The next day after the funerals, we were at it again getting closer to gangs we knew near to our construction projects in South Los Angeles. Like before, while most neighborhoods were clearly marked as gang territory, they were quiet.

It wasn't until 2 o'clock when we came upon the Pillage Green and they gave us one hell of a firefight. It took everything we had to stop them from firing at us from both sides of the street. Including a couple of our lethal drones… one shot down… And the other getting the shooter. If we hadn't had our heavy SWAT equipment we all would've been wounded. I got hit a couple of times. The second time it knocked my wind out. And Mel told me later that she was hit once.

"Really scared me! To think I would've died!"

I could see the concern in her eyes. This wasn't a shooting game. It was life or death. It was war. We had to have superior firepower and protection. Thankfully, we did.

Once inside their compound, we found two women and five children cowering in hiding. Mel talked with them and found out they had been kidnapped by the gang and made to serve them both physically and sexually. Mel told us she wanted us to take them in. One bothered me because she was heavily tattooed like the guys and I suspected her. Morgan told me that he would put her in custody and find out from the others if she was telling the truth.

The next day, we were closer to home. Also finding most of the streets where the Santa Monica gangs hung out to be quiet. But about 11 o'clock as we approached the headquarters for the Sophia 13 we faced another vicious battle. But with rockets and the tank we were able to take out their vehicles that came at us and we eventually rounded up four gang members, one of them a woman, who gave up after they saw their comrades dying and they were losing.

Sheriff Singh's jail was near full and we had to get ready to go to the Central Valley, so we decided to stop our gang cleanup operation for now. So far, we had only touched on about 10% of the gang area of the city. But we estimated about 25% were wiped out by the flood, if not the occupants who may have moved.

Moving into new territory for those displaced by the flooding would be difficult if they came upon other gang territory with food as scarce as it was. We had not encountered any of the Blods yet. We knew them to be very prevalent on the east side. But they were far enough away from the port that we could relax a little bit after what we'd done during the week.

Of course, I knew there were surprises coming. I just didn't know from whom, what, or where.

29

Gangs of Fresno—Santa Ana Fires

It was October and the girls were starting to show baby bumps. Stephanie was pregnant again. Still not telling who the father was. Rain to fill all the cisterns was but a month away, hopefully with the weather changing the way it was. The hurricane had quelled the drought but the dead grass and brush remained, dried out again after two months without rain.

For the most part, the harvest in the Central Valley, what little there was salvageable from field crops, was over but there were winter crops, like alfalfa and winter wheat that would need to be planted and cultivated if there were ways of harvesting and processing them for cattle feed and flour locally. Dairy production and honeybee harvest also continued through the winter. The biggest problem was having enough hands to do the work.

Most of the land became fallow from lack of cultivation. The wild returned rapidly as all the small creatures multiplied that survived the flood.

Two days before we were to leave, I gave Morgan a call.

He answered, "Sheriff Singh, Port of Los Angeles."

"Hello Morgan. It's Drake. How'd you like to come along with us this weekend to the Central Valley?"

"I don't know. I'd like to go along, but I'm not sure about the security that Derek and Wondah have rebuilt and whether my staff are up to being alone now that my cousin was killed in the line of duty."

"No better way to break them in than to give them more responsibility. When I found my parents gone I had to grow up immediately and take charge of our neighborhood or it would have fallen apart and everyone would have died only because no one would take charge and do something."

"You're right, Drake. I need to let my staff take charge so they can learn to take responsibility and I can leave and learn from what's happening in the Central Valley… A place I've never been."

"You'll like it. Can we count on you leaving from the port at 8 am on Saturday?"

"Okay, you've convinced me. I'll put someone I think I can trust in charge and join you. Are you taking the SWAT vehicles?"

"Wouldn't take anything less, but we are leaving the tank here because we can get tanks and other military vehicles close to Fresno."

I was glad that he accepted and would learn from the trip like I knew I would and needed.

We left that morning with my truck and a trailer, two hydrogen fueled SWAT trucks and a refrigerator truck filled with fish and seafood.

The Santa Ana winds were picking up as we left the city and the acrid smell of brushfires was in the air. While the hurricane flooding had stemmed the drought in the Valley, the hillsides of surrounding mountains where water had run off very quickly remained bone dry and now burned unhindered by firefighting crews.

When we arrived at the Grapevine we could see fires burning on both sides of the road. There was a smoky haze in the air but no smoke yet crossing the road to affect our visibility or breathing to drive on through and into the Central Valley.

We turned off after the 99 bypass of Bakersfield to Mondale because I wanted to introduce Morgan to Sheriff Alex Crockett. I wanted to ask him to come along and learn how to deal with gangs if he could, too.

But when we pulled up to where the roadblock had been, it was no longer there. We drove on to the clearly marked Sheriff's Department and pulled up. No one greeted us.

But when Morgan, Nick, Der, Mel and I entered the office, we were greeted by Deputy Ramirez like our first arrival. He rose from his seat behind the reception desk and came over to meet us.

"Where's Sheriff Crockett?" I asked.

Ramirez got a sad look on his face, shook his head side to side and replied, "He's dead. What's left of this town is in mourning. We buried him and five townspeople this morning. You've come at a very sad time for us."

"What happened?"

"About thirty gang members from Bakersfield snuck in here in the middle of the night two days ago and started killing and robbing people until we all woke up and Alex led the charge. We killed fifteen of them before they left with nothing. But they left us with more sorrow after all we've been through already."

I motioned Morgan forward to introduce him. "This is Sheriff Morgan Singh, our newly elected sheriff of Los Angeles County and the only law we have in our port village."

"Pleased to meet you, Sheriff," the deputy said with a strange look on his face seeing a uniformed sheriff in front of him with a black beard, a black turban and an obvious dark skinned Asian face.

"And to meet you," looking at his nameplate, "Deputy Luis Ramirez. You're the first small town sheriff's department that I've visited. Mind if I look around a bit because we are building ours right now."

"I guess you know our situation. We usually have about seven people here every day. But today, it's just Gloria, our dispatcher, and me. Our whole department is only five people after what has happened. The others are sleeping after the night shift."

"I just lost my first deputy, my cousin, shot by gang members a week ago. I know what you mean." Morgan shook his head up and down and his expression showed that he understood.

Some townspeople were called out to accept the seafood we had for them and Morgan toured the office briefly before we had to continue our journey. I offered Luis to come along, but he, understandably, said, "I can't, in good conscience with the threat we are under."

As we got underway I didn't tell the others, but thought, when we have the opportunity and depending on how well we do in Fresno, we would come back and see what we could do in Bakersfield. Bakersfield was much bigger than Fresno and probably had many more gangs. But then, we were in the process of taking on the gangs of L.A. A nearly impossible task.

We arrived at Grandpa Ralph's just before 4 o'clock and he was waiting for us with a big party. The Meyer brothers and Gladys were there along with other farmers that would be going with us the next day to Fresno.

The party ended and we went to bed early knowing we would have to get up early to go to Bob's Surplus to gather equipment and plan our attack. Gramps insisted on going along even though I told him it would be dangerous. We joined the Meyers and several other farmers in a convoy as we arrived at Bob's.

Bob Holcomb came out to greet us. Shook my hand and acknowledged Gramps.

"Glad you're here too, Ralph. I've decided that I'm going to drive one of the tanks. Three nights ago, they came and tried to break in. I lost one of my friends who heard the shooting and came to help out as I was firing at them. It's a damn shame. We've already lost so many."

I responded, "It never seems to quit. We are all losing good people to these gangs, time to get rid of them like we are doing in Los Angeles."

"I don't envy your task, but I'm glad you're here."

After I introduced everyone all around, Bob showed us two Korean War era Abrams tanks that were fully operational and fully armed. Derek, Monsour and Vik would man one of the tanks and Bob, Morgan and Bob's tank mechanic, José, in the other. I would drive the lead SWAT with Mel by my side. Vik was especially valuable as a veteran of the Russian army before coming to the United States.

After Der showed his skills with Bob aboard we were ready to move out. We left all of the vehicles behind except the two tanks and the two SWAT vehicles with all of the SWAT occupants in body armor, including Gramps because we knew we would get hit. I knew we would have to make sure that the tanks were not compromised because they could be death traps if stopped by losing a tread or hit with a Molotov cocktail, rocket or bomb.

When we arrived at Fresno, Bob knew where he was going and drove immediately to the west side to the headquarters of the Central Valley Blods. There were two machine gun equipped pickups out front and he blew them both away with two well placed shots from his big gun.

A couple of guns opened up on us but were quickly dispatched by a rocket from Derek. Bob broke through the gate to their parking lot and firing ceased. We got out and entered the place. Found five women and kids but the only men left were the ones that were firing at us and they were all dead. Nearby were the North 7. Their yard was open and there wasn't anyone alive around. We moved on to where the Young Brown Militia had a compound. They fired at us from three places and we returned fire until they didn't anymore. When we went inside we found only one woman with a baby to her breast. All of the gang members were dead.

By that time, everyone in Fresno had heard the firing and word had reached the several Bullhead affiliated gangs running drugs for the cartels through Central California. They descended upon us from all sides and we got in a firefight with them.

Unfortunately, even with machine guns on their pickup beds, they were outgunned and we destroyed five vehicles and killed about fifteen gang members. Our guys were hit seven times but no one was seriously injured. They were able to shake it off with nothing but deep bruises and soreness.

I watched in horror when some of the wounded gang members came out from where they had been with their hands up only to be mowed down by fire from the farmers that were with us.

I yelled to Cy, Jr., "What's going on? I thought we had a deal we weren't going to kill anyone unless it was in self-defense?"

He shrugged his shoulders. "Those guys lost kids to the drugs here in high school. I know, Rich and I tried a little marijuana, but didn't go any further once Dad found out."

I understood. "Yeah, Derek and I had the same problem."

About that time, we heard sirens wailing and two cars pulled up. One had Sheriff painted prominently on its side. A man stepped out holding a gun on us with a bullhorn.

"What's going on here! What are you doing in this county! Who are you?"

Bob Holcomb stuck his head up out of the tank hatch he was driving and yelled, "Harve! You're a little late for the party. We have just been eliminating your gang and drug problem."

He continued for our benefit. "Guys, this is Deputy Harvey Ford of the Fresno County Sheriff's Department. How is Sheriff Grant doing?"

"He's dead for months now. I had to assume the job, unfortunately. Pandemic got him along with a lot of others. It looks like you guys have pretty much wiped out all the gangs we have here. They've been terrorizing us and the surrounding farms ever since the pandemic hit. Let's go check out where they all hang out and see if there are any stragglers." He looked really tired but happy.

We followed Harvey to several places and entered. We got shot at three times and ended it very quickly. As we moved about town, people came out on the street and started waving and cheering like we were a military parade. They were also grateful.

I thought, *If only Los Angeles could be cleaned up this easily.* I knew it wasn't to be.

Grateful, too, were the farmers among us, because they knew they could bring their food into town now without having to deal with the gangs anymore.

The Fresno folk wanted us to stay and celebrate but we declined, although some of the farmers said they would come back to town that night for the celebration.

We pulled into Bob's Surplus a little after 4 pm and were back at Gramps's place by 4:30. The Meyer brothers invited us and others over there and Gladys was so glad to have her boys back safe. She gave us a feast before heading back to Gramps's for the night.

The next morning, we left early and made it back into town with edges of flame on hillsides and black smoke in the air all around. Sometimes nearly blinding and choking us as we drove through thick smoke blowing across the road. Santa Anas whipping at our high-profile SWAT vehicles, sometimes threatening to throw them off the road.

As we passed Santa Monica on our way to the port, Topanga State Park behind our compound was burning and there were fires all over L.A. fanned by the strong winds.

I wondered; *will it ever end?* I didn't know and I didn't know what would be waiting when we got to the port.

30

Troubles Never Cease

Seeing the fires in the Topanga State Park from the 405 got me worried. I asked Mel to give Daphne a call. "Daph, this is Mel. We're on our way back and saw the fires. Are you okay?"

"I am now, but we're all exhausted." "Fire?"

"Yes, two nights ago."

"What happened?"

"We went to bed worried because the windmill went to idle because of the high winds and the solar panels were rattling trying to break loose. Haven't had winds like that since the hurricane. The smell of smoke in the air grew stronger every hour. My bedroom has those huge windows overlooking the reserve and about 2 am I sensed something that woke me up and it was an orange glow in the east that was surreal. It looked like a fireball and I could feel the heat already. I called Wondah and she sent out the alarm to everyone. By that time, embers were flying over us and we were all scrambling to put them out when they landed in the yards where there was dry grass. Fortunately, our goats, cows and the bull had eaten most of the dry grass.

"It was worse here, so some of the youngsters from the compound came to my rescue with buckets to put out the embers that were landing everywhere in the backyard using the water from the pool. I was using the garden hose to wet down the walls to keep the fire from coming over them. For a while, the servant quarters by the back gate was threatened but we all pitched in and got that fire out. If our buildings hadn't had tile clay roofs and stucco covered sides, we would have lost several buildings. As it was we only lost a couple of sheds and backyard burned areas that we put out when it was finally over about 8 o'clock in the morning."

Mel acknowledged. "I feel bad that we weren't there to help out, but I'm glad that you were able to handle it. We are seeing a lot of homes still burning. And many more burned-out."

Mel and I looked at each other after she hung up.

I shook my head and said. "If it weren't for those who stayed back, we might be coming home to nothing." It was a sobering thought.

Thankfully, the closer we got to the port, the less we saw burned-out or burning buildings. Unfortunately, when we passed the airport that we had seen many times going back and forth from the compound to the port, the terminal was burning.

Damn! I thought, *I always wanted to fly.*

Thinking about how Derek and I had flown aerial surveys for construction projects and even, once, flew out to visit Gramps because his dad flew small planes. I drove those thoughts from my mind to what we would find at the port. I hoped, nothing new.

The first place we stopped was to drop off Morgan and then head down to the fish market to drop off the live animals I had and the frozen meat that we had to Van and Quoc to distribute to the community.

They wanted us to stick around for a seafood and steak party, but we had to decline, needing to get back to the compound to see what damage the fire had caused.

But before we left, we got a call from Morgan.

"We've got a situation. You remember that heavily tattooed woman we took into our jail? Well, my guys fed the three women with metal utensils. After they ate, that woman took a fork and they didn't notice. In the middle of the night, while the other two were asleep, she apparently held them down with her hand over their mouths and stabbed them in the neck repeatedly, initiating arterial bleeding one at a time. When our guys checked them in the morning there was blood all over the place and all over her.

She claimed … "I had to kill them; they were from rival gangs. They would have killed me… Given the chance."

"That's terrible, Morgan. What do you suggest we do?"

"I want to convene the judicial committee as soon as possible to see what they will want to do with the woman. I don't want her in the jail anymore. I don't want to give the men we have here any ideas."

"I agree, Morgan. Let me know what the committee recommends."

The judicial committee met that afternoon and decided to use the woman as an example. After a brief trial with gruesome picture evidence placed before a jury, the defendant was declared guilty of first-degree murder and the judge ordered her execution.

The next day all of the prisoners from the jail and the jail on the ship were brought to the rear of the ship. Where a crowd of people from the community had also gathered.

Morgan had gathered a team of five volunteers for a firing squad all armed with AR-15s. They wore black masks and black long-sleeved hoodies like many criminals did for robberies so that they wouldn't be readily recognized.

With the woman placed on the rail at the rear of the ship and asked whether she wanted to wear a blindfold or not, she refused. At that point, the judge read the order to execute, and, when given the signal by Sheriff Morgan, all five of the firing squad opened up at the same time firing a burst of rounds, literally tearing her apart.

Just before they opened fire, she realized what was happening and screamed, "Noooo!" As bullets ripped her face off and the scream was halted before ever finishing. The bloody mess that was left fell to the deck.

The crowd watching gasped loudly at what they saw. Those detained with a front row seat could see what kind of justice they could expect if they were found to be a murderer. One reason why the justice committee wanted them to go back into the city and tell their gangs what they had seen. Five were released with food and water that very same day.

Morgan gave two of the male inmates rubber gloves and asked them to throw the woman's mangled body over the rail. An unceremonious burial at sea where the crabs and fishes were waiting for a meal. The blood would draw sharks. They could be seen in a feeding frenzy a few minutes later for those who looked.

Two days later, with more volunteers and eight SWAT vehicles we continued our sweep to clear the area of gangs within a 20-mile radius of the port and our compound.

As quickly as they came, the Santa Anas left and Ray, Derek, and I surveyed the hillsides behind the compound. It was remarkable how most of the wildlife seemed to have escaped and were actually foraging in the burned-out areas finding seeds and shoots that had been exposed by the fire along with dead bugs and worms that were easy to find and eat.

31

Thanksgiving Hell

Everywhere among the village inhabitants, pregnancies were seen with obvious baby bumps and ravenous appetites. Melody was growing more than the others but insisted on going on the raids. She wouldn't let me tell her that she was endangering both herself and the child.

Even Dani Steffensen, first mate of the Rambler, was pregnant. I didn't dare ask her who the father was. The ship had a strict rule against cohabitation among the crew, but all bets were off after the pandemic, obviously. Other members of the crew were showing baby bumps and the hotel was full of girls as young as fourteen showing pregnancy. The village would grow because it was the natural order of things no rules could control. We would need young people to repair the damage. I was happy to be a new father at 18. What a responsibility!

We continued our raids to gang locations into mid-November. Finally, removing all that we were aware of within 20 miles of the compound and port. It wasn't without casualties. We lost two volunteers who were killed when bullets from gang members penetrated their armor between their helmet and their vest. Twelve of us received wounds to arms, hands, legs and feet. I ended up with sore ribs after being hit twice. Some of us even got broken ribs if hit by a shotgun slug.

Throughout the campaign that lasted nearly a month with many skirmishes and some firefights, we rescued thirty-five women and children and even some men who were being held by the gangs either as hostages or slaves. And our jails swelled with six women and three men we couldn't trust kept for observation and interrogation until we could. They all were emaciated and begged for help.

Gathering up all the survivors with medical skills or training we staffed the village Medical Center to take our sick and wounded, relieving the infirmary on the Rambler that had been overloaded for so very long. Stragglers kept trickling in, some from the distant suburbs and as far as the San Fernando Valley in the north and Irvine in the south. They all told us that they had heard we had food, clean water and a safe place to live. The one from the south told us perilous tales of crossing the flood damaged area of the Los Angeles River basin. Freeway pillars about to fall down with gaping holes in the roadway.

Our two dead were given honorary funerals at sea for their service. They had friends that they had made during their brief time with us, but fortunately the two men were alone when they came to us originally with no family alive that they knew of. But we kept good records in the village offices of all of our villagers, in case relatives did show up looking for their kin.

As we opened up sections of the medical center, a survivor medical technician who had never done ultrasound scans took a look at the instruction book for the machine. She told the health and medical committee she thought she could operate the machine correctly, both from her training and understanding of the process.

She was assigned to the job. Soon, there was a long line of women wanting to have her look at their pregnancies. Mel wasn't the first, but she was one of the first to get an image and invited Flower and me to come along.

Melody's anxiety grew, as we approached the room after being called from the waiting room. "Dre, I hope everything's going to be okay. Remember that Martha put the stethoscope on me and heard something strange about the heartbeat?"

"Don't worry. You seem really healthy and you're growing faster than the others. Everything will be all right."

As we entered the door the medical technician, a Chinese lady named An, had Melody come over to the table. But first, she had her sit on the table while she checked her blood pressure and put a stethoscope on her.

An said, "You seem to have an abnormal heartbeat. I don't recall ever hearing this in training. It sounds like two heartbeats."

"Twins?" Melody was surprised. "Oh my God!" And Flower laughed. "Mommy, I hope I have a sister?"

"Let's take a look at the 3D ultrasound and AI evaluation." I was as excited as she was.

Melanie got on the table and the technician conducted the ultrasound with everyone watching on the big, curved screen overhead projecting the 3D image. The image was very clear of two fetuses with one normal and the other one breach in perfect symmetry with their arms and legs moving freely.

Flower was jumping up and down, Mel was crying, and I was assured that the future of the village was not in survivors, but in future generations from babies born like this–starting over. We asked and got a copy of the ultrasound sent to us so that we could show everyone the fantastic results.

In spite of the growing drought that had grown worse for several years, our backyard and rooftop gardens continued to provide the necessary vegetables and greens that we all needed for a balanced diet. Thanks to our irrigation systems that even provided water for fruit and nut trees, keeping them alive and producing for us.

The drought had been interrupted some years occasionally by downpours that created more landslides and flooding, but nothing like what the hurricane had back in July. We didn't know how much rain we would get when the rains came this fall or not. It was necessary to make sure we had a steady and reliable source of fresh water. I looked to the Los Angeles River for that. After the hurricane and flood, it had been flowing cleaner each week and it didn't dry up so far like it had before.

Ray found that the water at the Santa Monica pier had cleaned up enough so that fish were returning to shelter under its shadow and feed on what grew on the pilings. With his net, he was able to bring fresh fish to our tables every few days. With kids, he also gathered mussels from the pilings and clams from the sand. Shrimp were caught where creeks entered the Pacific. Something that hadn't been done in a long time in that area but was coming back already.

With all of that plenty and with children eager to return to normal, we had trick-or-treating in the compound over Halloween and we began to plan Thanksgiving celebrations. We were also thankful that even though so few of us survived, we were now thriving at the end of the first summer and really needed to celebrate.

At a town meeting, it was decided that each of the locations would have a Thanksgiving dinner at home. So, we planned a traditional Thanksgiving in the compound on Thursday, inviting others who wanted to come and join us.

On the following Saturday, the fish market planned a buffet of many dishes by all of the occupants in the village. It promised to be a wonderful affair with singing and dancing from live acts all day and into the evening as well as lots of Asian and other ethnic fish and seafood dishes.

And then on Sunday, everyone was invited to a formal champagne dinner in the Rambler's main dining room that would be fully waited on by Rambler staff and volunteers from the village, to wrap up the Thanksgiving weekend celebrations with movies in the theater after.

Two days before Thanksgiving it was a time of rut for California black tailed deer. When Ray, Der, Peter and I, along with a couple of other volunteer hunters, waited for the sun to come up, we found the deer had all gathered in a running creek bed about a quarter mile from the gate.

The bucks were all fueled with testosterone and more interested in the does that had also gathered to observe their champions and mate with them, than us. We snuck up on them easily upwind. We each picked out a buck and the five of us fired at the same time. We had fresh venison for our Thanksgiving dinner like the Pilgrims.

The next morning, we waited in a blind we made for the sun and a flock of tom turkeys that had also come to that stream to drink where we had observed them before. When they got within range, we opened up with shotguns and had five turkeys for our meal the next day. Along the way, we picked up some rabbits and quail as we returned to the compound with our kill to clean it.

On Thanksgiving, about 100 people joined us from the port and the Rambler, including Van and Quoc Nguyen, Captain Jens Jensen and his first mate, Dani Steffensen, and some of his mates, as well as Sheriff Morgan Singh, leaving the security of the port in the hands of newly trained deputies and guards.

To say everyone had a good time and went home with regrets for overeating would be an understatement. After it was all over, Mel and I went for a walk to try to get rid of all the excess and prepare for the feast to follow on Saturday. Nobody ate anything on Friday knowing what was to come.

Saturday came too soon and we left the compound to our electronics and booby-traps so that all of us could go to the fish market for the huge buffet that was available there. That party lasted well into the night and there were fireworks over the water everyone enjoyed, especially the children.

Once again, Sunday came too early. We fasted until about 4 o'clock when we closed the compound again and all of us went down to the ship to the main dining room. There, we were treated to anything on the menu, free-flowing champagne and exquisite desserts to go with the rich coffee and after dinner drinks.

But, we were in the middle of our main course at the captain's table while being serenaded by an orchestra of talented musicians gathered from survivors when we heard "popping" from off the ship and telephones began ringing.

I looked at Morgan as he answered his and I swear that his face turned white as he yelled at me and others, "They're breaching the gate! We've got to get going…!"

The deputies with him all jumped into action and ran for the dining room entrance. Mel and I were close behind. But we needed guns and it took a while for Captain Jensen to get to where the guns were stored and open it so that we could all get armed and loaded.

The deputies were already engaging the marauders with their pistols from the ship's railings but were no match for the AR-15s shooting from below. Most of those picking up weapons joined them at the rails shooting down with more firepower.

In the meantime, the intruders had driven down to the fish market and were helping themselves to food and throwing it into their pickups. If anyone fired at them from the hotel, they fired back. But worse, the two guards at the entrance to the ramp to the Rambler were soon killed and the marauders got into the lower deck crew passageways to the kitchens above and other parts of the ship.

All of the elderly, women, and children were escorted to the top floors and helped to hide in locked state rooms until it was clear to come out. The fear and panic as they rushed upstairs made a wave of desperate humanity with some stumbling and falling, screaming. Some of the elderly had to take the elevators and they were jammed. The crew locked the elevators as soon as the last elderly were safe for the moment to keep the attackers from using them.

With Captain Jensen's help, we fanned out with AR-15 automatic rifles and headed down all of the stairs, including the staff stairs that were very narrow.

We had to fight our way down as they came up. The sheriff and two deputies took the one main staircase. Mel and I, backed by some others, took the other main staircase. Fortunately, from our battles earlier, we knew how they would behave, but we were without our armor and no longer bulletproof. I feared for Mel and the babies and made her stay behind me as a shield.

As bursts of automatic weapons were heard throughout the ship, we watched for the slightest movement below as we descended slowly to make sure we had a deadly shot before pulling the trigger. We knew the attackers would fire wildly and if we stayed low they would miss us.

Before we got to the ramp on Deck 4, we were stepping over bodies of those we had shot. It was gruesome. Fortunately, some of the crew of the ship had brought bazookas to the rail and fired upon all of the pickups, destroying them and anyone still there, in or near them.

So those escaping our firing on them did not have their vehicles and were fired on from the rails of the ship and the hotel. When we got to the ramp where the two original guards lay dead and mutilated, we heard firing down the Deck 4 hallways, so Mel and I moved down the right one that curved gently with the ship's hull toward the bow and the sheriff and his deputies down the left one to the rear. These hallways were dangerous because any bullets fired would ricochet back down the hall. And could even reach someone around the curve a long distance away.

Fortunately, there was no one in that hall, although we heard firing behind us where Sheriff Morgan was. We came up behind two marauders firing up the crew stairs unaware of our coming and we quickly ended their attack.

Suddenly, I realized that I had been grazed because blood was flowing onto my right shoulder and a pain in my side turned out to be a bullet that went straight through. Everything got dark and the last thing I saw was Mel reaching for me as I fell.

❧⊱⊰❧

32

Christmas Approaches Without Rain

I woke up groggy and realized that my hands were being held. On the right, I saw Mel holding my right hand and on the other side Daph, holding my left. I was in the Rambler infirmary from my surroundings and was about to ask what happened when…

Mel spoke for me. "We thought you were a goner. You were bleeding so badly. A bullet ricocheted from behind and struck you just above and behind your right ear. The force of it gave you a concussion and you were bleeding profusely from the three-inch gash the spinning bullet gouged in your head. And then, you were bleeding both front and back from your abdomen where a bullet went through.

"The crew members who were fighting the guys at the base of the stairs that we shot, came down and saw me trying to hold you up as you fell. They ripped off their white shirts they had been wearing as waiters a short while before to make bandages. And then, all four of us carried you to the stairs and up one deck here to the infirmary."

I wanted to know. "How long have I been out?" I struggled to whisper through my brain fog.

"Three days." Daph said. "I was coming down the stairs with some of our people who had been hiding on the 16th deck with me when I saw you being carried down the hall on Deck 5 and had to help. They were setting up a triage and you were one of the lucky ones that got this bed. Others had to lie on the floor until they were moved to empty crew rooms nearby. It was a lot of confusion."

"Then what happened?" I was eager to find out and my voice was stronger.

Mel continued. "We couldn't get a pulse on you and your blood pressure was nonexistent. The medical assistant here quickly checked our blood types and hooked us up to giving blood to you as well as giving you an IV feed with a saline solution. They were totally out of plasma. We all crossed our fingers."

Daphne continued. "Both of us gave all the blood we could, considering we were pregnant and did not want to deprive our babies. There were others here needing blood, too, but we insisted on our blood going to you, hoping to save you from the state you were in. After getting your transfusion, you were on a heart and lung breathing machine used on the ship for emergencies when passengers had heart attacks. As soon as your vitals finally stabilized and you were sleeping, we had to give the machine up for others."

"Sleep some more, now, you need rest." Mel patted my hand and both of them kissed me on both cheeks. I dozed off.

Five hours later, I was awake again and wanted to get up. The girls were gone and the guy tending to the three of us in the room told me, "You can't get up yet. You need more blood."

I told him, "You can go shove your blood, you know where. I am leaving." I got up off the bed and immediately collapsed to the floor.

Down there for a minute, that lightheadedness disappeared. This time, I got up on one knee with my right hand on the bed and then gradually stood up while making sure I had my left hand reach out for the doorframe, and then, the hall walls. I took a few slow steps, until my rhythm of walking took me to the elevator and I took it down one floor to the ramp that was surprisingly clean except for bullet holes that had already been filled with spackling compound to be repainted.

The bright sunlight struck me as I teetered on the ramp but kept walking all the way to the torn up village and sheriff's office looking like it needed a frontal renovation. There, I found Morgan working on restoring monitors with one arm in a sling from a bullet he took in the shoulder.

I was starting to feel a bit dizzy again, so I sat down and he quickly got me a sports drink that went down well despite my parched lips and made me feel a bit better.

The first thing you said to me after, "Hi Dre," was, "I'm sorry, but I'm afraid that bullet that grazed your head was mine. I missed a bad guy on the other end of the hall."

"That's okay, Morgan, I've been so lucky so far. These are my first battle wounds. They probably won't be the last." We both chuckled in agreement.

I asked Morgan, "Any answers as to why they came in and who they were?"

"The only deputy here who survived said they took in and temporarily jailed a couple of Blods from Pasadena. Following procedure, they let them go the day before Thanksgiving with food and water. Checking all of these bodies they all have markings of Blods."

"Our generosity backfired on us?"

"I'm afraid so. Unless we can get it on the Internet, executing the wounded we have here… There are only three… Won't deter them. But maybe, just maybe, that one truck and ten of them we estimate that got away, have realized we mean business and won't come killing and looting again."

"I'll bet on that. Have you got a phone I can use? I've got to call and get someone to come and get me so that I can see how things are at home."

"They're just fine and from the looks of you, you do need more rest and iron rich food… You're still very pale."

I dozed off on a bench until Ray came to pick me up, and then, I slept the whole way to the compound. When I got there, Martha gave me nourishing soup and I went to bed again for two more days until I felt better and good enough for a swim with Mel when the midday sun warmed up the pool in the afternoon before another cool clear night with no rain.

By December 10th, I was back alternating my days working with Der on construction projects at the village to repair the damage caused by the attack on Thanksgiving and attending to what was needed to keep our compound in fresh food.

Each day, I worried more as our cisterns started to run out. Eventually, the utility committee formed a crew to drive milk and fire trucks to several reservoirs to get water. Each convoy was escorted by a SWAT security team, but there were no attacks. All was peaceful.

Martha, Wondah and Steph incorporated some of the Christmas stories into their studies to the delight of the children. Each child was asked to create a list of what they would like for Christmas. On the 20th, we went shopping. While most of the major stores had been looted, toys had been overlooked in some and the rest could be found in the homes if one could stomach going into a home and finding long decomposed bodies as we looked through closets and places where the things on our list might be.

In our search to find some fitting clothes for Flower as well as dolls and electronic gadgets she liked; Mel started to have labor pains. They were spaced like she remembered from Flower, telling me…

"I'm sorry, Dre, but we have to go. I'm going to have these two rascals that have been beating up on me the last few days."

I wasn't sorry. "Okay, let's get to the truck. Would you like to go home or to the Med Center?"

"As much as I would like to have them at home, I think it best that we go to the hospital where they have everything in case we have any problems."

It wasn't long before we reached the hospital and got to the maternity ward. It had been busy already, with seven recent births, two of which were premature and in incubators. We settled into a private room and waited.

Ten hours later, Melody's contractions had reached the point where she was in great pain and needed to deliver. I called the only baby doctor we had there, a young Chinese woman gynecologist.

She asked, "Do you want to have an epidural?"

Melody just shook her head, "No," and clinched her teeth in pain.

Ann Ma, from her nameplate, began trying to help Melody manually in her struggle to give birth. She announced, "One of the babies is a breach, but I think I can maneuver the one whose head is in the right direction and pull him out."

I doubted that Melody heard her as she struggled to hold back her screams. and winced when I saw how far the doctor had her arms inside trying to get one of the babies to come out. Finally, after what seemed like minutes of struggle, he did, a loud boy with distinct African American features who weighed a whopping 7.1 lbs. and had a very healthy yell.

But it wasn't over. Dr. Ma still had to turn the other baby around so that it could come out. This one had my features smeared with red blood and also had a healthy yell. But his weight of 6.9 lbs. was a bit shy of his older brother. I was overjoyed. I was a father, and I was only nineteen!

Melody finally was relaxed after that ordeal and smiled broadly as Dr. Ma brought each baby to her arms, amazed at her accomplishment.

I immediately got on the phone and called Derek. He answered… "Der, you won't believe this but you're a father!"

"What?…What are you saying?"

"I'm saying that you are a father and so am I. Mel just gave birth to twins. A black boy and a white boy. Yours is biggest and the oldest. So, you beat me at the punch. You had better get down here and greet your son."

"My son? Where?"

"The Med Center, the maternity ward we restored to function."

"I'll be right there. I'm not far away, working on the village office building."

೪೫ಬಿ೧೫

33

Christmas Arrives

Derek arrived within ten minutes and was totally surprised to see a little boy, Mel's first born and his, as well. It hit him like a ton of bricks.

"Can't believe it… Can't believe it…!" Derek exclaimed as Melody handed his son to him to hold and view. The child's features, definitely telling him it was his son without a doubt.

"That's another thing you beat me with, Der…" I chuckled and gave him a high five with his free hand. "But I came in a close second." We all laughed.

"I guess I'll have to start learning how to be a father rather than all this electronics stuff that Wondah's teaching me." Looking resigned.

"You and me both. At least Mel is experienced with these things."

Smiling, "I sure am, and the best thing you two can do during these early months is stay out of the way except at night when you can help with bottle feeding and diapering."

That didn't sound too good. I knew we would have two rug rats to deal with, trying to get into everything and learn construction way before their time.

Two days later, Mel and our sons came back to the compound where she decided to set up a nursery for all of the young mothers to share so that most could work the projects during the day.

The next day, Wondah started having labor pains and we rushed her to the medical center from the nursery. She had a beautiful baby girl that told Derek he was a father again.

Der gushed upon holding his first daughter whom they christened Wonder. "I hope she's as smart as you are, baby."

Wondah laughed. "We'll see, we'll see… honey." She reached for his hand and her eyes misted over from happiness.

The next few days were filled with making sure that the children, both at the compound and at the port, were entertained and gifted so that they didn't feel so lost for having lost parents and brothers and sisters in the pandemic.

And there were new arrivals. On the 20th, Selma Lopez gave birth to a boy that she christened Hector, Jr. named after her father. Like Stephanie, she didn't reveal who the real father was.

She took the boy in at the nursery so that Selma could continue to work with her father every day on the many sheet rock jobs there were both at the compound and the port after the massacre.

On the 23rd, Frances Hastings gave birth after a difficult labor that lasted four days until she had a cesarean to remove the girl. She admitted that Viktor Sarnoff had eased her pain for losing her husband in the pandemic and that he was the father.

Ironically, a day later Viktoria Sarnoff, Viktor's wife, had a boy. Since Frances was forty and Viktoria was forty-one, both pregnancies were a surprise but welcomed with full-term and healthy babies.

On the 27th, Sean Nguyen, an unmarried sister of Van's, surprised both Van and Quoc with a boy from a brief affair with her fifteen-year-old nephew, Quoc.

Throughout the Christmas holidays leading up and through the New Year 2033, the village birthed thirty-two new inhabitants. Three sets of twins, three stillbirths, and two, too young, mothers died.

The first post pandemic generation would become part of the New World within twenty years and hopefully, change it for the better.

Remembering what happened at Thanksgiving, the compound, the Rambler, and the port held low-key Christmas celebrations with carolers for the sick and aging, and gift-giving for the children. Security was at an all- time high and no incidents were reported, except Sheriff Morgan put two rowdy fishermen in jail who got drunk and started fighting.

There were fireworks at midnight from the Rambler and hotel, but once again, security was very high. What we had to celebrate was all the people that were saved from dying of thirst or starvation in a city that was filled with goods to plunder, but very soon lacked fresh water and healthy food to eat.

Derek and I, along with all of the members of our small compound community, like Wondah, Martha, Melody and Daphne, were very proud of our contribution to surviving to a time when the rains would come again to the Los Angeles basin.

Unfortunately, our New Year's celebration was dampened a bit by the lack of rain.

But on January 3, as we drove down to the Rambler to welcome Dani's first birth, the sky opened up.

Earlier that day, Dani Steffensen had twins, a boy and a girl. The father was none other than the captain of the Rambler, Jens Jensen. While the boy looked just like Jens's baby pictures, the girl had other features.

Jens asked her, feeling a bit guilty with a wife and two daughters back home that he had lost touch with, in Denmark, "Was there someone else beside me?"

Feeling pressured, Dani confessed. "One night, I complimented our chef, Carlos Rodriguez, about his peach cobbler. He invited me into the kitchen and into a storeroom where we both got carried away. Afterword, he told me not to tell his wife who works in the laundry. And I promised not to."

"Okay, I promise to provide for them both. And if my wife and daughters are gone, I promise to marry you."

He bent down and kissed her in front of us. We all promised not to tell anyone. Humbled by what the pandemic had wrought.

By the time we returned, the streets were flooded and we had great difficulty getting back to the compound for three days. More roads were washed out. I could see a huge effort with too few hands to try to rebuild the roads and to restore infrastructure like the water system that was both contaminated and broken in so many places.

꧁❧☙꧂

34

When It Rains It Pours

Rain like this was to be expected. The United States Congress finally got its act together in 2027 and passed the historic War on Climate Change bill. The law changed everything as far as the direction the government was taking towards eliminating fossil fuels altogether with a combination of incentives and rebates. Also, allowing business and individual taxpayers to finally be able to literally get off the grid.

Most didn't and retained their grid connection to the various electric providers and producers, who had to all be 100% carbon free except for their equipment manufacture requiring some fossil fuels to be processed and made for the effort.

As a result, by the New Year 2033, about 80% of the homes and businesses in the greater Los Angeles area had solar power equivalent to daily usage. With about 60% having battery storage of one kind or another for up to three days without the sun. Making our job easier when renovating property for the village to grow.

Only about 40% of the homes and businesses had wind power, largely because of the danger involved even though the installations were usually on rooftops away from all but occasional workmen. Both solar arrays and windmills were subject to damage from lightning, ice and the occasional windstorm that had become much more severe, like the hurricane of mid-summer 2032.

When United States finally followed the rest of the world in 2027, it was already too late to stop global warming and the consequences to the climate. Megatons of methane had been released from the melting permafrost, warming oceans of the polar regions. A condition that only a drastic reduction in the using population, like the pandemic of 2032, created any hope that humankind and all life on the planet would make it to the year 2100.

Our fathers and the Hutchins and Jones Construction Company had shifted gears from making earthquake tolerant high-rise energy consuming buildings to massive solar, wind and water retention projects all over the L.A. area even before 2020. Derek and I were masters at this kind of construction and recycling demolished construction materials; we had made our compound and the port nearly completely off the grid after the pandemic and never stopped.

So, drought like we had the summer before stretching well the beyond normal November rains had become the new normal during the latter 20th and the earlier 21st century. Like the hurricane and the flood aftermath, as well as, the January flooding now. We had to be prepared for all kinds of weather never experienced before. And come up with ways to stop erosion and landslides.

The urgent need was for roads to be maintained while flooding continually eroded them. But all we could do during this rainy weather was haul gravel to fill the collapsed areas of the streets and clean debris out of storm inlets that were dammed by it. Under the current conditions, pouring of concrete and proper repair would have to wait for warmer, sunny days to come.

But the shortest way between the compound and the port had to be kept open because our babies and their mothers needed access to the medical center and our daily work required a lot of commuting back-and-forth. Especially for town meetings every Friday night.

It took us two weeks to get the roads open to the port with a combination of detours and with makeshift repairs. But those repairs had to be constantly maintained while it continued to rain.

The good news was that all of our catchment systems had full cisterns by January 10. But we were beginning to think that we needed to more than double that capacity if we were going to make it through the droughts to come. More and more, I thought about bringing water from the Los Angeles River, but those thoughts had to be postponed dealing with what was currently demanded.

Derek and I had a hard time setting schedules with so much to be done. Fortunately, we gained volunteers to do the work almost every day requiring them to be taught how to do things they didn't have experienced skills in.

More good news was how well the space-based, solar powered, and AI- run satellite Internet grid worked and continued to provide G6 connectivity to everywhere in the world. While many business websites disappeared, many stayed open, run by AI for the foreseeable future, allowing searches for almost anything to continue. Even defunct local businesses that could be scavenged or renovated.

Email spam and scams nearly disappeared and there were no more irritating software updates or requests for monthly payments for services no longer rendered. Without updates, software and hardware lasted much longer for users. Wondah estimated that there was enough in stores that weren't looted, homes with no occupants but the dead, and warehouses to last the village until the end of the century.

The same was true of most consumer items. We formed a recycling committee to determine what to do and how to keep recycled demolition materials and even consumer items that wore out or were broken. Regulations had prevented putting anything in the sewers except biodegradable materials like sewage.

Plastics and electronics were warehoused for the possibility of future recycling. Animal dung was gathered and used for fertilizer along with bones and unused parts from both animal and fish processing. Plant and vegetable waste for cooking processing was routed to compost bins that we constructed for every garden in the entire compound and the village. A natural way to make fertilizer and maintain garden soil health.

Similarly, everywhere we processed meat, like the Santa Monica pier and the fish market, we built smoking sheds from salvaged lumber and created smoke with salvaged wood that littered the beaches. We scavenged drying appliances, radiating appliances and ways of canning fruit for storing harvested garden seasonal abundance.

Throughout the village, individuals took upon themselves to create small businesses and even commandeer some of the nearby shopping centers to set up those businesses like hair salons, taverns, restaurants, martial arts studios, and the like. Restoring the monetary system for these businesses seemed paramount.

When the community met the first Friday in January, Mayor Roberts had on the agenda the establishment of a fire department at the defunct port fire department where much of the equipment had been vandalized. Some former volunteer firefighters and former Fire Chief, Eric LaRosa, thirty-three, of the Torrance, Los Angeles Fire Department #1 volunteered to start up his department again and get the Harbor Department #40 working on the water right at the port.

Also on the agenda was the establishment of a money system. Everyone agreed to sticking to the United States way of doing things, financially. Locally, there was a credit union and branch bank.

Fortunately, in the village was one bank vice president of the Golden State Bank & Trust, Dorothy Chung, 47, and two employees of a credit union, one manager, Elsie Cook, and a cashier Henry Hines. They were already part of the financial committee. They were charged with reopening the Seafarers Federal Credit Union to serve the financial needs of the community. It was agreed to continue bartering, but also to allow the use of cash and checks, for now, to do financial dealings.

The financial committee decided they would oversee the operation and make corrections in the rules as things progressed. It was not known if major national banks or even brokerages, were still in business. Some of their websites still operated. Wondah was charged with finding out if any of them were still doing business. I doubted it.

It was agreed that any wealth that the community gathered as a whole, either by salvaging, scavenging or by earning, would be shared equally among the citizens of the village. That included treasure that could be located, but not hoarded, by individuals.

It was a difficult task to oversee, but necessary if the village was to grow economically and to join the rest of the United States in commerce again. More connections would be made with other parts of the United States and the world that was, hopefully, recovering. Some would be useful for us for regional trade.

Meanwhile, all of our water catchment systems were overflowing and there was much need for more wind turbines because the dark skies made power production with solar panels sketchy.

Still, the thought of a safe and stable water and sewer system stayed on my mind. How would I accomplish it along with all the other renovation and restoration projects that our firm would have to take on in the coming months, rain or shine, I didn't know?

∾₧₧∾

35

A Dismal, Down Time

By the time February came around, even in days of repairing roads and working inside on renovations and restorations of businesses and homes, the constant rain and dreary weather was taking its toll.

Still, they came trickling in. Those who had found out in various ways that we were prospering. So many having to resort to drastic means, too unspeakable for some to talk about, like cannibalism. Necessary in order to survive the long drought with dirty water and little or nothing but canned food to survive on if they could find it.

I woke up one night and found that Mel was not in my bed. She wasn't with the twins either, they were sleeping quietly. I heard her crying in the bathroom.

I stuck my head through the door and asked, "What's wrong, Mel?"

She answered, "I don't know. I can't sleep and it isn't the boys. I just don't feel well. Everything is getting to me." She started crying again.

I tried to console her, but she would have none of it.

Mel was suffering from postpartum syndrome that no amount of my encouragement could relieve. Women seemed to be taking it harder than men. Many of them staying at home doing menial tasks while their men went to work with us. Or, in the case of the fishermen, heading out into the storms that came every few days, not knowing whether their men would return with fish or at all. The weather was that bad and feelings were so on edge.

At a town meeting a mental health committee was formed by calling on all of those who had been counselors, therapists or otherwise engaged in helping people mentally, to get together. Charged by Mayor Roberts with coming up with ways of helping those suffering from post-pandemic loss or just the dreariness of rain without sunshine day after day.

To make matters worse, in our compound our solar panels were useless without sunshine. With only the power from our windmills, about one half of what we needed to run our houses, we had to cut back on electricity use and light wood fires in our fireplaces on cold nights to help warm our houses. Sometimes we slept in front of the fireplace.

To meet the growing demand for counseling, the mental health committee created groups for group therapy sessions where everyone could share their experiences with others of a similar problem and get encouragement on how to leave those bad memories behind for a better life ahead. Group membership was made voluntary, but everyone suffering was encouraged to attend.

Melody began attending a group and it seemed to help when we talked at night after she returned and we had the twins with us overnight. Daphne soon joined the group with Melody because she was having trouble coping with her baby's needs and the lack of sunshine for so long.

Soon, Stephanie joined, too. It put a strain on Martha, but the babies were in the nursery and all she had to deal with was teaching the kids in her small school where outdoor activities were hampered by all the rain.

And then, I got a call from Gramps.

"Drake, is that you? My reception ain't so good."

"I see you Gramps. What's going on?"

"I'm staying at the Meyer's place again. The rain just won't quit and the entire valley is flooding again. I never, never, Sonny, have seen anything like it."

I could see him shaking his face as his image broke up and came back like a bad connection.

"I guess that means we won't be able to come there again until everything dries out in the spring."

"That's what I'm calling about. If this keeps up, we won't be able to grow anything or even have anything of value to trade with you. A damn shame!"

"We knew it was coming for a long time. Maybe when we get there, we can raise your house and provide you with raised greenhouses so food can be produced all year round. Maybe even raise the barn floor for your animals."

"Those are great ideas. But this old guy can't do any of them without your help. I have to leave now… Just saying…"

"You hang in there, like you always have. We'll be there before you know it with some solutions for you and the other farmers. After all, that's what the Hutchins family is famous for… Rolling with the punches… Right?"

"If you say so, Drake, I'm a believer, but this old body of mine won't be able to do much to make it happen."

"Before I leave the phone, Melody had twin boys. They are your great-grandchildren and will be the ones who make things right. I'll see to it." I flash sent him some pictures of them.

"Well, Sonny, it sure looks like a good thing can come out of a bad situation." He was grinning mischievously in his flickering image like a ghost coming and going.

We said our goodbyes and I had to tell Mel. I didn't want to give her any more bad news to contemplate. So, I just told her that I talked to Gramps, and he was pleased to see the twins and would look for us to come in the spring when it dried out. I will admit I lied a bit, but I didn't want to upset her any more than she was. She and so many others needed to heal until that California sun came back again.

All the rain was causing a lot of mudslides and washed out streets. All of the properties on our side of the street were losing a little bit on the back of the property overlooking the Pacific; our reason for being here in the first place. The soft ground was heavily soaked with water, even though most of what fell ran off and down the cliff behind. Just another worry that nagged me.

Each day, we repaired the roads with gravel and were often able to re-store some really nice house that we picked out in a neighborhood close to the port and begin to go to work. Inside, we cleared out any bodies we found and buried them in the backyard. Usually, we could find their names and ages on paperwork in the house. Sometimes on computers and cell phones left behind.

We made little concrete monuments with bronze plaques commem-orating where they were buried, but the primary reason for burying them there was to allow their bodies to replenish the soil like for thousands of years before we segregated them into cemeteries and mausoleums.

We removed all the junk from the house and kept what was usable or beautiful. Personal information and DNA samples of the previous owners was carefully kept and stored in case there was an inquiry from family. We completely cleaned out and fumigated any creatures that had started to take over in the short time since the occupants died.

Every house we got ready for reoccupation was already called for by someone tired of living in the hotel or the ship and wanted a place of their own again. The deeds they were granted were contingent upon the possible return of the occupants and/or family from other parts of the country or world. Where legal proceedings would determine who had right to the property.

And there were those who wished to return to their previous properties in the port area. In some of those cases, they wished to move into a better house on their street or acquire the next-door neighbor's houses to make their property and their houses bigger. With so much vacant property going unclaimed, a lot was possible and we were doing it, one project at a time, with multiple crews doing the work.

For those who wished to move back to their homes in neighborhoods far from the port, Derek and I told them we couldn't help them now. And we didn't know when we could. To have them live outside of the security of the growing village and its facilities would be dangerous and unhealthy.

We had some very wealthy people who wished to return to their retreats in the Hollywood Hills or other wealthy enclaves like the downtown high- rises and stylish lofts. Of course, anyone was free to go back to their homes, but we couldn't guarantee their safety or that they would be able to sustain themselves.

With the way the weather had been, our greatest obstacle was the deterioration of the roads and utility infrastructure. The heavy rains had brought down many hillsides across roads all over town. We weren't ready to clear those slides and rebuild those roads anytime soon.

So, each day, Der and I headed out to various projects and got people working on them, taking their minds off what they had lost in favor of what they could make of their new lives without those missing family and friends that supported them before but no longer could.

സ❦ᘏᑤ❦ᖾ

36

Flying High

The morning of February 28, 2033, I took a look at the list of re-modeling work and saw something unusual. Something like we hadn't done before. I gave the requester, Harlan Cole, a call.

"Hello, Harlan, this is Drake Hutchins calling about your project. Yours is quite unusual. Just what is it you want to do?"

"Hi, Drake, I guess we haven't met. I grew up in Hawthorne and stuck it out when my parents and brother died in the pandemic through all of last summer until October when I came to the ship and they took me in."

"We have similar stories. But I see another name on your application for your project."

"That's Crystal Han, the daughter of a Chinese importer here in LA, also from Hawthorne. We dated in high school and were surprised to find each other on the ship. She's 20 and I'm 22. We had the captain marry us on December 15th. We need to have some babies and that's why we want to move to the airport, LAX."

I was amused. "You want to move to the Los Angeles International Airport? Are you kidding me?"

"No, I'm not. My father was an aircraft mechanic who worked for GMG Studios and maintained their fleet of aircraft. We want to turn the 2nd floor VIP lounge of the GMG hanger into our home. We will need a water catchment system and more electricity so that we can live there, maintain the airplanes and fly them."

I was no longer amused, I was intrigued. "You fly planes?"

"Every spare moment I had when not in school. I worked with my dad on the airplanes. And, as soon as I was able, I took lessons and earned my private pilot's license at sixteen and my commercial license at eight-een."

"I see that you could be very useful to the village and to me. I need to get a better handle on the condition of the city these days. Taking pictures from the air is the only way to do that. You could be a big help."

"Yes, we can help each other. When can you start?"

"Since you are at the top of the list right now, can you be at the site at 9 am today to survey what we are going to do?"

"Yes, my wife and I should be able to catch one of the village's cabs to Building 37 at LAX. And meet you there."

"Okay, Derek, my partner and I, will meet you at Building 37 in two hours."

Mel had to go to a counseling circle, so I gave Der a call. When he heard what we were going to do, he dropped everything he was going to do that day and joined me. We took my service truck to the airport. The first time either of us had been to the airport since the pandemic.

We were somewhat familiar with the private area of LAX because our fathers often rented planes to fly out of there for various construction projects. Even hired helicopters to deliver materials to some difficult places to get materials into by truck.

I was always fascinated with the airport and flying but only got to ride along a few times on private jets and smaller, propeller aircraft flown by high school friends, contractors and even occasionally, on vacations. Thinking that I might fly myself someday because I was already hang-gliding off the cliffs and finding it very enjoyable.

As we drove in on the road leading to the main terminal, there were some abandoned vehicles, but the whole place was eerily quiet, unlike it was during previous visits, bustling night and day.

As we drove past the buildings, some appeared to be vandalized, but when we arrived at our destination the building looked untouched except for a door open that we drove up to and parked.

We entered the building. It had two parts: a huge hangar filled with a number of planes, large and small, and at least one helicopter from what I could see and a VIP area on the 2nd floor to our right.

I yelled upstairs. "Is anyone there!"

We got an instant reply. "Yes, it's me, Harlan and my wife Crystal. Just come on up the stairs. Crystal was a design student at UCLA. She's helping me work up the layout that we'll want to do to convert the VIP lounge into living quarters for us and our kids to come."

We reached the lavish 2nd floor lounge and it was very modern and beautifully appointed. Harlan and Crystal came over to greet us at the top of the stairs.

Harlan shook my hand and then introduced his wife, Crystal, to me. I held out my hand to her and was struck by her beauty and the way her hand embraced mine. I could see in her eyes that she seemed as equally entranced by me as I was by her. I was so unnerved I nearly clumsily replied, "Pleased to meet you, Crystal." I wondered if they knew I was in love… *Lust?*

Derek and I took a look at the floor plan that Crystal had created and it seemed like a very well-designed use of space that was enormous compared with most homes we had already done. Everything looked to be feasible and could be finished in about five weeks.

Of course, the most immediate need would be to mount both a wind turbine and solar panels to provide additional electricity to the whole building. There already were solar panels but they needed to be upgraded to provide more power.

With the discussion of the project over, Harlan offered… "Would you like to go flying?" The sky had cleared up between storms.

We were very busy, but both Derek and I really wanted to see what it was like from up there. We went back downstairs and it wasn't long before Harlan had a small twin-engine Jessna four-seat taxiing out of a hanger door he had opened.

We climbed into the plane. Derek sat alongside Harlan while Crystal and I sat behind. Above the idling engine's sound, I asked, "How come the building's in such good shape?"

Harlan explained. "After my parents died and I was well enough, I drove my car here and hid it in the hangar. I put up large "No Trespass Or You Will Be Shot" signs and stayed here. Whenever I heard people in the area, I would start shooting warning shots from the roof with my dad's rifle and thankfully, nobody ever shot back."

I smiled at Crystal when I heard what Harlan said and she smiled back in a way that was not about what Harlan said but more about me.

The engine revved up and we left the runway smoothly out over the port, buzzing it a bit, but not too close, knowing there were guns, perhaps, pointed at us as we surveyed. Der had called Morgan to tell him we were flying over. We then flew up the Los Angeles River basin, well out of its concrete banks showing extensive damage from the flood after the hurricane, including sections of freeway that were gone making it very difficult to cross the river except for a few street bridges that survived the flooding.

As the plane banked to the left, I felt Crystal grab my thigh as if to brace herself, but when I looked she winked at me and moved her hand up a little bit that gave me a different message.

While things got even hotter we flew over downtown and several burned-out buildings, open areas, and then on to the hills above Hollywood where we saw many landslides blocking roads to some of the more exclusive places making them rather inaccessible unless we were able to clear the roads of debris.

I continued to take pictures in spite of the messages that Crystal kept sending me throughout the flight until we returned to the airport. Upon landing, Derek said he had to leave, so I told him to take the truck and I would go back to the port with Harlan and Crystal when we were through.

After Derek left, Harlan said, "Why don't you two go upstairs and hammer out the details of the renovation. I need to do some routine maintenance on some of these planes that should take about an hour before our GoTo cab arrives from the port."

I said, "Okay. Call us when the cab arrives."

Crystal gave me a look and another wink, and I followed her upstairs, fully wondering what was going on as I watched her perfect behind move beautifully with every step.

When we reached the lounge area, she turned around, pulled me in close and said, "Let's talk," as she brushed her lips on mine.

I replied, "What's going on? I can't say I don't like what you're doing, I find you extremely exciting, but aren't you and Harlan just married?"

"We are. But I have a problem."

"You do? Are you promiscuous?"

"Not normally. I must say, seeing you may have changed things for me." She started nuzzling me more and I could feel her breasts moving against my chest. Earlier I noticed she wasn't wearing a bra.

She continued… "But that isn't my problem. We both want to have kids. Especially now when kids are needed. But we've been trying since well before we got married in December and so far I haven't gotten pregnant. But when I saw you, I couldn't help thinking…"

"You want me to…"

"See if it's me or him that can't conceive. And if I do, I want him to think that the child is his. I don't want him to lose the ego he had that attracted me to him in the first place. Even though I wish I had met you sooner. You seem to have much more going on." Her eyes were so sincere I had to believe her.

"I'm in a rather committed relationship and we had a baby in December, my first son. So, allow me to ask her first. But we are in a rather open relationship so I don't think she will complain. I see what you are doing to make Harlan feel good. But it might backfire on you in the future. It might be better to be honest and tell him."

"Let me do that… I'll consider it. In the meantime, I can't wait…"

She slid her hand down inside my belt line and kissed me deeply. She felt so good in my arms, tasted and smelled sweetly and I couldn't look at any part of her without being turned on.

An hour later, our cab arrived, and Harlan called us down to leave. When we arrived at the port, I had it drop me at one of our renovation projects trying to think of what I would tell Mel. I was glad we had rescued some of those self-driving taxis and kept them charged. Many people at port had no other way to get around our growing community.

37

A Change of Partners, Places

Dinner with others at the compound at Martha's had become a ritual for us to get together and discuss things in general. That evening, I talked of how we were going to be renovating a lounge at LAX into living quarters for Harlan Cole and his wife, Crystal Han. The facility would provide an opportunity for villagers to begin learning to fly and overcome the obstacles that so many damaged roads in the area presented.

Ray reported on how fishing was going and we were all grateful for the fish and seafood that he brought into the compound supplementing our stores of beef, goat, mutton, venison and pork that were beginning to run low after so long of not going to the Central Valley. It was a way for all of us to have the time to relax and eat during the long gray days of constant rain and erosion of our backyards on the west side.

But one thing remained on my mind and I didn't bring it up until Mel and I had put the twins to bed and were getting ready for bed ourselves. With no other way to express it, except, directly…

"Honey, something came up today that you need to know."

"Oh, what?" Mel seemed a bit amused by the mystery.

"Harlan's wife, Crystal, is such a beauty that I was immediately struck by her and her, by me."

"Oh… Tell me about it?"

"It was like, I know, this seems ridiculous, but, love at first sight."

"So… I think I've experienced that once or twice. But it always became what it really wasn't later."

"No, this is different, Mel. Already, she wants me to give her a baby. When we were alone this afternoon detailing what we will need for their floor plan she designed, I stopped short of giving her what she wanted. Told her that I wanted us to wait until I let you know… Didn't want to hurt you or our children."

For the first time in over a month, Mel chuckled. "You know Honey, the pandemic did me a big favor. It freed me from an oppressive husband and allowed me to be in charge of who I love and have sex with. That's a big deal. Why I'm content not to marry you. And I'll give that right, that freedom, right back to you. Ray has been eyeing me for some time. If you don't mind, I think I'm going to give him a little pleasure. He sure deserves it, for all he has done for us."

"So, you don't mind? What about the twins?"

"Don't worry about them. I hope to have a few more babies and plan to take care of every one of them, with their father present, or not. But I think they'll have many fathers to look up to, including you. Mentors to be like, or not."

"Thank you dear. The way we've been together and with the twins, I didn't expect you to be so open anymore."

"You may be feeling fatherly now that you have a son. But I need to tell you that you need to comfort Daph. I believe she had your daughter. I didn't tell you earlier, but she lost her little girl last night. Found her dead in the morning in her crib. You need to console her."

That morning at breakfast, Renée and Daphne weren't there. Ray was, and Mel sat next to him while I paid attention to the news that Wondah brought us that morning. Mostly about what the weather that winter was bringing to the northern half of the planet she gathered from the few places and satellite radar tracking major weather fronts.

What news there was, wasn't good. In the North, people were dying for not having stored enough food to make it through the winter, cold and flooding.

That night, when Mel went to Ray's house, with Martha and Steph's help, I put together a bouquet of flowers she had and arrived at Daph's house. It was dark and quiet. I knew all the codes so didn't set off any alarms. From the foyer, I could see a faint light coming from Daphne's familiar bedroom and quietly reached the top of the stairs and her door.

Renée and Daphne had made a little box as a coffin and wrapped the little girl warmly for her journey to the backyard. I approached cautiously so as not to startle them as they were busily writing down names that they might name her for her coffin and marker.

When I was close enough so they could smell the flowers, I gently said, "I'm so sorry that you lost her. I'm here to help."

"Oh, Dre!" Daph rose to her feet and came over to hug me. "I'm so glad you came. I don't know what to do!" She began crying on my shoulder.

"I know. At least, I think I know, how you feel. I felt that way after I got better and went into my sister's room to see her dead after I'd seen my parents. I've seen so much death; I've become hardened to it."

"I guess that's why you're here. I need you…" She led me to the bed-side to sit down with her where they had been writing down names.

Renée said, "Ever since Sean died, I haven't been able to think. I can't even think of an appropriate name for a little girl that only lived a few days." She was also feeling the pain of loss.

I took a look at the list and right away, a name caught my eye. "Isn't Darla the name of the little girl member of that classic 1930s serial, Our Gang?"

Renée replied, "I wrote that name. You saw those episodes, too?"

"Josh Jones, Der's father, showed us them on YouTube when we were about six years old. He wanted us to see how Buckwheat was treated amongst an integrated group of mostly poor, kids in Hollywood in the late 1930s to early 40s. We loved those episodes, built a fort and tried to form a gang ourselves."

"I would have loved to be in your gang." Daph whispered, clinging to me.

"We soon found real construction more fun and, I remember that our fort was 'No Girls Allowed.'" The girls giggled. The sadness was partially broken.

We started watching episodes until we had drunk the magnum of champagne and Renée told us that she was sleepy and going to bed.

Daph replied, "You've been sleeping with me these cold nights and there's no reason for you not to continue. It will be too lonely for you in your room. Stay with us."

We took off our shoes and crawled under the covers of the huge oval bed. It was a bit awkward at first with Daph at my chest and a woman older at twenty-eight, but still younger than Mel, Renée, cuddling up to my back. Until we got too warm and had taken off some clothes–Daphne more than Renée at first.

Before morning, with Daph's blessing, I found myself entering Renée's virgin territory with caution and love all around. The deal was sealed. Fates willing. When Daphne was able, they both wanted a child by me.

In the morning, we had a hot shower together, thanks to the wind turbine, and walked together to breakfast at Martha's. Life would begin again, no matter what, for those of us survivors in the village.

Mel was always there at breakfast, but every evening she went to Ray's house for the night, taking the twins with her.

Crystal and I were spending time during the day whenever we could steal a moment or two. And, every time we got together it got better. Her work was so superior on all of our projects, I was glad she was on board in the company.

She never mentioned whether she told Harlan or not. We didn't let our lovemaking get in the way of our work. We both were believers in working hard and playing hard, but that could be said for most of the members of the village.

Everyone was trying to make everything better for everyone else, including having babies for all those that were lost.

Two weeks later, the erosion on the backside of all of our west side cliff overhanging houses had reached a point where it had taken the end of my garden and some prize fruit trees. And was now threatening to take my swimming pool that we treasured so much for exercise and partying in the sun and rain.

It seemed like our compound was slipping away to the valley below one bit of loose, rain-soaked soil, at a time. Our walls were hanging out over the precipice and pieces of them were falling off. when the cantilevering of concrete blocks held together with reinforcing rods, concrete for mortar and covered with stucco, gave way. It was a relentless process that couldn't be stopped. I knew it, but...

I brought Der, Wondah, Crystal and Vik together at my house to see what we could do. After assessing the situation, Vik had an idea.

"We could use steel and place I-beams under the buildings, your pool, and the walls. The soil could fall away for some time before the steel cantilevers would be compromised, maybe over 100 years. Then, without enough support, the property would have to be abandoned."

Crystal replied. "In school we were told not to design buildings near cliffs that were not on solid bedrock. With solid bedrock, we could build cantilevered structures to and over, cliff sides. Is there any bedrock under us?"

"These homes were built in the 1930s when I don't think they considered bedrock or not. But the erosion clearly has been much faster recently in Derek's and my remembrance here. And, since the pandemic, it is moving about six inches a month–very scary. Am I right, Der?"

"My backyard is the same. I'd really hate to lose the gardens and fruit trees in Martha's yard. Some are nearly 100 years old and still producing excellent fruit. What do you think, Wondah?"

"Those aerial pictures that you took from the plane and the many that I've taken from drone excursions around the city, I'm seeing landslides everywhere. It just doesn't seem safe to build anywhere near a Pacific facing cliff–bedrock or not. They are eroding away at a rapid rate and will have catastrophic consequences in any major earthquake. We've had a few small quakes lately."

"I have a suggestion." Crystal said. "Why don't those of you on the west side of the street move to the airport. There are a couple of hotels close by that could be used as temporary quarters until we begin to renovate the 2nd floors of buildings like we are doing for Harlan and me.

"The buildings are mostly steel or aluminum frame, are strong against wind and earthquake and can catch a lot of water with large hanger roof surfaces for solar and wind power. The roads are good. There is a good sewer system and rainwater runoff system already."

I replied. "That's a great idea. It doesn't look like we can stay here much longer. If we move across the street, we will become crowded. While that may work on a temporary basis, we will need to bring it before everyone here for approval, and I think we should save everything we can… Like moving the fruit trees to the other side of the street, the gardens and everything else we can move. Eventually, we could move those same things to the airport." Everyone was agreeing that it was a good idea, when we felt a slight bump like an earthquake. Looking out the window, shaking a bit, we saw a section of the wall between my house and Martha's fall away. Adding to the urgency of what was now, top priority.

❧ ❦❧ ❧

38

Wide Open Spaces Traces

We began in earnest, the process of moving everyone and everything we could from the west side of the compound to the east. It wasn't an easy task.

The rain would not let up. Martha had lived her entire married life in that beautiful Spanish style home overlooking the Pacific with her husband, Jake. For her to leave her home at 82, if only just across the street, was almost as traumatic as losing Jake.

But then, she remembered hearing her grandmother tell of her rough life in Poland as a child and surviving Auschwitz. She calmed down enough to accept her fate of having to move her most precious things and plants across the street. The saturated soil made moving the plants a lot easier. But many would die with their roots and tops severely pruned.

Any work at all, removing fruit trees from the west side with or without heavy equipment like our 4 wheeler with a backhoe had to be severely anchored by either rope or chain to the firmest ground bedrock. In case of, while working, the ground would fall away underfoot. It happened a couple of times and people doing the work, including me, were saved when I fell. Only a few feet and was able to be pulled back up by the rope attached to my harness. Better safe than sorry. Our motto in construction.

I recall from high school classics for those of us going to college, something about, "Beware the Ides of March." In the classical case, it was a warning about Caesar's pending betrayal. In our case, I was beginning to think that the weather was betraying us, regardless of our plans.

Those moving, making their way to temporary shelter in the hotel we reopened near the airport, were hampered, along with our construction crews working in the airport with frequent street flooding. We had to use high wheeled vehicles when that occurred.

Even though there were thousands of vehicles available, the ones we had to use for construction, we didn't want to get caught in high water and disabled. We could always do something else while waiting out the flooding and did. There was much to do even while waiting for flooding waters to subside.

When torrential downpours occurred the flat terrain of the airport would flash flood. Sometimes as much as two feet before the water would drain off after. While the upstairs sections of the hangers we were renovating were safe, all of the planes that we wanted to keep in good running order and their service vehicles, were on the ground floor pavement and were repeatedly flooded. As long as the water didn't reach the fuselage we were okay. In some cases when the water did, the bodies were watertight and the planes floated. Like everything else in the L.A. area, survival was like a roll of the dice.

As expected, there was another pregnancy boom. The nurseries at the compound, the port and the ship were filled to the brim and required 24-hour a day care with substitute moms while their mothers were working. First, Mel got pregnant again. And then, some others in the compound who had given birth before, and finally, Daphne and Renée.

I began to wonder how many children I would have. I had no experience as a father but remembered how Josh and Dad got Derek and me doing construction at an early age. I will do that with my sons and daughters. We won't rebuild the city—they will.

One morning when they were getting ready to go to work in their newly remodeled airport home, Crystal took a pregnancy test and brought it to Harlan.

"Harlan, honey! I've got good news! Look what happened this morning! I took a pregnancy test. See… the color has changed. We're pregnant!" Harlan took a look and almost couldn't believe his eyes.

"Well, Crystal, it sure looks like it. You think it's because we're married? This change? Or is it something else?"

"What do you mean, Hon?"

"Do you think I haven't noticed how you and Dre are together? You seem like you can't wait to get out of my sight so that I can't see what you're doing. Well, I placed a few small cameras and have seen the two of you having sex… And then, you come home to me, all hot and bothered, and want to have sex with me!" Harlan's face was flushed red. He was clearly agitated.

"I'm sorry, Hon. Dre and I just have this thing, you know. But he's already got other women who want him to be their child's father. I can't blame them. Just something in him that attracted me. Dre's way of going about surviving this whole thing and bringing us all along with him.

"I love you. I always will. We could raise this child together, regardless if you are the father or not. Only a DNA test will be able to tell. And that may not be available for some time. I'm sorry for not telling you earlier."

Harlan saw how sincere Crystal was. "Okay, I think I understand. I like Dre. We are helping each other. I'll take responsibility for the kid. Whether he's mine or not. I deserve to have a child with my wife."

His look had shifted, but still showed that while he was trying to keep peace, he was still upset and trying to deal with it.

The next time we were together working on another airport residence, Crystal told me.

"Dre… I told him. He told me that he had us on some cameras that he planted. He's upset, but willing to go on with the plan we have. You may find him rather different how he deals with you now."

"I'm glad you told him. If he's angry, it'll blow over in time. In fact, we are flying this afternoon. I'll know then."

Whenever it quit raining and the runways were clear, Harlan was teaching me how to fly. We started with the Jessna, but there was a former Air Force helicopter pilot at the ship that he was working with to get a couple of the news helicopters working again, so we both could train on those.

We all met at the hangar for the GMG helicopter for a demonstration run at 2 pm. When I arrived, I saw her talking to Harlan and he introduced her to me. A tall black woman in jeans.

"Drake, this is Glorious Epps. She tells me that she's a career Air Force major flying helicopters. Glory was flying missions for the Air Force during the pandemic and found herself in the hospital when she couldn't leave a downtown hospital rooftop platform after delivering Amazonia-9 patients because she was too ill. She recovered and survived with other hospital survivors until November when Glorious arrived at the ship. Afraid to tell them too much because she wasn't sure how the others would receive her ability to fly helicopters or her being in the military as a single woman of high rank."

"Hello, Major Glorious…" I held out my hand to shake hers. A woman who looked about 30 with a hardened face of a career military person who had seen battle.

"That's a rather strange name, Glorious, but interesting. I'm glad you're here. Harlan and I want to be able to fly these helicopters and we hope you can help us do it."

"I'm often asked about my name. My father wanted to name me, Gloria. But my mother said that was too ordinary and came up with something unique… I'm glad. It's good to meet you personally, Drake. I've seen you at the ship many times and feel honored if I can help Harlan and you, not only fly, but fly a vehicle that can get you to the places that are becoming hard to get to. For the last three years, I was training young helicopter recruits. I can't wait to help out."

"Okay," Harlan said, I've been tinkering with this GMG beauty ever since we were flooded last week and I think I've got her working well again with a little grease on the suspension joints where the water had washed all the lubrication away. If you run down the safety check with me, Glory, we'll see if we can get this chopper in the air."

They started checking and I watched, trying to pick up as much as I could of this required procedure before leaving the ground. Helicopter pilots tended to have the shortest lives of all pilots even though most helicopter crashes were not as violent as plane crashes.

Regardless, flying could make you dead if you didn't make sure that all of the functions were working properly before taking off. Over the years, I remember many military and commercial helicopters going down. Sometimes, losing the entire crew and passengers.

It took about a half-hour and everything was found to be in good working order, thanks to Harlan's routine maintenance. We pushed the helicopter out of the hanger into the open and got in. Harlan sat up front with Glory. I sat behind her, watching her every move while I strapped myself in and put on the headphones so that I could converse with them above the beat of the rotors.

The turbojet engine roared into life and in an instant we were airborne over the hangar and headed south along the coast to examine what the storms had done to the beaches and shoreline. It was devastating. Where there were beaches, there was a lot of beach erosion and a tremendous amount of debris from boats, buildings, logs, and even whole trees crowding the sand in huge piles with each wave coming in bringing more.

Where the coast was cliffs, it was worse. Whole sections of the coast had fallen in taking any buildings or highways like Cal 1 with them. Traveling the coast on that highway might take a very long time. Whole lengths of the venerable old road would have to be rerouted and rebuilt.

Glory turned inland at Camp Pendleton and all we could see was snow topped hills of anything over 3000 feet and many, many mudslides and landslides destroying not only buildings, but the ability to travel main highways like 101 and the 5. Through L.A. proper the flooding was more devastating than with the hurricane, but somehow hadn't affected the port. Largely, because the prior flooding had created several more direct channels to the Pacific.

But it was when we got into the Hollywood Hills and all of the posh retreats in that area that we counted over 500 mudslides with so much destruction that it looked like it would take 50 years to repair and rebuild it all. As a construction guy, I couldn't believe it, but there it was, right below us. The Hollywood sign was left with only the H and the Y standing. The rest of the sign had slid downhill.

We landed a couple of times to get a better look and took some videos along the way to show to others. It was obvious we would need helicopters to get into some of these areas long before we would be able to rebuild the roads with heavy equipment. It was sad to see so much destroyed former beauty. I knew we would try to make it even more beautiful in time.

And then, we flew north to Santa Barbara and followed the coast back to the airport. There was more of the same and it was sickening to see. At least, our little foothold in what had been Los Angeles was still there. But for how long? I couldn't begin to guess. Just hoped that all of our work would turn things around for the better and not be destroyed by the tides of the weather and other calamities in the coming years.

૭∽ଌ୦ଓ∾ଐ

39

Clearing Skies vs Tensions

It was well into April when the constant storm fronts stopped battering the California coast and dropping heavy rainfall into the interior with epic floods that even surpassed the hurricane of the summer before.

I could begin to see more clearly the path forward, but it would take the talent of all of our village citizens to move any closer to what we had known before the pandemic struck the year before.

Derek, Harlan and I were all learning how to fly helicopters from Glorious while Harlan was teaching Derek and me how to fly, not only small prop planes, but 535s, so we could carry people to and from other parts of the country or countries if we wished. It was a lot to learn while we were trying to do other work, but both of us were quick learners, excited with what we would be doing with those skills.

Nonetheless, flying a helicopter and a light plane under visual rules required a whole different set of muscle reflex action that we had to remember, depending on the vehicle we were in. Every single one had different characteristics. It wasn't like going from driving a car to driving heavy equipment. Much harder, more detailed and dangerous. Recent AI improvements helped a great deal. Made flying safer for us.

Among others, the residence that we had built for Mel and me for our growing family to use at the airport, was finally finished so that I could move out of staying temporarily with Daphne and Renée. Then, I got a phone call.

It was from Mel.

"I came by Martha's to pick up Ron and Reg and take them to our new place. When I got there, Steph said that Daphne had picked them up. I called Daph and she said that you are now staying with Renée and her so she is going to take care of all of your kids!"

I could see how agitated she was. "I've got her on the line. Tell her she can't do that!"

I entered the three-way call with trepidation. "Daph? What are you doing with Mel's kids?"

"She's off with Ray every night, from what I hear. They would be much better off here with the three of us."

"Mel and I just finished our home at the airport. It's time I moved out from staying with you and reestablished my home there."

"But we have a much better place for you. And the kids and you could stay here in the compound and not abandon us."

Mel interrupted. "Those boys are mine. I gave them life, not you! Tell her, Dre, she has no right to my children!"

"Mel's right, Daph. Those may be my sons, or at least Ron, but you have no right to take them from Mel just because I've been there in the house comforting both of you. Mel's their mother! Don't you see?"

"But I lost Darla. Renée and I need babies. And we want you to be the father, Dre. Please!" She began pleading.

"I'm okay with that, Daph, I will support any children of mine. But you must be reasonable about how my children are raised. You'll have to let me decide who stays where. now, those two boys need to be with Mel and me— tonight."

Renée stepped in and put her arms around Daphne as she started crying uncontrollably.

I drove back to the compound, picked up Mel at Martha's, and we walked to the estate to pick up our boys. I wondered if I needed one of Morgan's deputies with us. Frankly, I wasn't ready for any confrontation.

Once again, there was no one at the front door. But we could hear wailing coming from upstairs. And it was coming from the boys and Daphne… With her the loudest. We found Daphne in the bed with her arms around Ronald and Reginald in a grip that was making them upset.

Mel and I approached her from both sides while Renée stood off to the side with a frightened look on her face, saying nothing.

Daph stopped crying and her face turned mean. "Don't you dare, they're mine." She gripped Ron a little tighter. I could see that he felt it and the way she was snarling.

I approached her as carefully as I could, crawling on the bed on my hands and knees and reaching out with my softest voice. "Com'n, Daph, let him go. You're hurting him!"

Mel approached from the other side. Daphne was jerking her head back-and-forth and glaring at both of us. Saying only, "No, no you don't… *Don't!"*

My hands reached Ron and I started stroking gently the sparse hair on his head with my left hand while taking a hold of his left leg with my right. I certainly didn't want to get in a tugging match with Daph over him. At this point, I could go no further without hurting him.

Mel reached the same impasse on the other side of the bed when Renée finally said something.

"Daph, don't do this. Dre and Mel have a right to their children. We'll get pregnant and have our own! Don't hurt the boys. Let them go."

After what seemed like a few more moments, Daphne gave in and let us take the boys. Renée rushed to her side and they both cried out loud as we left the room.

A couple of days later, I heard that they had invited both Ray and Derek to come to the estate. Ray declined, but Derek felt obligated. Wondah, wise to the whole situation, came to stay with us in our new digs. While she was there, she made it completely operated by our voices. It was nice, after a long day, to just relax and not have to run around opening and closing windows, turning lights on and off, or even running our entertainment. She was a wizard with that kind of stuff and a real jewel of a friend. Always had something new to show us in bed.

Gramps kept calling and wondering when we would be able to come back. I told him that based on the landslides we had seen we would have to use some heavy equipment coming with us to get back to the Valley and the flooding there would have to subside again before we could make it the whole way. I avoided telling him about coming by helicopter. Something that we planned to do as soon as I felt comfortable flying that far with passengers.

Work began in earnest creating rooftop greenhouses for growing food on hangar buildings at the airport. Many people came from the port hotel to help us with that task. The landslides we cleared provided lots of fresh topsoil and seaweed, shellfish and composted waste provided fertilizer so that we could get crops and food very soon after planting.

It was all a matter of prioritizing. During that very hectic time before we had all of the gardens in, learning to fly was postponed for a while. Many moves continued to take place, particularly from the port, moving away from the shore and flooding a few blocks, or moving to the airport where we were developing a suburb of the village that would be our primary way in and out of the area, eventually.

We found those with experience among the village to come and help us get the airport tower and communications running again so that we would have safer takeoffs and landings. Fortunately, we could grab manuals from the Internet and use them to learn how to run most of the equipment that hadn't run for a year and needed a new way of being powered and used. I didn't see commercial airlines starting up again anytime soon. But those hydrogen powered jet passenger planes would be flying again, soon, I hoped.

Captain Jensen of the Rambler was glad that people were able to leave the cabins and move into homes. Living on the ship without it going to new ports resulted in a kind of cabin fever for both the crew and temporary occupants from the pandemic.

He had serious plans to begin cruises to Catalina Island where he was in touch with survivors there, and then, venture south to San Diego and, if possible, to Mexico before the midsummer hurricanes would make that trip more dangerous. Trips north to Santa Barbara, Santa Cruz and San Francisco could be possible, too, as long as their tanks of methane had survived all the floods.

While the ship's infirmary remained staffed, Jensen had to train a whole new crew to safely run the ship at sea. He could run with fewer crew than when fully loaded, but he would have to more than double the crew that he had. So, he put them all doing training of recruits that wanted to help run the ship for its initial voyages.

Rambler's store of food had been depleted during the long wet winter. There was a need to restock in almost every category, especially wine and booze. While the warehouses that hadn't flooded still had more than enough staples, meat, and seafood, fresh vegetables and fruit was all depleted and would need to be restocked before they could go on any lengthy cruise where they might find hungry people to feed.

A suitable auditorium for holding village meetings was found at the medical complex and fitted with large interactive screens so that most of the residents could come to the meeting via the local area network that Wondah had created from the beginning, joining the compound with the port and the ship. All of the residents, still growing, could not be present in person, but they could participate and vote online.

I observed all the new life in our very busy nurseries and realized that

I had to get our schools refurbished for the next generation to go through an education far different from the one I had, but probably far more personal. I just hoped we were up to the task. I wanted to train a whole new generation of reclaimers and rebuilders.

40

A Busy Spring Turns Into Summer

The people in the hotel and the ship at the port, more and more, were tired of living in such close quarters and wished to move into some of the better properties inland from the port. That was understandable.

But Derek and I could not oversee all the projects to make it happen overnight. We also didn't want to get involved in the increasing politics of who gets what done. So, we formed a planning committee to do that and we focused on infrastructure.

With no time to lose, we established growing plots for fresh vegetables at the airport. With both solar and wind power to provide for the families that were moving there. Greenhouses with drip irrigation and air-conditioning to protect crops during the hot summers and cold rainy winters. Away from the runways but nearby, we planted many native fruit and nut trees that once were the staple of Orange County before all the suburbs were created.

The planning committee came up with a plan to take over the best homes, properties and businesses between the port and the airport to move into, one family at a time. It required the families that wanted to move to do a lot of sweat equity on their property before moving in. Crystal was extremely busy helping these families convert the layouts of the original homes and businesses into what they wanted to make them.

Derek and I managed work crews that developed over time and followed the layouts that Crystal provided in discussions with the eventual owners. There were some problems with theft, both by existing village people and the few gang members or outsiders that were still able to operate after all of the time since the pandemic destroyed most services, food and water. Sheriff Morgan Singh was very busy on those cases. For some, a path to rehabilitation was offered. Others were placed on work gangs with armed supervision. During this period, none were judged dangerous enough to deserve death by firing squad.

One day, Crystal and I had finished with the layout for three families in a rather large private hanger for Union Airlines VIP private flights when we began relaxing and enjoying each other on one of the king-size beds when Crystal's phone rang, rudely interrupting us. She picked up the phone and briefly, saw Harlan's face before it disappeared and the phone went blank.

She turned to me. "That's strange? I thought I saw Harlan, but then, without saying a word, he disappeared and the phone went dead? Do you think he's got video on us and is harassing us?"

"Oh, Crystal. Don't be paranoid. Maybe he just accidentally called you and then, just hung up and put the phone back in his pocket."

We resumed what we were doing for about five minutes and she was really getting into it when the damn phone rang again. She answered and saw a stranger in the viewscreen.

"Hello… Are you Crystal? This is Roger Worth in Pasadena. I just took this phone from a guy who's unconscious and all broken up in a helicopter that crashed right in front of us!"

Crystal screamed… "That's my husband, Harlan! Can you put him on?"

"No ma'am, I told you he's unconscious! It's going to take us some time to get him out of the wreckage, but he's still breathing. Just appears to be knocked out and has broken some bones."

"How can you use his phone?"

It was on when I found it here in the wreckage. Saw he was texting you so I figured you were important to him and called your number that he stored."

"Can you do anything for him?"

"First, we gotta get him out of wreckage. We don't have any place to take him. We have a nurse among our people and I sent a kid to go find her, but that's all we've got. Will just give him first aid and try to keep him alive. Can you get here?"

I interrupted… "This is Harlan's friend. To get an ambulance there would take several hours with the way the roads are, and we might not be able to get there at all. Harlan has been training me on the helicopters and I will try to get there as soon as I can, probably within the half hour after picking up some EMTs that can help. Hold tight and we will keep calling you. If anything changes in his condition, call us and let us know.

In the meantime, keep the phone on so we can track it. We already know where you are."

I called the Medical Center and two EMTs would be waiting for us at the rooftop helicopter platform. Crystal and I jumped in my truck and we raced back to their place where the GMG helicopter waited. We rolled it out of the hanger, both of us got in, and I took off.

We picked up the EMTs and were at the site within 15 minutes of leaving the hospital. There was a crowd of over 100 people below who moved out of the way when we landed in the street near where the crumpled Union Airlines helicopter crashed. The one that Harlan had repaired earlier in the day and took off leaving Crystal and me alone to play.

They had him out of the helicopter and on a stretcher with a woman tending to him. Harlan was in and out of consciousness and asking for Crystal. He smiled when he saw her come close and kiss him on the forehead. He tried to talk when the EMTs carried him quickly to the helicopter, but while sedated and stable, too sleepy to.

I invited Roger and the nurse to come with us. Roger insisted on a couple of other people to come along, too, so I agreed.

On the way, Roger told us what happened.

"We are about 200 people working together, trading and scavenging since that terrible pandemic last year. But we are running out of food supplies and about everything else. All that rain nearly did us in and we lost quite a few people to starvation, bad water and food poisoning.

"Lately, we been seeing planes and helicopters flying over and it gave us hope that we could be rescued. When we saw him flying low this afternoon, we all came out of our houses and started waving at him. And then, the engine quit with a loud bang and the helicopter spiraled down until it hit that streetlight and flipped upside down.

"But, you came! I can't believe there is a medical center operating in this area. What with all the gang activity we've had to fight off by arming ourselves and stopping them only after we killed many."

"Roger, we went through the same thing. From the minute I recovered from my bout with Amazonia-9, I was about growing food and hunting food as well as rebuilding, since my partner and I lost our fathers and mothers, but not their construction business. The pilot you helped save, Harlan, taught me to fly this helicopter less than a month ago."

In the setting sun, the port with the Rambler loomed ahead and I landed on the helicopter pad at the medical center where there were people running out to help get Harlan to emergency surgery. I promised Roger and the others that I would take them back and talk to Mayor Roberts about bringing his people to our village soon if they wanted to come under our terms.

Roger agreed and followed the nurse and the others after Harlan into the hospital. I came back later to fly them back to Pasadena and pick up some seriously ill from there to the hospital.

Harlan had a broken shoulder, several broken ribs, a concussion and his left femur was broken. It would be weeks before he would be out of the hospital and teaching flying again. We really needed him to do that. In the meantime, Derek and I, along with a couple of others that he had trained, took on flying functions even though we were all just beginners.

The next day, I flew to Pasadena again and brought back to the port ten new villagers who were in need of medical treatment for starvation and malnourishment. A route was found where we could go and get them within three hours and return with buses. So, after the severely malnourished and those who had medical problems from lack of medications were brought and treated by helicopter, the others came by bus. The village was growing again. I expected many more would come as we reached more areas of the greater L.A. area by helicopter and plane.

A group of the fishermen who no longer fished began creating grazing areas for cattle, sheep, goats and pigs. They did this by removing fences between properties, using their yards and backyards as places where the animals could graze safely. The grazing animals fertilized the soil in those areas. Chickens, geese, ducks and pigeons were everywhere. And so far, unregulated. Chased by feral cats and coyotes.

Trees bearing fruit or nuts were planted and protected from the grazing animals. Milking and slaughtering stations were set up on the property and some buildings, like garages and sheds, were used for housing animals in inclement weather. A bartering system was set up whereby the meat and milk producers could trade products with the fish market or use cash as the unit of trade.

Two grocery stores were repaired and opened. One to provide for the port and another to provide for the airport community. Staples were brought in from other stores and food warehouses that were located by Internet searches. Many who had small businesses before began to open abandoned ones in the area.

There was a team assigned to opening ship containers. Many of them contained staple food. But there was much spoilage and insect infestation making much of the food unsuitable for humans but good for some of the animals or fowl. The same was true with dated food supplies. Each one had to be checked if it could go beyond its sale date and still be safe. Many would last years. The rest went to compost.

Finally, the Central Valley had dried up enough for Derek, Melody and Wondah to join me on a flight to check on Gramps. He assured me that the road in front of his place was dry and smooth enough for me to land.

"The coast is clear, Sonny, come and see me," he pleaded on the phone.

I hadn't flown that far, yet. But Harlan was a good teacher and with Derek on the other controls, we both could check each other on this flight that might just be a round-trip without landing because of the condition of the road we were supposed to land on. With Harlan's blessing, we took off the next morning at 6 am to get the maximum benefit from daylight that day. Fortunately, it was a clear day after we rose above the morning fog and along our driving route there.

Before long we were flying over the Grapevine's mountain range and into the Central Valley. We could see evidence where the floodwaters had been. I circled friendly Mondale and tipped the wingtips back and forth in a kind of wave to those on the ground who hadn't seen anything but highflying military jets since the pandemic. We saw people waving back.

Before long, we came upon the Central Valley Aqueduct and saw so much destruction that the floodwaters had carried down to it. It was obvious that we would have to take the route through Mondale with trucks again because 99 was blocked by flood debris that wouldn't be removed anytime soon.

We safely landed on the road to Grandpa Ralph Hutchins's farm although it was much softer than expected. He rushed out of the house to greet us heartily.

"Hey guys," he squinted, "and gals. I knew you were coming by plane but it surely was a surprise when I heard you buzzing over and then landing right here in front of my house!"

I answered, "It's good to be back. But landing on your soft road was a little dicey. From what I can see, it looks like the improvements we made last year held up."

We reached each other and he hugged me, and then Derek, and then, shaking hands and hugging the girls.

"They sure did, Sonny. The water came right up to the first floor level again, but with the house jacked up and the livestock having raised pens we weathered all those storms and flooding much better than some others I talked to since the water receded. We still have all this mud problem that I hope you can help me with when you come again with trucks."

I wanted to know. "How did the Meyer brothers do?"

"They learned a lot from you. Did quite well. Have a lot of new arrivals that they want to share when you bring the trucks. When do you plan to do that?"

"As soon as we possibly can. But we have so many projects underway that getting away from all of them, even for a couple of days, will be difficult.

The road here may require more detours. We'll have to fly low all the way back to make sure we can get through without having help getting the roads open."

Gramps invited us inside and shared some of his homemade wine and cheese. Derek and I made sure we didn't drink very much, but the others enjoyed themselves and indulged quite a bit.

Using visual flight rules, we had to get going early to make it home well before dark. We wanted to taxi on down to the Meyer place, but when we got to the plane, it had sunk into the mud on the road and it took all of us to get it turned around and in position where it could possibly take off with all of us inside.

To get a good start, we went to the barn and got some plywood that we placed in front of the plane for about 30 feet. We then pushed the plane up on the plywood and all got in.

I applied the brakes and revved the engine to where it was pulling hard and released the brakes. It was nip and tuck when we hit the soft road accelerating off the plywood. We were nearly to the Meyer place before I attained enough speed to get airborne. We all sighed in relief when we finally were in the air and headed home. It would take a while before that road would handle heavy trucks.

I told everyone, "Next time we have conditions like this, we'll come by helicopter." I heard some chuckles from behind me.

Flying low on the way home, we buzzed a few folks who shook their fists at us as we passed, but I don't recall anyone shooting at us. We took a lot of videos of stretches of the road where flooding had left debris. And then later, when we got into the mountains leading into LA, we noted mudslides and landslides. Much more than we had seen earlier and found our way over, around or through.

We knew that it would take longer and much more difficult to get back to the Central Valley this year, but we were prepared to do it. Our growing village needed the trade.

41

Summer of Rebirth and Reconnection

With the rain over and the sun drying everything out, we mounted another convoy to the Central Valley. This time it was 25 vehicles and we had two excavators, a bulldozer and a grader on trailers to help us with the tough spots we noted and took pictures of on the trip back by plane.

Particularly, when we got into the Grapevine, we encountered landslide after slide. It took us two days to get through those so that we could continue. We left that heavy equipment behind with the operators to make the way even better for returning and drove, once again, through Mondale, sharing fish and seafood for what they had to offer us–just hospitality since most everything they had, had been flooded.

Once again, the Meyer brothers and their Mom, Gladys, were very happy to see us and told us that the measures we had taken the year before had saved much of their livestock and they were very grateful.

They had lined up a number of farmers who had commodities to trade for seafood. We had 10 refrigerated trucks. We enlisted the good people of Eunice to help us unload and load traded goods for a share of what was being traded. We finished by going to Fresno and trading there. Promising everyone that we would be back.

Gramps was part of the whole thing and always glad to see us. Our plan was to have regular runs back-and-forth from L.A. every week or so as crops developed throughout the summer. We all wanted to get back to normal, where the highways were filled with trucks carrying goods everywhere within the country and especially into and out of the greater L.A. area.

We stayed two days, and then, headed back to a load of work waiting. The drive back allowed me to think ahead. Wondering if we were going to be interrupted during the summer again with another hurricane. All I wanted was everyone to have working infrastructure and safety from what might come next from the weather. I just didn't know.

The first major project was to ensure that our sewage system was not spewing raw sewage into the ocean or onto the land but going through the right places and steps of cleaning to be re-released into the environment. We enlisted the help of Hans Hansen, the water systems engineer from the Rambler and did a search of anyone with city sewage treatment experience.

Rocky Palmer had been working with Wondah after his father's death to create a single database for the whole village so that we could make the best use of everyone through their resumes that we created and were able to search. We did one looking for sanitary sewer experience.

Fortunately, there were two former L.A. sewer plant workers in our midst: Fred Owens and Steve Adamski. They didn't know each other because they worked in different cities but we found them with sewage treatment experience and skills. We put Adamski in charge, Hansen as a technical advisor and had Crystal and Wondah join the three of them for the initial planning meetings.

The first job I gave them was to check out all of the sewer lines leaving LAX and what kind of sewer treatment that it was getting. They checked out all of the lines with snake cameras and all were working well. And then, they checked out the airport plant itself and recommended to me some measures needed to ensure that it was running properly. We enlisted some helpers to make sure that the plant had the power, chemicals and attention from routine maintenance that it needed to run properly.

Once that plant was working well, they began to tackle the plant that served the port. It had been damaged by the floods and needed a lot of work. I was glad I had Owens and Karpinski working on it because neither Derek nor I had any experience with city sewage treatment and what it required.

The next big project was to make sure that the growing village had a safe and dependable water supply through the old system—a much larger task. Fortunately, again, I found three people who had worked in public works: Sylvia Gaines, Frank Orchard and Randy Evans. I also provided them with crews to help them with their tasks. After planning sessions that included the unique knowledge of Hans Hansen, we decided to use a two-pronged approach.

Sylvia, an environmental water systems engineer, would work with Crystal and Hans to design a lift and gravity system to bring water from the now flowing freely, Los Angeles River into existing treatment plants providing potable water for the area. Reducing the need for cisterns, particularly during the long dry season. Orchard and Evans were assigned the job of checking the existing potable water mains for breaks with camera snakes and getting the plants that would be used up and running again. It was a project that would take several summers.

Derek and I spent our days hopping from project to project checking on their progress and getting workers trained to do the work. We spent a lot of time locating supplies and materials around town where they were stored in warehouses and yards. We sent armed convoys to those places to recover what we could find to make tools and materials for renovating or constructing new pipelines and other necessary treatment facilities designed by Sylvia and Hans.

We did much of the work at our company's work shed after we cleared out the flood debris and repaired essential tools for heavy metal work– cutting, welding, bending, grinding and polishing.

Approaching burnout, we decided to take time off when June came. Van and Quoc Nguyen had told us of encountering other fishermen as far north as Monterey and as far south as Mexico. Those fishermen told them about survivors trying to make a go of it both North and South.

So, we rounded up Crystal, Melody and Wondah and decided to do a little exploring. First, we flew up the coast all the way to Santa Barbara in the GMG helicopter. Arriving at the airport, we dropped down there to see if we could refuel and continue on, or have to return to L.A. Fortunately, while we found no one at the airport, we found fuel.

Arriving at San Jose airport, we noted that we saw people and crops being grown south of town with a settlement, but didn't stop, wanting to make another fuel stop. Once again, we found fuel but no one around to stop us from taking some to refuel.

Just before we started the twin turbo jets we heard vehicles coming and I saw them brandishing rifles. With the engines revving up we couldn't hear, but I could see flashes from their guns and knew they were shooting at us as I gained altitude as fast as I could to avoid getting damage to the helicopter.

I exclaimed, "Dammit! We didn't bring any firepower. Must remember to do that in the future."

Mel said, "I thought about it briefly. My bad…"

Der chipped in, "Yeah, we were lucky. We'd better be more careful on our next stop. Probably best to avoid SFO."

As we flew up the west side of the San Francisco Bay on the Peninsula, we noted people below in various settlements and landed in the Presidio in San Francisco. Wishing we had created some flyers to drop over those settlements.

The first thing we saw when landing was both crops and animals in the open areas before we saw any people. But soon, people came to greet us from all around cheering our arrival. They told us about their struggles and we told them about ours, for about an hour, before it was past noon and we had to head back.

But before we left, we felt the earth move under our feet and I asked Harold Stevens, the guy that seemed to be the leader of these pioneer San Franciscans, if it happened often. Harold said, "Yes, we've been getting a lot of tremors lately, much more than I remember, ever. I hope it isn't predicting the coming of the big one."

I answered, "I'm with you. That's all we need."

Crystal offered, "It sounds like an earthquake swarm: a predecessor to a larger earthquake. Based on earthquake history from my design classes, this area is way overdue for an earthquake like the one in 1906. Fortunately, most of your high-rises are designed to withstand earthquakes of catastrophic proportions, anchored in bed rock. I'm not sure about your bridges or any areas that are on landfill on the Bay."

We promised to come back and make arrangements to open a trade route between L.A. and San Francisco. Fortunately, all of the bridges were still intact and being used every day to get to Oakland across the Bay and Sausalito to the north. The Golden Gate Bridge was closing in on its 100th birthday in 2037.

MART was not operating, but the reduced traffic allowed vehicles to move easily where there wasn't road damage. We stopped briefly on the Stanford campus where there was also farming and grazing on the grounds and talked briefly with the people there, knowing we had to get back to L.A. by nightfall. They had the fuel we needed and we refilled there to get back to Santa Barbara safely.

Likewise, we stopped at that settlement south of San Jose and found them to be quite enterprising and healthy from their efforts. Once again we promised trade with them using 101 and 5 to come north.

When we got to Santa Barbara, there were people there at the airport because they heard us come and leave earlier in the day. They told us that they had been in touch with our fishermen and had learned about how our village was doing. By that time, it was nearly 4 o'clock in the afternoon. Once again, we talked a little while and promised trade before getting back to LAX just at sunset.

That laid the groundwork for flying planes to the airports where runways were photographed to see if they were clear and to establish a truck route to the north all the way to San Francisco, as well as the Central Valley. After a year, our wine reserves were running low and I knew we could replenish them and a lot of fruit and nut stores by doing commerce there and Napa Valley in the future.

At every stop, we shared business cards we had printed with telephone numbers and email addresses. When we arrived back that evening, every one of us had lots of call messages and emails to attend to. At this point, all we could do was promise. But it was a start. The roads had to be opened up first and any threats from gangs, desperate villagers, rural landowners and militia to deal with first.

In the meantime, Capt. Jensen was worried that his ship would be unable to cruise again if he didn't get it underway… and soon. He started out modestly, offering the village a Saturday cruise to Santa Catalina Island, just twenty-two miles away. With a skeleton crew that was half seasoned and the other half recently trained, they launched with 700 guests and 500 residence aboard. Taking off at 8 am that first Saturday morning for the hour and a half it took to arrive at Avalon and anchor offshore.

At first, there wasn't much activity onshore. But eventually, some people came down to the docks. Captain Jensen had already anchored and launched the first tender with about 50 people aboard to the docks. He was on that first tender and greeted the young people who came there as they cheered, shook his hand vigorously and hugged him. They didn't know that his crew was heavily armed, just in case.

It turned out there were only twenty-five survivors of the normally 4100 permanent residents. The pandemic had hit them hard, and without adequate medical facilities and no way to get to the mainland because of mandatory quarantine, most of the older people died. Those that survived had been struggling ever since, eating the native goats, seagulls and seals, as well as fish and other seafood that the island was famous for. Some were malnourished and most were deeply in mourning. The hurricane had destroyed many houses and their electrical system–making everything more dire.

At the end of the day, most of those young inhabitants took the tender to the Rambler for medical attention. Jensen promised those that stayed that he would send people who could repair and get their electrical system and water supply rebuilt and working so that all of the survivors could return. And perhaps, some people of the village who would want to live on the island as well.

At our village meeting, I thanked Captain Jensen for what he had done and told him that I would join him on a cruise there or north where they would find friendly and eager people at Santa Barbara and San Francisco. He agreed to begin scheduling longer cruises to friendly ports.

The next morning after the meeting, I launched an armed road repair convoy to take 101 all the way to San Jose. I included three food trucks for the security guard and drivers, operators, as well as food for inland settlements that may not have had access to food after the pandemic.

We all rested for a day, and then, decided on a more difficult trip south for the next day in the GMG helicopter again.

42

A Time To Explore

A year had passed since the epidemic. I couldn't believe how much I had grown up… We all had, those of my generation who suddenly had to take charge of our lives because so many of our parents, siblings, friends and relatives were dead and the whole structure of society we depended upon suddenly cut off by the lack of people in the mix just doing what they always did–their part in a civilized society. Cut off to a point where we all had to change what we were doing just to survive.

And we survived, perhaps thrived compared to other places. But I have to give credit to where we live, here in a rather temperate climate compared to some other parts of the country. And by the sea, a good source of food for us. But we've had our share of bad weather disrupting our efforts to rebuild and repopulate the area.

And, speaking of repopulating the area, I couldn't believe I may be the father of three children already when my plan was not to get married until well after I graduated from college. I still don't believe I'm a father, even though I see my sons with Mel almost every day before I rush to do whatever I'm going to be doing all day, and then, I see them again at night. So thankful there are those willing to take care of them while Mel and I work at getting things back together and working again all day without them.

But the twins are sleeping soundly all through the night now and showing signs of talking, crawling and getting to become a nuisance around the house until they're off to nursery and out of our hair. All the more reason to be more careful in everything I do. It's hard, taking on flying planes and helicopters with only half of the training that most people get.

The five of us are scheduled to leave south on the GMG helicopter tomorrow, so I have to get my sleep because I will be the principal pilot again with Derek there as copilot if needed.

Morning came and we were off at 8 am, I headed south along the coast where we had gone with Harlan before to San Diego. All was going well until all of a sudden, a stealth Marine helicopter appeared at our side with me barely able to see a guy in the heavily darkened window hand signaling something to me.

Our radio suddenly came alive… "You are violating military airspace. If you don't follow us around our airspace to the south, we will have to shoot you down, or preferred, force you down and hold you prisoner!"

I clicked on the microphone and replied. "Roger that. We will follow you to the south. We are headed for San Diego and beyond."

The ultra-sleek helicopter moved in front of me and flew painfully slow for its ability out to sea about ten nautical miles, and then turned south for about thirty miles, until we were allowed to fly back to the coast just north of San Diego. The last radio admonition was, "When you return, if inland, be sure to stay more than ten miles from the coast or you will be intercepted again."

We all heard as clearly as if from a loudspeaker that the military had returned to Camp Pendleton and had locked it down, for now. Until now, we had only seen highflying planes we assumed were military although we had put out large signs telling anyone who could see them from the sky that we were open for business at LAX for any arrivals, military or not.

That encounter was a little unnerving and we all sighed a bit when we saw a small settlement of people and buzzed them in San Diego, dropping flyers and business cards. The Naval Air Station looked abandoned but I was afraid to stop there unless it was an emergency to get fuel. Hoped to find fuel so that we could go to the tip of Baja and back picking up fuel again on the way.

We made a call to Barbara Roberts but got no answer except that, "Barbara's mailbox is full." An email did not even go through. But we would keep trying later to see if Jerry's auntie was still alive and could take him in someday. But it looked bleak.

Once again, we were on our way to points south. If we couldn't get fuel at Ensenada, we would have to return to L.A. I crossed my fingers but didn't let the rest of them know my concern.

When the Ensenada airport appeared, it looked clear of any people. We landed where we knew there would be aircraft fuel for our twin turbojets. Within a few minutes we had broken into a fuel storage tank and refilled our helicopter tanks when we heard them coming….

Pickups were arriving from both sides and we didn't have time to get into the chopper and take off. Derek, Melody and Wondah just raised their weapons high to signal to the approaching pickups that we were armed and ready to defend ourselves. I joined in with a white cloth I was wiping up some spilled aircraft fuel with. Waiving its weighted ingredients above my head to the man standing up in the lead pickup. The one who seemed like to be in charge.

It was a standoff and I heard someone yelling in English above Spanish voices, "It's okay! We're here to greet you as friends. We want to know if you're going to be able to help us. We need help and you're the first to have come to our aid!"

We put our guns down, but kept them handy, just in case. A fellow in a straw hat, Hawaiian shirt, and khaki shorts, jumped out of the front of the leading Jeep and ran up to us with his hand out to shake hands… Announcing his name… "Hello, I'm retired commander Alfred Flood of the U.S. Navy… Are we ever glad to see you. About half of our survivors here are American and the other half natives… Mostly those who worked with us or for us. We were a very close community and still are. Except for the sea and shore there isn't much food here in the desert so we are hurting for basics like flour. We haven't had tortillas for some time and it's starting to affect our population. You wouldn't happen to have any ground corn flour with you, would you?" He questioned with a wondering smile.

I answered, "I believe we don't, just lunch and some snacks. We have an operating cruise ship out of Los Angeles that can arrive here within a week with suppliers if you like. Please make a list of what you need and I will provide it to the captain when we get back and he can bring the food, medicine and other staples when he comes."

"That's amazing! We have some elderly that survived the pandemic and are desperate to help them. We are about out of everything, and, except for our hurricanes last summer are running out of water until this summer's storms come."

"The ship can provide you with those things. Hopefully you can give the ship some of your tropical seafood like your abundant squid, octopus, abalone and other delicacies."

"We will try. We want to stay healthy and are struggling with our diet."

Derek had put down his AR-20 and was using it as a support standing by the end of the barrel. He asked, "What about the cartels? Any trouble?"

"All last summer. But we were ready for them, knowing they were coming to get what we had left. We set up defenses on all the entries to town and killed a lot of them. They haven't been back since. The ones we shot were starving from the way they looked."

"What about further south? Is Cabo San Lucas safe?"

"Probably, we had only one attack from the south. All of our attackers came from either Tijuana, or overland from the other side of the peninsula–San Felipe. There is no water and fuel that way and no way to fix their vehicles if they break down."

They all gathered around and everyone chatted for a while. We promised that the ship would come and bring them whatever they needed if we had it. I told them that we would fly on down to Cabo and then return in a few hours to pick up their list and refuel. They thanked us profusely and we took off hopeful that we would find fuel at the airport at the tip of the Baja Peninsula.

That flight was the longest we had taken, about 200 miles, and we were running low on fuel when we arrived at the airport. There were people there and they were flying!

They didn't challenge us with our black helicopter with those large gold GMG letters on the side, knowing that we were probably movie people from Hollywood. But the handful of people that came out to greet us there were just as eager to make our acquaintance and see if we had anything that they needed dearly, like toilet paper and other essentials that they were unable to get from the few fishing boats that came by from across the Gulf in Mexico.

They were afraid to sail their sailboats for fear of pirates or fly there with their planes because of cartels. Some of which they'd also had to fight off who arrived in the middle of the night to harass them looking for money, of all things, when water and food was so dear.

We told them that the people in Ensenada were making a list of what they needed and we could also send the ship down to Cabo as well on the same trip with the same items. If there was anyone needing medical care, the ship might be able to help them in its infirmary or, they could take the ship back to Los Angeles and our medical center for more care if they needed it, even surgery. They told us they had done some surgeries under terrible conditions in their clinics without even anesthesia, at times.

After talking with them for about an hour, we took off again and, in another hour and a half, arrived back at Ensenada. Once again, Commander Flood came out to greet us with the others and a long list of what they needed, including quantities.

I told them that we would try to get everything on the list but couldn't guarantee and might add some things to the list that they would find useful. I told them that we had been down to Cabo San Lucas and they had similar needs. And then, Flood had a surprise…

"I know this is imposing, but we've got two of our citizens here who are in dire need of medical help. Would you mind taking them back with you to get to your medical center?"

"We have another row of seats. What are their conditions?"

"The first one, twenty-two-year-old Sunny James, has been struggling with a hernia for about six months. We don't have any way of operating on it. And fifty-seven-year-old Rebecca McKenzie is suffering severe anemia and we tried everything but can't seem to get her blood count high enough. She may die on us any day now."

I surveyed the others, and told him, "Okay, we can take them. Are they here?"

He nodded, and from the vehicles the two ailing people were being helped towards our helicopter. We shook hands again, helped our passengers get in their seats, gave them some snacks and water that they both needed, badly, and took off.

This time, I flew inland to bypass much of Tijuana and San Diego to get pictures of the 15 to see how the roads were down that way. But it looked like we wouldn't be going that way anytime soon because the 15 passed right by Camp Pendleton where we had been accosted and told to stay well clear of. It would be hard to detour around with a fleet of trucks in those mountains. It was late afternoon when we arrived at the helipad at the Port Medical Center and delivered our critical passengers who were both sleeping peacefully from the food we had given them. That evening, I called Captain Jensen.

"Jens, this is Drake, calling for a favor. Now that I see your first cruise to Santa Catalina has been a success, I'd like to suggest you going further.

Today, some of us flew down to Escanaba and Cabo San Lucas. We didn't stop at San Diego because there is a Naval Air Station there and we were intercepted by Marine helicopters when we got close to Camp Pendleton. Those two Baja communities are in need of supplies that we can provide. The only way to provide them would be to have your ship bring them in the quantities needed."

"I was thinking the same thing after talking it over with the fisherman who had been traveling up and down the coast. Our people here would certainly like to have a summer cruise in either direction. and before the summer hurricanes start in the Pacific off the coast of Mexico, it would be wise to go there first."

"I'm glad we're thinking the same thing. Our hard-working people need a break. And nothing better than to go to that sunny paradise and view orca, whales and dolphin along the way. Maybe, a night observation of the feeding of the squid in the Gulf of California."

"We would have to outfit the ship for a longer trip, and perhaps, more passengers."

"I will dispatch crews to find the items that the two communities are requesting from known warehouses and stores that weren't looted. It might take a week or so."

"I agree. Depending upon what is requested, if you send me the list, I might be able to find some of the items in our warehouses. I will also outfit the infirmary to take on immediate health concerns for those that need it, and to aid in those that we might bring back to go to our medical center. I can see the exchange of bodies. Some of our folks may want to go there and stay. I don't think that immigration laws will apply anymore for some time."

"Okay, it's a deal. Thanks for your help. We'll get on it right away."

We both hung up and I felt good, being able to help the two expatriate communities south of the border Californians cherished so much. Mel listened the whole time and agreed wholeheartedly while nursing the boys.

The next morning, after discussion with village leaders, we dispatched crews to secure the items on the list for both communities and take them to the ship for transport south. I briefly checked on Harlan. He was recovering quite well but it would be some time, with rehab, before he would be up and walking enough to be able to fly planes again.

I had been thinking about checking the two routes east by jet all the way to the southeast along the 10, maybe Texas, and to the east through Las Vegas, Denver and beyond to the Great Plains for grains and other commodities. But without Harlan, I didn't want to take a chance flying one of those business jets yet.

As soon as everything was set for the cruise south, I thought I would take the gang again flying the Jessna Cryon I was familiar with, to Las Vegas, to start.

✎⊰⧓⊱✎

43

Into the Barrens

We stayed around long enough to see that the Rambler was loaded with enough of the essentials needed by the two Baja communities and 300 of the village inhabitants for a five day cruise to the tip of the Baja Peninsula and back. Something that would probably be repeated until the summer hurricanes made it impossible to go there safely.

The Starliner high-speed train to and from Las Vegas that opened in 2030 had been a huge success. However, air travel from L.A. and San Francisco, and the use of the 15 had dwindled except for trucking. The towns along the way that provided basic automobile services, quick stops and long- term and short-term rental housing for both travelers and the down and out suffered greatly. Truck stops and motels were the only real source of income along those Indians trail turned superhighways.

Barstow, at the intersection of the 15 and the 40, had become overrun by gangs and was in the strong grip of the Sinaloa Cartel. The truck stops there and along the other little towns became very dangerous with lots of trucks hijacked. I suspected trying to run our trucks through there would be difficult if the gangs were still in control. Like all public transportation in and out of LA, the Starliner was shut down from our aerial reconnaissance earlier and wouldn't be operating for a long time to come.

Instead, we flew the Diplomat II twin turbo prop from USA Aerospace's hanger, because it had a range far beyond the helicopter and could land on highways or level fields if necessary. It was a ten passenger model. We used that extra space to carry essentials as gifts and key first aid and medical supplies that we thought might be needed from the list we got from Ensenada. We weren't sure there would be anywhere where we could get aviation fuel we needed. So, we had to have a long-range plane and the 3000 mile range of the dual fuel tanks made the Diplomat a good choice.

Once again, we took off at 8 am for Las Vegas to return the same day.

This time, Derek flew because he was more experienced with twin turbo prop planes than I was. Wondah and Crystal took detailed photography from each side of the plane that we needed to make sure, or not, that we could run trucks to the Upper Midwest.

This time, thinking about what would happen to the twins, or the one growing in Mel, she decided to stay home rather than face any danger. We invited Daph to go with us because she knew some showbusiness people in Las Vegas. She eagerly agreed to go along, concerned about her friends, even though she was pregnant again from Ray.

We flew the familiar 15 to Victorville and saw thousands of vacant vehicles stalled that had attempted to leave L.A. the year before and didn't make it very far. There were some encampments, but they were deserted as well. As we approached Barstow, Derek climbed to 5000 feet. We took high resolution pictures and videos over the city because of what we had heard about the gangs there. I didn't want anyone shooting at us. The videos would show us human activity on the ground. A way we could assess who was still alive and moving around at all the little towns and encampments along the way. We saw some activity–pickups with guns mounted.

From there, we slowed our flight and flew low enough to capture more detail and video. Like before Barstow with the stalled cars leaving LA, on the other side, the stalled cars and encampments were all headed toward L.A. Truck stops and turnouts at Basin, Baker, Halloran Springs, Mountain Pass (where it was cooler) and Primm at the border with Nevada were crammed with all sorts of vehicles and encampments.

But there wasn't any movement, any life, in any of them. Clearing the freeway would be a major undertaking even if Barstow could be cleared of its criminal element. Gasoline and diesel fuel would probably be nonexistent. We would probably have to bring tanker trucks to refill some truck stops. We flew on.

Arriving at Las Vegas after an hour and a half we circled the city and saw virtually no life. I could only surmise that once the stores and warehouses had been looted and the casinos trashed, the lack of food and water within a couple of months had driven the remaining residents to head into the desert in both directions. Only to run into a dead-end at Barstow with nowhere to go to get gasoline, food, and water after the easy stuff was gone. We could only imagine how terrible their situation was. Some probably still lived but we wouldn't know until we got there on the ground.

We talked about it as we flew along and realized that it might be quite a while before we could safely get to Vegas and if we did, we might not find anyone to work with us there at all. No way to refuel trucks if we tried to go beyond on the 70 to Denver and beyond that to the Great Plains. The Central Valley could provide all that the Great Plains could, for now. Unless we could find some people, trying to revive Las Vegas from what little water there was there naturally, seemed like it wasn't worth it.

But Derek said, "We've got a lot of fuel and flying time left. Why don't we follow the Colorado River south to the 10 and take that back to Los Angeles?"

I agreed, "That's a good idea, Der. But let's look at Lake Mead first. It's the closest major source of freshwater. If there's anyone still in this area, they would be there."

It was a short five minutes to Lake Mead. Before we arrived we could see a major encampment by the lake… A small village. We flew over cautiously at first, using our cameras to see if we were drawing any fire.

We saw a lot of people come out of campers and tents and start waving. Then, we flew over very low. There seemed to be 300-400 people.

There was a stretch of road clear enough for us to land, so we did. Ending up about a quarter mile from where the people were at, what looked like, a thrown together checkpoint that was unoccupied. By the time we came to a stop many were coming in all kinds of vehicles.

We got out of the plane to greet them with automatic rifles in hand as the first people came up and shook our hands and then began hugging us. All were asking, "Where are you from? How did you get here to find us?"

We told them that we were from Los Angeles and the village we were building there with and for the survivors of the pandemic. They told us a terrible tale of how those that survived looted all the food and money they could find in the stores, warehouses, and casinos. It got to be very violent. City services disappeared and during the middle of the summer when the hurricane dumped flooding waters, the water system broke down.

With little or no uncontaminated water, a couple of weeks after the flood, they fled to Lake Mead because that was the only source of safe freshwater in the whole area. They had set up checkpoints on the road that were heavily armed because the gangs that were left in the city tried to make raids on what they had. And they had to hold them off. Many died at the checkpoints, but the campgrounds remained secure.

They told us there was no food left in the city and what they had was running out. Their greenhouses couldn't grow enough. Their only source of new meat was fish and hunting what little game the desert and Lake Mead provided. There were already squabbles breaking out among campers over what little there was. They were really desperate.

We asked if there were any leaders that we could talk to. No one volunteered. But almost everyone wanted to go back with us. We told them that we would see about bringing food by some form of airlift. It would take a while, maybe a year, before we could reach them by road, but we would try to do it sooner and bring food from the Central Valley.

There was a rumbling among the campers and we tried to calm them down. Finally, with so many wanting to go back with us, I laid down the law, backed by Daphne, who couldn't find any of her friends, Derek, Crystal and Wondah with AR-20s.

I brandished my Glock and yelled, "Everyone calm down! We will do the best we can. We can take four of your people needing urgent medical care. But that's it! We will see if in the coming weeks we can airdrop food for you. But that's it. Take it or leave it. That's all we can do."

We unloaded all the food and supplies we had and there was a mad rush to pick out things from it. Some even opened the food and started eating. I warned them again to calm down, raising our rifles. They backed off and one or two came forward to take the supplies as we unloaded them.

The crowd calmed down and brought four people. A woman and a man in their 50s with severe malnutrition and a man in his 20s with three infected bullet wounds and a woman in her 30s who was very pregnant. We loaded them in the plane, promised again to be back and bring the four back, and took off… Glad we got out of there without being overrun by the crowd just to get our airplane.

From there, Derek followed the Colorado River south through several small reservoirs until we reached the 10. We couldn't stop anymore, but we saw several communities with people as we flew over low and waved our wings to greet them. There were three Native American communities that seemed to be the most normal. While Lake Havasu City was the largest community, it appeared to be abandoned. But across the lake in California, that community showed life and crops being grown.

Sustainability seemed to be the survival factor. The ability to grow food along the Colorado River and to keep livestock. Something the natives always had done. But most of the elderly residents that chose this part of the desert to live relied heavily on grocery stores and city services no longer available. The same elderly were most susceptible to the pandemic.

Left without any support, the younger people probably drove off trying to find somewhere where they could survive and the elderly probably died terrible deaths. I couldn't imagine how many died in all these thriving desert communities like Las Vegas and Lake Havasu City. Some probably committed suicide rather than face certain dehydration after the water ran out. Others who had water, after there was no food anymore and they were dying of starvation.

We decided that we would only make contact and drop food to desperate communities until the roads were open and armed convoys could deliver food and other essentials like gasoline to these remote desert areas to anyone who was still alive and had anything to offer in return while eking out a living/surviving.

At the 10, we flew east for a few miles and noted that there was a line of stalled cars and makeshift camps, all abandoned just like we saw coming out of Las Vegas, apparently leaving Phoenix for L.A. Without irrigation, what had been crops along the 10 had reverted back to desert again with lots of tumbleweed as the only vegetation.

Returning toward L.A. again, we noted that the stalled vehicles were coming out of the L.A. area, basically, to collide in the middle of the desert with no gasoline, way to charge electric vehicles, and worst of all, no food and no water. I imagined how many died on those roads to nowhere and it must've been staggering.

I knew when we cleared the roads we would find lots of bodies or skeletons after the desert creatures had picked them clean. It really made me thankful that we lived where we did and were able to grow food from day one. Something so many of these people couldn't but risked their lives to try to find it and died trying to. What a shame.

Palm Springs, the only major city before reaching San Bernardino, was the same, abandoned. But we saw some life in the mountains where homesteaders had established self-sustaining places to live. To open up commerce east of Los Angeles would have to wait. I wasn't sure if we would be a part of it or not.

We were back in the village and landed on the Medical Center helipad to deliver our four malnourished, pregnant and injured. The pregnant lady delivered within a couple of days. And the young man had four bullets removed from his body instead of three, got antibiotics and was doing much better. As were the two that were malnourished to the point where they had already sustained some organ damage and would require hospitalization for a long time before they could be airlifted back with food to the Lake Mead community.

Within a week after returning from Baja, the Rambler took on a load of essential supplies and passengers and cruised north to San Francisco. After staying there for two days, returned, stopping at Santa Cruz and Santa Barbara. Captain Jensen was pleased with the fruit, nuts and wine they were able to acquire in trade in San Francisco. While there, they encountered a couple of small earthquakes like we had.

I was glad that through the cruises our hard-working village people were able to leave the city and all that hard work occasionally for a few days. Similar to those of us who had learned from Harlan how to fly. But, as I looked at what needed to be done yet, it was staggering.

44

Barstow

In the following weeks as we moved into another hot, dry summer, we established regular runs into the Central Valley to both barter trade and make cash transactions, depending on the commodity involved. Some of our village people traveled there to work on the farms and learn more about growing in the L.A. area from the farmers they worked for.

Soon, more farms and communities got involved and a network of support stretched all the way to Stockton. However, fuel oil was difficult to find from the stores in underground tanks at truck stops and storage depots.

More and more, only electric vehicles run by the sun or by batteries charged by the sun and wind had to do the job. There was no other choice, because all of the refineries in the state weren't working and pipelines no longer carried fuel oil throughout the state. We trucked fuel oil from L.A. for a while, but stopped knowing that we would have to conserve what we had for machines we had that would only run on fuel oil to help reconstruct the city.

While there was a lot of solar panels available and wiring, batteries were at a premium. That was one of the first manufacturing plants we re-opened in L.A. The former Sure-Fire battery company had recycled batteries prior to the pandemic but was shut down.

We engaged a couple of chemists who had joined the village to see if we could get the company restarted. At first, only producing a few batteries from recycled batteries that we'd salvage from throughout the city. Gradually, working day and night, the chemists got that production going again and we were able to ship batteries and solar panels, along with complete wind power units to the Central Valley.

There were problems. Having inexperienced people working with hazardous materials caused some health problems. Worst of all, we had batteries explode or catch fire. When that happened, people were burned and equipment sometimes completely destroyed.

Although there was an overabundance of vehicles that we could use and reuse, there was no immediate way of manufacturing new ones, just modifying all the ones we had and getting them back on the road. Once back on the road, maintaining them for as long as we could–especially the electric ones. Although we had warehouses full of them, I could see time having an effect on our tires and eventually, having them all go bad from oxygen deterioration. A tire plant somewhere in California would have to start up again. The Council put our chemists to work on that problem, too.

We established regular flights to Lake Mead, Lake Havasu City, some of the Indian communities, and Palm Springs.

People in the mountains, camps and homesteads would come to these places on a regular schedule to trade and/or buy supplies that we would bring from lists that they emailed if they had an Internet connection.

Everyone could use SatGrid, established by 2027, and G6 to eliminate all the need for ground-based, cable-based Internet connection run by AI for the foreseeable future with solar power in orbit. We were very grateful for that. But there were those who still gave us handwritten lists to bring on the next supply run.

The problem with Barstow remained. At a meeting of the Council, we decided to attempt to contact the military for help with the problem. After sending several emails, we received an email from Vice Admiral William Wortham telling us they would help us with gunships out of Camp Pendleton when we were ready for the help.

It took several emails with General Colin Parker at Pendleton before the details were worked out. The plan was to use two of those stealth helicopter gunships to force the cartel members to surrender in Barstow. We were to call them when we got close with a contingent of armored vehicles. The idea was not to destroy the city in order to rout out the bad guys. I hoped it would go that way. In our previous experience they always fought back viciously to their death.

We sent a convoy of armored trucks and two police buses to carry any prisoners back to L.A. that we might apprehend. First, we had to clear the mass of vehicles that hindered our progress just getting to Barstow. It took about a week sending bulldozers, graders, tow trucks and others, to both clear the road of slides and deal with the abandoned vehicles. Moving them to places where we might later reclaim them, while opening the road for truck travel in the future.

Our aerial photographs had shown a major truck stop checkpoint on the 15 about a mile before Barstow where all of the stalled vehicles jammed up trying to enter the city started. That mile into the city was clear but controlled by whoever was in control of the city.

With no traffic, that checkpoint had been long abandoned after serving its initial purpose–a roadblock to rob, kill or enslave those trying to come through the city on the 15.

So, we planned on clearing the road about 5 miles away even though the gangs could probably hear the work going on at that distance. And then, when we made the final push, we would have trucks with the ability to push any vehicles in our way out of the way quickly as we proceeded to the outskirts of Barstow.

But, as our crews came within about seven miles, they drew fire. Their security detail had to move in and kill three gang members recognized by their tattoos and destroy their pickup with a rocket. The security detail then moved on pickups coming from town and killed all of the gang members there with a couple of rockets, followed by cleaning up and coming to a stop just out of assault rifle firing range from the scattering of buildings entering town.

The road clearing crew made a hasty retreat and we planned to make our assault of Barstow the next day, leaving L.A. at 6 am to be in place by noon. At 1200 military time, we called for assistance and two of the stealth helicopter gunships appeared overhead and swooped down on the city with loudspeakers blaring… Both in Spanish and in English… "Surrender to the authorities waiting outside your city immediately or we will destroy the city and you in it!" With earth-shattering effect by demonstration, just short of a sonic boom.

To show their firepower, both fired rockets into nearby open desert with tremendous explosions and plumes of fire that encompassed about half of the entire city in a single blast. The sound and fury were overwhelming and earthshaking. Scared even our people waiting to move in. I was one of them. Had me shaking in my boots.

Soon, pickup trucks carrying men, women and children came out onto the highway with their hands up. Except for innocent women and children, the total gang and cartel members left amounted to only twelve. We put the seventeen women and children in one of the buses. And those, including two women with tattoos and other indications they were hard-core gang members, in the other bus under heavy guard.

As we entered the city, we caught fire from two snipers. One of our amateur soldiers exposed himself enough for the sniper to shoot him in the shoulder.

To our amazement, along with the emaciated cartel leaders, towns-people, about thirty of them of all ages came out and hugged us as their conquering saviors. Most had been kept as servants by the cartel to serve them by scavenging up and down the highways, bringing them gasoline, food, money and whatever else they could find in cars and campgrounds just for the privilege of keeping them alive to go out again in the hot sun for another day of life.

We gave those few survivors of that terrible ordeal of over a year all that we had of our food and medicine and promised them that trucks would be coming through with lots of supplies very soon.

We told the townspeople now that Barstow was cleared and the 15, 40 and other highways and roads would be open, they needed to open the major truck stop right outside of town again to serve those trucks coming and going.

A thorough search was done using the townspeople to help and the city was declared clear. We had captured all of the bad guys. But we didn't want to take them back to the village where they could cause problems.

After the successful mission was over, I got in contact with General Parker by telephone.

"General Parker, thanks to your gunships, the cartel members and gang members surrendered with very little resistance. We put that down easily. However, we have an even dozen of the leaders in custody as well as their seventeen women and children that we really don't want to bring back to Los Angeles where they may become a problem in the future."

Colin Parker answered. "We understand. We've got that problem all over the country. We will take them off your hands at LAX when you get there. After we interrogate them here in Camp Pendleton, we will try and deal with the worst here. The rest, we will take to Mexico where we have an agreement to deliver them to authorities or to, in the case of the proven innocent women and children, to the surviving Mexican communities of their choice."

"We will let you know when we have arrived at LAX. We greatly appreciate your taking these people off our hands. We want our village to be free of past alliances that may cause danger to our citizens still trying to recover."

"If any of those young citizens of yours wants to join the proud, the brave, the Marines, I would appreciate it if you let them know we are taking recruits."

"Okay, fair enough. I will announce that to everyone at our next village meeting."

When I hung up, I breathed a sigh of relief along with the others listening in on the conversation.

"That's one problem we won't have to deal with." The others shook their heads in agreement.

As promised, when our buses arrived at LAX, large transport helicopters arrived and separated the innocent from the clearly tattooed into different ships and they took off with us hopeful of never seeing them again. Our road clearing crew was on the road again the next day and truck convoys soon followed. Eventually, reaching Lake Mead, down the highways leading to settlements along the Colorado River and back to Palm Springs, into Pasadena where a roadway was cleared all the way to the port.

We were ready, if possible to receive container ships from other parts of the world again. Quite an accomplishment in only a year and a half. But we were faced with new challenges. One of those was people who had homesteaded for the year but had given up and hitched rides on the supply trucks back to sign into the village and become citizens of a city like they originally despised and left.

With newcomers, we were growing, but with newcomers, we had new problems.

♋ℬↃϾℬ⚭

45

Return to Some Normalcy

While cruises to Cabo San Lucas were interrupted during the summer by Pacific hurricanes of immense power, only one reached the area of San Diego and Camp Pendleton, causing some destruction, lots of flooding. Also, much inland rain was beneficial to the Central Valley and even to the desert regions of Arizona and Nevada. Each year now they were getting more water than ever, creating lakes and oases where there weren't before. Just dried, alkaline valleys with little or no vegetation.

We discovered settlements of people who had fled their cities in these places growing food and animals. More survivors than we thought initially, but still not very many. The whole climate of the desert Southwest had changed, making it more livable than before. The Colorado River was once again flooding much of the area in the spring, as well bringing it to life, starting with wildflowers and willow trees along the paths where there was nothing but dry gulches before.

More and more businesses and some manufacturing companies were opened during the summer. But we were still primarily salvaging what was left of the former city's stored wealth of almost everything imaginable. Most of that we had no use for anymore but were willing to keep available for some future time when we would get back to it.

Of utmost importance was reopening a nearby junior college and expanding it into a university. Using AI, providing everything from post high school education in the trades to doctorates.

All this stretched our meager workforce to the limit. But, everyone was working far more than they did before the pandemic with the joy of being able to do whatever they wanted to do. All helping to move the village ahead.

When I asked for volunteers, I always got them. Especially for ventures into new territory. By the end of the summer, we had trained 30 pilots and Harlan was back doing most of the teaching. We were getting ready to fly great distances by jets to get to the rest of the country and see how they were doing. Much better in person rather than just the Internet.

We got some gist of what was happening from the Internet. There were some news channels opened that had news from across the country in a ramshackle arrangement between various cities that had resurgence like ours. But it was tough everywhere.

People were still dying from lack of food and clean water. There were many places where there were as many new births as we had, creating large nurseries for us at the airport, on the ship, and the port area. Where surrogates took care of the children while the parents were out doing whatever they were doing that day, to be returned to them in the evening.

By September, Ron and Reg were walking and talking. Starting to get into things. Ahead of other children their age, like Derek and I had. We had record crops from all of our greenhouses and were able to share with the people in the desert. Especially, seafood that they craved because they were a long way from the sea and could only get freshwater fish from the Colorado River when it wasn't flooding.

We celebrated Thanksgiving with more thankfulness than ever before for our good fortune and how we were able to help others that were recovering, but not as well as we were. Ray and Daphne celebrated the arrival of Marilyn in mid-December and Stephanie, a son she named, Spike. There were several other births to members of the village to the new year.

But it was after the New Year 2034, that a whole new second round of babies appeared from the mothers who had had babies the first year. As soon as they felt able, got pregnant again. Adding to our growing population of babies that needed caring for in the nurseries, and the soon to be developed, preschools. These children have no memory of the hardship of the pandemic and after. They would take on our world the way it was and prosper in it.

I just knew it, one night, after we put the twins to bed and were breastfeeding little Missy, born just after the new year, Mel confessed…

"You know Dre, she is so wonderful. And Ron and Reg are so smart and active. I just love babies, don't you?"

"I do. But I want to see them grow up. Perhaps, too soon. They are all so unique."

"I've been talking to the other mothers. We are all in agreement that we have as many babies as we can. That will mean that we probably will be away from some of the other work we've been doing with all of these children to look after, but it will be best, don't you think?"

"It sure will. We need kids. The whole country needs kids. These kids will bring the world back to the way it was, but better, not us. We will be worn out by the time we're 50. There are times I wonder if I can keep up the pace that I have in the past year and a half."

"Now, now, you're not going to abandon me, are you? Will I have to go to others to get this job done?" She taunted, and then laughed.

"You have and didn't let me stop you in the past," I taunted back.

That was the nature of our open relationship. Melody seemed to need variety. And more than just Crystal needed my attention when it came to the need to have babies. Some of them wanted me to be their only, but I always told them that I was bonded to Mel but willing to help. They had to agree or I wouldn't come to their beds. It was really with mixed feelings that I got women pregnant who I would never be with and probably not even know the children I fathered. It was a strange time we were in.

The rains were relentless that year and one cold and rainy day in March we were called to the hospital. Martha Rosenberg had suffered a devastating heart attack while at her elementary school and was clinging to life. Those of us from the former compound who could make it crowded around her bed and wished her well.

She died at 6:35 pm that evening with most of us still around her bed. Her last words were… "I only wish Jake was here to see what we have done. But I guess I'm going to see him now." She closed her eyes and never opened them again.

I thought of all the mornings we gathered to plan in her dining room while she fixed us fabulous breakfasts with whatever she had at the time to feed us. We all would miss her much longer and more deeply than any other of us from the village. She had been that special to our recovery from the devastation of our families and our lives by the pandemic.

On the contrary, in spite of a good summer of good crops and harvest, the flooding was back and the constant storms with cold, dreary days and nights did not seem to get to Grandpa Ralph.

Gramps was overjoyed that Derek and I were taking the lead in helping both Los Angeles and the Central Valley get back on its feet. He seemed to be rejuvenated by our helping him save his house and his animals. Welcomed us heartily every time we came. In February, I even flew in on a seaplane and floated right up to the house to his great joy and surprise. But I had to leave the same day because another storm was coming in.

Once again, things dried up by April, and the convoys were able to run again. What was noticeable was the lack of any attacks from gangs or citizen militias. Everyone was so grateful that the trucks were running and there was life in the remote desert regions again that it was all cooperation and trade. Where there was nothing to trade, it was outright charity. We all had more than we needed. Why not share it with those that didn't?

The Internet gave us some inkling that there was an attempt to start the government working again. We didn't know if we would have representation or not, but we made a few inquiries and by June 2034, Harlan flew a contingent of us to Washington DC. We met with the Secretary of State who was acting as president from the line of succession. Cyrus Greene had been quick to gather the surviving members of the Congress and Supreme Court with the help of the military. Bringing some of them to Washington DC to reestablish a United States government again.

In his office in the White House, Dr. Green asked us to send five representatives and two senators that would be duly elected from California in the first election since martial law was declared and he was put in charge. He told us that rebuilding the government for the entire country would take some time because some parts of the country were doing better than others and elections were his priority as well as trying to provide for those who were malnourished, starving or without clean water.

Told us, "I haven't slept since this whole thing started. You don't know how I want to hold a presidential election and leave this office for my family who need me."

He started crying. We reassured him that we would have elections according to the federal schedule in California as soon as we could get those set up and send the representatives and senators after the fall 2034 election. We told him that we would have to use Internet voting because the state was vast and getting to the polls would be impossible for some.

President Greene agreed. "We will send guidelines for Internet voting as soon as we have them prepared. We will use AI to make sure there is no election fraud."

When we returned, our mayor, Joan Roberts and treasurer, Seymour Kaufman, immediately established committees to set up local elections and provide guidelines and ballots for elections up and down the recovering county precincts in California.

We knew that we couldn't include everyone in the vote for the fall of 2034 or even all of the potential candidates. But it was a start and we had to get representative government from the entire country back in place, until a new census would determine what ratio of representatives would be elected to the House.

Derek and I, after our brief trip with ten others to Washington DC and our meeting with the president, decided that our services would best be focused on Hutchins and Jones Construction Company and the rebuilding of Los Angeles for the near future. We spent a lot of time getting subcontractors operating again in all of the fields of construction. Getting them to use the best techniques and materials to make whatever we rejuvenated or built from scratch would serve the village for a long time.

In November, 2034, we elected the slate of senators and congressmen that the president had requested. Harlan flew them to Washington to begin to serve their terms in January when a new president had been elected and Cyrus Greene handed over the responsibility of President of the United States to Sylvia Wilkinson, a former federal judge and graduate of Radcliffe and the Stanford School of Law.

In the spring of 2035, the 70 was finally cleared all the way to Denver and trucks begin traveling coast-to-coast. While most of the trucks were solar, natural gas or fuel-cell powered, a couple of refineries in Texas got to working again so there was fuel oil for those trucks, trains and barges that were still so vital to begin moving products and commodities around the country again. It would take a few more years before the rail systems could be fully operated and made sustainable again. We began a subcommittee to work on planning the CalBulletLiner that originally was planned to run from San Diego to the Canadian border. Our initial work was to open the 300 mile- per-hour electric train between San Francisco and the Village. A task that would take several years.

We were spread so thin that work had to be delayed and priorities set by the Town Council. I knew there were bumps in the road ahead. I just didn't know what they would be.

46

The Big One

They started in late summer… Tremors like we experienced on our first trip to San Francisco. Through our contacts there, after we felt it on August 29 at 2:29 pm, we learned they had the biggest earthquake since San Francisco's in 1906 at 7.8 estimated on the Richter scale. Government seismic sensors were still working along the coast through the satellite system and operated by AI. We also learned that this one was 7.6 and centered on the San Andreas Fault at the Crystal Springs Reservoir, 15 miles south of the City.

The Council immediately got in touch with the group in San Francisco we were trading with and they told us the bad news. Many of the older buildings built just after the 1906 earthquake out of wood had collapsed and those buildings rebuilt after the Loma Prieta earthquake in 1989 as well. Especially, in the fill areas along the San Francisco Bay where the subsoil turned liquid and everything came down that had been built or rebuilt since then.

Fortunately, the settlements, most occupying the more solid bedrock areas anticipating earthquakes had survived with a few deaths and injuries. Only five major high-rises came down in the City… None of them lived in–thank goodness.

Broken gas lines caused some fires to break out and broken water lines caused a lot of structural damage where water was still in the mains, washing out streets and foundations from under buildings. But San Francisco did not burn this time, or any of the other cities except Richmond where huge oil and gas tanks ruptured.

The roads and streets had been cleared of abandoned vehicles across to Oakland, down the Peninsula and across the Golden Gate to Marin County where there were settlements of survivors, too. But getting to those cities and towns was another matter.

The Golden Gate Bridge suffered some damage and was a regular "Galloping Gertie" from those who saw it undulating during the earthquake and took videos. The damage was mostly from about 15 vertical cables holding the bridge that snapped. Something that the local government wouldn't be able to get fixed very soon if at all, making the bridge very unstable and fearful to cross.

Worse, the Bay Bridge with its 2013 rebuilt Eastern Span was completely blocked by both older and newer sections of the roadway dropping into the Bay. Much worse than the Loma Prieta damage that resulted in the rebuilding. The San Mateo Bridge also lost several sections making it impassable. El Camino Real and US 101 were badly damaged in many places and would have to be repaired.

But, worst of all, the Crystal Springs Reservoir, built 300 yards from the epicenter of the earthquake in 1888, that had stubbornly withstood many earthquakes since with very little damage, finally broke. The resulting surge of water and earthquake took out the buttresses of the Father Sierra Freeway as the water surged eighty feet high down the San Mateo Creek to the Bay.

While earlier flooding from heavy rain had caused damage all along El Camino and US 101 that was being repaired, the floodwaters from the broken dam were a half-mile wide when they reached El Camino and destroyed everything in their path. Fortunately, there were no settlements, only vacant buildings…

But all three major thoroughfares were completely washed out leaving the Peninsula cut in half with only the badly damaged and dangerous Skyline Drive linking San Francisco with the South Bay cities passable. Cal 1 was completely destroyed, too, and would take a very long time to rebuild with much of its Peninsula length fallen into the sea or covered with huge landslides.

To add insult to the injury already caused by the earthquake, there was a tsunami that left the San Francisco Bay nearly empty, and then, overflowing, destroying much of the remaining 101 and everything close to the shore, especially those areas of fill that were developed. At the south end of the Bay, the water sloshed out and overcame a settlement in San Jose, crushing and drowning many according to eyewitness accounts and videos.

With that news, we put a plan into action. As the tremors, some thought to be aftershocks from the San Francisco quake, continued, we tested all the tsunami alarms and found them working. We set up evacuation plans and routes for those living in the port and in low-lying areas like we were living at LAX, only 129 feet above sea level.

Knowing that all of our planes were at that level and the hangers were all susceptible to collapsing if a wave hit them, we created an evacuation plan using the planes. Most of the 43 trained pilots were living like us, above hangers and the rest were living close by. As the tremors continued and grew, every time we were away from home doing construction work, Derek and I worried that we wouldn't be able to save our planes being far from them.

Fortunately, at 5:37 am on October 17, Mel and I were thrown from our bed and the twins were screaming after being thrown back and forth in their crib. There was no time to call anyone, but we grabbed our clothes.

I yelled, "Mel, take the kids, I'll follow with our escape packs."

I slung one pack on my back and grabbed the other by the straps and ran downstairs to get to the NJN Studio helicopter waiting in the hanger with the other planes below, also stocked with emergency supplies.

There was no time to call anyone. The tsunami alarms were blaring up and down the coast and if the earthquake wasn't enough to get people fleeing the lower areas, the tsunami sirens did.

As Mel got the twins and our packs into the helicopter, I tried its hanger power door and it didn't open. It was jammed! I yelled…

"Mel! Mel! Come and help me! The door is jammed… Help me try to lift it!"

Melody joined me, but although we both strained as hard as we could, we couldn't open the door even when I tried a crowbar underneath to lift it. It wouldn't move. The door next to it wouldn't open either. We were trapped! While I figured we could ride out a tsunami if we had to, I saw another opportunity. I told Mel, "Quick, pull the blocks from the wheels of the CN40."

It was a twin-engine commuter with a lot of power. I hopped in the cockpit and turned on the twin engines. As soon as Mel got the blocks pulled, I revved up the engines, released the brake and drove right through its aluminum door with a loud crash. I could see the propellers breaking off cutting through the door as the door collapsed on the windscreen and stayed there while the plane taxied off at an angle to the right carrying the door with it.

I was pumped so full of adrenaline that I didn't even notice that I had bent the yoke in my hands upon impact, the plane accelerated and decelerated so quickly. But I was unhurt, forced the jammed cockpit door open with my shoulder and jumped out.

It took both of us to line the helicopter up with a battery-powered jockey to move the helicopter into position and out of the hanger. We saw two people running by that didn't have a plane and I yelled out with the loudspeaker, "Do you want a ride?"

At first they shook their heads, "No," and continued running towards their car, but suddenly, turned around and waved as I was starting to warm up the engines. Apparently they thought better of trying to save their car and outrun a possible tsunami coming for higher ground.

With them, neighbors just starting to learn to fly, aboard, we took off. But I didn't head for our ultimate destination just yet. We circled and watched as I saw other planes taking off and checked to see Derek fly out with the executive jet Wondah and he had invited us to join them on.

In the distance on the coast as the sun was coming up, we saw the water leave the coast for what seemed like minutes, but then, come rushing back in a monstrous wave. It was surreal to watch and record with our cinema-grade cameras.

By that time, most of the planes had left on crowded runways. Finally, we saw Harlan with a 989-8 leaving the hangar with a load of airport housing residents who didn't fly as the first wave broke and surged across the runways about four feet high, catching Harlan and the plane mid take-off but at a speed that guaranteed they would make it to the air.

With all the planes that were leaving also gone, we flew south amid other planes and helicopters who were also watching and videoing what they saw. Only to find the Rambler, just offshore aground on the sea bottom as the first wave receded under it and the second wave loomed ahead over its bow.

The wave crested high over the bow and caught the ship listing a bit to the right side with no water for support as the bow was violently lifted by the wave and thrust backward as its engines struggled to overcome the wave and save the ship from being washed back up on the shore.

When the sea lowered again there was enough water so that the Rambler made good time and the next wave, the strongest, was only about ten feet high to the liner but about sixty feet high when it hit the fish market and brought the hotel down.

I exclaimed to Mel, our passengers and boys, "Oh my God! What a tragedy! I sure hope everybody got out all right."

"At least the Rambler made it. I'm glad we got video. Nobody would believe if we hadn't seen it happening."

I turned our helicopter to our destination not far away, noting along the way that some of the downtown L.A. skyscrapers had fallen even though they were generally earthquake proof. We arrived at Ontario International Airport (ONT) amid a traffic jam of planes and helicopters from LAX. We were very relieved to see the 989-8 prominently parked by the terminal.

We learned later that not all of the planes made it. Derek, Melody, Wondah and I, after putting the boys with their LAX nursery attendants, flew back to LAX to assess the damage and see whether or not the planes could return. Some of the hangers had collapsed, but ours, set back behind others because it was closer to Airport Boulevard, wasn't damaged other than those jammed doors.

There was a lot of debris on the runways, but we saw some other helicopters arriving with people jumping out and going to get their electric jockeys to help them move that debris off the runways ASAP.

But a number of the people that lived there with us would not be coming back because their hangers had fallen and probably wouldn't be worth rebuilding right away. Some planes in the hangers like ours, escaped damage, but in those where the water came up higher than the bottom of the fuselage, there would be some that would need to be cleaned and/or restored before flying.

Now that the rainy season was soon upon us, I began to think that it would take some time before we would be able to get things running again like they were during the summer. We had trucks all along the roads that were now unable to come into or go out of the L.A. area again. I began to wonder if our challenges would ever allow us to get back to normal again.

Gramps was calling, so I answered the phone.

৯~৯৩৫৫৫

47

Aftermath

Grandpa Hutchins had felt the earthquake and was just curious about how it had been for us. I told him… "Gramps, it was centered just offshore from here. We had to evacuate forty-two planes and helicopters from the airport. The whole place was flooded up to nine feet, and we are all exhausted already."

"Oh my gosh! That sounds much worse than I thought."

"It is. It looks like we won't be able to get trucks to you anytime soon, or even fly out, there's so much to do."

"I understand Sonny, I'll let you get back to work like you always do. You are in my thoughts at times like this."

Gramps hung up without allowing me to say goodbye.

It wasn't until the day after, amid frequent aftershocks, that Mayor Roberts was able to call a meeting at the Medical Center auditorium, mostly via videoconference because so many of the populace were isolated and unable to come to the auditorium in person, including those of us who were trying to restore our lives at LAX.

As soon as we arrived back at the airport, we joined the other helicopter pilots and passengers in trying to get the runways free of debris as soon as possible. It was already about noon and we had a lot of work to do if everyone was going to get back before dark.

Thanks to the abundance of electric pushback tugs that survived being waterlogged, we dragged most of the debris off the runway we were using very quickly. But some of the larger things, like whole boats, required multiple tugs and even the use of helicopters to get them out of the way or even lifted all the way to the water again.

With debris lining the runway, it wasn't exactly safe in case any of the unexperienced pilots didn't stay on the runway while landing. Unfortunately, the families at ONT were all anxious to see how their homes survived and couldn't stay very long at that airport because there were no facilities working… Not even fresh water available except in the emergency packs everyone had, bottled. No food beyond what they had brought, either.

One by one, planes started coming back–all of them, except two that veered off the runway and hit debris without any injuries, fortunately, landed safely. Only to find that aftershocks made chills run up and down our spines every time they occurred thinking the worst thought… Is an even worse quake eminent? Should we camp out and not go back into our homes?

We ended up taking in two families until their apartments could be repaired or rebuilt: the Pope family of four and the Alexander family of six, so we had four toddlers and three on the way. As I surveyed the scene and talked to Crystal and Der, we had our work cut out for us in the coming weeks as the rains would get stronger every day. The worst time of the year to begin restoration of recently damaged housing here.

Some of them would have to wait months. Our initial survey indicated that about 20% of the hangars and apartments would have to be demolished and rebuilt. The rest would have to be worked on from minor repairs like our hanger doors to major repairs and reconstruction.

Rather than rebuilding the hangers, unless needed for planes, we planned to house those displaced in the main terminal if they didn't want to move into houses near the airport. Fortunately, the earlier fire at the terminal was put out by the sprinkler system and there was only minor damage that could be tolerated by those displaced.

The meeting was delayed until 9 am to give people more time to get there physically, or, if they couldn't, set up their viewing screens to connect and share with all the others. And, vote if necessary. Finally, Mel and I, along with the two families that shared our apartment, saw a harried looking Mayor Roberts pop onto the eight foot wide screen and bring the meeting to order.

"I want to thank you all for bearing with me for not getting to you until now. And, especially for all you have done from your good nature to help others in our community in our time of great need. We don't know how many have died, but the number of those with minor cuts and bruises to major crushing wounds coming into the medical center is growing as I speak.

"As for those of us in City Hall, now destroyed, as soon as the tsunami warning blew, we evacuated to our planned evacuation storefront on higher ground and have been trying to get it operating ever since. Moving the police station and jail was the hardest. Sheriff Singh, can you fill us in on that?"

Morgan, showing gray hair he didn't have before on his ample black beard, appeared on the screen.

"First of all, we had our own emergency. So, responding to your many 911 calls will have to wait until we can marshal resources to do that. As soon as the tsunami warning went off, we had to move a lot of equipment, and most important, prisoners, to an alternate jail at the old police station in Gardenia. That site was vandalized and we are working to get it operating with the equipment we brought and gathering more.

"Unfortunately, one of the vans we had hauling prisoners with a single deputy driver-guard, was overcome very close to our new destination by one or more of the five prisoners Deputy Chang was carrying and died.

"Through a sensor we tracked the van to the middle of Watts where it was abandoned. The prisoners were some of the most violent that we had imprisoned rather than executing, because they hadn't gone to trial yet.

"Fortunately, they are far from most of our population. Unfortunately, they may be on the prowl for water, food, clothes and weapons. Please give us a call if you see any of them–heavily tattooed or in orange clothing–do not approach them but give us a call on 911. We will respond as soon as we can under the circumstances caused by the earthquake and aftershocks."

There was a flurry of questions for the chief, but Joan interrupted and told everyone, "I'm sorry, but we can't take questions right now, I suggest that you send an email to the chief and he will decide which of your questions he will answer and whether your concerns are high priority or not, considering his staffing and the earthquake."

And then, she asked Captain Jensen to make a report from the Rambler, floating just off Santa Catalina Island. Conducting some rescues of the few survivors of the quake and tsunami there. Waves had reached 300 feet and nearly swamped the entire island. Destroying almost everything on it that was still intact after the earthquake and tore all of the buildings and infrastructure apart.

"We were docked at the port when the earthquake threw me out of my bed as the Rambler whipped from side to side as though hit by a rogue wave. I knew immediately what it was. There was no time for me to dress, so I slipped on my pants and ran barefoot to the bridge to get the engines started just as the tsunami warning started blaring.

"Some of our residents were running out the gangway to the dock and heading for higher ground. Fortunately, the port men we had assigned to release the mooring lines were in place just-in-time. I put slack in the lines so they could be lifted off their bollards. Once that was done, I revved the engines full forward and retrieved the lines as we left the dock and lifted the gangway as we left with people scrambling off the gangway or back into the ship. Those men who lifted the mooring lines on the dock ran for higher ground without any chance of getting on board.

"Our engines are very powerful, but it takes a bit to get this huge ship underway. We lost precious time as we gained speed. Soon though, we reached our maximum thirty kilometers the Rambler is capable of; faster than I'd ever run her.

I could feel the sea falling out from under us as we followed it down going top speed and more until there wasn't enough water to support us and we came close to running aground, starting to list to the right. I was afraid we were going to tip over when there appeared ahead a massive wave building in front of us and it was at least fifty feet tall when it hit the bow and we were thrust upward near vertical as water reached the bridge with huge force.

"Those of us on the bridge fell backward and some were injured hitting the back wall, being hit by flying objects or cut by broken glass. Throughout the Rambler we had people falling wherever they were. In state rooms, people were crushed by their beds. In larger rooms like our dining rooms, people fell great distances, some to their death. Others, hit by tables and chairs causing lots of injury and death. On the decks, those that were unable to hang on or in the path of the wave were swept overboard.

"I was at the wheel and managed to hang onto it. Then, keep the ship into the wave as we climbed up over it onto the top of the wave in the manner of couple of seconds that seemed like an eternity.

The second wave resulted from another drop in the Pacific around us but was only about twenty feet and we rose over that with little damage or injury. I understand that the third wave on the shore was the greatest but it was only about a foot by the time it reached where we were, about fifteen nautical miles offshore and free from any more waves, aftershocks or greater earthquakes or tsunamis that would follow.

"We have lots of damage caused by flying objects like tables in the dining room and other larger pieces that weren't tied down. There's lots of broken windows and glass everywhere.

"Our infirmary was badly damaged, but is very busy with broken bones, cuts and bruises. We have left the dead where they are for a mass funeral and burial at sea tomorrow. I will forward a list of those who died and who were injured as soon as I can get it done. The whole ship is a bloody mess!"

The good captain had to pause and openly cry. A few moments later, after drying his tears with a handkerchief, he continued…

"For the rest of the ship that is able, everyone is cleaning up all they can. Our food storage areas are a real mess. Everything was stored for rough seas, but not the type of jolting, gravity driven experience that I never had in my life and hope I never have again.

"We are worried about Dani's pregnancy since she fell about 10 feet against the back wall of the bridge and we are not sure without an operating ultrasound, whether her fetus, at eight months, will make it. She has broken ribs that are very painful.

"We are anchored off Santa Catalina for as long as it takes to see if we can find a dock that will be able to take us. I understand our dock at the port was destroyed and will need to be rebuilt. For now, we will repair and wait. But we don't have enough fuel to do any rescues or relocate people up and down the coast." He stopped talking and started crying again.

Mayor Roberts interrupted, "Thank you for that report. We are all stunned by the loss of life and the damage you describe. I don't know what it would've been like if we had lost the Rambler that has been such a mainstay for us since the pandemic. Are there any fishing boats out there that can tell us anything about the fleet?"

Quoc Nguyen with his father, Van, behind him appeared on the screen…

"We were offshore of Santa Barbara when our sonar detected the quake and we heard shoreline tsunami alarms going off. By radio, we have learned that most of the fishing fleet was out to sea like us in the Laughing Minnow and weren't caught by the tsunami waves.

"But those that were docked or close offshore fishing and didn't have enough time to get to calmer waters were either swamped, carried far inland or dragged out to sea–helping some survive. But we fear lots of loss of life and injury–lost fishing boats–perhaps ten."

I heard the mayor say, "Drake, can you tell us about the airport situation and your plans for reconstruction?"

Still shaken by what I heard from the others; I wasn't prepared to answer. I came to my senses and answered.

"Crystal and I have surveyed. We believe that about 20% of the hangers converted to housing have been destroyed and will need to be rebuilt. Our plan is to house the displaced occupants in the main terminal or two nearby hotels until we can rebuild or relocate them. About 10% of the rest of the hangers are livable, but have major damage and about 70%, like ours, have minor damage that can be fixed rather quickly."

"In the hangers that sustained little damage like two of our jammed hanger doors, most of the airplanes and helicopters that remained may need cleaning or minor repairs. Flooding that occurred throughout the whole airport complex to about 6 feet at the third wave. Most of the 42 pilots that flew to Ontario International have returned with their passengers because there's no water or food at that terminal.

Unfortunately, two of the smaller planes crashed when they veered off the runway we had cleared while landing and hit debris. No one was injured but both of those planes are out of commission. All in all, we fared better than I thought we would.

"Unfortunately, I'm faced with a priority problem with all the debris removal, demolition, renovation and construction ahead. While Crystal and I might be able to do all the planning, we lack manpower to manage and do the work.

"So, we will have to send you our priority list when we get it finished after reading all the damage reports on the ground and seeing the images from the air. I understand that the dock for the Rambler will have to be rebuilt, but I don't think it would be wise to rebuild the hotel.

"We probably should rebuild/relocate the fish market and access to it for fishing boats, while trying to protect it from future tsunamis if that is possible. Infrastructure will take high priority as well as clearing roadways. It's a massive task that will require everyone's help to get done."

The task I had exhausted me just to describe it and I wasn't sure that

I was up to what we would have to do to bring us back where we were just a week ago. I stopped to shed my own tears for what we all needed.

Would it ever stop, this punishment? I didn't know.

And then, the phone rang just after the meeting was over… It was Daphne!

As Crystal, Harlan, Mel and the Popes and Alexanders who were staying with us looked on the screen, Daph told us…

"It was terrible! Like everybody else, we were thrown from our beds and scrambled for clothes and something to hang onto. There was a terrible roar just outside. And, as it got lighter, I walked out on the front verandah very carefully because it had partially fallen away to see that everything on the west side of the street facing the ocean had fallen away! Derek's house, Martha's house, your house and all the rest!" She paused to cry and catch her breath.

"Even the street was cracked and damaged, making it difficult to leave here for fear of aftershocks and losing more of the street. Those that live on the east side lost parts of their backyards and were mightily shaken like we all were. Can you come to rescue us?" She pleaded.

"You know, I'm up to my ears in alligators, but we've got to see that damage ourselves. I'll see if Der and Wondah can come along, and we'll drop everything to take the helicopter up there. We will evacuate anyone who needs to leave. We are already full here but will make room for those that have to leave."

I shook my head in disbelief and said, "I'm sure glad that Martha is no longer alive to hear what happened. We'd better get going…"

48

Overcoming Depression

Amid clouds building, we arrived at the compound to discover for ourselves the shocking truth. While the drive through the compound to the cul-de-sac at the end was still there, all our homes on the west side of that street where we had grown up and recovered quite well from the pandemic, were gone! Gone in the inevitable creep of the West Coast of California falling into the sea.

And, the east side of the ridge that the compound was built on was also showing some decay with parts of the backyards and back fences fallen off in the valley between the next ridge subdivision. It was like that all over, destroyed roads, collapsed buildings, and chances that much of what was damaged or nearly destroyed would probably not be worth rebuilding again.

We landed in the courtyard in front of the mansion, but inside the fence where Daphne, Renée and their in-and-out consorts lived. As we exited the helicopter and ran to greet them coming out of the house, another aftershock reminded us that this whole ridge probably shouldn't be inhabited anymore. Part of the verandah roof and upstairs balcony had fallen in front of the entrance and we had to walk around it to get into the house. Once inside, we could see extensive damage to the circular stairway and almost everything on shelves or hanging on the walls that had come down, along with portions of the walls, themselves. It was a real mess. They needed to evacuate.

Both of the girls were a real mess, too. They were wailing…

Daph declared, "Dre, what are we going to do? I don't think we can live here anymore."

While Mel hugged her and Wondah hugged Renée, all of them pregnant, I tried to answer.

"The only thing I can think of, Daph, is for you and Renée and everyone else living on this block to come with us and stay in the LAX terminal until we can find some temporary housing for you, and then, find a place or places for you. I'm overwhelmed with work, but I'll try to find something for you along with all the others that need help with housing."

My eyes grew misty and I couldn't hold back my feelings anymore. I thought I was going to lose it, but I knew that I had to get these people out of there–soon. So, I sucked in my stomach and tried not to vomit.

We walked through the gate to see the large cracks that were very prominent on the west side of the street, but less so on the east. Our friends were coming out of those houses. Steph and Flower, Mel's oldest who had been staying with Martha, but now taken in by Ray. Rocky and Crystal Palmer, some of the mainstays of our construction company. Selma Lopez, who had been working with Steph and Martha. Ray Dugas, who had been taking care of the girls since Martha passed. Finally, Vik, Viky and Pete Sarnoff, ironworkers and an essential part of the Hutchins and Jones Construction Company, too.

While it was terrible that they all had to be evacuated, it was probably a good thing that they were relocating to the airport. Everyone could leave together for the construction sites each day rather than drive from the compound. One of the first jobs for the Palmers and their crew would be to come up with a way to capitalize on the coming rains to provide hot water to the airport terminal bathrooms where the temporary residents could find some semblance of group bath convenience.

It took four trips back-and-forth carrying them and their belongings they put together trying to make their new home more like home, with the promise that they could come back later when they found alternative housing and get their furniture and other, reasonable personal items that they loved.

As the rains began, the whole village fell into depression and found it very hard to get up in the morning in the gloom and began to eat the elephant that lay before them. Just to make it somewhat like the village was before the earthquake and tsunami changed things, seemed insurmountable.

The counseling circles were growing, and Melody and I attended regularly to try to help me with my inability to figure out how to proceed with so much to do and so few to do the work. One of the things that came out of the counseling session was this: by working hard at physical labor, everyone said, "For a little while, I forgot what was troubling me as I focused on getting something done… A little accomplishment in the many accomplishments I would have to do to make things more normal again."

Like they had to initially, get past the loss of friends and loved ones in the pandemic, the bad circumstances after, and the earthquake.

I began with making sure that all the power sources were working, water and sewer lines were not damaged, plugged or otherwise not working. And that all of the greenhouses were working and had someone to maintain them –mostly the children–to produce fresh vegetables and greens for the com-munity. While the animals had initially been frightened by the earthquake and some swept out to sea by the tsunami, the green grass and new plant growth of the rainy season was a boon to health and growth. Most of them still had a warmer, drier place to go in and out of the cold, mud and wet.

So, we still had adequate fish, seafood, meat, milk, eggs, vegetables and fruit from our higher ground warehouses and food stores. It just took a little tweaking here and there to get things working at full production during the rainy season. Ray told me that most of the Santa Monica Pier and nearly all of the luxury beachfront homes were completely destroyed.

"I will see if I can start another net fishing operation near the airport so that we can have fresh fish while we are camping out. The roads are impassable to get to the Santa Monica beach anyway."

We had a rather subdued Thanksgiving and Christmas celebrations but celebrated a lot of second and first birthdays during that period and got the streets between the airport and the medical center in good shape by using gravel and blacktop to fill cracks and placing culverts where water had tried to make gullies across streets from heavy rains and flooding.

Like children always have, those little guys and gals were having the time of their life with their siblings and friends and didn't have a care in the world when it came to all the hardships that we adults were going through. Those birthday parties were great morale boosters for all of us. We tried to do something special for each one… More helpful for us adults than the kids.

***

The rainy season wasn't as happy and as good as we matured, so all of this time we spent whittling away at problems. Fortunately, the weather cycle changed, and we went into a winter with little rain and snow on the mountains. Little by little, we were able to open up more roadways and make them easier and safer to travel, even if we had to slow down for the bumps created by temporary patches to the road surface. By mid-summer we had opened a route to the Central Valley so trucks could roll again and we were able to rescue the four trucks that had to be abandoned on the road and their drivers picked up by helicopter and brought back to the village.

They were really happy when the drivers returned and found their trucks still in good shape. Some of their cargos, if they were refrigerated, were not, and it was a terrible, sickening job to clean them out.

The inmates that escaped while being evacuated came back, one at a time, because they were cold, wet and starving. They were immediately assigned to daily roadwork crews and locked up at night. Something they gladly did for better food and fresh air… Even though sometimes it was pouring rain.

The guy who had killed Deputy Chang did not return. One of the others told Sheriff Singh, "Ricardo committed suicide rather than starve or give himself up. He was one hard-core mutha. Glad I ain't like him."

Being unable to use most of the elevated sections of the highways made travel take much longer and less predictable, timewise. Fortunately, the old roads before they were elevated, were still there. After removing all the rubble and repairing all the cracks and gullies, our trucks could move quite quickly unhampered by the traffic that originally required the freeways to be built in the first place. They would be a long time being rebuilt. But even these old roads had washed-out bridges and culverts to deal with. All we could do in the beginning was just makeshift work or devise a detour around the problem.

It was another long and dry summer. Fortunately, most of our cisterns had completely filled by the end of the rainy season and were able to supply our crops and homes with water. In a few cases we had to haul water again from various lakes that were now crystal clear and full of fish and other wildlife that we hunted for additional food. Derek, Ray and I savored those times we went hunting because it took us away from the grind of daily construction jobs and the worries that were endless.

There were more births and pregnancies. All of these babies and toddlers were a real joy but could be a pain and they got into our computers or papers that were left around the house. Of course, we had to get dogs and cats and there were many, many strays to choose from. If one didn't work out for one reason or another we could put it back out in the wild and get another one, usually a puppy or kitten so it wouldn't develop any bad habits before we taught them.

One day I told the twins in a jovial way, "While you were still in Mommy's tummy, we had to shoot dogs and cats just to get something to eat." Suddenly they both started crying and ran off calling out, "Mommy… Mommy! Daddy said he's going to kill Jax and Penelope! He says we are going to eat them!"

While Mel comforted them and they hid against her growing belly, I tried to apologize and tell them that I didn't mean "our" pets. But it was to no avail, until a couple days later, they came back and jumped up on my lap while watching streaming movies after a long hard day's work. I wondered if they were going to be sissies and unable to take on what it would take to run the company after Derek and I are gone.

49

Putting the Pieces Back Together

May 2037: Five years after the pandemic changed the world.

It has been quite a struggle but we have made progress. The village has doubled in size over the years. People have come from all over for the safety, convenience and general benefzits living in a community like Los Angeles. A climate and location it always had that made L.A. so great in the first place.

As a result, we've made progress because of the people that joined our construction company and started other companies doing all kinds of things that needed to be done to reestablish some semblance of the life we had before the pandemic and provided by California. The two "Great Ones" as we call the earthquakes that set our progress back but didn't totally defeat us like it seemed in the beginning, three years ago, they would have.

With no real port except the damaged one in San Diego, Captain Jens Jensen and Dani, his wife, came ashore by a tender boat to a town meeting shortly after the tsunami and made the following announcement for everyone who was there or online to hear… Jens appeared haggard and tired, but was dressed in his full white captain's uniform.

"I want to first tell you that it has been amazing to be a part of this community for the past two years as we worked together and recovered from probably the greatest tragedy that has hit our world–ever. But the earthquake and tsunami has struck a blow to the port and my ship that is nearly insurmountable.

"I have been in touch with our corporation in Denmark and have decided, the first thing in spring, to take the Northern Passage back to the Rambler's birthplace on a river in Germany. To be refitted with a reduced crew they have there to do the work."

There was a collective gasp among the people in the audience as they heard the news. Having been dependent upon the ship for so many things for so long. When the good captain sensed their concern, he raised his hand to stop the murmuring and spoke again…

"Please don't despair… Any of my shipmates, my crew who want to stay here, can. And any of you who wish to take the long voyage can certainly join us in the journey that will require you to work as hard as you ever have to make sure that we make it with so many windows out through the frigid waters full of icebergs until we reach the North Sea open water again by July if everything goes well. But the Rambler is a good ship and still one of the fastest and most maneuverable of cruise ships, ever. I think we will make the trip there and back within three years, maybe four."

With that there was a cheer from the audience and as soon as the meeting was over, several people came to the stage to sign up for the trip and to help with the refitting half a world away.

And, I'm pleased to write that it took us only a short while to reestablish the fish market after we removed debris from the destroyed hotel and moved the few people that still had lived there to housing in neighborhoods beyond the elevation the tsunami had reached.

Rebuilding the port to accept the Rambler when it came back earlier this year required removing a lot of debris in the channel and a lot of concrete work to restore the pier from both earthquake and tsunami damage. It is so good to have the ship back with even some new people from Germany and other parts of Europe wishing to come to Southern California with our increasing droughts and periods of hurricanes and rain. Not to mention, earthquakes. But I believe more big ones are a long way off, given our history of earthquake cycles.

Hutchins and Jones Construction Company is the only one in town, except for some loyal subcontractors who managed to survive and continue to work with us. And, we have engaged in a tremendous public works project funded only by money stolen from all the coffers in all the bank's safe-deposit boxes, unclaimed, to help pay all of the people who had to learn new trades and work very hard to rebuild, better than before, our town from a village to someday, a great metropolis again.

Carlos and Jerry are now both seventeen and have married. They both plan to become subcontractors for us. Carlos as a civil engineer and Jerry as a landscape architect. They are a big help to us and taking a lot of responsibility at an early age.

We have been opening, first the highways through town, and then, streets, as necessary, so that commerce can continue using many driverless, solar powered vehicles and taxis that our meager automotive repair people can make roadworthy.

One of our greatest accomplishments, about three years ago, was being able to get driverless, AI operated, eighteen-wheelers on the road coast-to-coast that are solar powered. With a normal range of about 600 miles on a charge, whenever there are periods of no sun, they just park by the side of the road until their batteries are fully charged again and then continue on automatically to their next destination that may or may not be occupied by humans. Robots and drones do much of the loading and off-loading and distribution for us as well.

Our nurseries and preschools have continued to grow. Mel and I, not only have Ron and Reg who are four and already showing Derek and me how to run our operations with their skillful toys, like flying drones as skillfully as any of us oldsters; she has also given us Mindy, three, Chase, two, Cindy, one and a boy we hope to call, Rake, due in about four months.

In addition, I have about fifteen other kids who I won't bore you with all of their names and ages from women who needed a helping hand and needed children to help them reestablish their lives again, overcoming depression and giving them purpose and hope. I promise to support every one of them financially, if need be. In preschool, they are all playing together and studying together as one big happy family.

We are reopening elementary schools for the expected surge of young students to come. In the meantime, using what is still operating on the Internet, our preschools are using smart technology and AI to enhance the minds of these young children in ways that we never imagined when Derek and I were in school. We may have some Einsteins, Steve Jobs or Elon Musks already in their midst, soaking up knowledge we can't believe as we work on mundane nuts and bolts projects getting things working again.

We now have every available helicopter in the Los Angeles area flying with pilots and five without. But also, countless drones doing daily deliveries of many things up to fifty pounds and other duties like canvassing areas for infrastructure repairs.

We are a very busy community these days but not in the way we were before the pandemic. Most of us go to our place of work in the morning and return in the evening to relax and unwind. But they're no more long commutes and busy business office activity during the days.

Actually, it's quite quiet and a place where wildlife is flourishing in all the new open spaces along with our domestic animals grazing. It is an almost pastoral scene going back to the beginning of Los Angeles over 500 years ago. The parks we are creating and linking together throughout the area will ensure that wildlife will have an equal footing with humans.

Ray, Derek, Carlos and I relax some evenings after a hard day's work by taking the helicopter up to the abandoned estate at the end of the compound to look for quail, emu and ostrich eggs, shoot some of the birds in season, help reduce the growing population of wild pigs, and bag an occasional blacktail buck. If the bear become a problem, we kill them for food because their population is growing and stable.

The same with other predators, like bobcat and cougar. When they become a threat to our village people and children we find it best to eliminate them. The food is always welcome for its freshness and taste. Nothing goes to waste when we render an animal for food and other purposes. Some of the native American tribes in California have been showing us how to do that.

During the spring while egg hunting, we bring the kids because they always find it a lot of fun along with helping us pick mushrooms, locate tasty cactus, and other wild food that we can add to our diet. Ron and Reg have become part of our fall deer and bear hunting, although we have to carry them sometimes when they grow tired of walking through the chaparral hills with us.

For the last three years we have launched weeklong hunting expeditions including over 100 of our Village people to the Sierras. There, we can hunt mountain goat and elk along with what we hunt in the coastal ranges. Of course, we always stop by to see Gramps along the way.

Grandpa Ralph Hendricks is thriving since he took in the seventeen-year-old orphan, Rosalie (Rose), the only family member that survived from the gang in town. Two years ago, they were blessed with a new arrival, Abilene (Able), and the farmhouse no longer looks like an old hermit bachelor pad.

Gramps always reminds me, "I don't know who he looks like more,

Dre, you or Julio Iglesias… from the way he yells, I think he's going to be a singer."

And then, he chuckles loudly, a proud father again after all these years. We have sent our representatives and senators to Washington, but they mostly remain here and work through the Internet. Like everything else, websites that were still active after the pandemic have begun to fail for lack of maintenance. We wish we could enlist the genius of Augie Palmer, but Wondah, assisted by Rocky Palmer, are doing the task of locating some major servers in town. And then, attempting to restore some websites and create new ones for our use with AI assistance.

Washington assures us that our greatly downsized military are doing great work helping others throughout the world recover using our warships and planes. They are also drawing on funds from banks all over to fund projects on the order of the New Deal to help us get the railroads back working, refineries working to provide all of the synthetics and chemicals we have become so dependent upon. But only the ones that can be recycled and are not harmful to the ecosystem. As well as help decentralize power sources because the grid in most places no longer operates.

We have to give the people assurance that everyone who survived is moved to safer places to live as the droughts, wildfires, violent storms and resulting floods ravage more and more of the country. These weather threats won't be turned around until we can lower the carbon dioxide in the atmosphere. Something that happened almost overnight when the pandemic occurred but needs to be enhanced if we are going to make it to the 21st century without everyone and every animal, bird and insect dying along with fish and aquatic life in the rivers and seas.

It's a daunting task to turn things around, but from what I hear worldwide, everyone, everywhere, is doing it in a cooperative way. So many wars have ended while survivors from warring factions are now cooperating with each other. I hate to say it too soon, but it's a great time to be alive.

❧ ❦❧ ❦ ❧

50

Thriving Amid Horrific Climate Change

May 2042: Ten years after the pandemic changed the world.

The weather has gotten progressively worse. We had a period of drought that ran most of 2036 through 2040. Fortunately, the Los Angeles River didn't run dry until August 2039. By that time, the California Aquifer had recovered enough so that we were able to draw fresh water from deep wells to keep us in water for domestic use as well as keep our crops, fruit and nut trees from dying and water for our livestock.

We had two hurricanes, one in 2036 and the other, last year that dumped a year's worth of rain, destroyed buildings and threatened our people. Last year, we clocked winds of 160 mph, tearing away at our solar panels, windmills and rooftop greenhouses. They all required a lot of repair after it was over.

We lost two people who were hit by flying debris, three others from lightning strikes, and two from unfortunate drowning caused by vehicles caught in floods. It was impossible to be outside in the hurricanes, so most, like us, hunkered down in the safest part of our living areas. Thankfully, the Internet and radar told us well enough in advance that it was coming.

We lost others, five adults and three children when self-flying or navigation systems failed. And three more from batteries failing and the flash fires that burned the occupants so badly they couldn't survive. Accidents at work injured about 50 people and killed two. AI has been a big help in improving safety wherever heavy work is done.

Melody has had seven more kids, although two of them are clearly from Harlan and Ray.

She tells me, "Dre, now that I'm 39, I think it's time for me to stop having babies. I've been lucky so far, with two sets of twins and all these others, breast-feeding Art, to taking Ron and Reg to work with us in the afternoons. I don't want to have any kids with disabilities like some are getting, having kids over 40. I believe I've done my part."

"Mel, you've done more than your part. How you managed to mother all of those kids while pregnant most of the time and still work with Der and me almost every day is amazing… Why I love you more than ever."

"Dre, I think I'll get fixed… My tubes tied. You know how I love sex, both with you and with some others who make me feel young even though most of them are much younger than me, like you. I'm going to have fun as long as I can because this world is stressful and whenever I'm with a man I feel all that stress gone for a while. Helps me sleep better, too. Now that Jens is back from Germany and running cruises all the way to Acapulco, I'm thinking of joining him and having a little fun with him and Dani… What do you think?"

"What do I think? Do I have a choice?" I laughed. "Dani is such a Scandinavian fox. If you can interest Jens and all of us sharing the captain's quarters on a trip to Acapulco, I'm all for it."

"But will you still love me after you've gone blonde?" She teased… "Have you forgotten about Daph and at least three others, as blonde and blue-eyed as they get."

"There's something about Ray's red hair makes me think of King Harry of Great Britain. Oh, I love that guy."

"We counting coup?"

"No, just reminiscing and looking forward to what's possible. Maybe some of those, Hollywood types."

"It sure is nice that the movie industry is back up and running, producing new streaming movies for the world through the World Wide Web. Never thought that would happen so quickly. But we sure had a bunch of unknown screenwriters, directors, actors, and production people that survived and have restarted what I thought they would not be able to do so soon.

"Daph's found her way there and I'm glad. She was floundering for a while not knowing what she would do. It's good to see her starting some of these new productions. Starring in some of them, too."

"And Flower… I'm so proud of her. At seventeen and already two years into her college studies in the dramatic arts. Living downtown with her boyfriend and my two grandchildren, Jetson, 16 months and already get-ting into everything like a two year-old and Sparkle who is the image of me when I was three months old." She sighed happily.

"Kiss me honey. We'd better get some sleep. Another big day ahead and I've got to give Art his midnight feeding."

We kissed, and I rolled over to fall asleep. Later, I felt her spooning me as we turned together like we always did when we were sleeping together. Laughed when we watched videos of it from our overhead camera–every half hour or so, turning in unison as though we instinctively knew what to do in our sleep.

Melody had given us, in addition to Ron and Reg, nine, Mindy, eight, Chase, seven, Cindy, six, Rake, five, Celeste, four, Rob and Rand, three, Star, two, Gaye, two, King, one and Art, four months. Seven of those were mine and the rest knew who their fathers were. With all those kids in the house, I was glad that our two boarding families from the earthquake had found suitable homes nearby above the potential tsunami line of the future.

Speaking of the future, like St. Helens in the last century, Mount Rainier blew its top in 2037 and the pyroclastic flow reached all the way to Seattle, causing about 500 deaths and setting back that community like the earthquake here set back ours. Mount Lassen has become active again with flowing lava endangering the 5 and the community below.

Fortunately, we were able to send driverless trucks filled with supportive supplies as well as mobile homes for those without homes, until they got back on their feet like we did. With the 5 open all the way to Canada, it was a blow to have it cut off again, but that was one of the projects that we were starting to do far from our home village here in L.A.

All of the nine-year-olds, the first of the generation we call, The Pandemic Generation, get up early every morning, have a hearty breakfast and then take care of their animals and crops before heading off to school until noon. After a hearty lunch, they take off for various afternoon work. Some work with their parents, like Ron and Reg, but many try out different work to see what they like to do and what they might end up spending their lives doing as varied as playing music, writing, engaging in the the-ater, as well as so many trades that need young workers with so much re-building to do.

Ron and Reg have become part of our construction crew. They run drones checking on the progress of construction and its quality with detailed photos. They help us maintaining our hardware and software for our computers and all of our temporary construction offices, usually on wheels, and run errands in cars, trucks and even planes that are all self-driving / flying with AI operation where they can practice their driving and flying skills without worry by us.

The AI always takes over if they get in a dangerous situation like driving too fast or flying towards potential obstacles like highline wires or landing too steeply. Even landing the planes if they sense any potential failure of the plane parts for any reason, whether it be the motor, wheels and tires, batteries, computers or even parts of the skin of the aircraft coming loose.

We have refocused our construction projects away from remodeling and revamping homes for those displaced to rebuilding the freeways, starting with redesigning some to be more earthquake resistant before rebuilding. There is not much traffic that needs them now, in the future they will speed driverless loads throughout the city once again like before the pandemic but without the heavy commuter, workaday and leisure loads that snarled traffic before.

Our workforce had become stretched even thinner, so the village declared a four day work week, so that all of the people could spend three days a week with their families doing whatever they wanted to do. With our helicopters and planes readily available, they could leave town and enjoy some other location of their choice and come back ready to work again after their days away from all that struggle to make things right.

Supplies like sheet rock and concrete, as well as parts for vehicles and planes, by now had all been removed from supply houses and manufacturers. All the new vehicles had replaced those that failed and the ones that failed had to be cannibalized for parts for the ones that were in operation. Small shops were started to make supplies like sheetrock and concrete again. But it took a new way of not using too much raw material and relying heavily on recycling, rather than burying so much of the debris everywhere that was being hauled away, piece by piece.

The nine-year-olds were now in middle schools we opened, but their accelerated online based curricula from sources like KenduAcademy.edu were already placing them in college-level instruction. The ability of AI tutoring each individual as though they had a personal tutor was amazing in the way it empowered all of our young children to be much more than all of the generations before who had to endure middle school with boring teachers and the kinds of bullying and classmate misbehavior that had become the norm for preteens heading into even more disruptive years trying to grow up. Our kids were enhancing their talents rather than experimenting with social misbehavior–a great relief.

We even got to open some of Disney Land so that our children could once again enjoy the delights that place always provided. Mel and I, along with Harlan and Crystal had flown as far as Disney World in Florida for three days of fun in the sun there. Working with a greatly reduced staff, Disney World still had much fun and was maintaining its Safari Land so well that all the animals out from Africa were thriving and protected from occasional hurricanes and floods. Human like robots replaced all the wonderful characters that had been played by human actors, like Mickey and Minnie Mouse.

Nearby, NASA was beginning to send probes to Mars and astronauts to the Moon to start mining there. Miners were rotated in and out often to keep them from the dangers of staying too long at 1/6 gravity and the radiation unimpeded that required them to live in the dark underground. Underground there was protection and water but not much natural sensory enjoyment, except by streaming videos from Earth onto the walls making them appear to be earthlike with day and night sensation and simulating actual earth environments. Part of the regimen of exercise required that they experience Earth gravity four hours each day or suffer the aftereffects of light gravity when they returned to Earth rotating out after 2 years or so.

Gramps, Ralph Hutchins, now 92, but showing no signs of slowing down, had found great help from his son, Able, seven, and other young kids he hired from the village to tend to his garden and fruit trees while he imparted his wisdom and knowledge of farming to a generation that would repopulate the entire Central Valley. Of course, Rosalie was a big part of allowing him to be able to interact with the kids every day.

Gramps and Able joined us in the hunts for seasonal duck, geese and quail along the San Joaquin watershed, as well as capturing and killing feral hogs. Later in the fall, they joined us for hunts and trout fishing in the Sierras. Our three boys, 2nd cousins, became fast friends for life with Able through those camping and hunting trips.

The few scientists that were still working on atmospheric data, told us through the Internet that there had been a drastic drop in CO_2 release into the atmosphere in spite of so many wildfires and industrial fires that burned uncontrolled from 2032 to 2035.

Unfortunately, methane release from permafrost melting in the Arctic continues to keep the global temperature high for the near future, in spite of indications that a new Ice Age may be upon the Earth because of the orientation of the axis of the earth that often changed regularly.

With no way of predicting how the weather would go, only the most adaptable species on the planet were able to respond to the changes, while so many were dying out until the United States and some other countries have begun to create greenhouses and zoos along with DNA repositories all over the world to try to save as many species as we can until the Earth climate stabilizes again.

So many species have required that we create an ark for them in several different ways. The Swedish seed repository created many years ago will be a huge help with replanting species of plants that have already gone extinct. Replanting those plants will relieve pressure on all the animals and birds that have depended upon those foods to survive in the past.

The leveling off of the climate swings where it was about 1990 is not expected until 2100 or even later. While some of us survivors may live long enough to see the day, many will not, and even we may not know at that time, whether the climate will settle down for any long period. It is only a guesstimate now.

All we can hope for is doing our best so that future generations will not have to suffer and work like we have. But in our suffering, we have lived more than most people live a lifetime in the last ten years.

At only twenty-nine, both Derek and I are looking forward to what we might be able to accomplish in the future… If we live that long…

৵৽৵৽

51

A World Totally Changed

May 2062: Twenty years after the pandemic changed the world.

It is hard to believe how the world and we have changed in the twenty years since the pandemic forced us to rethink who we were and why we were here. I can't believe while Derek and I are thirty-eight, Ron and Reg are now nineteen and have taken over the day-to-day operation of Hutchins and Jones Construction.

Leaving Derek and me semiretired, but still heavily involved in planning what to do next. Most of it has been to counter the horrific climate change and its consequences I'm seeing from the 20th century now wreaking havoc on the 21st and all of our young people's lives.

Not only have both of the boys… I still call them boys, although each of them has children since they were senventeen and I have three grandchildren… taken on full responsibility for construction projects that I only dreamed of in their industries…

But, they both also have advanced degrees. Ron has a doctorate in mineralogy and Reg, a doctorate in astrophysics, leading our company into the space-based manufacturing that we are doing in addition to general, sustainable construction.

But let me first tell you about the climate. While we have noted that the CO2 in the atmosphere has begun to decline rapidly and some parts of the Arctic permafrost have returned with increasing cold spells during the winters, during the past decade we have seen some of the greatest droughts that history has ever recorded.

More violent storms requiring new scales of severity, hurricanes, tornadoes and derechos making much of the North American and Asian continents very dangerous places to live, except underground or in steel structures able to withstand 200 mile an hour wind and hail the size of cantaloupes. Hail has killed more animals, birds and humans than the previous yearly climate killer, lightning, in the last decade.

Shortly after the Great One Two in the L.A. area, while we were re-build-ing the fish market and the dock for the Rambler, we noted a rapid water rise. Wondah informed us that the ice cap covering Greenland had com-pletely collapsed and so had parts of the continent ice of Antarctica, as seen from space.

The exposed bedrock grew green during the long summers for the first time, ever, in recorded history. Projections were for the oceans to rise 69 feet and we have noted forty-five feet so far in LA–rebuilding and restor-ing ac-cordingly. We have been resorting to floating docks rather than rigid ones built on bedrock to accommodate these water level changes so rapidly happening.

The bad news is that most of the California beaches are gone because it takes at least a thousand years to create a sand beach. The rising water is now crashing, sometimes, very violent waves, against the crumbling coastal heights, making the scenic Cal 1 totally unrepairable in most places. With coastal avalanches and cave-ins on the rise.

The bad news continues with global photos showing so many of the world's islands simply disappearing under the waves. To be gone for a thousand years more unless an Ice Age comes along again soon. Many of those islands protected by coastal reefs or mangroves, all gone now.

Coastal cities around the world, despite heroic effort to save them like Miami, Amsterdam, Venice, New Orleans, Sydney, New York City and London were for naught.

While the Santa Catalina Island remains, the popular Cayman Islands are gone along with many others like the Florida Keys that existed for centuries just a few feet above the, mostly calm, ocean waves.

Sea water leaking into the volcanoes in the Azores, caused one to erupt in 2057 with a massive landslide of half of the island. We have reports that a 100 foot tsunami hit the East Coast from St. John's, Newfoundland to Miami, killing many of that growing population and setting the US government back again with Washington DC under fifty feet of water and the classic buildings like the Capitol and museums destroyed. Those that survived have vowed to rebuild, but I think it will take a long time and require us to get involved at some point.

The good news is that the kelp forest off the coast of California has more than doubled in size, making fish and other aquatic life that live there much more common and providing us with food and fertilizer in abundance for our greenhouses and changing palates of taste.

While many of our young people have become vegetarians, our meat diets have also included much more wild game, fish and insects than ever before the pandemic. Some species have suffered greatly from climate change, others are more adaptive and have reproduced by the millions like Brahman cattle and bison in the Great Plains making them good sources of wild natural food with few chemicals in their bodies.

Our government, before the tsunami, was back up and running, concentrating on recovery, reintroducing key manufacturing, often through cottage industries that have sprung up making things that are needed for reconstruction and moving forward.

Most of the governments in the world have also started back up and no longer are at war. Some of the poorest areas hit hard by drought or flooding have called on our military to help them recover. But our military budget has been redirected mostly towards climate mitigation, space exploration and scientific discovery, making it less likely to step in on disasters. Studies have shown that many people during disasters have tremendous resilience and have recovered without help.

We are engaged in removing hazardous waste by sending it on a course towards the Sun. Have done limited mining on the Moon and Mars to provide resources here on Earth that would require additional devastating mining our fragile ecosystems can no longer tolerate. These initiatives were unheard of before the epidemic changed everything.

We have restored all of the freeways but they are mostly used for heavy hauling and lightly traveled. Many of the railroads in the country are now running solar/wind powered trains with AI running the lead locomotives that spot and stop them long before they reach any anomaly ahead, spotted by cameras, laser radar and infrared detectors.

Not only are the trains and trucks running without people; we have had very few train and truck accidents in recent years. The West Coast Bullet Liner, WCBL, is completed from Vancouver to San Diego. With plans for it to run down the West Coast of Mexico all the way to Mexico City in the next ten years. Additional expansion will take it to Edmonton and Saskatoon across Canada later.

AI taxis carry most people around town. But there are also AI assisted personal aircraft that fill the skies along with drones of many kinds. Their AI functions result in following paths of least resistance amid other flying objects, wires, buildings, poles and other structures that have caused accidents in the past.

These AI devices are not completely foolproof. We have had accidents, but they are much fewer than when we had planes, helicopters and drones flown by highly trained humans with autopilot assists. We humans are just too slow and unreliable when it comes to determining all kinds of potential hazards while at speed. When AI fails so rarely, human intervention has been known to save lives, too.

Because of the redistribution of wealth and the available property left idle because so many people of wealth and ownership died, most of the residents of LAX, like us, have left for some of the more palatial compounds formally owned by the stars and moguls, CEOs and other captains of industry, the arts and business.

We have relocated our family to join Daph and her consorts at her Uncle Louie's retreat in the Hollywood Hills. It suits our outdoor lifestyle much better and the children just love roaming the woods whenever they have free time to do so.

Efforts to save species have accelerated and been improved. In our greenhouses we are growing exotic plants and fungus in mass quantities, not only for food but for preservation when they can be replanted in the wild once the climate settles down again to a more constant and viable seasonal pattern.

One of our most and fervent efforts is to maintain coral that have been destroyed by rising waters and high water temperatures forcing many fish, mollusks, mammals and other sea creatures to modify their patterns of life or migration routes in a remarkable way that we didn't foresee.

Many species prosper in spite of the loss of so many others. Life, especially of those of us who are human or intelligent like dolphins and the apes, are very adaptable and can change rapidly when necessary in order to not only survive but thrive–like we have done in the face of some, seemingly impossible, challenges.

I believe I will live, now that I am thirty-nine, to see the end of the century and the planned Earth-sized habitats built orbiting the sun within easy transport of the Earth. They will be built from asteroids and comets that are abundant to be mined. And also, to see the first deep space probes to find other suitable planets like the Earth in many stages of evolution that may or may not be anything like the Earth and far stranger than any fan-tasy we can dream of.

Gramps died last year just after waiting for his 102nd birthday before allowing us to give him euthanasia having, as he put it during the celebration with all of us around…

"It's really hard for me to believe what I've seen in my long life. And how I have overcome so many changes in recent years while so many others died and didn't get to see. I have to hand it to Derek and you, for coming to my rescue so many times when I thought all was lost and rewarding me with such a wonderful life here after all the trials and tribulations we've seen together.

"Tomorrow, when you put me to sleep for the last time, leaving all these aches, pains and irritations behind I don't want anymore, you'll be looking forward to a future that looks so bright for all in spite of what we've done to try to destroy our planet before. I plead guilty to being a part of that." He sighed and began to cough… one of the reasons he wanted to go away… from smoking in his youth. It kept coming back after multiple transplants.

After several of his favorite margaritas made fresh from his own lemons and tequila from agave grown on the farm and distilled in the village, he grew sleepy and went to bed early from his 102 birthday party looking forward to the next day.

On the morning of July 4, 2061, we woke Gramps up to a rather, late for him, breakfast of steak and eggs, helped him get dressed and into his AI assisted personal hovercraft for a spin around his growing 2000 acre farm. Most of the spring crops, like corn and alfalfa, were already harvested as the land became totally parched from the hot sun of summer drought.

Gramps returned to the shade of his 400-year-old oak tree in the yard and a lounge where we all gathered around and gave him his lethal dose of Fentanyl as he raised his last glass of margarita with all of us toasting him knowing that he would be passing painlessly.

Able, with the help of his mother, at seventeen, had already assumed running the growth and productivity of the farm using many hired helpers from the village. Derek and I were grateful to him for taking over stewardship of the Hutchins's foothold in the great Central Valley of California.

With our AI assistance for almost everything we did and many implants and bots making us healthier and more powerful in many physical, sensory and intellectual ways, the harsh climate of the earth no longer seemed insurmountable like it had just years before when the ecosystems were collapsing and extinctions increasing with no end in sight and few of us left from the pandemic to fight it.

I looked forward to a brighter future but had no idea except what AI was telling me what it would be.

～∞৪৩∞～

52

Leaving Earth to Evolve

2092: Fifty years after the pandemic changed the world.

I must apologize for not checking in earlier. I have been very busy in retirement and everything that I experience is now automatically picked up and placed in a cloud memory bank so that anyone with any interest in what Drake Hutchins did, is doing or will be doing in the future is easy to access by merely asking for my experience or opinion available in-stantly through your memory sources and connection to the World Wide Web of information. Soon to extend solar system wide, with some delays in response based on the limits of electromagnetic physics.

But I must complete this early, sometimes on paper, but mostly just a summary of events that have happened or may happen for the reader to close the pages on this book of a style from an earlier time when books were made by only the strong and powerful, making sure that their story was the only story that counted, while millions of humans were used as cannon fodder for war, wealth and power; kept under the spell of the cults of control like religion and political dogma.

Somewhere along the line, we have learned to defeat the fear of death. The primary driver of all of the cults that ever existed. The promise of something better after human death and after a life of struggle and misery. At sixty-eight, Derek and I still feel no older than twenty. In fact, in some ways, even better. We are not experiencing the loss of function as we age because any time any part of our bodies starts to deteriorate from age, they are replaced either by medication or surgery in painless ways that rejuvenate us and allow all of us in retirement to continue to do what we love to do without any health restraint.

Bots maintain our bodily systems better than our immune systems ever did. Gene therapy heads off potential disease, cures diseases, and regenerates whole bodily systems. Implants provide us super memory power and access to the cloud Internet by mere thought without having to use any devices anymore, like the obsolete cell phones, smart pads, and other electronic devices that required the use of rare minerals and created a lot of junk that needed to be recycled. Those of our generation are now generally what would be called in early science fiction, cyborgs. Our bodies so enhanced by AI technology, that we can live our complete lifespan without pain, insecurity or other concerns that have always held humans back from their full potential.

Hutchins and Jones Space Industries is in the process of building Earth 2 with many other firms, after completing Earth 1 just two years ago and learning so much from the process and the many failures. But, with AI help, all were overcome and the population there is growing. Those are mostly young people who are willing to take the risk of living off planet in an artificial planet colony and make it their home. They are the pioneers of 22nd century, just eight years off. The ones that will lead us off Earth in the future.

While we still have active research and mining projects on the Moon, Mars, and several moons of Jupiter and Saturn, including an outpost on the narrow temperate side of Mercury, where brave human solarnauts are making breakthroughs in understanding in very dangerous locations, we have given up any idea of colonizing any of these places. Largely, because of radiation and long-term gravity problems that make these places, while suitable for AI androids to operate in, very unhealthy for humans. Researchers are regularly rotated in and out of these places.

The village of Los Angeles has returned to a megalopolis of earthquake proof, sustainable buildings for work, home and leisure for 835,000 full-time residents. Most of the food is still locally grown from what remains of the city sprawl no longer there, returning to a more pas-toral or even wild environment for both pleasure and use as a source of recreation and food. The sky is more filled than ever with personal air-craft and birds. There hasn't been an accident in the last decade because of collision avoidance technology that is so good allowing toddlers to fly for fun. They grow up so fast now.

I instantly know I have sixty-five grandchildren and some twenty-three great-grandchildren. I could, from my cloud memory, reiterate them all but it would bore you. I treat them all with the same love when they come to me for various reasons. Some, just to see who their grandfather really is. And women still come to me and to Derek for children because of our success in life and they want our genes to continue in their line of children. Our generation of males who survived the pandemic have been both the first to enjoy and to be cursed with this urge to repopulate the planet. It is the women that are doing all the work and we greatly appreciate it with their powers of motherhood and caring.

But relocated Washington DC, in alliance with most of the world leaders, has decided that it is time that our growing population leave the planet for the colonies we are building, so the planet can heal and continue to evolve naturally. And, continue to surprise us with new life without our intervention. The plan is to allow the population of the Earth to only reach 1 billion. We have an accurate count of the world population at 800.2 mil-lion and rapidly growing.

The colonies are being built in Earth orbit around the Sun with stimulated gravity to take care of the rest of our population. Each new Earth replica will be able to maintain comfortably, a billion people. Each of us will be able to return to Earth occasionally to view our small planet and how it is changing. Those that stay on the planet will largely be researchers and scientists taking advantage of what evolution and geological and astronomical change is creating.

In the early 21st century we easily eliminated one of the major causes of Earth extinctions like the demise of the dinosaurs 65 million years ago by a huge meteor, creating the rise of mammals like us. All we had to do was simply nudge them slightly from their orbits around the Sun or planets that they are on.

Many of those asteroids and comets have also been corralled for use in our construction of model Earth replacement colonies. Making our near solar system safer all the time from unidentified flying objects traveling at high speeds. The rogue ones coming from deep space outside our solar system–the most dangerous ones.

All the nuclear waste from all of the bombs and closed nuclear power plants that have not been recycled have been sent to the Sun for disposal along with other scourges like non-biodegradable chemicals and plastics.

Cleaning the oceans and all of the land-based pollutants that have leached into the soil is an ongoing task that will continue well into the 22nd century. Nature has conquered some, but invasive species, insect, animal and vegetative kind, continue to plague ecosystems until proper predators can be found to control them naturally.

Freshwater ice is growing on Antarctica again and sea levels are showing some recession after reaching the predicted high of sixty-nine feet above pre-pandemic levels in the 20th century. The same is true of Greenland where the ice sheet there is growing as well as glaciers and all of the mountains with high enough elevation for glaciers to form. It is not known whether we would be going into another Ice Age or not, but that is one of the things that we will be studying carefully.

So far, while geological events like volcanoes erupting, earthquakes and tsunamis continue, we haven't had a super volcano, like Yellowstone, yet. But that is one good reason for moving our population to the where the environment can be controlled.

Of the several super volcanoes on Earth, any one of them can cause a major extinction event. To hedge against that, we will be moving earth fauna and flora to our experimental Earth planet colonies. Also, as a hedge against any major extinction event whether it be another Ice Ball Earth or Fiery Hell Earth like the planet Venus.

The Earth has a potential of 3 billion years of stable Sun energy before the Sun grows larger and consumes the Earth as it dies. None of us will live that long, but Arthur C. Clarke was right again when he predicted that the human race could expand exponentially into outer space without ever being able to consume all of the energy and matter that is available. Especially our growing knowledge of dark matter we can use.

While we have been somewhat of a parasite on our planet, that would not be so with an endless universe for us to migrate into without any resistance at all, just mighty cataclysm that we are just beginning to understand that makes our universe the way it is–very dangerous.

Welcoming us to explore and grow as long as we begin to understand what we have could be gone in an instant. All the more reason for us to leave the planet and find other places to live when our solar system is sucked into a black hole or simply struck by a pulsar.

Our compound in Hollywood Hills is being abandoned by our offspring and their offspring for the glamour and excitement of downtown

L.A. where all the action is. Making our village turned into a city one of the top attractions for those coming from all over the world to see.

It is time for me to turn the page on this report and hopefully, give you another account before Derek and I reach our extended lifespan and leave forever.

53

Colonizing Humans, Near and Far

May 2142: One hundred years after the pandemic changed the world.

This will be my last report of this kind. If you want to know more, you will need to use your memory capability to tap into mine in the cloud. You will be able to see much more of what I've experienced in my long legacy reaching to 118 after the 100th anniversary of the event that prob-ably saved our Earth rather than making things worse there.

I still feel like I am twenty. Derek, unfortunately, died two years ago from a gene related to sickle cells that those with ancestry from the African continent have as a hedge against malaria. It was cured in the last century by gene therapy. But the therapy that Derek received caused pancreatic failure and he was diagnosed too late for replacement. We were fortunate to have a large crowd of friends and family at his bedside when he died to hear his last words… "I love you all…"

We both had children up until about 110 when we agreed together to stop. My great-great grandchildren now number well over 100 and I'm having great-great-great grandchildren come visit me from time to time and we play old games like chess. I love to watch them beat me with their AI assistance and let them do it because they can.

Unfortunately, we lost Melody, too, six years ago at 123. She reached the point where transplants just weren't working anymore. And was glad to have had a career and children that reached around the world and touched nearly everyone. I miss her. Daphne and some of the original members of our neighborhood compound are still with us. The human lifespan has been increased to about 140, but the promise of eternal life is still beyond our capability although may be solved within this century the way things are rapidly changing.

We have been living on Earth 2 since 2122. Our extended family environment is very similar to Southern California except for the ocean and beloved beaches that were destroyed by climate change and are beginning to come back on Earth.

Here, oceans are only simulated and we can go surfing, scuba diving, whale communicating or deep-sea fishing, if we want. We also don't have any earthquakes except in amusement parks for the thrill. But at least once a year, I, with others, usually grandchildren, go back to Earth to explore what's happening there and often drop by to see what is happening to the village that is now largely a research center and fantasyland of more movie memorabilia than anywhere else.

I miss flying because for the past fifty years or so, I have only been riding while AI does all the trip planning, maintenance and piloting of every vehicle of all kinds from large to small, like electric gravity defying skate-boards and the like. I am riding perfectly safe and sound whether it be going back to Earth and then returning or even going to the Moon or Mars on an excursion with first class everything. We have the time, and the thrills are endless.

Earth 2 has over 1000 different environments like ours emulating various parts of the Earth environment from forests to deserts and everything in between. We can choose to change where we live if we want, anytime we want, and our servants, our working force of androids, will do that for us without question and without any plots to our well-being conjured up by old science fiction.

Androids are much preferred over human helpers who always seem to have an axe to grind or another. We also have the ability to take an elevator to zero gravity for the enjoyment that it brings: like swimming underwater without worrying about taking a breath. The opportunities for outdoor activity are endless and we are still experimenting and developing more.

The Earth elevator to space designed to save the tremendous energy it takes to move any kind of weight from the Earth surface to Earth orbit has been under construction for some time at several locations. So far, the construction has failed because of Earth's violent weather. As the weather improves over time, we expect the project to succeed and allow Earth to orbit and return for both humans and material to be very efficient and trouble free. Our power is drawn directly from the sun and enables us to power everything on the colony with ease as well as do necessary maintenance and upgrades/renovations that are required. Earth 3 is scheduled to be completed by 2145, a new record for completion of such a colossal project. Most of the occupants of Earth 1 will temporarily relo-cate there while renovations are done. While almost everything was accounted for, our oldest colony has suffered from micro meteors and failure to be fully protected from solar storm radiation flares.

Earth 2 was the first colony to have our own magnetic field that protects us from solar radiation much better than the shields built into Earth 1. When finished, Earth 1 will be as up to date as Earth 3. The displaced occupants will have a choice of living in either of those worlds. There is always pleasure in changing venues, having done it many times in my life.

But our greatest project is not a solar one. We have located over 132 planets that are in the magic habitable zone, or as we like to call it, the "Goldilocks Zone." These are planets that are a reasonable distance from their suns, more often two than one, are rocky in nature, have water and a reasonable, oxygen atmosphere. As well as other characteristics like age and particularly, size, because human DNA is conditioned to Earth gravity and planets of that size are the most desired for multiple reasons.

While it would be nice to travel the distances involved in a state of suspended aging like so many travels to distant planets have been depicted in science fiction, AI has determined for us the best way for us to inhabit other parts of the universe would be to send frozen fertilized embryo and/or frozen sperm and eggs on these long distances to places that may or may not be conducive for the birth of any of the population sent. Androids would run the ships for the entire distance until orbiting and analyzing the planet below to determine whether or not it would be safe to allow children to grow up and begin to live on the planet below.

In any case, we have designed the program and ships so that key individuals would be allowed to grow up on board in orbit until they reach maturity and have learned everything they can from the memory banks of their parents and the Earth to make wise decisions about how to intervene in the planet below's evolution and whether to populate it or not.

We expect many of these planets will not welcome human intervention. Although we hope that some will. In any event, our spaceships will be equipped for us to build colonies similar to what we have built here wherever we go in the universe.

So far, we have not figured out how to communicate in interstellar space. Our communication, traveling at the speed of light, is already inadequate in our solar system. Except for the memory banks of Earth on the motherships, there will be no interactive communication. Our seeds sent to the stars will never return or communicate with us. At least under the means of communication we have today. Hopefully, that problem will also be solved someday.

Der, Mel and I had seen tremendous changes in our lifetimes. Seeing and doing things that we never thought we would ever see or do. And the possibility of extending our lifespans far beyond what they are today seems eminently possible. As well as connecting with other intelligence in an alliance that is hoped-for. Rather than the ongoing fictional theme of continuing Earth-based wars in interstellar space.

So, I am closing the book with this passage for you all to ponder.

54

Epilogue

I am a realist, a technologist, and a bit of an idealist when it comes to science-fiction. But I leave fantasy out of it, although fantasy may be big among readers of bestsellers and theatergoers of blockbusters from nov-els about things that will never happen but are exciting because they are so seemingly dangerous and weird.

The universe is a very dangerous place and much weirder than we can currently understand. Why fantasy works so well in science fiction. Because, we really don't know what is actually out there, except what the best science can tell us at this point in time. All we know is it may be very strange or may be very logical and fit into our current mathematical formulae describing its physics. Black holes at the center of galaxies seem to be obvious but have only been proven recently… although the-orized for over 100 years.

However, in the 21st century in this case, the city of Los Angeles, potentially faces three great dangers… Another pandemic like 2020, climate change caused by global warming and geological activity along the Pacific Rim. I left out world war or an economic or other disaster, although they may happen as well–something unknown but expected or anticipated.

Fortunately, a simple experiment by NASA recently has shown that the threat from meteorites and comets that have caused past extinctions like the one 65 million years ago that killed the dinosaurs and created us can be easily thwarted. A rogue planet or planetoid coming from outside the solar system at a high rate of speed may be a different matter, but highly unlikely.

Predicting the future is dangerous because we can't foresee everything that is coming even though science fiction has done a good job for some of it. Some of what has happened has been missed by even the best scientists and futurists. Like the current rapid advance of artificial intelligence, AI, into everything that we do, creating concerns about what it will do to or for, humans.

No one predicted the World Wars I and II in the 20th century, a world-wide Great Depression, the development of the atomic bomb and atomic energy. Landing and bringing back 8 humans from the moon and the power of the Internet. Even the World Wide Web of the Internet effectively bringing about a rather troubling global village as predicted by Marshall McLuhan that has so many peaceful uses and dark ones as well.

I chose Drake Hutchins to be my alter ego. Having worked with black partners in higher education over the years, I chose Derek Jones as a partner for Drake like my twin brother was a partner when we were 18. I was already a very good drafter (in those days, draftsman) who could design and build almost anything I wanted.

Roger and I, by that time, had worked a number of jobs from picking beans at nine years old in the fields to factory work at seventeen where we built mobile homes and were asked by the superintendent to stay on in the fall rather than go on to college. We were hard-working innovators and pacesetters, something that people higher up valued and saw in us.

I wanted to be an architect and an astronaut. Both of them seemed to be within my reach at eighteen. So, I made the presumption that in the 21st century there would be young people like my brother and me, willing to take on the world with everything we had, regardless of what happened or was to come. Rising up from sickness with 90% of everyone around us we knew, dead. Simply just doing the best we could with the knowledge that we had.

Unfortunately, while I have visited Los Angeles briefly a few times, it has been a long time since I've been there. So, I may have, in spite of my research had some things about the city wrong. But this is fiction, and this is a future we cannot predict. Especially when we get to the 22nd century where all bets are off when it comes to what will happen then. Assuming we haven't destroyed the world with our ignorance and fascination with having children and wealth over everything else.

❧ ⃝ᔥᔦ⃝ ☙

About the Author

Dr. Ronald W. Hull is an engineer, educator, and author. Fascinated with history and technological development, he likes to incorporate both in his novels. Paralyzed at twenty in a surgical accident, Ron walked away from the hospital, and, with a special hand splint, began writing again and typing with one finger. After his master's degree, Ron started his career in the telecommunication industry. For thirty-nine years, after earning his doctorate, Dr. Hull worked in higher education as a professor of technology and management, and as a university administrator until retiring at 69.

Ron Hull has written poetry all his life. He now posts a poem a week on his website, http:/ronhullauthor.com/. Ron has traveled widely and experienced many cultures. Starting with his autobiography, he incorpo-rates his many experiences into his books. His topics are wide-ranging and global. Ron's first book, The Kaleidoscope Effect was a science fiction first contact novel that spanned thousands of years. Alone? the mirror of Kaleidoscope, is in its second edition. War's End was Dr. Hull's first venture into the action thriller novel genre. Based on the catastrophic premise of War's End, the American Mole trilogy is Ron's first attempt at a continuing story bridging several books: The Vespers, MS-13 and Aryan Nation. Ron has packaged his many short stories into three short storybooks.

Relying on an electric wheelchair and specially equipped van because of the effects of aging on his severe spinal injury, Ron uses computer technology to write and research his books. He resides in Houston Texas with his longtime partner, companion, and assistant, Beh.

Ronald W. Hull June 16, 2024 Houston, Texas USA
Ron's Place: http://ronhullauthor.com